I0638289

IMPERIUM BOOK 5

THE FIRES OF VULCAN

TRAVIS STARNES

Copyright © 2024 by Travis Starnes
All rights reserved.
No part of this publication may be reproduced, distributed, or transmitted in any form
or by any means, including photocopying, recording, or other electronic or mechanical
methods, without the prior written permission of the publisher, except as permitted by
U.S. copyright law.
The story, all names, characters, and incidents portrayed in this production are ficti-
tious. No identification with actual persons (living or deceased), places, buildings, and
products is intended or should be inferred.

Maps available at

https://tstarnes.com/book-series/imperium/

Signup to get free previews of upcoming books before they're released at

http://tstarnes.com/preview-notification-newsletter/

Contents

Chapter 1

North-Western Germania

Anyone who looked at Ky, Consul of Britannia and commander of the Britannic forces in Northern Europe, could tell he was an outsider. Even dressed in the traditional Roman garb, worn by most of the Legionnaires, Ky stood out as a man out of place. Everything about him from the almost bronze color of his skin and almond-shaped eyes, to the way he sat on a horse, said he didn't belong here ... mostly, because he didn't. He'd been born thousands of years from this now, as part of a society that had homogenized into more or less a single phenotype, with genetic engineering doing the rest. He'd spent his life training to fly fighters in the depths of space, strapped into a chair built to offset high acceleration, not sitting atop a horse, rebalancing every time the animal moved.

And yet, all of his men followed him as if he was sent by the gods. Of course, that was because many of them still thought he had been, no matter how often Ky tried to dissuade them of the notion.

A narrow valley stretched before him, thick with frost, hemmed in on both sides by steep, snow-capped peaks. They'd picked this area specifically because of its inhospitable terrain. While they'd dealt a major blow to the Carthaginians, there were still units out there, and he wasn't ready to put his out-manned legions and ragtag allies to the test until they had the training to operate well together.

They'd gotten the drop on the Carthaginians in the fall, mostly because the Carthaginians didn't realize Bomilcar had managed to turn so many of their previously conquered vassals against them. That secret was out now, however, which meant the next battle would be a stand-up fight.

Hopefully, by then he would have more rifles, enough to arm more than a century or two, but even with that, Ky wanted his local allies trained up as much as possible. That's why they were hiding in the mountains for the time being.

Each of the five tribes, or four tribes and one confederation of tribes, had set up camps at one end of the valley while Ky had established his legions at the other. There had been some early dustups between the locals and the Britannians, mostly over misunderstandings in customs, that would take time to clear up. Until then, Ky planned on keeping the two groups as separate as possible, except during training, which was what was happening today.

Ky looked across the rocky outcropping, surveying the scene below with a critical eye. The Anglii, whose lands were closest to the Carthaginians and whose men had been drafted into their armies the longest, were by far the most organized, drilling in tight formations with crisp, disciplined movements that gave Ky hope. While they were following the standard of the Phalanxes and not his legions, it was close enough that it wouldn't take long to train them to the point where he could incorporate them directly into his forces, giving him an additional almost half a legion without much effort.

Sadly, they were by far the best of his new allies, by a wide margin. By way of contrast, Ky looked to the Vandili, the second most organized and disciplined of the tribes, and saw warriors in a disorganized mass. Even when lined up, their formations would quickly go from ragged and sporadic, which was as good as they ever got, to a clump of warriors, each trying to see who could attack the enemy line first. Their tactics began and ended with throwing themselves headlong into the enemy lines, trusting in their superior prowess as warriors to win the day. While Ky would never doubt each man's abilities and knew that each was probably a skilled fighter, that made little difference when facing trained soldiers.

It only got more chaotic from there. At this rate, even if he could keep the tribes united and all fighting in the same direction, he'd lose four-fifths of his new allies after the first contact with the enemy.

Bomilcar grumbled from the horse next to Ky. He was as out of place as Ky was, although in a completely different way. Born and raised as part of one of the oldest families in Carthage, his adoption of Roman dress didn't make him fit in any more than Ky did. He could change his clothes, but nothing could change the hawkish features and bearing common to the ruling elite of the African nation that currently controlled most of the known world. They made an interesting pair.

The old general's face was twisted in a tight frown as he assessed the maneuvers below.

"An absolute mess," he muttered. "I talked to them over and over, but Aliverko was the only one who'd sit still long enough to listen. The rest are too impatient and take any kind of organized movement as the 'Carthaginian way.' They think, now that they've broken from their old masters, they can just go back to the way they used to do things. Never mind that they lost doing things that way the first time."

"You were the one who told me this was going to take time," Ky pointed out.

"I know, but I hoped that once they saw what we could do, they might ... I don't know, come to their senses."

"They didn't see much. Sure, they were impressed by the rifles, but other than that, they mostly watched us run from the Carthaginian army for days while we tried to find a suitable place to fight. And then, when we did fight, they can take credit for the win because of their sudden attack from the Carthaginian rear. They won't be believers until they see us fight for real."

"Which won't happen until the snows thaw and we start operations. We should focus our efforts on the Anglii for now. Get them integrated into the legions and ready to fight. We can put the other tribes in the rear as support, watching our flanks and supply lines until they're ready to train for real."

"You know that won't work. You've been in the same parleys I have. They all want to show they're the biggest, baddest bunch there is, ready to take on Carthage by themselves. If we elevate one of the groups above the rest, the other four will go home, or worse, decide we're a lost cause and rejoin the Carthaginians. And the Anglii aren't even close to being the largest of the tribes. Hell, the Alamanni confederation has nearly as many men ready to go under arms as we brought with us."

"Then what do we do? Because we can't go into battle like this," Bomilcar said, waving a hand at the valley where the Alamanni smashed into a line made up of Anarti and Istvaeones in their mock battle simulations. Men were going in every which direction and all semblance of battle lines disappeared completely.

Glancing sidelong at Bomilcar, Ky said, "Maybe we're looking at this the wrong way."

"That's what I was just saying," the Carthaginian said, a little frustrated.

"What I mean is, maybe we shouldn't be trying to fit them into the mold of the legions at all. Like you said, we should focus on only teaching the Anglii to fight as part of our legions. The rest we don't try to make them legionnaires at all, instead we try to play to their strengths."

"Which are?" Bomilcar asked, not bothering to hide his skepticism.

"Their knowledge of the land, superb ability as individual warriors, their courage and, you have to admit, impressive stamina, and their overall raw enthusiasm."

"And how, exactly, would we use those traits?"

"By employing them as partisan fighters."

"Most of these tribes have already been doing that for a while, which is why they have so few men to offer to the cause as it is. They've suffered horrible losses trying to pick off even the smallest groups of Carthaginians."

"I didn't mean doing it the way they have been doing it or even in the way you've seen it done before. I mean we train them in real, hit-and-run tactics," Ky said, and then held up a hand, stopping Bomilcar from protesting again. "I know you've spent a lot of time thinking about our new tactics, the line of battle, battle squares, and the like, but you haven't extended that to other, less direct modes of warfare. Consider what hit-and-run attacks will look like with muskets. Normally that kind of thing is a melee-specific form of combat, since arrows work best when massed, especially at smaller or more spread-out groups of soldiers like you find in a supply column. But muskets, even with their smaller range, will be deadly if fired from the trees. They are easier to train on, significantly more deadly than any arrow, and fast-firing. Imagine a group of even a couple of dozen warriors firing from the trees at a collection of soldiers in camp or marching along carrying supplies. They can cause all sorts of chaos and disruption in the Carthaginian ranks before disappearing back into the wilderness. This is the perfect terrain for that tactic."

"It's risky. They'd be spread pretty thin and at a massive numerical disadvantage at every step. And for what payoff? A few dozen dead soldiers here or there aren't going to impact the effectiveness of any single Carthaginian force."

"They're never going to come into contact with the Carthaginians directly, so numerical differences aren't going to matter. Small raiding bands will move much faster than any Carthaginian security detachment left behind to guard their supply lines, and if we coordinate the attacks, hitting the column again after their guards chase after the first force, they'll have to start absorbing the smaller losses to keep from getting torn to pieces."

Ky said and then paused, watching the men below gathering for another attempt at something like an organized charge.

"That's going to slow them down," he said, continuing once the groups started marching again. "If they bulk up one supply column, we hit any detachments or switch to picking at the flanks of their main column. The key is to keep eating away at their edges, forcing them to chase our allies into the wilderness here or there. That's actually going to be the hardest part. When the Carthaginians start focusing their forces, that's when our people will have to resist the urge to charge in. It's important they fade away. Not just to keep our losses down, but to ensure the Carthaginians chase them. Once a force either stops somewhere advantageous or gets whittled down enough by detaching security forces, we hit it with the better-trained part of our army."

"Even if that doesn't happen, the Germanic corpse, as their emperor likes to call it, has been picked pretty dry," Bomilcar said. "It's why we've been getting so many refugees. Food supplies are scarce, and it was already getting difficult to have armies operating in this region living off the land. Starvation is going to start being a problem for them."

"You said most of the forces sent to this area were levies from further south. Iberia, Greece, Persia, and the like, right?"

"Mostly. Any large army will have a core unit of real soldiers trained in Carthage proper, more as a security force to push their less voluntary comrades forward than anything else, but they also make up the best part of the fighting forces as well."

"Which probably also means they'll be fed the best, better than the men pulled from conquered lands and sent here. What are the chances that, if they're starved enough, they turn on their officers?"

"Not good. It's why the emperor pulls them from so far away," Bomilcar said. "If they revolt, they can't turn around and run to friendly villagers or go defend their families, and they know the emperor would have their entire village, not just their families, put to the sword if they raise a hand against him. He does it often enough, for even the smallest infractions, that they're regularly reminded of what could happen if they revolt. So no, I don't think they'll turn on their leaders."

"It doesn't matter. Food is going to be scarce and they won't be able to forage much, especially during the winter, so they're going to be forced to spread their men out to protect their supply lines. We'll be fighting smaller groups and it will sow confusion and doubt among their officers, which will make it easier to hit the larger groups. The more I think about it, the more I think this plan will work."

"Then I guess we need to change their training. Like you said, this will work better while snow is on the ground."

"Yep," Ky said and turned his horse to head back down the trail and into the valley.

Devnum

"Ky?" Lucilla said softly into the darkness. "Are you there?"

Even though they'd done this hundreds of times, at first it always felt a little strange to speak into the empty air, talking to herself as much as trying to contact Ky. Maybe it was because she had to wait until she was alone to speak to him, which usually meant waiting until she was alone in her quarters, in the dark. That had been even truer lately. As the daughter of the Emperor, she'd been able to steal moments here or there away from servants, guards, and petitioners to have quick conversations with her husband, who was usually days or even weeks ride away.

That was less true now that she was Empress of Britannia. Now there seemed to always be someone around. Men wanting to 'advise' her on whatever topic they had a personal interest in, hoping to sway her opinion. Servants trying to tend to her every need, even when she didn't need anything. Guards insistent that she was in constant danger of assassination, even at night, when she was locked in her rooms at the palace. It had given her a newfound appreciation of her father and how he'd managed to keep his sanity dealing with this over the years.

Thoughts of her father brought her attention back to the sorrow that had hung over her all evening, threatening to crush her, and the reason she'd been so anxious for time to speak to Ky.

She was about to repeat herself when his deep, soothing voice came through the small device he'd given her to put in her ear, allowing them to speak, no matter how far apart they were.

"I'm here," he said. "Is everything alright?"

Even at this distance, he could hear the pain in her voice. She liked a lot of things about her husband, from his exotic appearance to his warrior's heart, but most of all she loved how he listened to her. Not just her words, but everything underneath them too. She'd never found anyone, through all of the suitors her father had thrown at her over the years, that had matched her so completely.

"No, it's not. My father died tonight," she said.

"Ohh," Ky said. "Sophus didn't say anything."

"I was asked not to. She said she wanted to tell you," the flat voice of the artificial lifeform that lived in Ky's head said to him.

"I ... I just needed some time to deal with it before you asked about him or how I was doing. I know you'd mean well, but I've had a barrage of mourners offering me their condolences all night, and I just can't deal with any more right now."

Ky wanted to tell her he understood, but he didn't. Not really. He'd only been close with a handful of people in his life, and she was the only one he loved. Because of how children were raised in his former life, in genetic batches rather than with families, he never really knew his parents and certainly didn't think he'd feel anything if either of them died. And while he liked and admired the Emperor, he wouldn't go so far as to say he loved the man, let alone like his daughter must have.

"Then I won't say it. This was a matter of time, though. We both knew how sick he really was."

"I know, but it doesn't really help. I'll be fine. I know we have a lot to do, and the stakes are too high for me to fall apart."

"It's fine to mourn, I think. Take a few days maybe. It won't be the end of the war."

"If I was his son, maybe, but I'm my father's daughter," she said, her voice hardening. "There are already men looking at me with skepticism, sure that I'm not up to the job. They're convinced I'm weak, and too emotional to do what must be done as Empress. There's a reason I'm the first one in our history. I can't afford to show weakness, even now."

"That's ... awful."

"It's the way it is," she said, but then her tone softened again. "But tonight, I just need to talk. I have so much ... it feels like I'm going to burst."

"So much what?" Ky asked.

"Doubt, fear, sorrow, grief, anguish. All of it. I miss my father. Yes, he was the Emperor, but he was also the man on whose knees

I played as a little girl. I miss my family. It wasn't that long ago I had a family. A father and a brother. And now they're both gone, or effectively dead. Caesius might not be dead, but he's dead to me, which for right now, is close enough."

"You're not alone," Ky said. "I'm here."

"I know. I think that's the only thing helping me to keep it together. But you're so far away. I know I'm luckier than any woman back here while so many of our men are out there, on the continent, but I still wish you were here, holding me."

"I know. I wish the same thing."

"I'm also feeling doubt. Yes, I was already named Empress, but there was always the knowledge that he was still here. I could go to him, consult with him, get his wisdom. Now that he's gone, we're on our own. We have to figure this out by ourselves. I know I'm up to the task in my head, but in my heart, I'm afraid I won't live up to this moment. We are still balanced on the edge of a knife. This whole Empire of ours could fall apart at any time. Already, the Romans bicker with the Caledonians, who bicker with the Ulaid, who both bicker with the Romans. No one can agree on anything, and I'm just there, playing ... Sophus, what was that word you told me?"

"*Referee.*"

"Yes. I'm refereeing. And now that I hear myself say all this out loud, I think maybe they're right. Maybe I am too emotional to deal with the realities of leadership."

"That's bullshit," Ky said. "First, everyone has these kinds of fears. Anyone who's ever led men into combat or made decisions about the fates of others has second-guessed themselves. Those that don't are narcissists who believe they are always right, and they tend to have fairly dramatic downfalls. No one is perfect. The key is to manage those fears. Use them. Are they baseless or is there a lesson in there your mind is trying to direct you toward? If yes, fix it; if no, then know you gave it reasonable consideration and move on."

"I guess," she said, not sounding convinced.

"It isn't a guess. Do you know who never second-guessed themselves? Your brother. Silo. Decius. They all thought they could do no wrong. Now one of them is in exile and two are dead. Which shows you what unquestioning faith in yourself gets you. As for the rest, it's normal to feel anguish. Caring about people is what makes you a great leader. Your people are willing to trust you with their lives because they know you would never throw them away needlessly. They know you've thought about the repercussions and made the best decision you could. Are you under pressure? Yes. Do you have big shoes to fill? Also, yes; but you can do it. Hell, you held yourself together today, even after the news of your father's passing, until you were alone and free to let your guard down. That's real control that others, lesser men, would kill to have."

She made a small noise he recognized as her thinking noise. It was how she indicated that she was listening to him, but she was also thinking about what he said and her brain was too distracted to give him an immediate answer. It's one of the things he liked about her. She had a focus about her that he'd never seen the equal of. She would go quiet, synthesize a massive amount of data he'd have to give over to Sophus to consider, and then come up with an answer he'd never thought of.

Ky waited peacefully for a minute while she thought, almost picturing her face in his mind, scrunched up, brows furrowed, as she concentrated. The image made him smile and made him think of something.

"Just before I left, after your coronation, I sat and talked to your father for a while. He'd been drifting in and out, and the pain was starting to be a real problem, but all of a sudden he put his hand on my arm and told me a story. You were about seven. Your brother was ten, and he was trying to get the servants to be his legion. He was going to have them attack the pantry. What he didn't know was that you had convinced one of the steward's daughters to bring all of the chickens out of their pen to the side entrance of the courtyard. Apparently, you were upset that he'd yelled at the cooks the day before, because he didn't like his meal, and it upset you, because you liked them all. Your father added that the reason you liked the kitchen staff so much was because they snuck you treats when you came in while no one was looking, but he didn't want you to know he knew because you were worried he would punish them. He was kind of fading at that point, so it wasn't clear if he thought you were still seven at that point or if he meant he didn't want you to know that he knew back then because of your worry."

Ky took a breath, thinking back to the frail old man and how much joy he'd had in telling that story. It had made Ky realize that maybe he was missing more than just the intimate side of relationships, seeing how happy he was just thinking about his daughter. Lucilla didn't say anything while he paused, and Ky could tell she was completely wrapped up in what else her father had said.

"Anyway, you didn't want Caesius to harass them while they were working, so you decided to stand in front of the doorway, wooden sword in hand, telling him to back down. Caesius laughed at you and said he was going to have the servants attack you. Before he could give the order, though, you yelled a command and dozens of chickens came tearing in, wings flapping, your young accomplice behind them swinging a broom and yelling. The servants all ran, and he started getting pecked all over until he finally ran too. Your father had to punish you for injuring your brother, but, secretly, he was proud of you. Not only had you stood up to your brother and protected people who otherwise weren't allowed to protect themselves from him, but you'd created a distraction and outflanked him. He said he knew then that you were incredibly clever and had the makings of a great leader. He then went a little fuzzy and said he was sad your brother was going to be Emperor just because he was a boy and firstborn, and that you'd make a great Empress if you were allowed to take the throne. He really did have incredible faith in you."

"I'd forgotten all about that," Lucilla said, going a bit fuzzy herself as her voice drifted off while she remembered it. "Caesius was so angry. He tried to get my friend punished, but he never spent time with any servants except the ones who cared for us directly, so he couldn't be sure who she was, and weirdly, none of the other servants remembered seeing her, so they couldn't help. Even then, he never understood that you don't have authority just because you are proclaimed to be in charge. To really wield it, people have to *want* to obey you, not just have to. Otherwise, you never get their active participation or best work."

"See, that's what I mean. You're worried that you're not up to the task, and then you say something like that. You're a great leader, Lucilla, and the person who thought so the most was your father. He had no doubts when he passed the mantle to you."

"Thanks," she said after a minute, choking up a little on the word. "That really helps."

"Good," Ky said. "Now it's your turn. You tell me some stories about your father."

Carthage

The dying sunlight had begun to drop low, bathing the emperor's palace in a warm orange light. The torches lit along its perimeter added a flickering effect that made everything seem as if it was on fire. The hour wasn't chosen by mistake. To the Carthaginians, the underworld existed far to the east, beyond the rising sun, and was made up of two lands: one close to the sun, bathed in its light, a place of harmony and warmth, and one far from the sun, where darkness, cold, and hunger resided.

The noble and virtuous, who honored the Carthaginian gods and their avatar on Earth, would go to this closer place, ruled by Tanit, while those who dishonored the gods and their avatar, or those who were defeated by the Carthaginians in their gods' name, would go to the far place, ruled by Mot. The time between day and night was as close as humans could get to their gods' realm, existing in both warmth and cold.

On this day, the gods' avatar in the world, Imilcar Azor, the Emperor of Carthage, glared down from his dais at the pathetic creature kneeling in the center of the courtyard. Caesius Germanicus, traitorous son of the Roman Emperor, defector to Carthage, and sworn to serve the true emperor, was clothed in tattered rags, his feet bare and torn. He had promised to deliver his father's people to the emperor. Instead, due to his incompetence and arrogance, he had failed at every turn, with the new Britannic Empire in control of all of the British Isles and armies victorious in Barbaria itself, just across the small channel from the British Isles. Imilcar smiled to himself. This man was about to learn what many men had learned before him; the cost of disappointing their emperor.

The emperor stood, his purple robes swishing at his feet, and looked across at the collection of courtiers, generals, and noblemen gathered to witness what could happen to them if they too failed him.

"A year ago, you stood before me and pledged your eternal devotion," the emperor said, his voice booming, haughty, and self-righteous. "You pledged that you alone could ensure the downfall of your people, that you could get them to submit to my rule. You promised that your father and the evil spirit he named Consul would kneel before me."

He paused, letting his words sink in as his gaze swept over the courtiers in the courtyard before returning to the ragged form at its center.

"Instead, what did you bring me? Failure. Time and again, your proclamations of spies and loyalists turned out to be as hollow as your courage. You've shown that you are only capable of incompetence and insufferable arrogance. The British Isles, once firmly in our grasp, have slipped through our fingers because you were unable to bring us a single one of their new weapons. Unable to bring us a single piece of information that could be used to counter this evil spirit. Their armies now threaten our very shores, just across the Syrian Sea in Barbaria."

There was a rumble around the courtyard as men murmured their agreement with the emperor, that responsibility for their defeats lay with this traitor and, more importantly, none of them. The emperor raised a jewel-encrusted hand, causing the crowd to instantly fall quiet.

"The gods themselves have granted Carthage dominion over everything the sun touches, yet you chose to defy them. You squandered what resources you were given, lying and blocking our armies from their rightful victory. It is clear now that your promises were all lies. You still serve your father, sent here to utter falsehoods at every turn. And when it was clear your treachery could be hidden no longer, you filled a ship with as many valuables as you could steal and attempted to sail back to your people as a noble hero. Now, it is time for your treachery to be rewarded."

Caesius threw himself prostrate, hands outstretched on the ground, and pleaded, "No, lord of the known world, protector of the chosen people, I would never lie to you. I've only ever wanted to serve you. I was not fleeing. I wanted only to contact those still loyal to me, to get what you require. I thought if I could do it in person, I might …"

"Silence," the emperor bellowed, cutting Caesius off. "I've heard enough of your clever deceptions and false promises."

"Please," Caesius begged, tears streaming down his cheeks. "I only want to serve you. Have mercy …"

"Mercy?" Imilcar laughed, the crowd of sycophants laughing with him. "You dare ask for mercy? You should be honored. Your death will be remembered by everyone who hears of it. You will be a reminder for all time of what happens to anyone who fails me."

With a flick of his wrist guards rushed forward, grabbing Caesius by his arms and dragging him to a large, standing wooden planks in the shape of a giant X that had been set up just behind where he had been kneeling. As the emperor sat back on his throne, waving forward an attendant with a tray of fruit, a nail was driven through Caesius's hand, affixing it to a board.

The emperor delicately selected a grape, popping it into his mouth as the first strip of flesh was cut off of Caesius's body. The scream of the man who thought he would be Emperor, echoed across the courtyard.

Chapter 2

Port Invictus, Iberian Coast

Velius, Legate of the 7th Legion and overall commander of the Britannian forces, gazed across the small but still-growing port from the nearly completed battlements. In a matter of weeks, his men had moved the heavens and earth to complete these fortifications before the Carthaginians could bring new forces to bear, and he was immensely proud of them.

A curtain of sturdy stone walls, extending well out into the surf, protected the small port and helped create a breakwater for their new port at the same time. There was still much to do, of course. Almost all of their efforts had been focused on the curtain walls, trenches, and other obstacles in front of the port or the port facilities themselves, and very little had been focused on anything inside the port area. Outside of a few wooden warehouses, to keep the goods that were shipped in dry, there were no other standing buildings in the small city, and row after row of tents still made up the bulk of it.

While Velius would prefer to have some kind of roof over his head, he had spent most of his adult life on campaign and in the field, so tent living was at least consistent. Giving one more look over the soldiers turned construction workers, Velius and his guards headed toward the very large tents at the center of the nascent city. Inside, his commanders were already gathered.

Gordianus, his second in command, and Aelius had already started the council meeting, going over the basic updates from their assembled cohort tribunes, checking on supplies, progress on assigned tasks and patrols, and the men's morale. All this was important work, the necessary administration that kept the legion functioning. The prefect of each legion was the one who usually dealt with administrative matters, leaving the legate to work on the strategic ones, and Velius was not one to buck tradition when he didn't have to, so he waited patiently as Gordianus finished this section of their weekly commanders' council.

When his second finished his updates was when things varied from how they'd gone for the last several weeks.

Instead of congratulating his men on how well their commands were running, as he had the other times they'd met, Velius said, "Now that the port is mostly complete, it's time for us to start looking forward toward our ultimate mission here in Iberia. Namely, cutting a path from here to the Middle Sea to establish a port to take on the Carthaginians in the Middle Sea. Right now, we have the Carthaginians on their heels. We know they are already starting to rebuild their forces to try to dislodge us from the continent. Instead of sitting behind these walls, waiting for the Carthaginians to attack, I propose we take the fight to them. Not directly, since they are currently far across the tip of Iberia in Italy, but at least not give them as easy a target for their forces to converge on. While they have limited forces in this area, we should begin our push forward, following the mountain range toward the Middle Sea. If we move along the north side of the mountains, we will have a fairly secure southern flank to protect ourselves should their Iberian force move to intercept us."

"In winter, Legate?" Viridius, the tribune in command of the seventy-fifth cohort asked.

"I know it's not usually done and supplies will be a problem, but if we move quickly we can be to the Middle Sea port before the Carthaginians can counter our move. We will have won the Consul's objective in a single fell swoop."

"My lord, I think to say supplies will be a problem is understating the difficulties we will face," Gordianus said. "Besides the fact that the Carthaginians have cleared this area thoroughly, stripping every village that they didn't destroy to starvation levels before winter, we were also ordered by the Consul not to take from any of the locals, as we're trying to gain allies in this region instead of just replacing the Carthaginians. Even if we do pay for what we take, what use is our coin to farmers here when no one else in several days' walk in any direction has food to sell them? We will have to maintain a very long supply train across snow and ice, and partially along the mountainous coast until we get north of the Pyrenees. Do we have the men to maintain a force to attack the Carthaginians, protect those supply lines, and keep this port open?"

"Yes, as I said, supplies will be a problem, but I don't think it's insurmountable. Last year's harvests were the largest our Empire has ever seen, thanks to the Consul's improvements, and he has laid in a significant amount of supplies for both us and the northern force. What that means is that we can get all we're going to need through shipments coming in here. Yes, we'll have to split our legions to cover everything. I agree the bulk of our forces will have to guard our supply lines, which will be what I task your legion to do, Aelius," Velius said. "I will split my legion in half, with five cohorts remaining here at Port Invictus with Gordianus while I take the other five cohorts with me to attack the Carthaginians. The odds aren't as good as I would like, but I think the combination of the weakened Carthaginian forces and our new weapons will be enough to give us an advantage. Besides, the Consul promised to send us the newly reformed First Legion as soon as they're done training all the new recruits, under our first Caledonian legate to boot."

"In the spring, wouldn't all that still be true, except we'd have the First Legion here and we'd have less trouble keeping our men fed and warm?" Aelius asked.

"Scouting would also be a lot easier," Micon, his cavalry commander, added. "Most of our horsemen went with the northern army, and we have only a small force left, and as the weather worsens their visibility will drop to the point that it is likely we could miss seeing an approaching Carthaginian army. The rifles and cannons are powerful weapons, but they don't work when the enemy is right on top of us, which they would be in that instant. Our force multipliers, as the Consul calls them, wouldn't do us much good in those instances, and they would rip our men to shreds. The same is true of the men guarding our supply column, except the problem is made worse in that there are fewer of them. Your five cohorts will be tethered to a very thin line and will be all but blind until the weather starts to clear in the spring."

"Which is why we have to move fast. According to our last scouting reports before the snows started, the Carthaginians have pulled all the way back to their cities to the south on the Middle Sea coast at the other end of the Pyrenees. We also had a pretty accurate view of the forces they had on the continent before we began our invasion, and they're all accounted for. The only other forces they still have on the continent are way out in Greece dealing with an uprising there, which means a long march for them to meet us, or are up in eastern Germania, and they have the Consul to worry about. We also know they can't just rush forces in from Africa, since the armies we faced were made up of every unit they could scrape together to get their counter-invasion of Britain underway before winter. They're going to need time to pull men from the east, either here or in Africa, or to conscript more men. All of that means one thing. We have a window in which to act, but it's limited. If we sit back until the spring, we'll be fighting our way to the Middle Sea."

"What was the Consul's original plan?" Aelius asked.

"That we take and hold this position until spring, and then fight our way through, but he didn't envision a victory of this size. Yes, we knew with our weapons we'd win and get this foothold, but he thought we'd only push their men back and that we'd have to worry about armies in front of us. If we act quickly, that won't be a problem."

Velius waited a heartbeat, gathering his thoughts and looking at his commanders. They weren't afraid, he knew that. They were cautious, weighing the costs and rewards, which was what they should be doing. He knew a lot of commanders, especially those he'd had before Ky arrived, only wanted blind obedience to their orders and didn't tolerate subordinates questioning them, but he'd never believed in that. He wanted his men questioning him, poking holes in his plans. Yes, when he made a decision he wanted his men to obey and follow it, but they all knew these planning sessions were for asking questions and considering options.

They might, with the exception of Gordianus, have less experience in the field than him, but he'd never been one that believed that made their thoughts and suggestions any less valuable. Even if they were wrong, they might make a point he hadn't considered and improve his planning. It had worked for him so far, and he wasn't abandoning it now.

He was, however, still convinced he was right.

"I know this is risky. We all know we are outnumbered by the Carthaginians, and this is the worst time to be campaigning. I know supplies are going to be a problem, and our scouting is nearly non-existent. What I also know is that we have a chance to make a strike right now and take something that might require a year to take otherwise. The Carthaginians have a depth of reinforcements we can never amass, and the more time we give them, the more we'll be up against and the more men we will lose. If we move now, we'll have a port on the Middle Sea before the end of the winter. With our ships, we'll be able to hit the Carthaginians right as the spring campaign season starts and maybe end this entire war by summer. I think that's a risk we not only can take but must take."

"Do you think we can do this?" Aelius asked.

"I do. We have the best-trained soldiers, bar none, armed with weapons that cannot be matched. Trust your men and trust your commanders, and we'll see this through."

"Fine. Let's do it," Aelius said to the nods of the other commanders.

Factorium

Lucilla stepped down from the carriage, pressing a hand into the small of her back. The road to Devnum was still less than a year old, but it had already become pitted from the sheer volume of traffic between the two cities, causing her carriage to bounce and jostle the entire trip.

Although manpower was forever an issue, she was going to have to talk to Hortensius and the imperial architects about smoothing and regrading the road again, something they would probably have to do monthly to keep it from getting to this state so quickly. Although she did want a smoother ride for herself, considering how often she was required to come out this far, she was mostly thinking about the shipments of gunpowder. Even in its caked form, the dust from it could be deadly, as they had found out the previous spring. She didn't want to risk losing entire carriages of that valuable resource if there happened to be an unexpected spark, which could sometimes happen.

As with every trip to Factorium, it felt like the place had grown since her last visit. She felt certain that if Hortensius had his way all of Britannia would be one large factory, and that he was actively working to make that happen. The city was as loud as ever, with the sounds of hammers, yelling, and pounding punctuated by an occasional high whistle sound from his steam engines, which had begun to pop up in more factories now that Hortensius had seen the value in how much more efficient they could make his work.

After completing a few more twists to work out the knot in her back, she motioned her guard forward so they could gently move the workers who stopped to gawk at her out of her way. Despite her frequent trips, she still managed to get the workers stopping to stare or even crowding to see what she was doing on every visit. It had actually gotten worse since she was crowned Empress. If she had her way, she'd stop and talk to all of these people, the very lifeblood of the Empire, but that wasn't allowed. Twice she'd been attacked by a Carthaginian plant or insurgent in a crowd of loyal citizens, once very nearly losing her life as a result. Only the small creatures Ky had placed inside her had kept her alive and healed her from the blade that had been plunged into her chest. So now, she was forced to maintain a bubble between herself and her people, which she bitterly disliked.

Today, she headed towards the guarded archive building, an assistant carrying a large case full of new documents, where Hortensius was meeting her. Besides the security of the documents, with the new steam engines, she found it difficult to hold detailed conversations inside his factories, like they had done previously, so most of their meetings now happened here.

"Your Imperial Majesty," Hortensius said, bending into a deep bow as soon as she entered the building.

"Stop that," she admonished, still finding all the pomp directed at her highly uncomfortable, and knowing he was doing it precisely because she found it unpleasant. "You've never been one to stand on ceremony, and you have too much to do to waste time genuflecting."

"Yes, Your Magnificence," he said, straightening, his eyes dancing with laughter.

All Lucilla could do was roll hers in return. The old manufacturer had a childlike humor about him sometimes, and he relished poking fun at her. She actually enjoyed his teasing, although she'd never tell him that it was because it made her feel more like herself, a regular person and not some prop.

"In spite of your insolence, I brought you presents," she said, directing her aide to set the documents on the large table set up in the center of the room.

Gaius, the young man, was one of Ramirus's, although the spymaster hadn't told her that directly. She knew he was trying to protect her, ensuring that her aide, who worked closely with her, was both loyal and trained to protect her should her guards fail, but she didn't like how frequently her father's henchmen tried to manipulate her.

"Thank you, Gaius. Please wait outside," she said, ignoring the conflicted expression he made every time she ordered him out of her presence.

"You should be nicer to the boy," Hortensius admonished her.

"Sometimes the hovering gets a little suffocating. I know Ramirus is just trying to protect me, but I wish he'd instruct his minions to be a little less enthusiastic in performing their responsibilities."

"I'm pretty sure his instructions are the exact opposite. There are probably blood oaths for those given the glory of protecting their Empress," Hortensius said with a grin. "Now, show me what you brought."

Ignoring his jibe, she spread the papers out and said, "Two new projects for you. The good news is that neither of these will require you to develop any new technologies. These are just extensions of what we already have, so you just have to work out the manufacturing of the prototypes, test them, and figure out the production lines. We also won't need the kinds of volumes for either of these as we do for the rifles and cannons, so they shouldn't be that much of a burden."

Hortensius made a mindless humming sound, his eyes already taking in the sheets of diagrams and instructions on making Ky and Sophus's new inventions.

"I'm not so sure about that statement. This one calls for a lot of fabric," he said, pointing at the diagrams in front of him. "We will at least need some kind of fabric manufacturing facility to put out anything more than a small amount. We already have a weaving factory here, but they are producing clothes and uniforms for the legions, sailcloth, and cartridges, and are pretty close to capacity."

"I stand corrected. It will not require you to change your processes, but it might require an increase in capacity. Better?"

"Much. So, I'm looking over these directions and yes, you're right, it does seem to be a simple repurposing of the processes we already have. What it doesn't seem to include is an explanation of why. While I'm always willing to make things on faith, knowing you and the Consul will eventually explain things to me, I usually have some idea of what I'm making, if not how it is intended to work. On this one, I can't fathom its use at all. If I'm to make it, I'll have to test its parts to ensure I know they each work independently and together, and I'm not sure I can do that this time. I'm talking about this one with all the fabric, of course. The scaled-down steam engine is self-explanatory enough, although I question how it could be more effective than the current version since it will have a smaller boiler and hence less steam."

"This is actually the original goal for the steam engine, but Ky felt it would be easier to build the larger version first and then scale it down, especially since the larger version could be used to increase efficiency in your factories. The smaller steam engine is intended to be installed on a mobile platform with connected wheels called a train, where the pistons from the steam engine turn the wheels, propelling it. According to Ky, it will be able to pull a massive amount of weight, closer to what the new ships he's designed can carry, and go faster than any team of horses. I'm not clear on how he's going to achieve that, but he seems pretty confident in its capabilities."

She didn't include Sophus's explanation involving laid-out roads of metal and wood, since she still didn't really understand how the whole system would work. There were times when she wished Hortensius was the one with the earpiece so he could talk directly to Sophus. There had been numerous times when she'd relayed an explanation from Sophus that had left her completely perplexed, only to have the manufacturer instantly understand Sophus's point. Not that she would ever willingly give up her ability to talk to Ky wherever he was. She just often felt underqualified to be the one to act as a go-between.

"I see. I'm sure the Consul knows what he's talking about, and it will all be revealed in time. I guess it's important to keep the weight of the engine down, but it still seems like you're going to have trouble generating enough power to overcome the friction created by so much weight. We'll both have to move forward on faith until he decides to explain to us why he's right. Now, about this mess with the fire pot and fabric."

"It's to allow one or two men to stand in the basket and be lifted hundreds of feet in the air. He intends to use it for aerial reconnaissance, much like ... a bird would," Lucilla stumbled, almost revealing information about Ky's drone.

A few people had seen the drone in action, and they trusted Hortensius explicitly, but when it came to Ky's magical items from his time, they both agreed it was best to keep it to themselves as much as possible.

"What? How? I ... how?" Hortensius stammered. "That's impossible, and the Consul thinks he can do it with some fabric and a small fire?"

He began to flip through all the pages, trying to see if he missed something. Lucilla sympathized with him, but she'd seen the drone hover off the ground on its own.

"Yes. I don't fully understand his explanation, but I'll do my best to share it," she said, speaking slowly to try and grasp what Sophus was saying before relaying those words to Hortensius. "There are a few things you have to accept to understand how it works, and the first is that hot air is lighter than colder air. This can be seen in how smoke drifts up and doesn't fall back down but levels out high above you. It does this because it is hotter than the air around it. The same is true in the summer when it is cooler if you lie on the floor and in the winter when the heat from your stove makes your head and body warm, but your feet remain cold."

"I haven't really thought about that. I guess it makes sense, although smoke also breaks apart as it moves away from the fire, so it could be that it's just separating until it's no longer visible."

"Umm ... that is part of it, but then why wouldn't the smoke drop to the floor like water before it spreads out or mist before the sun burns it off," Lucilla said, passing on Sophus's Socratic defense. "You can even see it in practice. If you drop a leaf from high above a fire, it doesn't fall into the fire but rises with the smoke."

"Yes, I guess that is a point."

"That is the basic principle behind this device, which is called a hot air balloon. The fabric is made into a very large ball with a small opening. The basket holding the fire pot is attached underneath the opening. As the fire pot heats the air around it, the air rises up into the enclosed ball of fabric, pushing the cold air down and out, until the fabric is completely filled with hot air. The hot air will actually continue to move higher, and it will push the fabric out until it is taut on all sides. When the balloon is full, it will lift off the ground, lifting the attached fire pot, which continues to heat the air. When the air is allowed to cool, it will start to equalize in temperature with the air around it, and the entire thing will gently fall back down."

"But the air is able to lift people?"

"Yes, and that's why there has to be so much fabric. It takes a lot of heated air to be able to lift that much weight. When it's stretched out, it will be a huge ball in the sky. The fire pot is designed to increase or decrease the heat output, and there will be additional coal on board for the person operating it, called a pilot, to generate more heat if they need to go higher. The basket will be attached to a cable that is connected to a winch below, so the balloon can be retrieved without having to let it crash into the ground. However, if they are cut loose, the pilot can slowly close off the fire pot, reducing the heat steadily, and they can descend on their own. Without being attached, the wind will carry it in an unpredictable direction, which is why a cable is the preferable method. Once we have it, our legions can launch the balloon and see much further than any horseman, allowing us to observe enemy movements from above. It may not always be useful when our armies are moving, but during sieges or when the enemy lines are close by, we will be able to always know what the enemy is doing."

"It still seems impossible that a bunch of air could lift people into the sky," Hortensius said. "But you and the Consul have never steered me wrong. If you and the Consul say this will work, then who am I to argue."

"Thank you, my friend," she said, putting her hand flat on top of his.

Being Empress, or the daughter of the Emperor before that, meant she didn't have the luxury of friends. Besides the obvious security problem, most people trying to get close to power were doing so because they wanted to either take or control that power. That made it hard to gauge the motivations of everyone. Hortensius was one of those rare souls who seemed to have little interest in ruling or power. As long as he had what he needed for his workshops, he was a happy man. Which was one of the reasons Lucilla didn't mind these trips to see him. It was a nice respite from the viper pit that was the palace complex.

"I know you're stretched thin," she continued. "And the rifles, cannons, and gunpowder remain your priority, but these items will both have a big impact on the war, especially the scaled-down steam engine, since it will allow us to move goods across the country so much faster. Both need to be done preferably by this summer.""You're right, we are very short on manpower, but that is always the case, isn't it? Don't worry, Your Majesty. I won't let you down."

Chapter 3

Carthage

Tabnit marched through the massive bronze doors leading into the emperor's throne room, his polished armor and red cloak swishing around his ankles with each step. His upright walk didn't give any indication of the bone-deep exhaustion he was feeling. He had been in Cairo five days ago, putting down another pointless revolt by the Israelites, when he received the summons to be at the capital within five days. It had taken almost eighteen hours a day in the saddle, changing horses numerous times, to meet that deadline, but everyone who served the emperor long enough knew the penalty for disobeying even impossible orders.

If he had forgotten that, the string of flayed corpses on the walls were an apt reminder. Although unrecognizable, he knew one was his former commander, sent to lead troops in Hispania preparing to re-invade the British Isles and deal with the Roman upstarts. Although Tabnit had been elevated to his own command and dispatched to Egypt before that failure, he couldn't help but be concerned that his association with his former commander was enough to seal his own fate. Of course, running in fear would probably result in the same outcome, except his family would be there with him. Better to stand before the emperor and hope he was feeling reasonable today.

The throne room itself was impressive, especially compared with the courtyard beyond, with its permanent dark stain left from the scores of men who met their end there at the emperor's command. The long room was flanked by a series of massive, imported marble columns, disappearing into the shadows of the vaulted ceiling. At the end of the long hall, lit by braziers of scented oil, loomed the emperor's throne upon a towering dais.

Tabnit approached the base of the dais, falling to one knee as etiquette demanded, his eyes downcast. He had only been in the emperor's presence once before, but minions waited outside the outer doors telling anyone who entered the protocols and warning of the consequences if they forget them.

Time stretched for what seemed like forever as the emperor remained silent, letting the tension build. Tabnit could feel his gaze like a physical weight, assessing him. That, in itself, was actually a good sign. The general had heard about some of the audiences that had ended with the person in his position hanging on the wall, and the tales all involved nearly-instant yelling and abominations, not silence. Tabnit hoped that, if the emperor was trying to make him uneasy, he was doing it for some reason other than terrorizing him before his death.

After the long, pregnant pause, the emperor finally spoke, his voice echoing in the empty hall. "I understand you have fought in Hispania and Germania."

"Yes, Your Majesty," he said, looking up but remaining kneeling. "My previous command was in Hispania last year, and I spent most of my early days in the armies pacifying the northern Germanics."

Another long pause. "I see. And you have been in Egypt since then?"

"Yes, Great One."

"What do you know of what has been happening in the west with the Romans and Britannians?"

It was Tabnit's turn to pause. How he answered that question was tricky. If he made it sound like the empire was doing poorly, he could be declared disloyal or of defeatist thinking, either of which could end this audience abruptly ... and fatally.

"I know some commanders in those areas have not been performing their duties adequately, allowing the Romans to gain control of that small island."

The emperor leaned forward, his eyes full of fire, and said, "It is worse than that, General. The Romans have developed new weapons that produce great clouds of smoke, thunder, and fire. Weapons that can tear through armor and flesh as if they were nothing. It is like nothing we've ever seen."

As always, Tabnit's first thoughts were how such a weapon would be used tactically. The advantage to the Romans was obvious, as something like that could negate his own people's numerical superiority and send the less well-trained conscripts, that made up the bulk of every Carthaginian army, into flight.

"How long have these weapons been employed, Your Majesty?"

The emperor waved a hand dismissively. "The specifics do not matter. What matters is that they were employed against both our fleets, trying to reclaim the British Isles, and our armies, sent to stop the invasion of Hispania, destroying both utterly. I will not tolerate such losses again, General."

Tabnit inclined his head, still unsure of where he fit in this conversation, and said, "Of course not, Your Majesty."

The emperor settled back into his throne, steepling his fingers, and commanded, "I have been gathering a new army, one that will dwarf the force sent against the British Isles. You will lead this army into Hispania and crush the Romans beneath your heel, destroying their new weapons and all traces of resistance. You will take whatever losses are required to accomplish this, General Tabnit. The only outcome I will accept is total victory."

Tabnit kept his features neutral through sheer force of will alone. The emperor described a situation where other armies, who also outnumbered the Romans, were completely destroyed, and now he was being ordered to run into the jaws of the same beast and hope to win just because he had more meat to feed it.

Tabnit bowed his head, choosing his words carefully, "Your Majesty, I beg your forgiveness, but how am I to succeed where others have failed against such a formidable foe?"

The emperor's eyes flashed with anger, his fat hands gripping the arms of his throne. "You defy my orders, General Tabnit?"

"No, Your Majesty," Tabnit said hastily. "I merely wish to understand how I might gain victory where none who have come before me have prevailed. The Romans' new weapons provide them a nearly insurmountable advantage."

The emperor studied him for a long moment, then settled back into his throne, his unnerving gaze never wavering from Tabnit's.

"You are right to recognize the threat these weapons pose," he growled. "Fortunately, we have acquired new weapons of our own from lands to the east, weapons that will counter those of the Romans. They have not yet arrived in full, but once they do, you will have the means to overcome the Roman dogs."

Tabnit couldn't help but wonder what those weapons could be. If they were something as powerful as what had been described, why hadn't they gotten their hands on them before? It wasn't like the emperor was holding back or wanted to keep casualties of their enemies low in the past. Still, he'd survived asking one question. He doubted he'd survive a second.

Instead, he said, "I am grateful to hear that, Your Majesty. With such weapons in hand, victory will be within our grasp."

Even the pause had been too much, it seemed.

Used to immediate obedience, the emperor jabbed a finger at him and said, "See that it is, General Tabnit. I did not elevate you to this position to hear defeatist talk and doubting questions."

Tabnit bowed lower, genuflecting, and said, "My apologies, Your Majesty. I weep at the faith you have placed in me. I will not fail you."

"See that you don't, General. If you fail, if you allow those Roman dogs to defeat you as they have others, the price will not be yours alone to pay. Your family will accompany you into the afterlife to witness your failure for eternity. You dying on the field of battle won't save them from my wrath."

Tabnit had faced death in battle countless times. He'd had Germanic axes fall a breath's span from his face and arrows impact close enough to cut his ear. None of those experiences sent a shiver of fear down his spine like hearing this threat from the emperor. His death, he could handle. The death of his wife and two sons, however, he could not. And yet, this had always been the threat hanging over everyone who lived in the emperor's shadow. Success was always rewarded with a harder task and failure with brutal punishments. It was their reality. So far, Tabnit had not only survived that reality but thrived in it. He would just have to continue to do so, for his family's sake.

The emperor finally looked away from him, since the audience started entering the throne room, waving a dismissive, meaty hand, saying, "Enough. You march in one month's time. Go now and prepare."

Tabnit finally stood, bowing as he backed away.

"By your will, Your Majesty."

When he reached the appropriate distance, Tabnit turned, already thinking about the task ahead. He was nearly at the ornate doors when the emperor's voice reached him with one last warning.

"Do not forget what hangs in the balance, General."

Devnum

Medb, once Queen of Connacht and now Princess, through marriage, of the Ulaid, sat at the plain wooden table in their quarters, staring out of the window at the orange sky as the sun dipped below the horizon, the dying light reflecting through her curly red hair.

Quarters. She should think of it as it really was. A prison. Nicer than any dungeon, true, but a far step down from the luxury she once lived in.

Here she sat, day after day, waiting for the fool child Cormac to return from whatever lesson he had that day, learning to be a king. That wasn't fair, really. Cormac wasn't a bad man. She'd been saddled with, and sometimes even saddled herself with, many suitors over the years. It was the curse of being a woman in power. Men always felt she needed a man to guide her and saw her ability to bear children as her primary function in life.

Of the men she'd taken on as consorts over the years, Cormac was probably the best option so far. Of course, this time she was his consort and he was in line for power instead of her, but it had kept her neck off the executioner's block and had given her time to figure out how to reclaim what was rightfully hers. She was surprised when she thought of her new husband warmly. He might be naive, but he wasn't a fool like Fergus, and he wasn't a coward like her first husband. He listened to her intently, never belittling her opinion because she was a woman, and he was eager to learn … in all arenas.

She was considering keeping him once she reclaimed her throne. While his family's hold on their throne was new, and therefore still tenuous, the people seemed to like him, and he would make it easier to keep them in line. Besides, he was cute.

As if her thoughts summoned him, Cormac Cond Logas, Prince of the Ulaid and current representative of his government in the Britannian capital, came striding in. Today he was wearing the current style of Britannian segmented armor that he wore when he was in the field with the legions instead of the simple tunic he was forced to wear when observing and learning from politicians. It also explained his good mood since, like all boys, he preferred holding a sword over reading scrolls any day.

"You are stunning," he said, stopping to admire her in the light.

"You're just smitten," she replied, giving the thin, off-set smile that seemed to work best on him.

She got up from the table and came around to begin helping unstrap his armor. Men liked it when women served them, and he sighed as she began tugging on the buckles and leather holding the metal in place.

"That is true," he said, placing an arm around her, cupping a hand on her bottom.

"As much as I appreciate your enthusiasm," she said, removing the hand. "It makes helping you with your armor harder."

Cormac held both hands in the air comically, saying, "Point taken. Who am I to stop you from undressing me?"

She had to hand it to him. He had enthusiasm … and stamina. Unfortunately, she'd already worked out her current plan of attack for today, and she needed him talking. As much as she enjoyed other methods of controlling him, not all of the methods had the same uses, and she'd already had him wrapped around her finger. Today she needed to get him angry and focused.

"How were the legions today?" she asked, trying to get him talking.

Only two things would distract Cormac from their bed. Talking about how he should be in charge and talking about the legions.

"Good, actually. Normally, I don't think much of taking farmers and tradesmen and putting them in armor, since they tend to make poor warriors, but the Romans really have worked out a system for building an army using the simplest of people. Both legions should be ready to travel to the continent by the spring."

"Such praise? From what you said yesterday, it felt like there were things you thought they were doing wrong. Was today that much better?"

"It was, actually. Last week they were just … I don't know, not moving fast enough. Or I thought they weren't, but Llassar said to wait and I'd see there was a point to how they were preparing the men, and he was right. I'm just used to how we did things at home, which I'll admit is a completely different way of fighting. Seeing the whole process, it starts to make more sense."

Medb frowned, but quickly hid her reaction and said, "I see. It is heartening to hear we're in good hands then. I was starting to worry about our fate in this war, hearing you talk about how slow and timid the Romans were in everything they do. I've just found real joy in you, and now I'm afraid I might lose it all if they allow the Carthaginians to return to the island."

Cormac pressed a hand to her cheek, looking at her lovingly, and said, "I would never let them hurt you."

"I know, and it's one of the reasons I've fallen for you, but … I just want to know everything that can be done is being done. You'd tell me if it wasn't, wouldn't you?"

"I would. And yes, they still move too slowly. You're right about that. Seeing these men today, they are ready to take the field now, and then more men could be put into training. The legions are on the continent now where there is a lot more manpower available. If they started conscripting those men, sending them back for training now, we'd have four more legions in the spring instead of just two."

"Have you made that suggestion to Llassar?" Medb pressed.

"I have, but he never listens to me. I tried to explain that now, this year, we have the Carthaginians where we want them. They're spread too thin and have been pulling men from lands they control that are further and further away, based on the knowledge we have gained from prisoners we've taken. They need to start conscripting and training more men for their armies, but even with their style of fighting, that will take some time. If we pressed now, or at least as soon as the snows started to melt, with everything we have, we could be in Carthage by summer, before they had a chance to put together new forces. They're just too cautious about everything, really. They don't understand that aggression is what's going to win this war. And they've got this hang-up about conscripted soldiers that is … frankly, perplexing."

He paused, but Medb could feel him building into a solid rant, and waited patiently, not wanting him to lose his anger.

"How do they think they can win anything if they aren't using the people they free to continue the fight? This decision that only volunteers will fight in the legions is a weakness. And I know there are men in both the Senate and the legions who agree with me. They have all this manpower in the factories and growing crops, and all these soldier prisoners just sitting in tents, doing nothing all day. If they took all those men and put them in the factories and the fields, forcing them to work, they could take all the free people and conscript them into the legions. We'd have thousands more men under arms in a day. But the Consul's womanly laws against slavery stop them. It's foolish."

Medb pursed her lips, her face a facade of worry and concern.

"I can't believe they won't listen to you. I gave my kingdom over to the Carthaginians because I saw that we didn't have the power to stop them, and it was all I could do to save my people. The Britannians have that power, but if they're too afraid to do what must be done, then I've just thrown myself and my people into the jaws a second time. I wish they'd come to their senses and realize the opportunity they're throwing away, ignoring what's right in front of them."

"I know. I'm not giving up, though. I'll convince them. If the alternative is losing you, I would carry the world on my back if that's what I had to do."

"I know you would. You have such a strong heart; it's why I'm so frustrated. I don't even think they know how lucky they are. If you decided your people made a mistake and wanted your kingdom free and on its own, like it was before the Britannians forced your father into that agreement, it would be the end of this Empire. With your people mixed in with theirs and what you know about war, you could create an insurgency that would rip the Romans to pieces. And yet, instead of listening to you ... taking you seriously, they just ignore you."

"Well, I don't know about that. There are benefits to our union. Their new weapons and the things they are still adding, make not only their armies powerful, but everything a little stronger. I've seen the Imperial Senate at work, and we do have a fair voice, I think, especially since the Caledonians are more like us than the Romans. Several times the Roman position was rejected in favor of the one we wanted. I think we've made the right call; they just need to start making better decisions militarily."

Medb took his armor and turned her back to put it on the rack where it was stored, so it would not warp or bend, and so she could hide the disapproval on her face. Cormac was naive, but he wasn't an idiot, and that was making this harder than it should have been. He had anger, which she could stoke and fuel, but getting him to turn it on his new allies was proving more of a challenge than she'd thought it would be.

"Ohh, I know there are benefits," she said, taking his hand and sitting him at the small table so she could serve him food she'd had a servant bring up from the kitchens when she'd seen the men returning from training. "I guess what I meant was that the new Empress doesn't seem to recognize talent when it's presented to her. What did she say when you presented these ideas to her directly."

"Ohh, I haven't ... I'm not ..."

"She hasn't invited you for a consultation? But you are the direct representative of one-third of the Empire. I know Llassar has meetings with her regularly as the Caledonian representative. Why wouldn't she give you the same honor?"

"I ... I don't know," he said, obviously never considering the slight before.

"Do you think Llassar has been keeping you from her? I mean, your father placed him in charge of your training, so maybe they all think that makes you just some kind of apprentice, and not a real leader."

"They don't think that," he said defensively.

"Ohh, I know," she said soothingly, sitting next to him, putting an arm around his middle. "I was just trying to come up with some explanation of why you would be slighted so. You are one of the most talented men I've ever met, I just wish they'd listen to you more, take advantage of your skills. It's selfish, I know, since that wish is partly for my own safety and partly for my desire to see you with the status you deserve, since I'm no longer a queen and can give in to simpler desires now, like wanting to see my husband receive the recognition he deserves."

"Thank you," he said, setting down his spoon and putting his arm around her. "Truly, I've never had someone with this much faith in me before, and ... I appreciate you. Don't worry, I won't let you down. I'll make them see me."

"Good. That's all I ask. Now, finish your meal so I can welcome my warrior home properly," she said, letting her arm drop lower, her hand resting on a muscly haunch.

Cormac gave her a lecherous glance, and Medb looked away, partly to maintain the demure attitude men seemed to like, and partly to get a handle on the overwhelming urge to roll her eyes.

Men were so easily led!

Chapter 4

North-Western Germania

Ky crept through the snow-covered forest, Vandili and Istvaeones tribesmen moving with equal stealth on either side of him. A dozen men in total, they were the ones who'd shown the best marksmanship with the new muskets over the last three weeks of training. Each was seasoned in fighting and hunting in the thick Germanic woods, and five knew this very area like the back of their hands.

It was easy to see their skill with each slow, precise step. Only Ky's augmented hearing could make out the crunch of snow under their heavily padded boots, which were quiet enough to be drowned out by the sound of the breeze rustling through the snow-capped trees.

The Carthaginians, on the other hand, seemed to be making no attempt to hide their presence. Even without his drone, soaring above the treetops, Ky would have known where the supply-laden wagons and the assigned guards were, a few hundred yards ahead. Horses stomping, loudly complaining men, and the clanking of metal marked their position for the world to hear.

There were about a hundred of them in total, with maybe fifty guards and as many laborers and drivers moving supplies needed for one of the nearby Carthaginian forces his Germanic allies had been shadowing.

A handful of minutes later, Ky could see them himself through the dense foliage. Five carts were slowly being moved by straining four-horse teams, pulling hard at their traces, hauling the laden vehicles over ruts and divots in the horse path. Two soldiers flanked either side of each cart, with the remainder split evenly in front or behind the small supply convoy. They looked miserable in the cold, and by their light brown skin tone, Ky pegged them as conscripted men from the Middle East or North Africa, making them particularly unprepared for working and fighting in these conditions.

Ky understood the reasoning behind sending conscripts far away from areas they were familiar with, to help maintain discipline, but if they were smart they should have swapped Germanics with those areas they controlled near the Ural Mountains, to at least keep from fighting at a disadvantage. Of course, a society like the Carthaginians had other priorities than those Ky would have in their place.

Ky held up a hand, stopping his well-spread-out team. They'd trained for the last week on how to operate as a unit, which had been easier than Ky expected. They were used to fighting like this and weren't the screaming barbarians that the Romans in his legions had pegged them as. Ky only had to learn their hand signals, which for him and Sophus had been child's play, to be able to lead them.

After giving one last appraising glance at the convoy, he signaled for five of the men to hold where they were while the rest moved laterally, spreading out to where the wagon train would be in a few minutes. After keeping two men with him, Ky sent the remaining five to where the head of the column would be in a few minutes at their current pace.

Waiting, he glanced at the man nearest him. Wulfram, an Istvaeones under-chieftain, was a towering German with fiery red hair and a beard to match. The man gave Ky a nod in answer to the unspoken question. The tribesmen were ready.

Ky gripped his rifle, noticeably different from the muskets designed after the Napoleonic era patterns due to its slightly longer length and thinner barrel. Kneeling, he raised his rifle, holding it unnaturally steady, as if it sat on a shelf. His allies followed suit, albeit without the same aptitude. Ky could feel their eyes on him as he looked through the trees and the drone simultaneously, Sophus drawing lines marking when the Carthaginians would cross into his trap. The group targeting the rear of the convoy was slightly off and would be partially blocked from their target by the rear wagon, but there was nothing to do about it now.

The crack of his rifle exploded like thunder, shattering the relative stillness of the forest, followed by a dozen muskets firing almost as one. Ten guards in total fell dead, struck by the deadly hail of lead balls erupting from the trees. Only two of his men missed, which was about what Ky had expected. Even with muskets, at this range, it didn't take a marksman to kill someone.

The harnessed horses shrieked, rearing at the cacophony of gunfire, a sound the beasts had never encountered before. Their handlers fought to control the panicked animals as chaos descended upon the makeshift road.

Guardsmen scrambled for their weapons, but the coordinated volley had caught them completely by surprise. Not that it mattered. Spears and shields offered little defense against Ky's modern firearms, especially not at this range. Seconds passed while the confused men tried to figure out what was happening. None of them had been among the mostly dead men who they'd fought near the river two months ago, and hearing tales about firearms is very different than experiencing them firsthand for the first time.

The second volley ripped into more guardsmen. Slightly worse accuracy this time, with only eight falling. The tribesmen had their blood up, and excited men tended to have lower accuracy.

By the time Ky and his men had reloaded and a third volley ripped through their targets, the Carthaginians had finally worked out where the attack was coming from. Between the wall of smoke starting to build between the tribesmen and the Carthaginians and the long tongues of flame leaping out of a dozen weapons at once, it shouldn't have been difficult to work out.

Several of the remaining guards propelled arrows blindly toward the gun smoke, but their shots went wild. Ky had anticipated as much, and his men were well concealed behind dense foliage. Still, two tribesmen cried out as arrows found their marks, though neither injury seemed immediately life-threatening.

A handful of the guards, not armed with ranged weapons, regrouped, rallying with shouts and gesturing angrily with spears as they attempted to launch a counterattack. Their courage was admirable but misplaced. Muskets erupted again, cutting the would-be attackers down before they'd advanced more than a few paces. The rest wavered, exchanging panicked glances, unwilling to share their comrades' fate.

With the bulk of the guards dead or wounded, the survivors abandoned any thought of a second charge. Their only hope lay in escape or defense. The guards and the mostly unscathed laborers scrambled behind the wagons, using the vehicles as makeshift barricades. The few armed with bows loosed another futile volley, more to distract their attackers than out of any real hope of inflicting damage.

They, however, didn't move before yet another volley of fire exploded into their midst, killing even more guards. Only ten guards remained, plus roughly fifty unarmed laborers and wagon drivers. Ky watched the guards take up defensive positions behind the wagons through the drone footage as he reloaded, considering their positions.

One of the injured tribesmen had already picked his musket back up, an arrow sticking out of his side, giving Ky eleven men. He was starting to formulate a plan to surround the Carthaginians and demand their surrender when his new allies took the decision out of his hands.

Ky cursed under his breath as the tribesmen surged forward with a roar.

"Hold," he called out in the Anglii dialect, the language the selected men all shared.

They ignored him completely, crashing through the foliage, axes, and bayonets held high. The guards rallied, bracing to meet the oncoming tide of fur-clad barbarians while the laborers and wagon drivers shrieked, some running and others diving under the wagons, hoping for some kind of cover. The lead horse team apparently decided the sight of screaming warriors was too much and bolted down the path, taking the wagon with it. The men unlucky enough to seek shelter under that particular wagon were then trampled or crushed to death by hooves and wagon wheels, leaving mangled bodies behind.

Ky emerged from the tree line, rifle raised, but there was little he could do now except wade into the fray. The tribesmen fell upon the guards with a fury, fueled by years of privation and abuse suffered at the hands of the Carthaginians. Axes and bayonets clashed with spears and shields.

Wulfram leaped forward, his massive axe swinging to hack a guardsman's shield in two, following through to bury the blade in the man's chest. He wrenched it free, roaring triumphantly, only to jerk as a spear caught him in the thigh. The red-bearded German stumbled but remained standing as Ky brought up his rifle and fired, sending the assailant tumbling backward into the trees on the other side of the path.

In a matter of moments, the guards were all cut down. Ky could see that one other tribesman had been hit, this one fatally with a spear in the chest, but that was the extent of the Germanic losses. The guardsmen had fallen to a man.

Then they moved on to the laborers, who were shown no mercy as they were cut down without a chance to flee or beg for their lives. Ky shoved through the combatants, trying to halt the slaughter, but it was a losing battle.

In minutes, the fighting was over. A few of the unarmed men managed to surrender, and a few more made it into the trees, running for their lives, but more than eighty men lay dead. Bodies and wreckage littered the forest floor, staining the snow and mud crimson. The tribesmen stood amid the carnage, chests heaving, weapons and furs splattered with gore.

Seeing there were no more men to kill, they raised their axes and muskets into the air, shouting their triumph. Ky was never one to back down from a fight, but after the guards were dead, this stopped being a battle and became a massacre. He knew he'd have to accept some brutality, fighting in a war in this time period, especially this war where one side had brutalized the other for so long, and he knew he would be hard-pressed to find a single combatant without a score to settle.

"Let me look at your leg," Ky said to Wulfram, pointing at the bleeding appendage.

"It's nothing," the tribesman said, slapping Ky on the back. "Enjoy the victory. We slaughtered them like animals, and these supplies will feed several villages through the winter. Today is a great day, and your weapons have proven to be as powerful as you promised."

"It won't always be this easy," Ky said. "They're still shocked when they hear firearms for the first time. As they get used to fighting against them, they'll realize the limits of the damage we can do and how long it takes us to reload. Had they charged after the first volley, we would have only been able to get off one more round, and then we would have been engaged by three times our number in hand-to-hand combat. Even your warriors, as great as they are, wouldn't stand up to those numbers."

"Then we bring more men," Wulfram said. "You said the best thing we could do to contribute to the war, if we didn't want to fight in your silly lines, is to raid their supplies and smaller units when we find them. We will do that. With your muskets, we will slaughter them by the hundreds. Their gods will weep at the sight."

"These weapons aren't magic, Wulfram. Give yourself more room; don't try to wipe them out every time. It worked this time only because of their surprise. Unless you have superior numbers, hit them and fade away. Even with these guns, you can still lose if you're overconfident."

"We're not afraid to die," he said, puffing out.

"I know that, and I'm not doubting your bravery. I'd prefer, however, that you didn't die. To paraphrase someone from my homeland, instead of dying for your people, I'd rather you make those bastards die instead."

"Ha," Wulfram said, slapping Ky hard on the back. "That's good. Yes, we will make them die. And these supplies will feed several villages that the death worshipers stripped bare. A few more victories like this and some of our people might even make it through the winter."

Even as he talked, his men, at least those not stripping the dead of valuables, were getting the remaining wagons turned around, starting them back north.

"Be careful. I wasn't expecting them to have this many men in this area, or that they would have collected this much from the local villages. There must be a larger force out here than we expected, and they must be pushing toward our armies even though winter has set in. Spread your patrols out more and try to cover a larger area, but be careful. You could easily stumble onto a force too large to handle."

"We'll be careful. These people don't know how to operate in the winter or in forests. They stumble along, loud and blind. We can hear them long before we see them, and only an idiot would be surprised by them."

"Not all of them will be like that. If they have some of their core troops, they will be more skilled than this. They might also have people who are used to this kind of terrain. Don't get overconfident."

Wulfram just shrugged and limped off, essentially ending their conversation. Ky, however, was still concerned. They only had a limited number of muskets, most of which had gone to the Anglii, who were being rolled into the legions. Eventually, they'd replace those with rifles, and their muskets could go to the irregular forces, but they needed time, which was something they might not get if the Carthaginians were continuing their operations into the winter.

His only hope was that these guerrilla attacks would slow them down, or that their force was small enough that he would have time to prepare for them and to finish their new allies' training.

Devnum

Valdar looked at his commanders as the last of the captains, minus Hakon, whose ship was currently assigned to guard Port Invictus, arrived in the dockside meeting hall. They were an odd collection. Mostly Scandi, although a few Romans and Caledonians had managed to prove knowledgeable enough about the sea to make their way into the small but growing ranks of new shipmasters.

It had taken those Romans some time to forget the nonsense they learned about oars and galleys and to learn to sail a real ship, but any of the men selected to sail one of the Britannic Empire's new caravels had to show they were adaptable enough to master the skills. Although trade continued, the waters became more treacherous with an increase in large storms and even some icebergs as you sailed up the Scandi coast. That, coupled with additional hazards caused by ice buildup aboard the ships, would slow the pace of naval operations considerably over the next several months.

Valdar wasn't one to waste time, however. If they weren't going to be chasing and sinking Carthaginians, he was going to get in as much training as possible while time allowed. Some of the newer ships' crews had only been working their vessels for a few months, which had their ships lagging behind in fleet-scale operations.

"Thank you for joining us," Valdar said as the last two captains finally arrived, shaking water and frost off their large fur coats. "I trust winter has not dulled your spirits too greatly."

"This isn't winter," Einar, captain of the Aquila, said. "I was thinking about sitting on the sand and basking in the warmth of the sun."

"Yes, we get it. The north is cold and our winters are for old women," Fabius, one of the newest captains and the only Roman among them, grumbled.

Fabius was slated to be the captain of one of the new caravels available in the spring, and he and his crew had been training with Einar on the Aquila. The Roman was too stuck in tradition and still held a lot of the old prejudices about Roman superiority, which had led to Einar's continual taunting of him. Although it hadn't come to blows, Valdar was moving Fabius and his men to the Seadreki next week to train with Dag, who had more patience with that kind of thing.

Honestly, if the Empress hadn't requested he begin finding placements from Romans, Caledonians, and even Germanics to command some of the ships, he would have put Fabius back on the beach. As it was, he had little choice. Fabius, for all his prejudices and flaws, was still the best ship captain the Romans could muster and had been quick to adapt from galley-style ship mastering to that of the new, deep-hulled, sail-driven vessels.

"There isn't time for that anyway," Valdar said, brushing past the small spat. "Lucan tells me the new caravels will be launched by spring, meaning our fleet will be up to twelve ships, giving us enough to leave some here to patrol and support the invasion forces, and to have the rest start wider operations against the Carthaginians."

"So we finally get to fight," Alfhildr, the only woman and most aggressive of their number, said.

"We get to take the fight to them, yes. To do that, however, we need to be ready to begin as soon as the newest ships launch. Provisioning our forces in the north won't be an issue, but stretching our lines to supply Port Invictus and the Middle Sea may prove to be difficult. Additionally, running supplies and reinforcements to the legions, guarding shipping routes, and launching an expedition as far as the Middle Sea is going to spread us thin."

"Supplying the northern army shouldn't be difficult," Einar said. "They are only a few days' sail at most, and our people control most of those waters. Other than some minor piracy, there isn't much to guard in that area, especially now that Yrsa is making merchant runs in his armed schooner through there."

"If we push into the Middle Sea, do we need to protect our shipping routes?" Kvasir, captain of the Pollux, asked. "Especially if they have the new sails, they should be able to outrun any pirates or Carthaginians they come across."

"Even if we push into the Middle Sea, the ocean is a big place. We won't be able to stop the Carthaginians if they decide to keep bringing the fight here."

"At least not until more of those schooners are ready. If more of our merchants had armed ships, they would be able to fight off anyone who might come for them," Ingvarr, the man selected to lead the Hrafn, one of the new caravels, said.

"At two to three a year, it will be a long time before that's reality," Lucan, the imperial shipwright, said.

"What about outfitting more of the existing merchants with the new sail plans? Can we increase their speed without slowing the new construction?"

"Possibly," Lucan said, looking off as he began mental calculations. "We're working on setting up a refitting section on the Londinium docks, since we're limited on how much more we can expand here. It will be some time before we can do any new construction there, but we can at least move most of the maintenance and upgrading work there. It should be ready in the next month. We face some challenges. Every industry is demanding more resources, and Hortensius has begun negotiations with some of the cloth manufacturers, which could slow down getting the sails we need, let alone putting them on ships. He has the ear of the Empress and is one of her favorites, so if he asks for it, she will probably give it to him. That isn't our biggest problem, however. Our biggest problem is going to be manpower. The entire Empire is short-staffed, from the legions to the factories to the fields. We're still getting a fair number of immigrants, but it takes time for the Praetorians to weed out possible Carthaginian infiltrators, and everyone is fighting over those laborers who do get through the evaluation."

"This will be a problem for a while, and we need to get more creative with our solutions. What if you sent an agent to the continent itself, in areas already cleared by the northern army? It's dangerous, but they could go to villages and recruit workers directly. Since they're recruiting from the villages, the chance of infiltrators would be low, meaning we could probably convince Faenius to allow them in without going through one of the relocation points. We could also start incentivizing the workers who are coming in now, or even some that are in other industries. Offering higher pay, lodging, whatever."

"As soon as we start doing that, Hortensius and the rest will match what we do, driving up costs while only boosting our manpower a little bit in the beginning before they match us."

"But it will give us a boost. Unlike the shipbuilding, the refitting isn't infinite. Eventually, all the Roman, Ulaid, and Caledonian ships that already existed will be converted," Valdar pointed out.

"At which point we will have to build more capacity for building new ships in Londinium, since the refitting is only a temporary measure. The Consul has already promised larger merchant vessels that will dwarf even the caravels. If demand for the schooners is any indication, we will never run out of requests for new ships, especially if the Empire keeps footing the bill for their construction as it is now."

"Doesn't that agreement force the captains getting new ships to be conscripted for work by us anytime we need them?" Egil, captain of the Bolvastr, asked.

"For a time," Lucan confirmed. "But not indefinitely, and that setup was only a stopgap. I don't know how long the Empress is going to continue to make that offer. With everything that's happening, the treasury must already be running a little thin."

"That isn't our problem," Valdar said. "Our problem is dealing with the mission assigned to us. Protect Britannic shipping, support the armies on the continent, and sink as much Carthaginian shipping as possible, and we need to find a way to do this."

"I'll look into sending someone to start bringing in our own workforce. It won't be long before the various manufacturers follow us in doing that, and I can't imagine what the Germanic reaction will be as we start siphoning off their labor, but it will help us a little. I think we can shave a few weeks off the construction of the new slips in Londinium and maybe get a dozen ships retrofitted a month."

"Do the best you can," Valdar said. "I'll talk to the treasurer and, if possible, the Empress to see if I can't free up some supplies and manpower. I'll also talk to them about Hortensius and the weavers. I might not have her ear the way Hortensius does, but she knows how critical what we're doing is. I can only hope she listens to us. Until then, captains, make sure your ships are ready to sail as soon as the ice thaws and have our new crews as prepared as possible when their ships roll off the docks. They need to be able to sail and shoot as well as any of our existing crews by then. I want to be on the sail by spring, and I don't want to hear any excuses as to why we aren't ready. Steal, beg, or borrow anything you have to. Do you understand?"

The captains all nodded their agreement, although Lucan was looking much less confident. To be fair, he'd be left here, on this island with the people they'd be begging and stealing from, while his captains could put an ocean between themselves and the angry manufacturers left behind.

"Good. Then let's get to it."

Chapter 5

"... your crops are purchased, and make sure the larger farms can't mandate which growers a market is required to buy from. Will that suffice?" Lucilla said, trying to maintain her focus in spite of the last five hours spent listening to dozens of petitioners.

"Yes, Empress. Your wisdom is an example to all of us," the farmer said, starting to genuflect.

"There's no need for that. We're all citizens here. Just ensure you treat your employees well and sell at a fair price, and you will have honored me enough."

"Thank you again, Empress," the man said, still bowing slightly before hustling out of the room.

She'd never understand how her father did this, hour after hour, without losing his sanity. She agreed with his policy of having set times to personally hear the complaints of average citizens, both so her people knew she was listening and to keep an ear to what was happening in her Empire, aside from what her spies and advisors told her. It's why she kept the practice her father had started in the first place. She just hadn't been prepared for the toll it would take on her. True, she'd sat in for him when he'd fallen ill, but the volume of petitioners had been less when people heard they weren't seeing their ruler directly. Now that she was Empress, the volume had increased dramatically.

"Who's next?" she asked Gaius.

"The Flamen Dialis, Lucius Vesnius Sacerdos," the young man replied.

Lucilla sighed and squeezed her eyes shut. While she understood the need to meet with the average citizen and didn't mind it except for how long audience days could drag on, this was one audience she wished she could have denied. Pompous, overbearing, and paternalistic in the worst ways, the Flamen Dialis was almost certainly here to complain, as he had numerous times before.

He was, however, the highest religious figure in Devnum, and the Roman state as a whole, and not someone she could just ignore.

"Send him in," she said, leaning back and putting on her political battle face.

The doors opened and Vesnius marched in, posture rigid, nose so far in the air she thought he might topple over backward. The purple of his traditional toga, a symbol of his office, swished around him as he marched up to the small dais her throne sat upon, a mound of golden bracelets and jewelry jingling softly as he moved.

"Pontifex Maximus, to what do I owe the pleasure?" she asked, greeting him.

His expression remained somber, as pompous as ever, "I have come to speak on behalf of the gods and all the people of Rome. There are concerns which can no longer remain unvoiced."

"What are the gods concerned about today?"

Vesnius frowned. If she'd been less tired, she would have worded that differently and not had it come off so flippantly.

"The gods are concerned with everything, Empress, and they have begun to show their displeasure as of late. Two blights have broken out among the largest farms, and a calf was born with no eyes this week, warnings from Jupiter of what is to come if we continue on the path we're currently on."

"Considering Jupiter sent us his sword to lead our people to freedom, what path, exactly, is he concerned about?"

"The Empire is changing, and at an unprecedented pace. Your father altered much in his time, allowing barbarians into our lands as equals," he said, a hint of distaste coloring the last word. "But he at least upheld our traditions, the values that have made Rome great. There are those who now fear too much is being lost, absorbed into this new ... amalgamation you and your consort seem so intent on forging."

"We are fighting for survival, and our strength has come in joining with our Caledonian and Ulaid allies. My father understood this. We honor the values of our ancestors by using them to build a greater society, and by recognizing that the traditions and values of our new allies aren't that different from our own. We are stronger, together, than we ever were facing the Carthaginians by ourselves."

"With respect, change brings uncertainty, and uncertainty brings fear. The people look to the gods for spiritual guidance in times of turmoil," Vesnius said, sighing heavily. "New temples to foreign gods have begun to spring up in our cities. They worship these invading gods as if they are equals of Jupiter and Mars. It's not just their gods. Their traditions clash with ours, their people refuse to honor the values we hold most dear, even in our cities. This Britannic Empire you seek to build ... it risks becoming unrecognizable. Is our survival worth abandoning who we are?"

"I disagree with your very premise. Allowing our allies or others to follow their own traditions doesn't make ours any less valid. If you speak to someone who worships different gods than you, does that make your beliefs any less true or your worship somehow less valuable to the gods? My father welcomed progress, including advancements in health and infrastructure. The gods bless innovation, not just tradition. Have faith in our people's character."

"Your father may have started us down this path, Empress, but the responsibility now lies with you. These foreign gods and traditions are an affront. If you insist on honoring them as our own, then I must consider refusing to conduct any state religious ceremonies."

Lucilla frowned and said, "You would hold our religious traditions hostage? The gods demand our worship and will know if you're the one keeping them from their rightful homage."

Vesnius drew himself up, gold bracelets jingling, and said, "I am bound to serve the will of the gods, not the whims of any mortal ruler. My duty is to uphold their laws and ensure proper respect is paid. I cannot in good conscience support ceremonies meant to honor those who do not share our reverence for Jupiter and Mars."

Lucilla leaned back in her throne, meeting Vesnius's defiant gaze with one of her own.

"You would be making a grave mistake. Our cultural identity stems from our values, not just from tradition alone. We must adapt to survive and prosper," she said, trying one last time.

"Our traditions are our values. They have stood for centuries and define who we are as Romans," he said, putting particular emphasis on the final word. "I am bound to serve the gods, not any mortal ruler. My duty is to uphold their laws and ensure proper respect."

"And as ruler of Britannia and consort of the gods' own avatar, my duty is to my people," Lucilla said, rising and descending the dais to stand before him. "If you refuse to perform your sacred office, I will have no choice but to remove you and install someone who understands their place."

Vesnius blanched.

"Y-you would not dare!"

"I will do whatever is necessary to protect my people," Lucilla lifted her chin, gaze unwavering. "All of my people. Be they Roman, Caledonian, or Uliad. The choice is yours. Do your duty or step aside."

Vesnius swallowed, shifting nervously before finally saying, "I … You leave me little choice, Empress."

He tried his best to seem defiant, but she could see the fear behind his eyes. Men like this never thought they were vulnerable, believing everyone, even their monarch, had to back down to their will. They also all crumbled just like he did when they realized they weren't as indispensable as they thought they were.

"A wise decision. Our people look to these ceremonies for spiritual guidance, as you said yourself," she said, turning to walk back up to her dais, dismissing him.

No longer face to face with her, Vesnius finally found his courage, saying, "Do not mistake this for surrender, Empress. I will do as commanded, but I cannot condone the path you seem intent upon. Accommodating these outsiders risks taking Rome too far from tradition. You play a dangerous game, Empress. The sword the gods sent may cut both ways."

Lucilla turned, tensing at the implied threat.

"Is that meant as a warning or prophecy, Vesnius?" she asked, her eyes narrowing.

"Merely an observation. I have given my warning before. I pray you heed it, for the good of our people."

"The good of our people is why this path was chosen," Lucilla said. "If you cannot see that, I fear your council will be of little use in addressing the challenges to come. You should go, before that fear becomes a reality."

Vesnius looked furious but was wise enough to stay silent, bowing and finally taking his leave.

As soon as he was out of her sight, Lucilla sat down on her throne and laid her head back, sighing heavily. Men like Vesnius almost made this job not worth it. In spite of all the evidence in front of them, they couldn't escape the past. They'd rather see the world burn around them than accept even the smallest change.

"Please tell me that was the last one," she said to the ceiling.

"Actually, your majesty, Master Hortensius has just arrived in answer to your summons and is waiting outside," Gaius said hesitantly.

For a man who worked directly for Ramirus, Gaius certainly was jumpy at times. He also hadn't picked up on her moods or preferences yet, or he would have known that was good news. Hortensius was one of the few people in her Empire that she looked forward to seeing. As much as his enthusiasm could cause her problems, he was also a welcome presence and a pleasant palate cleanser after her last meeting.

"Good, I'll see him in my office," she said, smirking inwardly as she said the word, her thoughts instantly going to her absent husband.

There were a lot of things that reminded her of Ky every day, but it still amazed her how much he'd really changed Rome, even in small ways like the words they used. Before Ky arrived she would have called the room where she did the day-to-day work of governance, rather than granting audiences, her tablinum. When people heard him use his new word, however, it had been picked up to the point where she was using it, even subconsciously. It was like that in many areas. Small things he didn't even think about had become stylish for others to pick up and copy.

Even the chair she sat in, behind the table already stacked with papers, was one of his changes. High-backed, with supports for her arms, like a small, simple throne, had become the standard for seating over the stools her people usually used. Besides making everyone who owned one feel a little like an emperor themselves, the higher back gave support when sitting for long periods of time and was notably more comfortable. Carpenters across the city had been doing a big business making these. Another ripple from Ky's appearance.

Her thoughts of her husband were interrupted when Gaius opened the door and admitted Hortensius, who bowed as he crossed the threshold.

"Your Majesty, I came as soon as I received your missive, although I'm surprised you knew I was here. Your spymasters must be efficient to keep track of so many people at all times."

"They are efficient, but it wasn't anything as clandestine as that. You've been visiting every weaver in the city, buying up fabric, something which Valdar and Lucan complained to me about several days ago. Your purchases have started driving up the cost of sailcloth, and they're concerned they won't be able to get enough for their projects."

"Ohh, I hadn't even considered," he said, looking off distractedly for a moment as he thought it over. "It should only be a temporary problem. Besides buying fabric for some initial tests, I was also talking to several of the owners I know personally about moving their operations to Factorium and increasing our textile production to a larger, full-scale production, bringing several manufacturers under one roof. While they are a little resistant, since they each think they should have their own facility, I believe I'm making headway and should have the new factory under construction within the month. Please tell Lucan I will try to keep from buying much more cloth and will ensure that he is our top priority when the new facilities are ready."

"I will, but I didn't call you here to chastise you about that. I was planning another trip to Factorium with a new project for you, but since you were already in town I thought I could give it to you now, and you could relay Sorantius's portion to him, thus saving me the trip. I know I just piled new projects on you, but hearing about this additional one I realized it would actually end up saving both of us a lot of time traveling back and forth, so I thought it a worthwhile additional burden."

Hortensius was the only person who knew about her ability to talk to Ky over long distances, which meant she didn't have to hide the origin of her ideas, which was why she wanted to speak to him in private, since that was information she wasn't keen to get out to the public. Although she was fairly certain that some of her guards had figured it out already, even if they were less willing to share that information than Hortensius was.

"I am, of course, always at your service," he said, bowing even deeper than before, arms out wide in an overdramatic pose.

Shaking her head in amusement, Lucilla said, "Unlike the hot air balloons and scaled-down steam engine, this invention will require you to develop new processes, and it will require you to work closely with Sorantius, since parts of the system are chemically based. It's called a telegraph, and it is a way to send messages very quickly over long distances."

"Like the semaphore?" he asked.

"Kind of; but much, much faster and over much longer distances. My understanding is that a person on one end of a long wire, up to about one hundred mille passas long, sends a message by tapping on the device, using a type of code not dissimilar to the flag system used by the semaphore. That message almost instantly arrives at the receiving station on the other end of the wire, where the operator listens to the taps, which would be in the form of long and short taps, combined together to form letters. For locations close together, that message could go from, say, Factorium to Devnum, would be direct from one telegraph operator to another, while for further distances, say to Londinium, the message would have to be received and then relayed down the next stretch of wire, until it reached its destination, again, similar to the semaphore stations. Except where the semaphore station could take hours to transmit the signal, since each station has to be in visual range of the previous one, these can be much further apart, reducing the number of times the message has to be received and relayed. The three hours it takes to get a message from here to Londinium could happen in ten minutes, with the reply sent back in another ten minutes. What's more, with the proper protective coating, we could put the cable along the bottom of the sea, allowing us the same speed of communication to Emain Macha or one of the new ports being set up on the continent. Our forces in combat would be able to communicate news and requests to us quickly, without the need for couriers and messengers."

"That is ... exceptional. I can see why this would be something we'd want, and its advantage in nearly every aspect of our Empire is readily apparent. I am not clear on how taps on one end of a metal wire can travel so far to be received on the other. While it's true the vibrations can travel down something like that, anything over a few feet and wind or any kind of disturbance could hide or even cause false vibrations."

"It isn't vibrations, although you have the right idea, as it is something similar. It uses something called an electrical current."

"Electr... it sounds like the Greek word for amber, but clearly it isn't. I don't know this word."

"I didn't either. It comes from another new word, electricity. Ky gave a lot of explanations on what that means that I didn't really understand, but I included them in the papers I will give you. My basic understanding is that lightning in the sky is electricity, and there is a way we can harness a small part of that power and use it. This part of the lightning doesn't just travel through the air, but also travels through metal very easily, which is why it so often strikes metal items put on buildings. We will create a device that will make a small amount of this electricity. That electricity will travel down the wire, like a vibration, and it will cause something to happen on the other end of the wire. We can, apparently send short and long sections of the electricity, which creates a short or long vibration, as it were, that can be differentiated on the other end, and it all happens nearly instantly, from one end of the wire to the other."

"So the ... electricity," he said, trying out the new word, "travels through any metal until it reaches the other end of the wire?"

"Yes, although according to Ky copper is ideal for conducting electricity over long distances. We will also have to coat the wire in a processed material Ky called gutta-percha, which is made out of an extract from the flower he's sent Vandar's merchants to acquire. The hope is that by the time that arrives, we will be ready to use it right away."

"I see. And this device that generates the electricity, how does someone make a device capable of producing lightning, and how do we capture that without it destroying all of the equipment we build?"

"We won't be generating lightning. Rather, we will make only a very small portion of the electricity that lightning contains. It is still dangerous and has to be handled carefully, but it won't be like a lightning strike. There are chemicals that, when we stack certain metals in them, begin to produce small amounts of electricity as the chemicals react with the metals. From Ky's description, there aren't even any moving parts and it can all be held in one container, which he called a battery. A battery is needed at each telegraph station, so it will be something we need to continually produce, as it apparently loses its potency over time."

"Chemicals and metal plates that produce lightning. It boggles the mind."

"I don't fully understand it myself. But Ky provided diagrams and descriptions of how to construct these 'batteries' that generate electricity, along with the production of the assembly for sending the messages and the coated wire," she said, placing a stack of papers on the desk between them.

"Astounding," Hortensius said, leafing through the pages, scrutinizing the unfamiliar schematics and notes. After a few minutes of reading, he set the pages back on the desk and rubbed his temples, shaking his head.

"Your Majesty, I must admit to feeling rather overwhelmed. Between the textile mills, the steam engines, these new 'telegraph' assemblies, not to mention everything else my workshops produce, I fear I've taken on more than I can adequately oversee."

"I understand. We've asked a great deal of you, Hortensius, and you've delivered admirably. But we never intended for you to carry all this alone," she said, giving him a sympathetic look. "For this telegraph system in particular, much of the chemical and metallurgical work involved in producing these 'batteries' seems well-suited to Sorantius' expertise. Would delegating the entire project to him help lighten your load? You will still need to participate, but mostly just to produce the wire, which should be simple enough for your foreman. You might have to loan Sorantius some men able to assemble it, maybe some who worked on the steam engine, but the batteries and the coating of the wire, he should be able to handle it all. And we have the teams who assembled the semaphore stations that can manage the conversion to telegraph stations and the installation of the poles for holding the wire off the ground."

"Yes, that would help immensely," he said, placing his hands on the plans. "Sorantius has a gift for such work, and his skills would be invaluable in developing a viable power source for this technology. I'm sorry, I should have thought of that right away. It is a bad habit of mine; trying to personally handle every task you give me."

"The fact that you take so much personal responsibility is why we trust you with all of these projects," she said, reaching across the desk and putting a hand on his.

"Thank you, Your Majesty. Knowing you have confidence in me means a great deal."

Lucilla waved away his formality. "Never question it, my friend. Now, while you're still here, tell me about any other problems you are currently having. Let's see if we can't find a few other ways to lighten your load."

"That isn't necessary, Emp..."

"Maybe not," she said, interrupting him. "But it is a command from your Empress, and a request from your friend. Let me help you if I can."

Hortensius' grin returned as they discussed logistics and practical details. She couldn't help but feel a wave of affection for his enthusiasm. Even when stressed as he was today, Hortensius remained undaunted. After dealing with politics and the difficulties of ruling, his optimism and enthusiasm were a much-needed balm.

Chapter 6

Daramouda

Tabnit looked around at his assembled officers, a sea of attentive faces staring back at him over a large table set up to hold a massive map of the continent. Wooden markers were scattered across the map denoting the positions of armies, theirs and the invading Romans, and the largest settlements, mostly Carthaginian, but a few very large indigenous villages as well.

The city they were currently in was marked as one of the largest Carthaginian settlements, which was only partially true. Until a month ago, it had been a small port built to supply the troops operating east of the Alps and north of the Pyrenees mountains. After their losses in Hispania and the realization that they would need a much larger presence to defeat the Romans and their demonic new weapons, a massive expansion program had begun.

The task the emperor had saddled him with was, without a doubt, the most daunting he'd ever been given. Especially once he'd heard more first-hand accounts of the Romans' new weapons. The emperor and his advisers had given some detail, but Tabnit wasn't sure they knew the full extent of these weapons based on what he'd discovered since arriving in Daramouda. While the weapons from the Far East he was being given would help, unless the emperor vastly underestimated their power, Tabnit doubted they'd rival what he would be facing.

Still, it wasn't like he was given a choice. He had to find a way to defeat the Romans here and now, or he and everyone he'd ever known would suffer for it.

"I know most of you are shaken by what has happened over the last several months," Tabnit began, his voice steady. "Yes, the Romans' new weapons make them a formidable adversary. And yes, we have received a long string of defeats facing them. I am concerned, however, that some of you have taken that as an excuse to shirk from your duties in fear. With the exception of one commander who chose to keep his forces in the field and, even now, is fighting the Romans, the rest of you ran back here and have been cowering ever since."

He looked around the room, hard, making sure to impress upon each man his displeasure with their recent failures.

"This, I cannot abide. And neither can the emperor. Starting now, anyone turning from the enemy, shirking from their duty, will be made an example of. Do you understand?"

There was no surprise or shock among the gathered officers. This had always been the way of the empire. It was only a matter of degrees, of how seriously a given commander applied this command that varied.

"That being said, we have, until now, tried to continue fighting this war as we have fought all of our wars before, relying on raw power and our numbers to roll over and crush anyone who stood before us. I think it is clear that strategy no longer works, at least not against the Romans and their new weapons. To this end, we are going to have to adapt and find new ways to combat them. When I give orders I expect them to be followed, no matter if you understand why or agree with them. While I want my officers to show initiative in the field and I stand behind them, as the one in command in that moment to alter their direct orders as they see fit to win the battle at hand, if that alteration is to simply send your men headfirst into the jaws of the Roman line, hoping one last charge will break them, then I do not consider that initiative. I consider that stupidity. Do I make myself clear?"

Again, the men all nodded their understanding, although it was unclear how many actually grasped what he was ordering them to do. The hardest struggle he'd had with commanders was that merit rarely determined who got elevated to command in the emperor's service. Connections and kissing up to the right people was really all that was needed, which meant their forces often did not have the strongest military minds leading them. In the past, against like-armed people, that hadn't mattered, but they were no longer in the past.

"Now that we all understand each other we can get down to business. The emperor is pulling together as many men as he can, and we will be receiving large numbers of reinforcements over the next several months. I've already tasked the commanders of these forces to prepare for their arrival. Many of these men will not have been under arms before, and over the next several months as we continue to build our forces, I expect your unit commanders to drill them until they drop. I want these men in good enough shape to be able to fight effectively when we send them into battle."

The commanders he'd assigned to the job already knew their tasks, but he wanted to say it out loud for emphasis.

"We will not be sitting idle while that happens. I know many of you are not used to operating more than patrols and small punitive actions over the winter months, and I do not care. We currently outnumber the Romans, but they are building allies and are continuing to send men from their island. The longer we give them, the harder the battle we will face when things come to a head. To that end, I am sending General Matho north with fifteen thousand men, the bulk of what we have left here. You will rendezvous with General Ippar, who commands the smaller detachments and was dealing with a small insurrection north of the Danube when the Romans invaded. You are not to engage the Romans in a straight-up fight. They are currently being supplied from the coastline and relying heavily on those tribes that have defected to their side. We need to cut off that support. Burn any villages harboring even one Roman supporter, destroy supply lines, and harass them. I want their army to wither on the vine. If they cannot eat, it doesn't matter how powerful their weapons are. I say again, to make myself clear, do not assault their forces directly."

"I understand," Matho said with a slight bow of his head.

"Good. Once our reinforcements arrive, I will take them west to deal with the Romans in Hispania. For now, all of our forces will use this port as their base of supply. The emperor has fortified the mouth of the Syrian Sea as best as he could and forbidden any ships to travel beyond that to the west, since we can no longer trust any of our shipping to survive where the Romans can reach them. I've been promised the rate of supply here will increase and we will have what we need to achieve victory, but be aware our supply lines will now be much longer than any of you are used to. Take what you can from the locals and protect the shipments in your area as best you can. Secondly, there will be no reinforcements, at least for the foreseeable future. Every soldier that comes in will be going west when that army marches, leaving only a skeleton force behind. Your commands are on their own."

The commanders looked disturbed by that, but no one complained. One of the strengths of the Carthaginian army was that they ruled nearly everything their sight touched, which meant they were never far from supply and reinforcements. The recent turn of events, losing control of the seas and effectively losing control of northern Germania, was a new situation for them. And one no serving commander had ever had to face before.

"Commander Nabalsa, you are to take two alae of light infantry and one of cavalry north of the Pyrenees toward the Roman base of operations. We know they are sending messengers north along the coast and we've started to get word that they are sending raiding parties along the mountain range, possibly trying to push forward towards us during the winter. Avoid contact but keep them under observation and disrupt their supply lines. Burn their stores, poison their wells, and slaughter any villagers providing them aid. Do not engage them directly."

Nabalsa paled at the orders but nodded grimly. Tabnit understood the officer's worry. North of the mountains was better than south, where the terrain could be treacherous in this weather, but such a small detachment meant any actual combat against the Roman weapons would destroy them completely. He also needed to keep the Romans on their back foot as much as possible, guessing what their men were up to and keeping them from feeling a sense of safety before the traditional campaign season started.

His gaze shifted to Atar, a young but clever commander in charge of a fresh division of infantry supplemented by Numidian light cavalry. Atar looked eager to prove himself, his youthful confidence overshadowing a healthy fear of the coming fight.

"Atar, take your forces south across the plains of Hispania and cut up toward the Roman base from the south. Do not approach their base or forces, but make sure they do not try to go around the mountains in that direction and root out any potential allies they may call on if they start looking for support in that area."

"As you command," Atar said enthusiastically.

"Commander," Tabnit said, pausing until the young commander looked directly at him. "I want you to confirm you understand. You are not to assail the Roman base or the body of their armies directly. You are only authorized to harry small units and foraging parties, or local allies. Understood?"

Atar seemed annoyed, although if it was because Tabnit didn't trust him to decide that on his own or because he wanted to make a play for glory and Tabnit wasn't giving him a way to achieve that, the general wasn't sure.

"Yes, I understand."

"Good. Both of your forces will link back up with the main body when I march it west, directly to the Roman base. Your job is to keep them from making a move towards us before we're ready, and to keep them from flanking our forces or trying to dodge us once we move to engage."

The commanders saluted in unison. Tabnit placed his hands behind his back and studied all of the officers.

"You have your orders. Follow them without hesitation or mercy. The emperor demands results, and results he shall have," he said, his expression serious. "Make no mistake, this will be a bloody campaign. The Romans' weapons provide them an advantage we have yet to counter, and it is to be seen if the Eastern arms are up to that challenge. The price for removing them from the continent will be high."

Silence greeted his pronouncement, but his commanders needed to understand the full scope of what they faced if they hoped to succeed.

"I do not say this to foster fear or doubt but so you comprehend why your orders are as they are. We must weaken them through starvation and attrition before we meet them openly. Disrupt their supply lines, destroy their stores and allies, leave their army weakened and vulnerable by the time we are poised to strike.

The emperor has given us the means to reclaim our lands. Now we must have the will and resolve to see it done, no matter the sacrifice or cost. There can be no failure. Do your duty for the glory of the empire. Dismissed."

The commanders saluted sharply, fists to their chests, and filed from the tent. Tabnit watched them depart with a mixture of anticipation and resignation. The battle to come would test them all. By blood, steel, and slaughter, the Romans would be driven back to their little islands.

Factorium

Hortensius made his way through the cramped workspace, with its piping and huge containers so close together there was barely any room to walk between them. It made his own factories seem spacious by comparison, which he hadn't thought was possible.

In a tiny, enclosed room used as an office sat Sorantius, scribbling notes, his brow furrowed as he concentrated. Hortensius knocked on the door frame, causing Sorantius to look up suddenly, irritation plain on his face until he realized who was interrupting him.

"Is it that late already?" Sorantius said, looking around his windowless office.

"Yep. You said lunchtime."

"I know ... fine, fine, fine. I don't have anything for you on the battery yet. We're still testing the zinc sulfate and the copper sulfate to find the right levels of diluted metals. I'm also not happy with the design of the container to properly seal the mixtures in while affixing the channel for the zinc and copper plates. I'm also not happy with this salt bridge design. I've tested both mined salt and evaporated salt from seawater, and the concentration doesn't last long on the fabric, especially on rainy days. I'm looking at a metal casing for the parts exposed to air, although that means we will have to produce those here, pre-soak the fabric and then seal it with wax, and deliver it to stations that need it, which will be a hassle."

The chemist was in a mood and had started to build up a head of steam the more he talked about his issues. Hortensius had worked with him long enough to not be bothered by the man's abrupt personality, but he also knew Sorantius had a way of working himself into a fit when he got like this, which would make him harder to deal with.

"I'm confident you'll find the answer. We're still working on the copper wire and have to wait on the flowers Valdar sent a ship to retrieve to make the coating, so you have some time. I mostly wanted to see how you were getting on with those initial tests for the hot air balloon."

Although generally, that would have been something Hortensius would take on, in their last meeting, he'd asked Sorantius to take on more of the responsibility of testing the new inventions the Empress and Consul brought them and working with him more closely on their initial production, instead of just producing chemicals as needed.

Sorantius had been a little resistant at first, since his focus remained on his chemicals, which had been his primary interest even before he'd been introduced to the word they now used for his concoctions. Thankfully, the scientist, another new word Ky had introduced, in him and his desire to be one of the first to see these new ideas had won out.

As soon as he asked the question, it was clear from Sorantius's expression that the tests were not going as they had hoped.

"They are not going well. Not at all. The lift is nowhere near what your instructions indicated we should be getting," he said, throwing his hands in the air and starting to work himself up again. "The fabric is far too heavy and loses too much air both through the seams and the weave itself. I attempted to coat the fabric in a diluted wax solution, which helped a little with the air loss, but increased the weight even more, which was not good. Also, the wax began melting very quickly once the hot air began to build up in the balloon, which means that won't work as a long-term solution either. What we need is a much lighter yet more durable fabric with a significantly tighter weave, which I'm not sure is even possible."

Before Hortensius could say anything in response, Sorantius rolled on into his next issue.

"The ropes are also no good. The ones attaching the balloon to the gondola contraption are going to be both too weak to safely hold two passengers without fraying and snapping, and too heavy. I'm also concerned about this winch mechanism. As it rolls out, the rope is going to start badly fraying, and we don't want to lose the balloon after we launch it, sending it drifting to the gods only know where."

Hortensius opened his mouth again to respond, and again Sorantius barely paused for breath, continuing his tirade before Hortensius could manage a word.

"I've tried everything I could think of, and weight is a problem across the board. If we're going to carry two adults, one of the telegraph stations and its battery, and the heating system with additional coal, we can't also have a lot of weight in the material of the balloon itself."

Hortensius waited a beat, to make sure his friend was actually finished with his tirade, and then took the opportunity to finally interject.

"I may have an idea for the tether rope, at least from the ground to the balloon," he began.

Sorantius made a face, but Hortensius ignored him. He was used to Sorantius's abrasive nature and didn't let it bother him. He understood it came from a place of passion and focus, and the manufacturer appreciated the man's unique mind.

"We need to send a telegraph wire up anyway, and I have been concerned about having this wire running up to the balloon, loose in the wind and it getting tangled on something. I thought, instead, we could combine rope and cable around the telegraph wire with some kind of protection around the telegraph wire to protect it from being rubbed or twisted by the rope and cable. It'll add some weight, true, but should provide the strength we need to secure the balloon safely."

Sorantius shook his head, unimpressed, "A little heavier? It will be far too heavy! And it does nothing to address our real problem here ... the weight."

"It won't be that heavy. If we find the right fabric ..."

"Which doesn't exist," he said, throwing his arms up again in exasperation. "I've tried everything you brought me and even talked to some of the weavers themselves. Anything lighter than this will tear so easily it will be useless."

Sorantius took a deep breath, calmed himself, and said, "My apologies, Hortensius. I should not allow my frustrations to get the better of me."

"Think nothing of it," Hortensius said with a warm smile. "Perhaps it is time we seek assistance. Since the initial plans came from the Empress, she might have some insights on what fabric we should be using, or what we're doing wrong with the fabric that keeps it from working as intended."

Sorantius gave a skeptical look, "I've wondered about that. Before the Consul arrived, she showed little interest in natural philosophy. Now she's coming up with devices to allow man to fly and send messages across the country in seconds."

Hortensius nodded thoughtfully, even though he knew the truth that this was all coming from the Consul and simply being sent to the Empress through whatever power they shared to allow their mystic communication. Knowledge he'd been expressly commanded not to share with anyone else.

"It is a conundrum, to be sure," he said, obfuscating. "But before the Consul left, they had many discussions about inventions needed for the war and he gave her plans for a large number of new devices for us to work on. I believe she thinks that, if she were to give them to us all at once, we would become too excited and try and work on all of his designs simultaneously, spreading ourselves too thin, so instead she doles them out as we have the opportunity to take on new work. What I meant was that there's a chance something we could use might be in these designs she is hoarding."

"If she really does have a treasure trove of this type of knowledge, I really would like to get my hands on it, but yes ... that does sound like us, and she's probably right to not turn it all over to us at one time. Fine, let's message her and see if she has a secret she's been keeping from us. You know, I never thought I'd spend so much energy and time trying to construct a giant sack of air!"

Hortensius chuckled, "They have made life interesting. I will draft a request to the Empress detailing our fabric troubles and send it right away."

"Good. Now, unless you need anything else, I have real work to do," Sorantius said, although his annoyed expression couldn't hide the smirk behind it.

Sometimes, the man could have a sense of humor after all.

Chapter 7

North of the Pyrenees Mountains

Optio Quintus Tullus Hortalus pulled his woolen cloak tighter, though it provided scant protection against the biting cold. The icy wind howled and rolled down the mountain and across the rolling foothills, whipping powdery snow into swirling eddies. His leathers creaked as he trudged through the knee-deep drifts, one weary step after another.

Around him, the fifty legionnaires under his command slogged along in silence, heads bowed against the storm, walking as close to the wagons as possible in an attempt to block the wind. He knew they were miserable. It had been two days since they had slept in a proper camp or enjoyed a hot meal, and it would be at least two more full days before they reached the Seventh Legion's current camp. At least he hoped it was only two more days.

With the peaks of the Pyrenees to his right, he knew he was going in the right direction, but it was hard to tell distance in the thick drifts of snow, and it wouldn't be that hard to walk through their camp and not realize they'd passed their countrymen. He'd sent out riders, but only two of the four had returned, and those reported that they had been able to see little with the snow falling as hard as it was, and that they'd barely found their way back to his small unit.

He knew his supplies were vital for the legion, but his faith in the leaders who'd ordered this insane expedition had started to fail. If he was having this kind of trouble, how badly could the main body of the Seventh be faring, and would anyone be in a state to fight if they ever actually reached the Middle Sea?

"Come on lads, pick up the pace!" Quintus called out, injecting false enthusiasm into his voice. "I know you bastards are too tough to let a little snow slow you down."

There was a chuckle or two, that were almost lost in the wind, but they continued to slog forward hopelessly. Quintus clenched his jaw. He knew it was a long shot at this point, but his only other option was the heel of his boot, and their morale was already bad enough.

"I know you're all weary," he continued loudly. "But if we don't push on, a whole legion will be going hungry. The entire southern advance is relying on us, and I'm not going to let the gods-be-damned Carthaginians win this thing because of some weather."

That elicited a few mumbled responses, although some included choice words of exactly what the boys in the legion could feast on which seemed like … poor nutrition. They did pick up the pace a little bit though.

"Just imagine," Quintus went on, "a roaring fire in camp tonight when we arrive. Hot venison stew, freshly baked bread …"

At this, one of the legionnaires, Rufus, Quintus thought, lifted his head.

"With spiced wine?" he asked hoarsely.

"Spiced wine for all!" Quintus proclaimed, smiling beneath his frozen beard.

"I would kill for a slice of …" another legionnaire started to say when a javelin seemed to appear out of nowhere, striking the man square in the chest, taking him off his feet.

"Form square! Rifles ready!" Quintus yelled, reacting on instinct.

In spite of the cold and exhaustion, his men performed admirably, responding with speed and precision. Smoothly, they shifted into a box formation around the central wagons, two men deep on each line. Three more men fell as they formed up, javelins in their backs. A crack of gunfire rang out as the line solidified, the puff of smoke wisping into the blizzard's fury.

"Hold your fire," he called out, staring into the swirling snow. "Hold. First rank, **fire!**"

The first rank fired as one, a wall of lead smashing into the attackers, mostly men on foot, carrying swords and javelins. A swath of men fell, pitched backward as the lead, cone-shaped mini-balls struck them, and sometimes the man behind them fell as well. The enemy kept coming.

"Second rank, **fire!**" he yelled, even as the first rank reloaded.

A second wave of metal slashed into his forces, sweeping more men off their feet. Still, more enemy fighters continued to come into view. If he had enough men for a third rank, he could have held this rate of fire until the enemy broke and ran, but he didn't. At two ranks, he only had enough for six men on a side and two at each corner, which was a very small square. Taking that down to four on a side, he wouldn't have had the firepower on any side to push the enemy back.

The first rank finished reloading just as the Carthaginians got within sword range.

"**Fire! Fire!**" Quintus called out.

Their attackers fell, but the Carthaginian forces were on top of them.

"Prepare to receive charge!" Quintus commanded. "Hold formation!"

With a resounding crash, the skirmishers smashed into the square on all sides. Quintus fired his rifle once and then stabbed over the fighting men, catching an axe-wielding man in the chest, the sharp steel blade cutting through the weaker Carthaginian iron.

Some men in the second rank reloaded, but most were forced to lift their rifles to defend themselves as the Carthaginians pressed their attack. Here and there, a rifle fired, but for the most part, it was down to hand-to-hand combat, removing Britannia's greatest advantage.

"**Push them back!**" Quintus roared, even as he grunted, stabbing another man.

His men were falling in twos and threes, beginning to be pressed backward under the force of the assault. The numbers were finally too much. The Carthaginians overwhelmed the disciplined ranks, breaking the square. More of his men fell as they were pushed back toward the wagon.

Losing his sword, the Optio pulled his gladius, the last line of defense. He stabbed and slashed with controlled fury, dispatching two more enemies before they could close on him. All around him, the legionnaires fought for their lives as the Carthaginian tide crashed over them in a frenzy of violence.

Rufus clubbed a shrieking man with the stock of his rifle before his throat was sliced open. Another legionnaire was tackled from behind, disappearing beneath three enemies who hacked and stabbed with abandon.

"To me, form on me!" Quintus bellowed, seeing the end rapidly approaching.

No more than fifteen legionnaires remained standing, the rest dead or crippled in the blood-churned snow. With their backs to the wagons, the tattered remnants of Quintus's century formed a final desperate line. Men screamed as sword and spear points sought enemy flesh. A bearded axe man broke through, splitting a legionnaire's shield in two before burying the sharpened axe head in the man's face.

"For Britannia," Quintus screamed, ramming his gladius through the axe man's ribs before kicking the body back into the seething mass.

Though hemmed in on all sides by the Carthaginian horde, the legionnaires fought with exceptional bravery. Quintus felt a glimmer of pride in his men, even as he accepted that these were their final moments.

A hurled spear glanced off Quintus's shoulder, staggering him. Before he could recover, a burly swordsman hacked viciously at his head. Quintus barely managed to deflect the blow with his shield, the impact jarring his arm. With a burst of desperation, Quintus lunged and impaled his assailant under the sternum. Savagely ripping the gladius free in a spray of gore, he prepared to meet the next foe.

The remaining legionnaires were now down to five men, all sporting grievous wounds. They formed a tight circle, making the Carthaginians pay dearly every time they got too close. It wasn't enough. One legionnaire fell, then another.

'Three now,' Quintus thought, parrying a sword thrust from the left even as he kicked out at a spearman trying to flank them. The last two men fell, and Quintus stepped back again, bumping against the supply wagon. Still, he refused to yield, roaring in defiance as he fought on stubbornly. A hurled axe caught him in the thigh, but he barely staggered, fueled by rage and duty. With his free hand, he snatched up a fallen spear, wielding it alongside his gladius in a whirlwind of steel. Two more of the enemy fell beneath his blades before a blade smashed through his sword arm, nearly severing it.

Dropping his bloody sword, Quintus stabbed out with the acquired spear, weaker with each thrust as blood loss and fatigue slowed him. Finally, a spear caught him high in the chest. He coughed, feeling wetness choking him. With his final struggling breath, Quintus impaled one more foe before dropping to his knees and falling flat.

He could feel his life draining out into the snow. All around him, he could see the feet and legs of Carthaginians as they gathered up fallen rifles. His men had done so well. He wondered if anyone would find their bodies before the snow thawed. 'What an odd thing to wonder,' Quintus thought, and then the world faded away.

Devnum

Lucilla sank down onto the plush couch in her private quarters, exhausted. Dealing with the Senate was beyond tiring. She'd never met any men more pleased with hearing the sound of their own voices than those men. It wasn't just the Romans. The Caledonians and Ulaid senators were just as bad. Since they were from such different societies, she had to conclude it was just their being men that made them so narcissistic.

That wasn't fair, she thought after a second. She knew of one man who wasn't like that, and she could really stand to hear his voice.

"Ky, are you available to talk?" she spoke into the empty air around her.

A moment later, his deep, soothing tone came floating back to her, "For you, always."

She smiled wearily to herself, saying, "How are things progressing with the tribes?"

"We're making progress. After seeing how well the weapons worked in the first raid, they've really taken to it. Our biggest problem right now is getting them to slow the tempo down. They're burning through our gunpowder supplies, and a few have gotten overaggressive, taking on forces too large to handle, even with their guns. Still, the Carthaginians are in disarray, and they've started pulling back to shorten their supply lines, so our plan is working as intended. How was the Senate? Are Roti and Bredei still being pains in everyone's asses?"

"Gods, yes," she groaned. "But that's not the main thing I needed to talk to you about. I received a message from Hortensius and Sorantius about the balloon project. The wool fabric is proving too porous and heavy, and they wanted me to give them an alternative material they can use."

Ky made a thoughtful noise and said, "Hmm, I was worried about that. The fabric seemed to have too loose of a weave, but I'd hoped the new steam-powered looms would make things better."

"Apparently, it isn't enough, or at least not yet," Lucilla said.

"We could look at upgrading their processes to produce a more modern and durable wool fiber. It might not help with the weight, but it would allow a much tighter weave. The downside is that it's going to take some time because it requires a change from almost the ground up in their production chain."

"If it doesn't help with the weight, then what's the point of the upgrade?"

"Well, we'd have to also look at the rest of the design and figure out why the weight is such a problem."

"*I believe that may be my doing,*" Sophus said. "*My initial assessments for building the balloon were based on fabric quality and* technologies from the mid-nineteenth century and not the materials being produced in this time. Rerunning my model now, it is evident that there are major issues with the design and assumptions made about substituting wool and linen for cotton, and that the current fabric is inadequate for our needs."

"So our only option is to rework the entire textile industry from the ground up to make a more modern weave of wool fabric?" Ky asked. "Or is there something contemporary we could use instead?"

"Silk was used during the nineteenth century in many balloon designs, due to it being both strong and lightweight. However, it was ruled out during my initial designs due to the difficulty in obtaining the material in any significant quantity, as it is only produced in large quantities in Asia. The same is true of cotton, as the industry in North Africa is not capable of producing the required quantities or quality, and it is not easily accessible. Records indicate that India would be a viable source, but accessing it is limited by the same factors that limit access to silk."

"Yes," Ky said. "Silk and cotton are good. So all we can do is stop this project until the textile industry catches up to nineteenth-century quality, correct?"

"That assumption is not correct. There is a synthetic option available that can be produced with currently available raw materials and chemicals already developed and being produced, called viscose rayon. It was discounted in my initial calculations because it is less durable than wool or cotton, which is a concern for a system that requires a cohesive structural integrity. Even if we achieve a wool/viscose rayon blend, the percentages of mixed fibers would be difficult to control, and the end result would not achieve the same durability levels of locally developed wool. Given the new factors introduced, however, a viscose rayon/wool blend would be the most balanced option between speed of production and quality of the resulting fabric."

"When you say it's weaker, how much weaker?"

"It is difficult to quantify due to the non-uniform makeup of the threads after they are blended together. Without more modern blending techniques, which are well outside the capabilities of our current technological base, every batch of fabric will have a different ratio of synthetic to wool fiber. To ensure the weight remains low, the mixture has to ensure that the low end is no lower than a sixty percent synthetic-to-wool ratio.

Although it's impossible to predict the top-end ratio, modeling indicates it could be as high as eighty percent synthetic to wool."

"If it's so weak, can we chance it?" Lucilla asked.

She didn't follow everything they discussed, but she was able to keep up with the gist of the conversation, at least enough to understand the central problem facing them.

"I believe there is little other choice. It could take more than a year to overhaul the textiles industry with no guarantees that the new fabric will be any more efficient. In addition, the viscose rayon will hold the ammonium phosphate solution we plan to use for flame resistance longer than pure wool fabric would. As a note, this process will be more labor-intensive, but should not delay the overall timeframe of production."

"I guess there we have it," Ky said.

"Alright, I'll get it written up and sent over to them. Now, tell me about what you've been doing, and I don't want to hear about you going on any more assaults with only a handful of tribesmen to back you up," she said in a stern voice.

North of the Pyrenees Mountains

Velius paced back and forth within the confines of his command tent, the walls seeming to close in with each frustrated turn. Outside, the camp bustled with activity as the Seventh Legion prepared to break camp once more and continue their march east. A march that had been agonizingly slow to start with and was losing momentum with each passing day.

"Four weeks since we left Port Invictus," he muttered, more to himself than to Gordianus, who stood stoically near the tent entrance, hands clasped behind his back as he observed his commander. "Three weeks slogging through mud and snow, and we've barely made it halfway."

Velius paused in his pacing and met Gordianus' stoic gaze, "The supply trains can barely keep up in this terrain. Half our time is spent scouting paths wide enough for the ox carts. At this rate, we'll be lucky to reach the Middle Sea by summer."

Of course, he knew that wasn't fair. The only reason they were moving so slowly was because of the weather. As soon as the snows melted, they'd start making better headway. Knowing that didn't make him any less frustrated. He slammed a fist against the heavy wooden table that served as his desk, making the neatly arranged maps and scrolls jump.

"We need to pick up the pace."

"Unfortunately the harsh winter conditions continue to take a heavy toll, sir. We've lost over a hundred men to frostbite and exposure, and twice as many are too sick and weakened to fight," Gordianus replied. "The supply convoys also report repeated raids by Carthaginians. Three convoys have failed to report in entirely. We've lost a large percentage of our resupply, including food and replacement winter equipment. At this rate, the legion's combat effectiveness will be severely diminished well before we reach the Mediterranean, even if the weather does let up."

Velius cursed under his breath again, before saying out loud, "Very well. Dispatch riders to Port Invictus at once. We need additional reinforcements and supplies. Ensure they send enough forces to escort the supply trains. A century isn't enough."

Gordianus considered Velius' order for a moment before cautiously speaking up. "With respect, sir, I would urge caution before sending out additional forces as escorts. Our manpower is already stretched thin as it is."

Velius crossed his arms, his brow furrowing, "I'm aware of that, but clearly we can't leave our supplies unguarded. It's how we ended up in this situation."

"Again, with respect, we ended up in this situation because we decided to try and press across the neck of Hispania, in the shadow of the Pyrenees in the dead of winter, in express contradiction to what traditional strategy would suggest. Dispatching soldiers to escort each supply train would require stripping Port Invictus of a large percentage of the remaining forces and would probably still not be enough to follow your orders. We will almost certainly have to send a portion of the main body back to supplement the guards for our supply lines. We will be diminishing our fighting strength even further and make Port Invictus, our sole source of supply, vulnerable in return."

He gestured to the maps spread across the table, its markers askew from Velius's earlier tirade.

"Due to the weather, our forces are already dangerously strung out," Gordianus continued. "Unit cohesion is becoming a concern and the columns are dispersed and vulnerable because of it. Removing more men would leave us open to being picked apart piecemeal."

Pacing to the tent entrance, Velius gazed out at the bustling camp, mulling his options. The men were huddled in small clumps, sheltering from the cold as best they could. Behind the façade of military discipline, he could see the weariness in their eyes, the sag to their shoulders as they went about their tasks.

Turning back to Gordianus, Velius nodded reluctantly.

"You make a fair point," he said, returning to the planning table and bracing his hands on the edge.

Gordianus had never been one for hysterics or shirking from his duties, and the map was no help, since it only confirmed what his subordinate had been saying. His forces were spread out, starving, and bleeding. Even in a perfect campaign, manpower was his biggest concern. They couldn't afford to throw it away now, especially as it became clear there was no chance they'd reach their objective before the Carthaginians brought in reinforcements. All he would achieve would be to meet them at their strongest when he was at his weakest.

"Give the order to withdraw west to Port Invictus," he said wearily over his shoulder.

It had seemed like a good idea, a month ago back at their finished base. A quick dash across the neck of Hispania, a surprise attack, and victory. A plan which had turned to ash almost as soon as they began executing it.

"Do we then wait until the spring, and try again?" Gordianus asked.

The man always pressed for more information. He was a planner at heart, which is one of the reasons why Velius valued him so highly. Velius was spontaneous by nature, and he found Gordianus a good foil to hold his impulses in check. In hindsight, he should have listened to his subordinate when he'd argued against the entire expedition, but there was no taking that error back now.

"No. We can't just sit idly and wait for the Carthaginians to build up more strength before we go at them. We'll have to figure out a way to continue progress east to hold the corridor between us and the Middle Sea open for our invasion of Africa."

Gordianus saluted and left the tent to begin preparing the men for their withdrawal. Velius dropped back onto a stool, elbows on his knees, placing his head in his hands. He was a good enough general to admit when he was wrong, but this failure was going to cost lives. Instead of cutting off the continent while the Carthaginians were weak, they would have to face yet another massive army, outnumbered and alone.

Chapter 8

Devnum

Medb sipped her calda, a mixture of wine, spices, and warmed water that she found oddly pleasing in spite of herself, as she watched Cormac stand in front of the mirror, its clear and even glass reflection one of the several miracles she'd seen since coming to the capital, adjusting his tunic. The very sight of him preparing frustrated her. Another day of him wasting away as an observer in the Britannian Senate.

Months had passed since he'd been sent here to observe and act as his father's direct representative. It had seemed a real opportunity for her at the time, especially after the disappointment of learning she would be forced to marry him in order to keep her head. A chance to reclaim some of her lost power. Yet here they still sat, guests of the Empress, her naive husband still clung to notions of loyalty and duty.

Medb set her cup down loudly, the sharp sound breaking the silence.

"You seem weary of late, my love," she said, forcing gentle concern into her tone.

Cormac glanced over with a weak smile and said, "Just tired. The days in the Senate are long and boring."

Medb rose and went to him, placing a hand on his shoulder.

"I know this is not the purpose you hoped for when we came here," she said, suppressing her mounting frustration.

Cormac nodded reluctantly, "I know, but what can I do? I've argued that I'm wasting my talents, but Llassar and the Empress refuse to listen. I've made suggestions to improve the legions, but they are ignored or pushed away as ill-conceived. Until my father changes his mind or Llassar says I'm ready, all I can do is continue my lessons and do what I'm told."

She turned him gently to face her, meeting his eyes with feigned sympathy.

"Loyalty is an admirable quality, but you must not forget your own ambitions," she said gently. "When your father passes on and you take the throne, it must be as your own man and not some lapdog, seen doing everyone else's bidding."

"I'm not a lapdog," he said, stepping back slightly, angry.

She suppressed a frown. She'd pushed too hard.

"No, of course not. I meant just that you can't be seen to be one by your people. Do you disagree with how the army is run? Do you think the Senate is making the right decisions, giving away so much power to peasants and ex-slaves?"

"No, but father agrees with them. Or at least agrees to follow them."

"But that doesn't mean you have to peacefully do the same. You could change things if given the chance. With your skills, you could forge an unstoppable force," Medb said, stepping close, running a hand down his chest. "But they will never simply give you the chance to do it on your own."

Medb watched carefully as Cormac turned from the mirror, frustrated.

She placed a gentle hand on his shoulder. "I know this is not the purpose you hoped for when we came here. You should be on the battlefield, not locked away listening to old men."

"You keep pointing that out, but what can I do? I've tried to argue my case, but the Empress refuses to hear me. Llassar just keeps telling me to be patient. Until my father or Llassar give the order, my hands are tied," Cormac said bitterly.

"I know it's frustrating, but you can't be the only one who feels the empire's resources are being squandered. Surely you've met others who share your... frustrations? Men who understand the art of war as you do and chafe at inaction?" Medb asked, her other arm snaking around him, pressing herself against him. "I understand your reluctance. Your duty to your father comes first. But you must also think of the future... your future."

Pulling her arms back, she walked slowly around him, trailing a hand lightly across his shoulders. "Even a king needs allies. People whose loyalty is assured. That starts early, by making connections. By building relationships."

Cormac shifted uncomfortably, "What exactly are you suggesting?"

"I'm suggesting nothing improper. Merely that it would be prudent to ally yourself with those who share your... vision. Your goals for Ériu and the empire. Look around you! The empire squanders its resources, restrained by timid old men and former slaves in the Senate. The military command wastes your talents. Does this seem right to you?"

Corman walked away from her touch to stand next to the window, gazing thoughtfully down at the orderly streets of Devnum below. After a moment, he turned back to her.

"No. No, it doesn't," he admitted. "But I'm not sure what I can do about it. Not yet, anyway."

"Right now, you can have patience. Your time will come," she said, coming back to him and squeezing his arm reassuringly. "And when it does, it would be prudent to know exactly who your allies are. Both here and at home. Friends in the right places, who want what's best for you ... for Ériu."

Cormac nodded slowly, "You may be right. I have heard some complaints, but nothing concrete."

"Talk to these men. Listen to their concerns, find common ground. Share some of your own frustrations. Let them know you hear them and understand their complaints. Use these men to start building bridges. Making connections. The loyal men who will stand with you when change comes."

"I'll try," he said, his expression pensive. "You may be right. Perhaps I've been too passive."

"That's all I ask," Medb replied gently, touching his cheek. "You should be going. The day awaits."

Cormac nodded and headed for the door before pausing to look back at her, "Thank you, Medb. For the advice... and the confidence in me."

She smiled warmly in return. "Of course, my love."

After he left, Medb let her composure slip. Her smile faded into a scowl. Finally, some progress, she thought. But still so tentative. She would need to keep pushing him along.

Medb sighed, sinking into a chair. Patience was required, despite her frustration. Cormac was still too deferential, too naive. She needed him hungry for command, not dutifully awaiting it.

Still, she had finally gotten some of the seeds planted. She just needed to continue nurturing his ambition, his resentment. Then maybe, she could find a way back to where she belonged.

"How are we faring?" Valdar asked Haakon, his ship's purser, as he approached the man watching crates of supplies being loaded onto the Bellona.

Winter was coming to an end, and the snows had already begun to melt, but a cold breeze still blew off the ocean, cutting through his thick furs. The new ships were about to roll off the docks, and he would finally be able to begin the trip south to what the Romans called the Middle Sea, finally taking the fight to them instead of endless patrolling.

"All of the supplies, aside from food, for the new ships are ready. We're just waiting for the ships to be in the water, and I'll get them loaded. I've managed to set aside enough dried foods, and I've arranged with several plantations to get some of their last winter harvests, so we'll have some fresh food, at least for the start of the journey."

"Any problems?" Valdar asked, hearing an undertone in Haakon's voice despite the encouraging words.

"Yes. We're short on gunpowder. The imperial treasury has provided just a fraction of what was requested."

Valdar's expression darkened, "How little did they allocate?"

"Barely a fifth of the amount needed," Haakon said grimly. "I've managed to cut corners to amass a little more, but even with that, we won't even have half of what we projected we would need."

Cursing under his breath, Valdar paced in frustration.

"Damned bureaucrats. Don't they realize how critical those supplies are? Have we put in a request to the Empress directly?"

Haakon shook his head, "Not yet. I planned to once the tally was complete, and I knew exactly how much I was going to be able to pull together from other sources. But it's not looking promising."

"Remind the treasurer that control of the sea is critical to winning this war," Valdar said, gesturing out at the row of moored ships. "Without enough gunpowder, how can they expect us to sail into the heart of Carthaginian waters and interdict their shipping? They want us to slow the reinforcements to their armies on the continent, force them to march all the way around through Persia and Greece. We can't do that if we can't shoot at them."

Haakon just shrugged. He was, in his own way, a bureaucrat. Valdar knew it wasn't his job to make strategic decisions and was mostly venting his frustrations on the man.

"They keep telling me the legions take priority," Haakon said.

Valdar sighed and kicked a rough spot on the wooden planking.

"Don't worry, I'll take care of this," Valdar told Haakon firmly, leaving the man to carry on with his work.

The busy docks, with its cacophony of gulls crying overhead mingled with the shouts of foremen and laborers, fell behind as he passed through the massive sea gate and into the city proper. In spite of the cold wind and the last snow still clinging to the recently improved gutters, part of the Consul's health and public cleanliness decree, the streets were packed with merchants, citizens, and praetorians.

Valdar was used to the cramped space on the ship, where it was impossible to get more than a few steps from another man, but the shoulder-to-shoulder pushing in some sections of the thoroughfare was a bit much even for him. It was a relief when he got to the cordon that surrounded the palace, forming a protective ring around it. People were still allowed in, but after the insurrection, the praetorians were not letting crowds push too close to the buildings, controlling access to the empire's leaders.

Valdar, a frequent visitor and, supposedly, one of those leaders, was waved through without issue, left to find his own way to the treasurer's offices. For as important as Lurio was to the empire, keeping track of all the gold that moved through the capital and all the supplies the empire paid for, Valdar was always surprised by how empty his offices always were. Of course, the Empress didn't call on him and made the treasurer go to her whenever she needed something, still, Valdar had assumed there would be more people waiting to talk to the man.

Instead, a clerk waved him through, past rows of men tallying, to a small office in the back.

"Enter," came Lurio's brusque reply when Valdar knocked on the closed door.

Light filtered through the narrow windows overlooking the palace courtyard, the spartan furnishings and lack of decoration reflected the stoic treasurer's utilitarian nature.

Lurio sat scrutinizing pages at his heavy wooden desk, only briefly glancing up at Valdar.

"Admiral Valdar. To what do I owe the honor?" he said, his tone almost disinterested as he continued reading.

"I want to discuss the fleet's gunpowder allocation. Our current amount is dangerously inadequate for naval operations."

"As I told your man, that is what is available. The legions require the bulk of our resources. We have limited supplies, and no one is getting everything they've asked for."

Valdar bristled at the man's dismissive tone but maintained his composure.

"With respect, the Empress has ordered my fleet to take the fight into the heart of Carthaginian waters. Without sufficient gunpowder, the fleet cannot effectively blockade ports or engage enemy ships, which will leave the legions vulnerable. My request is part of their mission and in direct support of it."

Lurio set down the pages and finally looked up, meeting Valdar's gaze. "I understand its importance, but I do not set military strategy or priorities. I can only go by the decisions of the Empress and her commanders, who instructed me that the bulk of our supplies, and specifically gunpowder, was needed for the legions. As of now, we are still not producing enough to meet their requests.

According to their quartermasters, they believe I am indulging you and spending too much on gunnery practice, and they suggest reducing your allotment even further. If you want a change in the distributions, you're going to have to take it up with the Empress herself."

"I see," Valdar said. "I guess I'll do that."

He had hoped he could take care of this here and now, but he was willing to talk to whoever he needed to, up to and including the Empress, to get the materials his men needed.

"She's in Factorium today. You should speak to one of her aides about scheduling a time to see her," Lurio said as the admiral turned to make his way to the palace.

Valdar suppressed a groan. Nothing was ever easy.

Port Invictus

Velius stood before a large table on which a detailed map of Hispania was laid out. The bitter winter winds still howled outside, and the fire burning inside the large hearth of the command hall did little to warm the gathered men, none of whom seemed to care. After the disastrous failed march to the Middle Sea, they were eager to reassess their situation and come up with a new plan to accomplish their goal.

"The freezing rain and snow may persist a while longer, but soon the paths through these mountains will be passable again," Velius said. "That means the Carthaginians will start operating in force again, which limits our options for cutting and holding a corridor to the Middle Sea. I'd hoped outracing them over the winter would get us there, but since it didn't, we have to decide on a new tactic."

He looked around the table at the gathered faces, most of whom had argued against that plan. While Velius still stood by its validity, he knew its failure had shaken the confidence of some of the men.

"There is some good news, however. While we were gone, we received the final shipment of rifles and cannons along with enough gunpowder to fully arm the Third Legion, meaning that all of our forces will be properly armed for the coming fight, which does give us options for what we're going to do next."

"It sounds like you have a plan already," Auspex pointed out.

It was said without emotion or accusation, but Velius knew his fellow legate had been the most opposed to his previous plan, and could feel the unspoken accusation in it. Auspex was one of the youngest legates in the legions, but he tended towards a more carefully measured approach to war than Velius did, leading the two to clash often.

"I do," Velius said, leaning over the map again to trace his finger on a line just north of the Pyrenees towards the coast of the Middle Sea. "I propose we divide our forces and fortify seven positions along this route at intervals under twenty mille-passes. I know this means, at the very best, one and a half cohorts per position, which wouldn't be enough to defend any of them from a full-scale attack by the Carthaginians and no manpower to react to anything outside of defending these positions. That's why what I want to do is construct a series of small, defensible forts manned by a cohort each, leaving three cohorts here at Port Invictus, and an entire legion free as a mobile force to react as needed."

"The interconnected forts would be a day's march from each other, meaning any fort except the one closest to the Middle Sea would be able to be reinforced from the forts on either side of it, which should be enough to allow the still mobile legion to counter the Carthaginian movement and force the enemy to stretch their supply lines far enough to stay out of reach of our forts. In return, our own supply lines will be protected, as any convoy will be in sight of one of the forts and never out of the protection of their forces."

"Which legion did you plan on splitting up?" Aelius asked.

"I'd split up the Ninth Legion, leaving you to be based here with three of your cohorts," Velius said, giving the legate the answer he was probably fearing. "You won't be out of contact with them, however. We'll also establish a semaphore system between the forts for communication. This will allow the forts to communicate with each other and the forces in the field, helping coordinate our defense and reinforce where needed. We'll also provide some cavalry support to each fort to maintain scout patrols that should increase the time we have to arrange support and, if things work well, get our mobile force to the location in time, pinning the Carthaginians between that legion and the fortification. With both armed with cannons and rifles, the effect could be deadly."

"Even if we do not manage a decisive blow, all we need to do is hold the forts across this line," Velius said, tapping his finger on the Middle Sea coastline depicted on the map. "That leaves just the Carthaginian port to take, which will be the responsibility of the Northern Army, although if we do remove any mobile Carthaginian forces, we might be able to achieve that too. Either way, we will have secured our main objective and established a protective corridor across to the Middle Sea."

"Wouldn't this spread us out too thinly?" Aelius asked. "With less than five hundred men at each fort, the Carthaginians have the manpower to surround multiple forts, keeping them from coming to each other's aid, wiping out at least one of them before we can get our mobile force on the scene. It's also possible that, even if the forts on either side send men to respond to the threat, they will not have, collectively, enough manpower to defeat the Carthaginian numbers. The disparity in manpower has always been our biggest issue in fighting them, and this makes the problem worse."

"Yes, that is a concern, and why I didn't pick this tactic at first, even though we would have been able to build in more safety had we done it in winter instead of waiting until the beginning of spring to build our forts. We have enough cannons to arm each fort with ten pieces each, and rifles for every man. You saw what we did to the Carthaginians with six cannons and a single legion armed with rifles in the fall, and we didn't have walls to protect us. The Consul is always talking about how these weapons are a force multiplier, and we've seen it in action. I'm just suggesting that we use that to our advantage."

"Five thousand rifles is very different than five hundred, though," Gordianus said.

"That's true. I'm not saying this isn't a risk, but anything we do is a risk. The alternative is we march one or one and a half legions across to their port on the Middle Sea and attack it, leaving the remainder here, but I don't think that achieves our goals. They can still move forces up from southern Hispania, and we have a hundred and twenty mille-passes uncovered between the two positions even if we do take the Middle Sea base. The cohort is only a start. We are expecting a third legion in reinforcements sometime this summer, which should be when the last forts go under construction, which means we can at least double our man-power at each if need be, or have two mobile forces. Also, the Consul should be starting his campaign to fight south to us with our new Germanic allies in support, which will alleviate pressure from that direction. By itself, yes, this is a risky proposal, but our operations aren't isolated."

"What happens if we lose a fort?" Gordianus asked.

"Then we replace it and reinforce. We go after the force that they sent. The Carthaginians have larger forces, but they aren't infinite and we aren't the only ones they're fighting. They're also going to have a harder time getting men into the fight here once our fleets start clearing the Middle Sea. We only need to buy time for the Consul to bring his army to us and for our new legions to arrive."

"Like I said, I know this is a risk. If you have a better idea to achieve our goal, I'm open to suggestions."

The commanders looked at each other, maybe hoping someone else would have a response, but no one did. Velius had spent a lot of time on the problem during the retreat from his failed winter campaign, and this was the only thing he could come up with that would achieve his goal. He was confident now that none of his subordinates could counter it either.

"It seems we are decided then," Velius said, looking around the table. "During the construction phase, I want all of the cohorts that will be assigned to man the forts to make up a protective force for the men building the forts. As a fort is finished, we will peel off the cohort assigned to that fort. I will also keep the Seventh operating in the area of each fort as well, to ensure we have no disruption of their construction. Have your quartermasters start their logistics planning. We'll need to identify resupply points and organize convoys to keep each fort continually provisioned. I want a full projection of needs and a provisional schedule ready by tomorrow."

Turning to his chief engineer, Velius said, "Coordinate with Gordianus' team and start planning the fortifications. We need defensible perimeter walls with firing platforms for the cannon crews. Include barracks, supply warehouses, stables, everything required to sustain five hundred men long-term and capable of holding twice that many as needed. I want draft plans drawn up within the week."

"I won't lie, this will be difficult and dangerous work. But if we succeed, we secure our supply lines and open the path inland. We don't have to defeat their whole army, just hold the line long enough for reinforcements to shift the odds in our favor. I have faith that together, we can accomplish this."

The men nodded. They were professionals and once the decision was made, he knew each would do their best to ensure the plan was carried to fruition.

"Very good. We all have our assignments. Let's get started."

Chapter 9

Devnum

It had taken almost two weeks following his meeting with Lurio for him to get to see the Empress. After her return from Factorium, there had been some kind of crisis in Caledonia that she had to deal with in person, all the time they were getting closer and closer to the day he needed to be underway, still without getting the supplies he needed for the expedition.

Now that he was here, though, he almost wanted to turn around and go back to his ships. The last time he'd dealt directly with her, she was just Lucilla, the Emperor's daughter, and they'd met on his turf, at the docks, surrounded by swearing workmen and salt air. Now she was the Empress, and he was walking through halls surrounded by ornate tapestries and marble statues. He was a simple sailor at heart, and all this finery and politics seemed designed to unnerve him.

The point was made even clearer when he was escorted into the Empress's audience chamber, where she sat on a gilded throne atop a raised dais, guards armed with rifles and gladii flanking the room, their eyes following him as he walked. She wasn't alone, either. Ramirus, the Imperial Spymaster, was there as well, standing next to the throne, his hawk-like gaze boring into Valdar.

"I understand you have something urgent that needs addressing," the Empress said.

"Yes, Your Majesty. The fleet stands ready for our mission to the Middle Sea. However ..." he said and then hesitated, gathering his courage. "Forgive my bluntness, but we have not been allocated sufficient supplies to carry out your wishes. I've spoken to Lurio, who made it clear that we've been given everything that is available and that there are no options for additional support. While I understand there are many factors that have to be considered where the supplies are concerned, I do not have enough gunpowder to carry out your orders, and I do not want to take my ships into the Middle Sea, far from support, and have them destroyed. The resources already put into these ships are vast, and we cannot throw them away simply because a clerk was too tight-fisted to properly outfit them."

Valdar swallowed; worried that he might have been a little too blunt. He knew she wasn't like other potentates he'd addressed before, apt to kill the messenger, but a monarch was a monarch, and they could be temperamental.

Lucilla frowned, but her tone remained level in spite of his directness, "Supplies are short for everyone, Admiral. Winter and the Carthaginians have disrupted our supply lines, and we've already had several notable losses on the continent even before this year's campaign season has begun."

Valdar nodded and said, "I understand, Your Highness. But controlling the Middle Sea is vital to cut off Carthaginian reinforcements. I'm telling you now, I cannot do that with the supplies I've been given."

Ramirus spoke up and said, "Reallocating supplies weakens land forces, Admiral. Perhaps a delay ..."

"Each day we delay is another day for Carthage to strengthen their position!" Valdar insisted. "Once we control the sea, coastal raids can keep their armies in check. Until then, more of their men will pour onto the continent."

Lucilla held up a hand, stopping Ramirus from responding, and asked, "And is gunpowder the only thing you're requesting?"

"No, Your Majesty. Once we start sailing, some private shipping will need to be appropriated to support my men and resupply us as we conduct operations. There will be no friendly ports nearby to rely on, at least not until the Consul achieves his goal and takes a port on the Middle Sea. I've started speaking to the captains, but they are understandably reticent. Without an imperial decree, I'm not sure we'll have enough ships to keep the fleet supplied, especially since the supply ships we do have are currently being held here to ferry supplies to Germania and Port Invictus."

Lucilla tilted her head thoughtfully, considering the admiral's words. "The shipmasters have already lodged several complaints about how often we've pressed their vessels into imperial service, even with the payments they receive in compensation. And aside from their displeasure, the imperial treasury is not infinite, and supplying both land and naval forces is already straining our reserves."

"I understand their complaints, and even sympathize with them. I was a merchant myself, not that long ago, Your Majesty. But as long as the Carthaginians remain a threat, we face more dire concerns. They will find their businesses disrupted significantly more if we lose. The treasury, too, will find itself in far worse straits if the enemy manages to land soldiers on our shores again."

He stepped forward, hands spread imploringly, "Without naval dominance, the Carthaginians can continue ferrying endless reinforcements across the Middle Sea, and our forces on the continent will be swallowed by the sheer number of troops sent against them. Without my fleet to disrupt their supply lines and raid their coasts, our foothold on the continent may collapse."

Before she could respond, Ramirus cleared his throat, his expression grim. "Your Majesty, I've just received concerning news. My agents have reported signs of massive Carthaginian troop movements, and it is possible that a new, larger army has landed at a port in Gaul. Nothing is confirmed yet, which is why I was waiting to report it, but the admiral's warning may be moot. Our estimates indicate that it's the largest force we've seen yet, over two hundred and fifty thousand men strong, compared to our twenty-five thousand currently in service."

"How sure are you of those numbers?" Lucilla asked.

"As I said, Empress, we haven't confirmed it yet, and some may be double counting, as the reports are from different agents and not all of the forces are in one place. It seems as if the commander has split his forces, sending some north to face the Consul and some to Hispania. What we know for sure is that there has been a constant procession of ships across the Middle Sea, delivering men and supplies to their port in Gaul this winter."

"Which is why my mission is so important," Valdar said. "If we don't cut off the flow of reinforcements, we will never hold the continent. We pushed them off Britain because we blocked their fleet from reinforcing Londinium before it fell. If we hadn't, we would still be fighting here, on this island, against wave after wave of men crashing into us. The Carthaginians don't consider most of their soldiers to even be people. They're just slaves to them. And their deaths are nothing to them but offerings to their god. There is no amount of losses they aren't willing to take, which means we can't just outfight them. We have to cut them off, which is what I'm trying to do. And what I can't do if I don't get the gunpowder I need."

Lucilla drummed her fingers on the arm of her throne as she weighed Valdar's request. She didn't reply right away, but he could see the calculations churning behind her eyes as she examined every angle. Her gaze flicked to Ramirus, and he gave a slight nod. At least he seemed convinced, despite arguing against Valdar earlier.

In the end, there was only one choice.

"Very well, Admiral. You have convinced me. I will authorize Lurio to release the supplies you need, and I will urge Hortensius to increase production as much as possible, although until the nitrate pits in Ériu begin producing, I'm afraid we might already be at our max capacity on gunpowder production. As for the transport ships, I will issue the orders for their appropriation today."

"Thank you, Your Majesty," Valdar said, bowing low.

"Now that you have what you need, don't fail us. Stop their shipping whatever the cost."

Germania, North of the Rhine

Ky looked through the tree line at the distant Carthaginian supply depot. The small wooden fort stood silently in the wide clearing, bathed in moonlight. They'd received word of these small forts springing up near the Rhine in a shallow arc roughly across from the main territory of his largest allies and the only area they had successfully freed entirely from the Carthaginians. When put together with the army that had recently marched up from southern Gaul, it wasn't hard to figure out what the Carthaginians were doing.

So far, the enemy had been spread out, trying to counter the raids and uprisings happening across Germania, but they were gearing up for a larger, more concentrated push against any villages they could get to. Already, thousands of civilians had been marched south, many presumably conscripted into their forces and sent to Greece or Asia Minor to free up armies there to come west.

The hit-and-run raids by Ky's forces had done well, and the tribes not being folded into the legions had taken to them with enthusiasm, but they didn't have the manpower to face a concentrated push. Muskets could only go so far, especially when used the way most of the tribes preferred.

He'd begun receiving rifles for his legions, but he only had two full legions armed with rifles. That should still be enough to take on the Carthaginians, but so far the enemy hadn't been obliging him. Instead of starting a headlong attack, like they'd done before, the enemy was pushing their armies around his edges, cutting off supply lines and burning out or displacing anyone who might ally with the Britannians.

The larger Carthaginian armies were an issue when dealt with head-on, but they were just as much of a problem when spread out. Maybe even more so. Ky had managed to counter their size difference with technological force multipliers, but that only worked in head-on conflicts. He did not have enough men to meet them in all of the places the Carthaginians were attacking, especially since he couldn't afford to spread his own forces out, which would invite a counterstrike against those Ky left behind.

He also couldn't ignore the hits on his allies. Already the tribes had started expressing their dissatisfaction at their people being slaughtered or shipped south. The raids on supply lines had been helping slow the Carthaginians, but they needed to do more, which is why Ky found himself and his small band of Germanic tribesmen so deep in Carthaginian-held territory. If he was going to slow down the Carthaginian units roaming Germania, he had to do more than take wagon trains, and this supply depot was the first step.

The Carthaginians could probably replace these supplies, but it would take time, and it was the beginning of the planting season, which meant there wasn't a lot for their people to steal or forage. The more he choked off their supply, the more they had to pull back units or risk losing them.

Still, it wasn't going to be an easy task. He had two dozen Germans against a garrison of fifty-plus inside the small, hastily built wooden fort. Going over the wall, even of a lightly defended fortification like this, would be costly, so Ky waited and watched. A scout had reported a wagon train in the area, and based on earlier activity, Ky was pretty sure it was heading this way.

The hardest part was keeping Wulfram and his men holding in place just watching Carthaginians on the parapets and doing nothing. They only calmed down when the four horse-drawn carts loaded with supplies came rumbling down the wagon trail out of the forest and into view. This deep in Carthaginian territory, there were only a handful of guards, so it didn't raise any concerns as far as manpower went. It did, on the other hand, solve one big problem.

"We should move," Wulfram said over Ky's shoulder.

"Not yet," Ky said, not looking back. "We need the gate open."

"They will just close it before we close the distance."

"No, they won't."

Ky's eyes never left the gate. The wagon cart rolled up to the gate, and one of the men exchanged words with one of the guards up on the parapet. Finally, the gate started to move.

"Wait," Ky said, as the gate started to creep upward. "Wait. Now!"

Ky exploded from the tree line, moving at an inhuman pace, leaving the tribesmen behind him as if they were walking. He was halfway across the open ground before any of the Carthaginians noticed him, his gladius already in his hand. He passed the last wagon before anyone could even begin to shout.

He passed the nearest guards and smashed into the guard closest to the gate mechanism, his sword slamming through the man's armor and out his back with such force that the man hurled backward, off his feet. Only Ky's enhanced muscles allowed him to grip the weapon hard enough to keep from losing it as the man sailed away.

Next to the gate mechanism, Ky's foot kicked out into the block counterweight, hitting it hard enough to lodge it into the wooden post next to it, embedding the stone partially inside the wood, locking the gate open.

To their credit, the Carthaginian guards didn't let Ky's sudden, brutal assault stun them into inaction. The guards were already closing in on him as their comrade fell, circling around him. Ky didn't give them a chance, his blade sliced across the throat of the closest man, who crumpled with a wet gurgle.

Before the man even fell, Ky was already spinning, his blade darting out in the other direction, the steel cutting down two more men, who fell like freshly scythed wheat. Finally, the remaining two guards were on him, both screaming as they attacked. Ky blocked a clumsy overhead swing with enough power to break the weapon at the hilt, his blade cleaving into the man's skull.

This time, his weapon did get lodged, pulling out of his grip as the man fell backward. There wasn't time to retrieve it. Instead, as the guard's partner stepped forward, hoping to impale him, Ky stepped aside with blurring speed, his hand gripping the Carthaginian's wrist, brutally snapping it sideways as he ripped the man's weapon from him. The guard screamed in pain, only to be impaled through the heart with his own sword.

That took care of the last of the guards inside the gate, leaving only the men who'd come with the wagon train that Ky had ignored in his rush to keep the gate open. Ky turned to face them, just in time to hear the crack of muskets and see those men begin to drop.

Ky moved quickly to put a wagon between himself and the open field. He appreciated the assistance, but his allies' accuracy with the muskets wasn't something Ky wanted to bet his life on. The fight was short-lived, with Wulfram appearing a moment later, stepping over the bodies of the fallen guards. Several of his men were reloading, but the majority were pulling out swords and axes. All of them looked hungry for more action.

"You work quickly," Wulfram said, kicking one of the corpses out of his way.

A shout from across the fort's open ground drew their attention as a group of Carthaginians ran past stacked supplies, intent on taking the gate back and kicking out the attackers.

Wulfram wasted no time, hefting his axe and charging forward with a roar, with his men close behind. Ky followed, although at a more reasonable pace this time. Now that the gate was locked open, there was no reason to rush headlong into the enemy. Together, they crashed into the disorganized defenders.

Ky parried a wild sword swipe from a soldier, then lashed out to slice the man's leg out from under him. As the Carthaginian fell, Ky silenced him with a quick thrust through the throat. Beside him, Wulfram was an unstoppable force, his axe cleaving shields and helmets with equal ease. A musket barked here or there, but the majority of the work was done with sword and axe.

Within minutes, the remaining defenders were dead or had thrown down their weapons in surrender, which didn't save them from their comrades' fates. The tribesmen were brutal in their treatment of the Carthaginians, offering no quarter in every fight Ky had seen thus far.

All around, his allies were smashing open crates and barrels, dumping out the contents. Sacks of grain, salted meats, tools, and other necessities were seized from storage and destroyed with something almost like glee.

Most of the supplies were foodstuffs designed to survive the winter and to be easily transported to men on the march. Hard-baked and dried bread, the Romans would have called bucellatum, dried meat, and pickled vegetables were all being destroyed. Piles were already burning, sending harsh smoke snaking into the sky.

"It's a shame we have to destroy all of this," Wulfram said. "The supplies we've taken from their wagons have fed many, most of whom are starving after these bastards took everything they had."

"I know," Ky said sympathetically. "We're deep in their territory and there's no way to carry out more than a handful of supplies. This year, the Carthaginians will have more to worry about than stealing from your families, though. Every bit of supplies we destroy now will make it harder for them to fight tomorrow."

Wulfram sighed deeply but did not argue. He turned and buried his axe into a barrel, releasing a flood of pickled vegetables across the ground.

Soon, the raiding party had broken open every container, scattering the contents to be ruined by exposure. The horses from the supply wagons were cut loose, denying their use to the enemy. The air was thick with smoke, causing most of the men to back away from the impressive bonfire they'd constructed.

It had taken time to destroy everything, but Ky wanted to make sure they left nothing for the troops in this area to use. They were almost finished hurling the last of the supplies from the newly arrived wagons into the fire when a cry rang out from the fort's parapet. The lookout he had posted was waving his arms and pointing frantically westward.

Ky vaulted up to join the man, making a leap that would have astounded them had they had time to be impressed. Instead, the lookout turned to the tree line, pointing. Sure enough, men had begun to appear from the trees. A lot of men.

How had so many arrived so quickly? He'd set his drone to provide overwatch, but Sophus hadn't alerted him to anything. Maybe it was the dense tree cover and the wet ground. Whatever the reason, explanations would have to wait. The enemy was almost upon them and he had to act fast.

Ky swore under his breath as he took in the size of the approaching force. At least two hundred men were advancing through the trees, far more than he and his small raiding party could hope to fend off.

"Form up!" he shouted to the tribesmen below.

There wasn't even anything to hide behind, since they'd burned everything that wasn't nailed down. Only the wagons still in the entrance offered any kind of cover, and that position was too easy to flank. At least inside the fort, the enemy had to funnel through one opening, protecting their flanks.

The men scrambled to obey, taking up positions as best they could and leveling their muskets at the open gate. Ky leaped down from the parapet, landing cat-like on the fort's earthen rampart.

"I make fifty, maybe sixty coming through that gate initially," Wulfram said as Ky reached his side. "We cannot hold them."

"Focus your shots and make them count," was the only advice he could give.

The first rank of Carthaginian soldiers came charging through the open gate, spears leading the way. A ragged volley of musket fire erupted from the tribesmen. It was impressive ... and futile. For every Carthaginian that fell, another stepped over their body and continued pressing forward.

"Back!" Ky ordered as the men reloaded.

The press of the incoming soldiers was inexorable. They moved slowly, but his men were running out of room and would shortly be impaled on the wall of spears.

Ky calculated the odds, and it wasn't good. He could see some of his allies looking at the rear wall of the fort, calculating if they could get over it and into the forest. The window to escape was short, however.

Another crash of muskets fired, pushing the Carthaginians back slightly. There wasn't going to be time for a third. There also wasn't going to be time to climb over the back wall. There was one other option.

Ky pulled his sidearm. It had been a full year since the last time he used it, carefully saving his ammunition to use in an emergency.

If anything counted as an emergency, it was now. Thankfully, the weapon was designed to last for decades without maintenance and the ammunition would take a hundred years to lose efficacy.

Ky fired, a ball of green plasma expanding out of the weapon and rolling toward the wooden palisade walls. The intense heat, that had melted stone the last time he'd used it, completely vaporized a five-meter section of the wood planking, blowing the undestroyed parts outwards and setting the wall on either side on fire.

The Carthaginian line actually paused at the sight. Only a few people in this time had seen the modern weapon in action and survived to talk about it, and none of them were present here. The soldiers might have become acquainted enough with firearms to keep from running from them, but this was several magnitudes beyond that, and their brains needed a moment to catch up.

None fled, however, which is why Ky hadn't just used it against the soldiers. He could have probably destroyed this entire unit with just his sidearm, but that would expend the last of his ammunition, and he still felt there might be a time he would need it. This way only required one round.

"Retreat!" Ky yelled, pulling the men nearest him and pointing them toward the newly appeared exit.

Seeing their prey fleeing, the Carthaginians' fear faded, their line breaking slightly as they rushed forward. It was a short sprint to the trees and none of the Carthaginians had made it around the side yet, with the bulk of the soldiers trying to make their way through the gate. The Carthaginians were nearly on top of them, though, and their panicked retreat into the trees might not be enough if the pursuit continued.

Most of the men were moving fast, but Wulfram and four of his lieutenants stopped, turning to face the oncoming Carthaginians. Ky started to object, to tell him to get moving, but Wulfram cut him off.

"Get my men out of here. Tell our people what we did today," he yelled over his shoulder.

With that, the giant of a man, his beard matching the color of the flames around him, charged straight into the Carthaginian line, his lieutenants in tow. The disorganized line of Carthaginians fell back at the sudden, brutal assault, clearly not expecting the counterattack. Ky gave the man one last glance, seeing the mass of soldiers swallow him up, and fled after the running men toward the forest.

Reaching the forest edge, Ky risked a glance back, but all he could see was burning wood. The wall around the hole he'd made had started to collapse, mostly blocking their escape route. It would take time for the Carthaginians to get organized and come after them, and maybe more if their men got caught in the quickly growing bonfire that used to be a small supply fort.

With a pang of regret, Ky plunged into the trees. They'd achieved their goal, disrupting Carthaginian supplies for the forces they were bringing in, but the cost had been high. Overextended and ambitious, he'd misjudged how quickly the enemy could react, and brave men paid the price.

Chapter 10

Factorium

Lucilla's carriage rattled down the cobbled road, the rhythmic clopping of the horses' hooves filling the air. The newly added stones were a step above the worn down and pitted dirt track, but it was still anything but smooth. A bright side was that the jostling kept her from dwelling on a growing list of pressures that were building on her. She didn't know if her father had felt these things when he was alone, the worry and fear of not living up to his responsibilities and allowing his people to come to ruin.

Most of the time, she was able to avoid her uneasiness and those darker thoughts by continuous forward movement. It was the one upside of being Empress. She stayed so busy that she didn't have time to dwell. It was moments like this, where she had several hours to herself, away from courtiers and petitioners, that were the problem. She had too much time with her own thoughts.

Ky was so busy, out with their new allies, directing their hit-and-run tactics, that he didn't have time to talk to her, to keep her distracted from herself. Worse, he'd become something else for her to fret over as he kept putting himself in life-and-death situations like the almost fatal raid Sophus had told her about. Instead of a balm, he'd become another worry. Which is why, for once, she didn't mind being thrown around in the carriage, having to brace herself for most of the ride. It was a welcome distraction.

The carriage didn't take long to arrive at Factorium. The message she'd received from Hortensius had a sense of urgency behind it, asking for a meeting as soon as she could manage it. Considering all of the projects he had going and the continued pressure on gunpowder production that was causing so many problems, she had made this her priority.

Oddly, Sorantius was the one waiting for her outside of Hortensius's factory, instead of the manufacturer himself. They usually met at Hortensius's place simply because he had a larger office with enough room for the three of them. Sorantius, for whatever reason, preferred his office to be almost cave-like and had requested it to be designed that way when they'd built his factory.

"Your Majesty," Sorantius said with a cursory bow. "Hortensius is already inside."

She nodded, following him through the heavy iron doors into the vast complex. All around them, workbenches were strewn with intricate mechanical parts and half-finished contraptions. The air smelled of oil and burning coal. She'd given firm instructions, long ago, that when she was there she didn't want any of the workers or artificers to stop what they were doing to bow or give any of the traditional displays of respect and deference to her. It had taken time to convince the workers she was serious, but over her many trips, they had finally started taking it seriously. Other than a side glance or whispered word to another worker, everyone kept doing what they were doing, ignoring her presence.

They found Hortensius in his office, furiously scribbling notes and muttering to himself. He sprang to his feet when Lucilla entered.

"Ah, Your Majesty," he exclaimed. "Please, do come in."

Lucilla settled herself into a chair across from him and said, "Your message sounded urgent. What can I do for you?"

Hortensius leaned forward, his expression grave. "Yes, yes. First, though, I can report that the viscose rayon tests went exceptionally well. The fabric holds air and provides the strength we need for the balloons and seems strong enough when blended with the wool to be usable. I'm not sure I'd want to use it if the other side had weapons with the range of our rifles, but in this environment, it is more than acceptable."

"That is welcome news," Lucilla said.

She still didn't quite understand what Sophus and Ky wanted them for. They'd explained to her the advantages of them and how they differed from using mounted scouts, and she did know how useful Ky's drone was during battle, but that she could see right away. Any messages from the balloon would have to be sent down, received on the ground, and a messenger sent with the information. Which added a delay that didn't exist with his drone. Still, both felt it would help them, and she was willing to make anything work that might keep Ky a little safer.

Which is why it was good news that the replacement material was working as they'd hoped. Ky had sounded dubious that the new material would be strong enough to be a workable substitute even after they'd started working on the project.

"However," Hortensius continued, "to produce the quantities required for an entire fleet of balloons, substantial expansion of my facilities is needed. Specifically, this will be a major textile operation, with large warehouses for raw materials, rows of spinning and weaving machines, and facilities for washing and coating the fabrics in this waterproofing mixture with room to dry it afterward. What we have here now is a very small operation, geared towards more traditional styles of textile production, which we will retain to continue producing materials for clothing and the like for the legions. Which means what I'm asking for is an entirely new facility."

"In addition," Sorantius added, "this process consumes a large amount of the acids we've been producing, which means I will need to expand my facility to make room for the vats and piping for that. We'll also need to move the pulping factory in Devnum, which has mostly been producing pulp for making paper, here so we can expand it and convert it from water to steam power, which is yet another facility we'll need to build."

"Our concern," Hortensius continued, picking the explanation back up from Sorantius, "is that we do not have the labor here to build these facilities or to staff them once they are finished. This is a very large expansion of our works, and we were told by Lurio, the last time we sent a request for manpower, that there was no more to be had. Which is why we contacted you. We could make the materials needed using our existing factories, but that will delay and slow down production in other areas, as we'd have to divert manpower and factory space from those other projects to this one."

Lucilla found herself nodding slowly as she listened. She wasn't surprised by the request. Manpower was the one thing every area of the Empire needed more of and the thing they had the least of. It was a regular topic of conversation in every meeting she had, regardless of the industry or the work being discussed.

"I see," she said, thinking. "I agree you need new facilities. Nearly everything you two are working on is critical, and the goal is to add to what we are producing, not take away from those areas. We can't let any of your other projects fall behind just because you're given a new project to work on. The problem is, I recently allocated additional workers to assist Admiral Valdar in preparing his fleet for the upcoming naval expedition and to expand the gunpowder production, of which we've been having significant shortfalls. This means there isn't much in the way of labor to be had."

She rose and paced the room, pulling gently on her lower lip as she thought.

"I'm not sure where we're going to find what you need. I've robbed and begged manpower to the point where the entire Empire is stretched thin. The armies are asking daily about their reinforcements, especially Velius, who is well outnumbered in Hispania. Valdar is pushing hard to get his expedition to the Middle Sea to support them, and we still have hundreds of vital building projects in Rome alone, which is the least of the construction needed. Ulaid has not yet rebuilt from all the damage the Carthaginians did there, and the kingdoms that it absorbed were nearly destroyed in the process. They need magnitudes more men for rebuilding than we do here, which is already putting a strain on us."

"I may be able to postpone some of the less critical projects and redirect that labor force here temporarily," Hortensius suggested tentatively. "It's not ideal, but it could get us started on the initial phases."

"No," Lucilla said, stopping her pacing. "None of your projects are less crucial. Even the ones that seem like it, such as the production of civilian equipment like the heavy plows, are crucial.

We need that to increase food and the like. We are shipping a lot of it to our new allies as part of our bargain with them. And what is being bought and traded by merchants is bringing in tax revenues we desperately need to pay for all of this. None of your operations are less critical, and we don't have room for you to postpone anything."

"We could implement longer work shifts," Sorantius offered. "Have the men put in extra hours each day. I know it's dangerous with the hazardous materials we work with, but desperation may demand some calculated risks."

"No," Lucilla said firmly. "I understand the impulse, but we can't afford to start losing our trained manpower to accidents caused by exhaustion. Pushing them harder will only lead to more mistakes, injuries, and deaths, which will set us back further. The worst thing we could do is make rash decisions that lead to a disaster that makes things worse."

Lucilla frowned as she turned to face them. "For now, I will reach out quietly to see what I can shift here without causing turmoil elsewhere. Maybe I can scrape some bodies from less vital projects."

It was more pressure she was taking on herself, but she needed these two men focused on the tasks at hand. Clearly, it had been weighing on them, because the pair exchanged relieved glances at having the responsibility taken from them.

"You're not off the hook that easily," she said. "Keep working on ideas to increase our labor pool. That's the real solution. We need more able workers, not just overworked ones. You are the two smartest men in the entire Empire, and I'm counting on you to help me solve this problem."

"We'll figure out something, your majesty," Hortensius said.

"I know you will," she said, not sure if she was trying to reassure them, or herself.

Northern Germania

A scream sounded out, a little louder than the other cries of desperation and pain, before suddenly being silenced forever. General Matho, assigned the duty of pacifying the tribesmen rebelling against the emperor and pushing the Roman army helping them back into the sea, sat passively on his horse, watching the carnage. Around him, soldiers were dragging villagers from their homes, cutting most of them down without mercy then and there. The few that weren't slaughtered right away had a worse fate in store for them as his men vented their frustrations and anger on the unlucky few before making their tribute to Hexitas.

Thatched roofs were burning, some collapsing into the houses creating a massive bonfire, filling the air with dark smoke. The houses that weren't burning, yet, would be as soon as his men went through them, looting anything that might be valuable.

He felt no pity or remorse for what he had to do. This is what happened to people who aided the rebels in raiding his supply lines and even an entire supply base. The loss of that supply depot was a hard blow, one he intended to repay tenfold. These peasants chose their fate when they provided aid to the invading Britannian forces. Their public punishment would serve as a warning to any who dared assist the enemy.

A young woman with a babe in arms ran past Matho's horse, sobbing, only to be cut down by a laughing soldier. Matho's face remained impassive at the child's violent death. It was up to him to pacify Germania, and he was not going to let Tabnit or his emperor down. He would achieve his goal even if he had to slaughter every last one of these barbarians to do it.

The sound of a clash of blades drew his attention to a cottage across the dirt path. A young villager, maybe ten years old, tried in vain to defend his home, swinging his axe at the soldier who was attempting to gain entry. His bravery was commendable, if foolish, Matho thought as the soldier cut the young man down where he stood, followed by screams coming from inside the hut.

The carnage around him slowed, as only the villagers who'd managed to hide were found and pulled into the streets to share their neighbors' fates. An officer, his armor splattered in gore, gave commands to a group of soldiers who ran into the trees nearby, presumably looking for any villagers that might have tried to flee by hiding there, before turning and making his way toward Matho. Stepping over bodies, he stopped next to the general's horse, slapping his chest in salute.

"We are just about done, General. All of the locals have been eliminated as instructed, and the last of their huts will be put to the torch. Nothing's left."

Matho surveyed the devastating aftermath with satisfaction. Mangled corpses littered the ground, and thick smoke blotted out the sun.

"Well done, Commander. Have your men check every hut that is not burning. No one is to be left alive. And send for Edom. Have him come here."

"It will be done, General," the commander said resolutely.

He hadn't seen his second in command for some time, but it was becoming increasingly hard to pick out any individual soldiers in the growing haze of smoke. The soldier must have known where he was, however, because only a few minutes passed before Edom appeared through the smoke, guiding his horse toward Matho.

"You sent for me, General?" Edom asked, bowing his head deferentially.

"Yes. You've done good work here, but our orders are to raze every village within a day's ride of our outpost. Take a detachment of men at once to the nearby villages to the west. If there is any suspicion that a single person in that village has aided the rebels in any way, you are to show no mercy. All inhabitants, men, women, children, and elderly, must be eliminated without exception, and every building and hut is to be burned to the ground. I want nothing left untouched."

The man had a grim expression but simply nodded in response, "It will be done, General."

"Your men may loot what they can before burning the buildings. With the losses suffered lately, morale is down. A few trinkets should help. Don't load up on anything not easily carried, however. There are many villages in rebellion against us, and I don't want your force to be slowed down with unneeded supplies. Understood?"

"Perfectly, General," the man said, and then hesitated.

Most officers had the notion of questioning their orders beaten out of them early in their careers, so it was rare for a man to do more than acknowledge his orders and hurry to carry them out. Matho, however, wasn't as rigid as some of the older commanders. He allowed some discussion, at least from commanders who'd shown they had a brain in their skulls. Of course, once he'd made his word final, he could be as hard on questions to his authority as any other general in the emperor's armies.

"Speak freely if you have concerns, Commander."

"Between having to supply us and the main army in Daramouda and the raids on the supply convoys, we are having trouble keeping the men fed. Most of what we are getting is coming from what we can take from villages like this one. In a few months, they will start harvesting, and we'll be able to replenish some of our supplies. Burning these villages means nothing will be harvested, which leaves us nothing to forage."

"I made a similar point to Tabnit when he sent orders to begin reprisals against villages in rebellion, but examples must be made. We cannot destroy the Roman army sitting north of us if we are continually being bitten by these raids all along our sides. If they have to start protecting all of their villages from our reprisals, they can't also be attacking us, and these people should start thinking twice about helping them in the future."

"I see," Edom said, not indicating whether he agreed with the thought process or not.

Not that his agreement was required.

"Go. The sooner we burn these people out, the sooner we can continue our march to take the Romans on directly."

Wheeling smartly, the officer strode towards his waiting men, barking orders. Mounting up, the company of soldiers thundered from the ravaged village. Between their actions and what Matho was planning to the east, they would spread fear across Germania, quenching any rebellion and clearing the way for the army's main task.

Devnum

Lucilla's head hung down as she listened to Valdar launch into his reasoning for the third time. They'd been going round and round for the last hour, and so far, neither man wanted to budge. She could, of course, just tell them to shut up and command them to do exactly what they needed to do, but she found that tactic had minimal usefulness. These men were both dedicated to the Empire and were trying to do what they personally felt was best for it. If this went on much longer, she'd make the decision for them, probably one neither man would find fair. She still held out a tiny amount of hope that they'd come to their senses and make up their minds on their own before that, however.

"Your Majesty, I implore you to understand the urgency of the situation," Valdar said. "While we appreciate you listening to us about the gunpowder, we are still critically short in other areas, and no matter how many times we petition the Imperial Treasurer, we're told we've been given everything the Empire can spare. We need more. More of everything essential to wage this fight. The allotment of fabric for canvases is insufficient for this long of a voyage, and our plank timber stock for making repairs while underway is incredibly low. We will run through the supplies given to us after one or two engagements and, considering none of our supply ships will be able to reach us deep in Carthaginian waters, we will be forced to return home to resupply well before accomplishing our mission."

"Admiral, you know as well as I that the Imperial treasury cannot sustain such expenditures indefinitely. This year's military budget is already overdrawn," Lurio said, turning to Lucilla, his expression etched with apology. "Your Majesty, I fear Admiral Valdar asks too much. We are stretched too thin. For every resource I give him, we have to take away from someone else, all of whom demand with equal tenacity how poorly they are being supplied and begging I take from the navy to give them more."

"Gentlemen, surely we can reach a compromise here," she said gently. "The navy's needs are valid, but so are the limitations we face. I need the two of you to reach some kind of agreeable middle ground."

Valdar's weathered face softened hopefully, while Lurio still appeared unconvinced. Lucilla opened her mouth to continue when there was a knock at the chamber doors, followed by one of her guards entering, handing a small, folded message to the Admiral, who read it quickly.

"The merchant ship we dispatched has returned from its special procurement mission," Valdar said, glancing up from the message in his hands. "The captain reports success in obtaining a large supply of the plant we sent him for. The one the Consul called Russian dandelion. He says the ship's hold is filled to bursting with the harvested plants."

Lucilla's face brightened at the news, "That's excellent news! We have multiple projects waiting on that shipment. Tell your man well done. Lurio, make sure he and his crew are paid right away for the shipment. I don't want any delays in getting it offloaded and into production."

"Of course, Your Majesty," Lurio said with a slight bow of his head. "Of course, we'll need to first ..."

"No. I appreciate your desire to keep everything accountable and well-managed, but time is of the essence. Pay them right away. Do you understand?"

"Yes, Your Majesty," the treasurer said, unable to completely hide his annoyance.

"I appreciate your willingness to humor me this time," she said, trying to soften the blow. "Now, about the plants themselves. I want half of the shipment sent directly to our greenhouses outside the city. Find an experienced farmer or agriculturalist to oversee cultivating and harvesting. We want to produce as many of these as we can as quickly as possible. Whatever the man needs to grow his plants, we'll give him. Is that understood?"

"Of course," Lurio said, bowing again.

"The other half should go to Factorium for immediate processing. I will send my man Cynwrig with it with instructions for Sorantius on how to properly process the plants and use the materials they produce. I will need a few hours to ... go through the Consul's notes and find the correct instructions," she said, making sure to include the fiction she and Ky devised on how she was able to give technical instruction for any of these new procedures.

In reality, she needed maybe an hour to transcribe all of the instructions Sophus would give her on how to turn these plants into rubber, which she believed was needed for the telegraph project, although Ky had mentioned several additional uses for it as well.

"Admiral, I know he just returned, but I'd like to get this captain back out on the seas as soon as possible to see if he can find more for us. Now that he knows the specific contacts to procure this, we need as much as we can get until we can start harvesting our own crops."

"I'll talk to him," Valdar said. "Now, about the supplies for the fleet ..."

"Yes, yes," Lucilla said, cutting him off. "I will get you some of what you asked for, although probably not everything you've asked for. I promise we will do all we can to ensure you're properly supplied. Will that suffice?"

The admiral clearly did not think it would and looked as if he wanted to argue the point more, but it was evident to everyone that she was done with this conversation and had moved on to the issue of the newly delivered flowers. She might have been willing to listen to the complaints from her subjects, more than most monarchs, but she was still Empress, and when she said she was done, they had little choice but to obey.

"Yes, Your Majesty."

"Good. Go deal with your ship captain while I get Cynwrig dispatched to Factorium."

Both men stood and bowed before hurrying out of the room to carry out her commands. 'Sometimes there are benefits to being Empress,' she thought before pulling out a blank piece of paper to begin writing down instructions for Sorantius.

Chapter 11

"Come," Lucilla said at the knock on the door to her quarters.

She'd been up all night writing out the rubber process details for Sorantius, and planned to get a late start on the day, after getting a few hours sleep. It occurred to her somewhere near dawn that Ky must have been doing this all those times he was locked in his quarters at night. She knew he'd told her that he could go much longer without sleep than anyone in this time, because of the alterations made to his body, which she still didn't really understand. It wasn't until she tried to do the same thing and felt the crushing weight of exhaustion that she really appreciated how well he continued to operate after spending so many nights with little sleep.

She was looking forward to at least a short nap, but she had one other thing she needed to attend to before she could rest. Thankfully, the person she needed to complete her last responsibility had finally arrived. The door opened as one of her guards, Rhys, she thought his name was, escorted Ramirus in.

"You sent for me, Your Majesty," the spymaster said, bowing low.

Lucilla waved a hand, "Please Ramirus, you were my father's longest serving advisor and have known me since before I could walk. Formalities aren't needed between us."

"Then, as an old family friend, might I mention how dreadful you look?" he said, an expression of concern on his face.

"Just the kind of thing a lady likes to hear in the morning."

"I ... You know that's not what I meant," he said, a bit flustered. "You look very tired. When's the last time you slept?"

"Yesterday, and I know. I plan on getting some rest as soon as we're done here. I had some things I needed to attend to that took longer than expected."

"Well, if I'm the one delaying you from proper sleep, why don't we get started so we can finish quickly?"

She couldn't stop the small smile that escaped. She teased him, but she knew of all of her advisors, he cared for her the most. He was closer to a cherished uncle than a simple advisor, really.

"Please," she said, feeling more tired by the minute. "I wouldn't have pushed so hard, but this is very important. I'm sure your people have already told you that our shipment of flowers from Asia arrived, the ones Ky requested."

"They have," he said, not bothering to deny he had people watching everything, both enemies and friends.

She knew he was watching her for sure, and not just through young Gaius. She suspected several of her household staff were placed there as an additional line of defense, and to keep their master informed on what was happening in the palace.

"We've officially run into a manpower problem, and this shipment will make the situation worse. Lurio tells me we are falling behind in multiple sectors and Hortensius and Sorantius have all but begged for additional labor to build new weaving and chemical facilities, and that was before the flowers arrived. We are stretched too thin, and I'm not sure how we're going to get through this. I've tried to work out the problem myself, but to no avail, and was hoping you might have some insight."

"I see," the older man said, his angular features creasing in thought. "There is one workforce we have available but so far haven't tapped into."

"Where?" Lucilla said, suspiciously.

"We have those camps just south of the city full of able-bodied men. They remain able-bodied because you and Ky have dedicated a not insignificant portion of our limited supplies to keep them fed and clothed. Right now, all of those men are just sitting around, waiting for the war to end, one way or the other. They could solve our manpower crisis, or at least the worker part of it."

"You're talking about the prisoners of war?" Lucilla demanded.

"Yes. Right now, they are a massive drain on our already strained resources. This would at least allow us to get some of our value back for everything we're doing to keep them fed and healthy."

"That sounds an awful lot like the servitude Ky specifically fought to get outlawed last year," Lucilla said, frowning. "How can we tell the landowners they must free their slaves and then we create our own?"

"It isn't the same. I don't doubt some of the more disgruntled landowners will try and paint it in that light, but it isn't. For one, these people will be released to return home as soon as the war is over. Before the Consul came, they would have simply been put to death or become slaves for the rest of their lives. We already have some prisoners working on construction gangs, so it's not unprecedented."

"That's different. Those men were given the chance to volunteer, and chose to do that work. The men still in the prisoner camps specifically chose not to work. Putting them to work regardless of what they want is tantamount to slavery."

"Tough," he said, meeting her expression without pleasure. "Empress, these men are here because they tried to destroy us. Each of those men had plans of raping and pillaging their way through this city until we Romans as a people no longer existed. I understand your compunction, but this isn't slavery. These men are treated better than any prisoner in any war I have ever heard of. Even if we make them work, they are still living better than half the people in the known world. They're fed, clothed, and kept safe from harm. They'll be allowed to return home when this is over. If our legions were to lose a battle, those men not slaughtered outright would be put in chains, dragged to some gods-forsaken land, and forced to live the rest of their days in backbreaking work living on barely enough food to stay alive, until they grow old and die, or are worked to death and die. Hell, most of these men were slaves in all but name, conscripted soldiers in the Carthaginian armies, fighting under the threat of the deaths of their families back home. They are living better now, as our prisoners, than they did as part of the Carthaginian army. It's your duty as Empress to make the hard decisions, to put your feelings aside to do what's best for the Empire. Things are safer now and everyone is feeling less pressure, but we are still in a fight for our lives and we must use every tool in our possession. These projects are all critical and need manpower. We have that manpower and we should use it, regardless of your personal feelings, or your feelings about what your husband might think. Respectfully."

He took a slight step back, dipping his head slightly, as his head of steam wound down. She knew her father had, at times, complained about being manhandled by Ramirus, but she hadn't experienced how forceful he could be until today. She felt like she was nine years old again, being lectured by her tutors for breaking some aspect of protocol.

Worse, he was right. She didn't like the idea mostly because she was worried about what she'd tell Ky when he found out she'd basically reinstated a form of slavery, but they were stretching to the point of breaking. If they didn't find a way to reduce their manpower shortage soon, things were going to start slipping, badly.

Lucilla pursed her lips, mulling over Ramirus's proposal.

"If we were to do this, how could we ensure we wouldn't be creating a security nightmare for ourselves? Gathering so many hostile prisoners outside the secured camps poses risks. They could attack their guards or, worse, slip away and become brigands or commit acts of sabotage. Most of our legions are away and the Praetorians are already stretched thin as it is."

Ramirus nodded thoughtfully. "That's a valid concern, Your Majesty. However, measures could be enacted to mitigate such risks. I know the Praetorians are stretched thin, but they continue to recruit, especially among the Germanics and Ulaid who've decided to settle here in Rome. We could extend their presence to provide additional security. We might also rotate a small detachment from the new training legion to guard work details. It would slow down the training, which I'm sure the Consul would have issues with, but if we take them out a century or two at a time, after they've completed most of the basic combat training and put them through a one-week session to learn the basics of security and guarding, they could do the job. We hold them for a month or two and then send them back to the legions to complete their training and ship out with the next batch to go to the continent. It would slow down what reinforcements the legions get, but the troops they do receive would be trained in security and have practical experience, which could be useful."

"You're right, the Consul will not like that," she said grimly. "At the same time, there will be a day when the war ends, and I imagine we will have to occupy at least the core Carthaginian territories for a time, to ensure that locals who feel allegiance to their emperor don't try and reinstate that empire."

She paused, staring at nothing, weighing all the options and consequences. Everything Ramirus had said was true, and they'd been left with little choice. They needed manpower if they were going to keep pushing to counter the growing Carthaginian manpower. That meant having to accept some rather unacceptable risks.

"Very well," she finally conceded. "Begin preparations to start using prisoners, those who will not be too big of a security issue, for building projects and look at setting up at least one of the factories in Factorium, maybe several close together, in a secure area, where prisoners can work inside on routine things that do not give away the secrets of our technology. But, I want measures in place to prevent security issues or mistreatment. And once the war ends, they are to be released immediately."

Ramirus bowed. "Of course, Your Majesty. I'll coordinate with the Praetorians about training legionnaires right away."

"Also coordinate with Hortensius on where this new manpower can be used, and about securing the factories."

"Of course," he said, bowing slightly again. "I'll see to it."

"May the gods grant us mercy," Lucilla whispered to herself as the spymaster left.

'The streets are full today,' Claudius thought as he and his squad of Praetorians marched through the crowded streets of Devnum on their mid-morning patrol.

He knew most of his fellow officers disliked this part of the job, pushing through the endless crowds of people and the packed market with its mixture of smells, but he actually enjoyed it. There was a feeling of excitement and optimism in the city that only grew by the day. Before the Sword had arrived and forged them into the Britannic Empire, everything had been gloomy and hopeless, since every citizen knew how close they were to being destroyed by the Carthaginians on their doorstep.

Back then, he'd been an apprentice blacksmith. He knew he'd been lucky, since most citizens had trouble finding any work outside of the legions, but he'd always hated the hot furnaces and backbreaking work. Which was probably why he found he loved talking to the people they were assigned to protect and patrolling the streets. He would take this any day over banging a hammer on metal for hours on end.

They pushed into one of the markets, which was one of the busier spots, since a better outlook for the future of the Empire didn't inspire the cheats and pickpockets to not steal what they could, when a commotion ahead drew his attention. At one end of the market, he could hear a swell of impassioned voices, loud enough to make out above the din of noise from the market itself.

Gesturing for his men to follow, he pushed through the crowd as fast as he could until they got to an area where the crowd opened up, forming a semicircle around a makeshift stage of upturned crates, atop which stood Vesnius, the Flamen Dialis, one arm raised in the air as he spoke ardently.

"Our great city falters under foreign influences that dilute the glory of Rome and threaten our way of life!" Vesnius declared, full of zealotry. "These outsiders must be expunged before they corrupt us further, bringing damnation upon our heads!"

Part of the crowd cheered while others, most of whom Claudius would have pegged as Caledonians, Ulaid, and even a few Germanics, from their dress, were equal parts angry and worried. They were right to be worried, considering how riled up many of the Romans, who made up the bulk of the crowd watching the preacher, were.

"We must cleanse our city and rid it of the corruption of their foreign influence. Until we began treating them like equals, the northerners lived in huts, in the dirt. They have no place among us, and they've made no attempt to become a part of us. All they want is our wealth, and they will stop at nothing to take it. They anger the gods, and allowing these people to remain, to taint our culture, threatens to bring our gods' wrath upon us. We must cast out these foreign vermin before they wholly corrupt our Empire!"

The crowd roared their approval, raising clenched fists. More Romans began to gather, drawn by the commotion, while most of the Caledonians and Ulaid began to slip away, rightfully fearing for their safety.

Knowing if he let this go on too long things could get out of hand, Claudius motioned for his men to remain where they were as he made his way to the preacher.

In hushed tones, Claudius said, "Pater patrum, I think it might be best if you conclude your speech and urge everyone to return home. The people are becoming agitated, and this could lead to an incident."

Vesnius scowled and loudly proclaimed, "I am the messenger of the gods, Praetorian. I will not stop until the people have heard their decree that Rome be cleaned of the non-Romans!"

Claudius suppressed a frustrated sigh and said, "Pater, please. I do not want anyone hurt, and this kind of talk can lead to a riot, especially here in the market."

"Then let them riot," Vesnius spat. "We have lived under a foreign yoke long enough. Let the true citizens vent their righteous anger on the interlopers."

Claudius suppressed another frustrated sigh as he motioned for his men to come forward. It was clear that Vesnius had no intention of ending his inflammatory speech voluntarily. The zealous priest was too caught up in his religious fervor to care about the potential consequences of his words.

As the Praetorians approached, Claudius raised his voice to address the crowd, "Citizens, for your own safety, I must insist you disperse immediately and return to your homes or places of business."

His announcement was met with angry shouts and jeers. The people were worked into a frenzy by Vesnius' fear-mongering rhetoric and had no desire to go anywhere. Claudius noticed more than a few fists clenched around makeshift weapons, boards, tools, even rocks picked up off the street. This situation could turn violent very quickly if he didn't gain control.

"I will not ask again," Claudius said firmly. "Anyone who does not clear this area immediately will be detained."

At this, Vesnius pointed an accusing finger at Claudius, "You dare to obstruct the will of the gods, Praetorian? I am their appointed messenger, and you seek to silence me through force! The gods will have their vengeance upon you for this!"

More angry shouts rose from the crowd. A small, late winter cabbage, probably grabbed off one of the market stalls, flew through the air, narrowly missing Claudius' head. Things were getting out of hand.

With no other options, he gave the order for his guards to forcibly disperse the mob. The Praetorians marched forward in tight formation, shields raised as they pushed back against the angry throng.

"Back! Get back!" Claudius shouted above the din.

The crowd cursed and shoved against the guards, but slowly gave ground under the inexorable advance. Vesnius scrambled down from his makeshift podium, glaring venomously at Claudius as he retreated.

"You will pay for this. If you refuse to stand for Rome, you will be treated as one of the invaders and dealt with the same," the priest threatened as he disappeared into the mass of bodies.

The Praetorians continued forcing the mob back, detaining those who resisted, receiving angry outbursts and protests in return. Rocks and debris rained down on the guards, along with a torrent of threats and warnings, but the firm shoving with their shields combined with the arrests had the desired effect. One by one, the agitators peeled away, slinking off resentfully. Soon, only the faithful few who'd been arrested remained.

The last few holdouts were slapped in irons and dragged away, the market seemed to revert back to its previous state, as if nothing had happened. The mob was ever fickle, able to be riled up in an instant, and to forget about that outrage just as fast.

Turning to Titus, one of his subordinates, Claudius said, "Report this incident to Tribune Faenius. Make sure he knows about the things the Flamen Dialis was saying and that I had to use force to disperse the mob."

Titus nodded, "Yes, sir, right away."

As his men resumed their patrol, Claudius couldn't help but feel uneasy. He'd thought he'd seen the end of this kind of scene with the death of the last of the insurgents. Of course, the fears and anger that the insurgences had spread were still there, under the surface, just waiting for someone like Vesnius to stir up, but he'd hoped no one would be stupid enough to do that again, considering the carnage and destruction the insurrection had brought.

This wasn't quite the same, since the priest wasn't calling for overthrowing the Empress, but it fed into the same fears and prejudices.

He just wished the Empress and her advisers could figure out a way to quell the unrest before it boiled over, because it would be people like Claudius and his men, out in the streets, who would have to deal with it when it did.

Chapter 12

Northern Germania

"They're all like this?" Ky asked, looking across the Rhine from the small hilltop they stood upon at what had once been a small village.

Dark plumes of smoke curled from the charred ruins and even from here, Ky could see bodies littering the ground, with no one left alive to bury them.

"The ones our people have actually seen, yes," Bomilcar said. "There are tales of more villages deeper inside Carthaginian territory getting the same fate or worse, since this was a raiding party and those were hit by full detachments from their armies. At least this is our understanding based on the stories we've heard from the handful of people who've managed to escape and run north."

"They're fighting to rule an area where they leave no people alive. What's the point?"

"'Lives are cheap' is a common saying among the emperor and his cronies. This was a common sentiment even toward my own people, but especially towards barbarians, which to the emperor is everyone who isn't a Carthaginian. If they win, they'll just bring people in from other areas they control and force them to settle here and work the land. There is some good news, at least. Since this was a smaller raiding party, a fair number of people escaped and made it to neighboring villages. They'll be able to rebuild."

"Come back to where their families and neighbors were murdered? I'm not sure they'd consider that good news."

"It's better than the alternative," Bomilcar pointed out. "And it's better than my other news. Our scouts have followed the trail of the Carthaginians. They crossed the river and are headed toward an Istvaeones village."

"Damn," Ky muttered.

"So far, the destroyed villages had been in areas still controlled by the Carthaginians, or at least in contested areas like the one we're looking at. If their raiders are headed toward an Istvaeones village, it will be the first time they attack one of their allies."

"I've sent riders to warn the village, but most of the Istvaeones men have already left our camps to return to their villages and get their families to safety," Bomilcar said, his expression grim. "They make up a significant portion of our raiding forces, which is going to slow our disruption of Carthaginian supply lines. I believe they intend to bring not just their families, but everyone they find to the north, abandoning their villages."

"In that kind of a hurry to escape, they won't be able to carry much, which means we're going to have to take them in as refugees. Some of the villages further north might take them in, but they're all short on supplies as well and the harvest is still two months away. They won't be able to feed all their people and care for the refugees too."

"We don't have the resources to handle them either," Bomilcar pointed out.

"I know. Send a rider back to the coast with a message explaining what's going on and arranging to have as much food and clothing as possible shipped to us. Also, have Valdar's merchants start trying to buy what they can and deliver it here. Lurio's going to have a stroke trying to find an additional money source to support this request, but Lucilla will see that it is taken care of."

Ky would actually message her as soon as they rode away from the scene and he had a quiet moment alone, but they had a fiction to maintain which meant sending a runner with the request. At least with the advance warning, she could start getting the supplies together, maybe even send Valdar's ship early saying it was based on her intuition.

It would still take time and they'd be stretched very thin until additional supplies arrived. They'd set out to make the Carthaginians struggle to keep their men fed and somehow, the Carthaginians had managed to turn the tables on them. Of course, the Carthaginians didn't have to worry about feeding and protecting civilians, so all they were concerned about was their own army.

"We can't stay on the defensive like this," Ky said at last. "With our raids slowing, they'll be able to increase how quickly they can build up forces while we have to divert rations from our men to feed civilians. Every day that passes we'll get weaker and they'll get stronger."

"We still don't have enough rifles to equip all of the men. Velius got the last shipment, which gives us only two equipped legions, not counting the muskets we handed out. Our supply of gunpowder is also lower than I'd like. The last shipments have been very light."

"I know," Ky said, thinking hard.

He didn't disagree with Lucilla's decision to transfer some of the gunpowder from his forces to Valdar. The Carthaginians had such a massive advantage in manpower, they could just keep throwing men at him, whittling away at him, unless he did something to slow down their reinforcements. Valdar was their only real shot at doing that.

"Which means we need to change our tactics," Bomilcar said.

"That sounds like you already have something in mind."

"I do. I didn't disagree with your original plan to use hit-and-run tactics. Considering the disparity in manpower and the fact that most of our men are still not armed with rifles, it was the prudent thing to do. Especially during winter while we were still training our allies and consolidating forces. We can't continue this tactic forever. No one has ever won picking at an opponent, slowly whittling away at them until they gave up, and we're not going to win that way here."

That might have been true in ancient times, but there had been points in history where guerrilla warfare worked, with the attacker eventually giving up and going home. Of course, there were just as many times, like the moon colony rebellion, when the other side giving up meant leveling every settlement and making the area uninhabitable before they left. Of course, that wasn't really possible with the current level of technology and it didn't make Bomilcar's point any less valid.

"So instead of using allies to hit and raid, what should we do?" Ky asked.

He'd actually already gone over some plans with Sophus, but none had jumped out at him yet. Sophus was invaluable and his ability to process tactical data was unmatched, at least in this era, but sentience had not come with the human ability to imagine and think outside the box.

"Instead of hit and run, we need to hit them directly. Draw them into open battle where our new rifles would give us an advantage. If we can funnel their army into a trap, we could decimate them with a single blow. Right now, the Carthaginian army is advancing along the Rhine toward the Istvaeones villages. If we position our forces to the southeast, we can lure them into the hilly country between the Rhine and Visurgis rivers."

"That plan has some risks," Ky said. "The land there isn't as mountainous as where we've been fighting. Yes, it's broken up by a lot of smaller rivers, but it's heavily wooded, which negates our advantages. We won't have clear lines of sight for our guns, which will allow them to get on top of us faster."

"That's true, but there are some clear areas and our people know exactly where those are. We can use the rivers to slow them down and keep them from outflanking us, hit them, and then pull back to the next one. If they try and pass us, instead of using the musket-armed tribes for raiding, we use them to pick at the edges of the enemy forces while they're moving through the forest. Their mounted units won't be able to run our people down and they won't be able to mass their archers. They'll have to turn to face the threat, at which point our allies pull back, bringing the Carthaginians against our main body, which is set up and focused on where they'll emerge from the trees. With our cannons and rifles, we can tear them apart and then pull back and do it again."

"We'd have to choose our ground very carefully. We need to find areas that are both open to attack and have rivers close enough to keep them from flanking us, which would also help us break contact as they get close."

"I've already picked several spots on their line of advance."

Ky considered his plan. They were short on rifles and gunpowder, and running low on either would put them in a dangerous position. They were also outnumbered, although not as badly as they had been in the past, since the bulk of the new Carthaginian forces were still near the Mediterranean. Still, they couldn't just keep waiting on supplies before attacking, not while the Carthaginians were threatening their new allies. They'd promised these tribes protection, and if they failed the first time one of the tribes was threatened, it would make any future promises that much weaker.

"Alright, let's start moving. Have the legions break camp and get ready to march. You're going to need to talk to the auxiliaries though. I've gone on enough of the raids now to see firsthand how ... energetic some of these tribesmen can be. It's imperative for them to know that they have a specific job, and that they can't just engage in all-out combat. If they don't break off, all we'll end up doing is losing their men without drawing the enemy into our attack."

"I know," Bomilcar said. "I've already talked to some of them, and I think they've had enough experience with the muskets to start to appreciate the advantage that they provide, but I'll continue to work with them as we move into position. I think they're capable of more tactical thinking than a lot of us give them credit for. It's one of the reasons I think this will work. The Carthaginians do not expect that kind of undertaking from them. They expect frontal assaults and retreats, and not much else. It will take some time for them to adapt to a change in the way the Germanic tribes fight, which is why I think this will work. If they see our men falling back, they will assume it's a retreat and will follow to crush them."

"I hope so," Ky said as he turned his horse away from the burning village. "For all our sakes."

Lucilla was running late. That morning's audiences had run long. As more migration continued into Roman territory, both from inside the Empire and those fleeing from the continent, friction between Romans and the new immigrants was on the rise. She had hoped that as the rate slowed, mostly because far fewer Germanics were immigrating, tensions would ease up. Instead, it seemed to be going the other way, with people taking what should have been petty disputes and escalating them to the point where the Empire itself had to be involved.

She had managed to settle most of the disputes and finish listening to all of her petitioners for the day, but she still had what was bound to be a quarrelsome meeting with Lurio to deal with. Ky had contacted her late the evening before with more troubling news. Beyond the need to find the supplies he was requesting, which in itself wasn't an easy task, she also had to find money for the new workers' camp, the increase in expenditures for better rations for prisoners they put to work, and money for all the building supplies for the new factories. Their resources were stretched incredibly thin, which Lurio reminded her about every time she met with him.

She was just starting to leave to meet him in her offices when a commotion at the chamber doors drew her attention. She could hear raised voices outside the doorway as her assistant Gaius entered, the look on his face telling her he had something to report.

"What's going on out there?" she asked.

"Praetorian Faenius is outside and wants to meet with you. He says it's urgent and can't wait," the young man responded.

Although technically all of her guards were members of the Praetorian Guard, they took their duty very seriously and let no one in her presence without her approval, not even their nominal commander. Of course, that might be because most of her guards had been made Praetorians only recently as part of a reorganization of the Empire to put all internal security under that organization. Her men had been protecting her for much longer than that and felt more personal loyalty to her than to the Praetorians. Not that she minded. While she knew Ramirus screened everyone accepted into the Guard closely and she trusted Faenius, many a ruler had been deposed by his own army, which is why the Praetorians had been formed in the first place. Now that they had a different mission, it was a little comforting to know she still had people whose sole responsibility was protecting her from the growing list of people who wanted to see her dead.

"Let him in," she commanded.

Gaius bowed and opened the door, saying a few quick words to the two men on the other side, who parted, admitting Faenius. The Praetorian swept into the room, his expression equal parts annoyance, probably at being kept waiting, and worried determination. One of the things she liked about the Praetorian was that he wasn't easily flustered, which was why it was notable to see him look troubled.

Approaching the dais and giving a slight bow, "Your Majesty, I apologize for the interruption, but a matter of some urgency has come to my attention."

At her gesture for him to continue, he said, "There was an incident this morning with the Flamen Dialis in one of the city markets. He was aggressively denouncing your recent policies allowing more immigrants into the city to a crowd of almost two hundred people. He called for violence in all but name against the 'foreign influence destroying our city,' as he put it. His words incensed the crowd, which began to grow violent. Several had to be forcibly dispersed and others arrested by my men."

She knew many Romans still viewed even the Caledonians and Ulaid with suspicion, as well as the growing number of Germanics that had been entering the country. It had been one of the points the insurrectionists had used to try and build a wedge in the new Empire. She'd hoped that view had died with the last of the insurrectionists, but the sentiment had taken root. More troubling was that Vesnius was involved. She'd hoped he would take her previous words more seriously and back away from his dangerous rhetoric, but clearly, he had not. Unlike the insurrectionists, who were generally in disfavor after the destruction in Devnum, the Flamen Dialis wielded significant influence over the populace. His inflammatory preaching risked igniting chaos within the city a second time. They'd survived one insurrection; it was unclear if they could survive another.

"This is the third incident this week," Faenius said, echoing her thoughts. "Each time, the crowds grow larger and more aggressive. Vesnius is tapping into underlying fears and resentments, and I am concerned about where this is headed."

"It seems Vesnius has decided to disregard my warnings about involving himself in political matters," Lucilla said, frowning.

Faenius nodded. "He does seem intent on stirring up the mob. My men can only do so much to keep the peace if he persists in riling up these crowds. So far, we've managed to quell the outbreaks more or less peacefully. Eventually, it will get out of hand, and there will be deaths, which will escalate things even further."

"What do you suggest we do?" Lucilla asked.

She already had a notion of what he wanted to do about the situation and what her response would be, but she liked to let her subordinates express themselves, instead of giving arbitrary rulings. Very often, they surprised her with opinions she didn't expect. Not this time, however.

"We should arrest him. If he isn't out there preaching, the mob will calm down."

Lucilla considered for a moment, just to make sure she was taking everything into account. Vesnius's position and importance to the people made him somewhat untouchable, which is why Faenius had come asking for permission instead of just arresting the man on his own initiative. She, however, disagreed with his assessment of the outcome. Vesnius's arrest wouldn't calm the population down. If anything, it would have the opposite effect. He would become a martyr, inciting more anger and violence from the people.

"No. That would be a mistake. For now, monitor him closely. He's always been difficult, but he's never been so vocally problematic before. There is a factor in this we are missing, and I want to know what it is before we make any rash actions. I want to know everywhere he goes, who he speaks to. Identify his inner circle, find out who is funding and supporting him."

Faenius made a face that either meant he didn't agree with her, or he hadn't considered that someone might be behind the scenes pulling Vesnius's strings. Either way, the Praetorian bowed and said, "It will be done, Your Majesty."

"Be discreet," Lucilla cautioned as Faenius turned to leave. "I don't want him alerted or driven underground just yet. We need to understand the full scope of this threat."

Faenius nodded and left. Although he did not have Ramirus's level of subterfuge, she'd found the Praetorian to be highly competent and trusted him to carry out her orders. Her problem was what to do with Vesnius once they knew the source and scope of his rabble-rousing.

There were political implications, both in what he was doing now and how he'd react when he was finally arrested, if it came to that. She would need to prepare carefully.

Vesnius wouldn't have had much success if there wasn't a deep well of fear and resentment against foreigners. It was the weak point in their new Empire. While the insurrection had been defeated, its ugly motivations clearly lingered. More work would need to be done to unify her citizens and ensure no demagogue could divide them again.

Chapter 13

Gaul, North of the Pyrenees

Velius stood on the edge of the bustling encampment, taking in the organized chaos of the construction site. All around him, the legionaries and auxiliaries were hard at work, digging with pickaxes and shovels, excavating trenches, and digging out foundations for the walls and towers of the half-finished fort. In the distance, beyond the tree line, came the sound of axes and falling trees as men worked to clear sightlines for the soon-to-be extension of their line of protective stations between Port Invictus and the Middle Sea.

Wagons loaded down with quarried stone and sand trundled past, destined for the mortar pits where the binding agent for the mighty walls was being mixed. By now, working on the third fort in the chain, they were making progress in developing a system to quickly build a fort, man it, and move on to the next, with his small force carrying all the tools and tradesmen necessary to make everything on-site as quickly as possible.

In spite of the swift progress, Velius was anxious. Partly, that concern was the same one he had every time he started building fortifications in enemy territory. Relying on mounted scouts, his information about the whereabouts of the various Carthaginian detachments was sketchy at best. They'd all but blundered into two groups of enemy scouts. Although the Carthaginians had quickly turned and run, the fact that they hadn't even known the enemy was that close bothered Velius.

So did the fact that they were running into scouts at all. Before, it had mostly been raiding parties, groups of a hundred or so men, nipping at his heels. These, however, had been actual scouts, detached from some larger force and not part of a small band of raiders. It meant the Carthaginians knew where he was, and the presence of a larger force needing its own scouts indicated an attack was likely imminent, which was why he was so eager to get this fort completed. Once the tree lines were cleared and the men were behind solid walls with cannon mounted in the casemates, they'd be difficult for all but the largest Carthaginian force to dislodge.

The location was good; a small hilltop with steady slopes up three sides and a sharp drop-off on the fourth that would help foil any attacker, slow any assault on the fort, and allow its defenders to fire down into the men climbing up it, increasing the chances of hitting someone during an attack.

Right now, though, it was barely a frame of a fort, with only the beginnings of a wall in place, surrounded by obscuring forest. They were vulnerable. He'd done his best to set his legionnaires up to have some defensive works to allow his men to fight if it came to it and give the workers a perimeter to run to safety. The biggest problem was he had to be prepared for an attack from any direction and he had to be ready on very short notice, because if things held to form, he wouldn't have a lot of time to react. Even with that, he'd still given up his biggest advantage ... range. Until the tree line was cleared farther back, they wouldn't be able to properly engage until the enemy was practically on top of them, which was going to make any fight harder.

The Consul had foreseen some of this in their training. Maybe not this exact scenario, but they'd worked on tactics for dealing with a massed enemy when they were within arrow range or closer. What made Velius so anxious was how many casualties they'd incurred during one of those simulated battles.

Turning, Velius looked to Crito, the chief engineer for the forts, as the man directed the workers, and fought the urge to go ask the man for yet another update. He'd already asked too many times that day, and the answer had always been the same. Velius knew he'd mostly be asking to try and assuage his own nerves, and that it'd be a futile gesture.

As if he'd willed it into existence, Velius's worst fears came true as his scouts and logging crews came barreling out of the forest, shouting alarms that a Carthaginian force was hot on their heels. To prove the point, a moment later, the first lines of Carthaginians marched out of the trees, weapons and armor glinting in the sunlight. He'd hoped they would have heard the army barreling down on them, but the sound had been broken up by the trees and covered by the sounds of construction all around him.

"Form ranks and fix bayonets! Prepare to fire! Front rank, lock shields," Velius commanded.

Legionaries scrambled into formation, rank upon rank arrayed in long neat lines, rifles ready at the shoulder behind the hastily arrayed defensive works which would slow, but definitely not stop, the horde of spear-armed men pouring out of the trees. Arrows whistled overhead as the Carthaginian archers let fly, the trajectory much flatter than he'd experienced before, almost coming up the slope instead of dropping down onto his men. This would be the first test of his forces in hand-to-hand combat armed with rifles instead of shields and gladii. Thankfully, the Consul had foreseen some of this and kept at least one row of shieldmen for the front of every unit. He'd hinted that, eventually, they'd transition to just lines of riflemen, which would have changed the calculus of the clash significantly.

"Artillery, fire at will!" Velius shouted.

The cannon along the line unleashed a thundering barrage in response, cannonballs tearing bloody gaps in the Carthaginian lines. It wasn't going to be enough. There were fewer than seventy yards between the tree line and his men. By the time they reloaded, the Carthaginians would be on top of them.

His men, however, performed admirably, breaking ranks slightly to allow the logging crews to flow through their mass and then reforming almost as quickly. It looked as though the entire mass of Carthaginians were only coming from one side, which would play in their favor, although he couldn't assume this was the only group of Carthaginians in the trees.

"Order the seventy-fifth cohort to send half their centuries around to support us."

He had to leave the units on his left and right intact, since there looked to be enough Carthaginians to flow around either side, but he could afford to peel some off the rear units which, hopefully, looked like they might go unengaged through the coming fight. His men formed a tight circle around the fort construction, which meant he wasn't going to be outflanked, at least not if he kept the line from breaking.

The Carthaginians had learned their lessons against cannon, and didn't flee as chunks of their force melted away. Instead, soldiers flowed in to fill the gaps created by the round shot tearing through them and continued to press forward.

"First rank, fire!" he shouted, followed by a clattering of rifle and thick smoke.

Unless the Carthaginians broke, he was only going to get one cycle of this use of the rifle, Velius thought as he yelled, "Second rank, fire."

More Carthaginians fell, but their line continued moving forward. With the added two centuries, Velius had seven hundred or so riflemen on this side of the circle, with the rest spread around the sides and rear. If he had to guess from the rows of men coming out of the trees, he was facing five or maybe even ten thousand Carthaginians. Even if every bullet hit true, and each hit a different man, he'd need fifteen or twenty volleys. Instead, he was going to get maybe three, which meant they were about to find out how these new bayonets fared against the long phalanx spears.

"Third rank, fire!" He shouted. "First row, brace for contact. Third row, reload and fire at will."

They'd trained for this. The first row dropped their rifles and held their shields tight, pulling gladii to fight in the old way. The second row changed the grip on their rifles, set to use them to deflect spears and stab over the shoulders of their comrades, while the third row reloaded, preparing to fire as they were able. They would also fill in for the second row as men fell. It had played out well in practice, but that had been with blunted poles and wooden rifles.

Through the lingering cannon and rifle smoke, Velius finally noticed why the Carthaginian arrows seemed to be coming in at an unexpected angle. Many of the archers in the rear weren't using traditional bows and arrows but were holding something that looked suspiciously like the arcuballista that the Consul had introduced before the Britannians had switched to rifles. It explained why the arrows were tearing through his men's armor, causing more casualties than they normally experienced in ranged attacks.

Highlighting the point was the interrupted cry of one of his aides as a bolt from one of the weapons slammed into his chest, knocking the man over backward. A part of Velius's mind wondered if they were some of the weapons the Empire had been selling off as a source of revenue or if they'd simply copied the design. Not that it mattered. At this range, they were almost as effective as his rifles and just as fast to fire.

The barrage intensified, raining death on the outnumbered defenders. All around Velius, men cried out as bolts punched through armor and burrowed into vulnerable flesh. The ranks wavered, recoiling under the brutal impacts.

Another bolt caught a legionary in the neck, dropping him instantly. The man next to him rushed to fill the gap, only to take a bolt to the shoulder, the force spinning him around before he collapsed. Velius watched helplessly as holes opened along the line. The losses were mounting at an alarming rate.

"Shields up!" Velius called to the first row.

The legionaries quickly overlapped their shields, forming a wall of wood and iron. It offered some protection from the deadly missiles, but the Consul's design had increased the efficacy of the weapons, and many bolts still punched through, hitting the man behind the shield.

Although it was doubtful they were going to break his line by using arrows alone, their phalanx still moved forward, and it was possible he'd lose enough men to give their spears the edge they needed.

"Target the skirmishers! Take out those arcuballista," Velius said, waving at the battery of cannon closest to him.

The crews swung their weapons around to point in the direction he indicated and let fly. Thunderous blasts echoed across the hillside and dirt fountained into the air amidst the Carthaginian ranks as shells smashed into the earth, obliterating men and weapons.

The arcuballista fire lessened slightly as shells tore through their ranks. It didn't stop their fire entirely, but it was enough to slow his losses. Once the phalanx reached his position, they'd have to stop firing anyway, to keep from hitting their own men.

All of the activity seemed to energize the Carthaginian spearmen, who picked up speed as they surged up the hill toward the Britannians. They crashed into the lines with frightening force, a tidal wave of flesh and sharpened steel. Shields splintered under the impacts. Spears thrust through gaps, impaling men where they stood. The Britannian line buckled and bowed under the overwhelming assault. Velius could hear the screams of the injured and dying over the din of battle, barely audible above the clamor of metal on metal.

The slope hindered the Carthaginians' progress, the wooden obstacles and defenses slowing their advance, breaking up their lines somewhat, and lessening the impact against his line. It didn't stop them, however, as the Carthaginians clawed over the impediments using tenacity and numbers alone.

Legionaries cried out as spears punctured armor and ripped into flesh. Boots skidded in the bloody mud as they were pushed back under the tide. Bodies began to pile up as men fell by the dozen. Chaos reigned. He caught glimpses of the slaughter through the press, legionaries being borne down and butchered beneath the tide, screams cut horribly short.

"Hold the line!" he called out, voice rising above the noise.

Around him, legionaries braced against the tide, bayonets flashing as they stabbed and parried. The rows behind them fired methodically into the mass, muzzle flashes reflecting off armor and shield.

In spite of their bravery and training, his men began to falter. This close, however, finally gave Velius a new option that he'd held off using until the right moment, waiting for the Carthaginian line to smash into his own, the soldiers behind beginning their normal tactic of pushing tight together, adding their weight to the steady press forward.

"Canister shot," he called out to his artillerymen. "Aim for their center."

The crews leaped into action, hands steady despite the chaos. They packed the cannons with metal cans stuffed full of lead balls and lit the fuses. Thunderous explosions resounded again from the hillside. Enormous sprays of metal shot ripped gaping holes in the Carthaginian formation, scything down hundreds of men in an instant. Firing down into the densely packed mass, nearly every projectile found flesh.

The Carthaginians reeled under the devastating impacts. Though they had grown accustomed to shells and rifles, they had never experienced canister shot like this before. It was as if the finger of an angry god had swept through their ranks, killing everything it touched.

All along the line, Carthaginian soldiers screamed as the metal shot shredded through them. Bodies piled up in mangled heaps. The phalanx formation wavered and threatened to break as men recoiled in terror. Velius saw his opportunity.

"Advance," he commanded.

The order caught his beleaguered men by surprise. Exhausted and outnumbered, they had been clinging to their defenses, struggling to hold against the endless tide crashing against them. But they were veterans, disciplined and battle-hardened. They did not hesitate for long. A guttural yell rose from their ranks as the legionnaires surged forward, the prospect of vengeance overcoming fatigue.

Shields slammed into the dazed Carthaginians, pushing them back and forcing them off balance. Bayonets followed, stabbing ruthlessly into any man who resisted. The charge gained momentum as triumphant yells mixed with screams of the dying.

The artillery crews reloaded feverishly and another ear-splitting volley of canister shot ripped through the Carthaginian ranks. The formation was coming apart now, order dissolving into panicked chaos under the withering blasts.

The Carthaginians fell back under the ferocious assault, cohesion evaporating. The advance turned into a panicked rout as men fled in terror before the vengeful legionaries. Cannon fire hounded them as they ran, shells tearing bloody swathes through their ranks.

Velius finally relaxed as the Carthaginian lines disintegrated, the organized phalanx reduced to a rabble fleeing for the tree line. Legionaries churned after the retreating Carthaginians, their disciplined bayonet line shattering the last vestiges of cohesion from the enemy ranks.

The din of battle faded, replaced by the moans of the wounded and dying. Britannian and Carthaginian bodies covered the torn earth.

"The enemy is in full retreat," Dexippus, tribune of the seventy-sixth cohort reported. "Orders, sir?"

"Send what horsemen we have after them. They are to harry the survivors, keep them from regrouping, but are to retreat at the first sign of organized resistance or if they get as far as the river. I doubt we'll be attacked again today, but pull the wounded back and have grave teams begin clearing the bodies, in case our men have to fight again."

Dexippus saluted and walked off, already barking orders. That done, Velius could turn his mind to the attack itself. It had happened so fast, he'd hardly had a chance to think, his focus being fully on stopping the surprise attack. It was a substantial force, to be sure. One that could have overwhelmed his defenses through the sheer weight of bodies alone.

But it was also a lot closer to his own number than they normally faced when the Carthaginians were the ones determining the time and place for an attack. The disparity in numbers was far short of the enemy's usual five or ten-to-one advantage.

Considering the skill the Carthaginian general had displayed so far, deftly foiling his plan to push through the winter, Velius doubted the reduced numbers were an oversight. If he had to guess, the goal hadn't been to seize or destroy the fort itself, although they probably would have taken it, if they'd been able to achieve that kind of victory. More likely, the enemy sought only to harass and delay construction. He knew their scouts had come across the first two, so they knew what he was up to by now.

Possibly, they were trying to allow time to muster far greater forces elsewhere before pressing the attack for real. Velius expected his men to be outnumbered, but considering how his plan required his men to be spread out along the line of forts, he couldn't afford to allow the enemy to mass its forces before his defenses were ready. Once all of his cannon and rifles were behind solid walls, they could counter much larger forces, or at least cause enough casualties to keep the Carthaginians from effectively crushing the whole line. Until all of the forts were up, however, he was vulnerable, which meant he needed to accelerate the construction of the rest of the forts.

With the sounds of battle fading behind the retreating Carthaginians, Velius turned back toward the half-finished fort, barking orders to the still-cowering workers as he went. There could be no pause, no respite. Not until the last of the forts were completed and manned.

Chapter 14

Devnum

Sorantius stepped off the carriage into the busy streets of Devnum, gazing around at the transformed city. Every time he came back to the city, he was amazed. A year and a half ago, Devnum had been a modest settlement, struggling under constant Carthaginian threat. Now it was the capital of a growing Empire and the center of technological innovation. The change was so much that a year ago Sorantius would never consider his particular interest in natural philosophy 'chemistry' and wouldn't have dreamed of a chemical industry, let alone heading one.

The city was a flurry of activity, with merchants hawking their wares, while labor crews worked diligently on expanding the infrastructure. What amazed Sorantius more than the city was its people with its blending of Romans, Britons, Gauls, and Germans. Such unity would have been unimaginable not long ago.

Reaching the imposing iron gates of the palace, he was waved through by the guards into the meticulously maintained palace grounds. While not as regular a visitor as Hortensius, the chemist had spent a fair amount of time here, either consulting with the Empress and the Consul or haggling with the tight-fisted Lurio. Today, however, he was here to see the Empress. Having been assigned the bulk of the responsibility for getting the telegraph project she'd described to them up and running, he'd run into some problems that he hadn't been able to sort out. Normally, he brought those troubles to Hortensius, since he'd had a longer track record working with the Consul and Empress to sort out issues such as this, but the manufacturer was running into issues with his own projects at the moment.

Instead of a normal audience chamber, he was ushered, by a servant, into a room that he hadn't been in before, passing Ramirus as he entered. Aside from the large table, his eyes were immediately drawn to a large map of the Empire tacked to the far wall. The Empress stood next to it, studying the marked positions of legions and settlements, ignoring him for a moment as he imagined she worked through whatever her previous meeting had involved. He waited patiently and was rewarded with a warm smile when she finally did turn away from the map to acknowledge him.

"Empress," he said with a respectful bow of his head.

Lucilla gestured to the chairs around the central table. "Please, have a seat Sorantius. I wasn't aware you were in town. What brings you to see me, today?"

He settled into a chair, hands fidgeting with a scrap of parchment.

"I hadn't planned on being here, but every time I tried to put my message into words I couldn't quite seem to explain the issue thoroughly, so I thought it best if I just come as the messenger myself."

"A reasonable solution," she said.

"It's the prototype for the battery for the telegraph you described to us. I built it as your instructions specified, but I can't seem to get them to maintain a consistent output as noted in your instructions. You described what happens when they provide too much ... I think the word you used was power, and that is what sometimes happens, although sometimes we get the opposite of that effect, where the containers might as well be filled with simple water for all of the reaction that happens."

"Do you have thoughts on why that is?" she asked.

Sometimes Sorantius couldn't tell if she was actually asking for more information or if she was simply employing the Greek method of teaching, where they asked questions rather than simply giving the answers being sought.

"I've done a fair amount of testing, and as far as I can tell the problem lies with the salt-soaked fabric connecting the two cells, although that's just a guess. I have tried both lowering and raising the levels of salt saturation in the fabric, but neither produced the desired consistent output. Too little salt, and the cells barely react at all, as if they are disconnected. Too much, and the reaction becomes volatile and uncontrolled. While I know this is outside your instructions, it did give me some insight into how this process you described works and is what led me to believe the salt bridge, as you called it, is the problem."

Lucilla tapped her chin thoughtfully, "What materials have you tried for the salt bridge aside from fabric?"

"Just the fabric, as per your original instructions. I thought any deviations might lead me astray."

"Of course, of course," Lucilla nodded. "I'm just trying to understand what you have tried so far to determine where the trouble might lie. And the salt, what type are you using?"

"Both mined and evaporated and both applied directly as well as putting it in water and then soaking the cloth in the water."

"I see," she said, and then fell silent.

He waited while she considered everything he'd said. As with the other times he's talked over matters like this with her, Sorantius was impressed with how quickly the Empress seemed to grasp the concepts, since this was all at the edge of his scientific understanding. He had been training as a natural philosopher since childhood, which at least gave him a basis to begin to understand these matters. She, on the other hand, had grown up learning how to lead, with a focus on politics and diplomacy. He doubted any other politicians he might meet would be nearly as adept at understanding these types of subjects.

"It does sound like the salt bridge is deteriorating too rapidly as the salt evaporates, which would lead to fluctuations in transmission power," she said when she finally spoke.

Lucilla fell silent again, her eyes going unfocused in that familiar way that signaled she was having one of her long pauses where it seemed like she was listening to some unheard voice. Although Hortensius had dismissed the thought when Sorantius privately brought it up, he couldn't help but wonder if she was actually listening to guidance from the gods. It would explain how she was able to come up with such wild leaps in logic and ingenious solutions that he would have never conceived of on his own. She always had some excuse ready, claiming she had seen a mention of something in the Consul's notes, but Sorantius had never found evidence to back up her claims. He suspected Hortensius knew more than he let on as well, based on the way the man denied Sorantius' suspicions a little too forcefully.

Sorantius shifted in his seat. He was always unsure of what to do when she got like this. He didn't want to stare or draw attention to it, but he also didn't want to interrupt her, either to break her concentration before she thought of a solution ... or on the off chance that she really was communing with the gods.

"I believe adding ammonium nitrate to the salt solution may help sustain the salt saturation within the fabric," Lucilla suggested suddenly, as her eyes refocused on him.

Sorantius furrowed his brow skeptically. Ammonium nitrate was not a compound he had considered for this application. While intriguing, he was unsure of the merits in this situation.

"Why would that help?" he asked, as usual, forgetting the pleasantries as he became more focused on an issue.

"Ammonium nitrate has unique properties that allow it to readily absorb water while also retaining soluble salts. When added to the salt solution, it should act as a sort of sponge within the fabric, holding the salt in place longer before it evaporates. This should allow for more sustained conductivity between the battery cells."

"I see. I've only ever seen nitrate used in the gunpowder process or making the new fertilizer the Consul described, and have been hesitant to experiment further with it, considering what it does when combined with the other components of gunpowder. If what you say about it slowing evaporation is true, I can think of a few other uses I'd like to test. However, that brings us to a new issue. We are currently struggling to get enough nitrate to produce gunpowder, let alone anything else. I've had to put producing fertilizer on hold until the military needs decline. How am I going to get enough to support making the batteries if we can't get enough for anything else?"

"I'll take care of that end. We should have more coming in by the end of summer when the first Ulaid pits begin producing, which will reduce our shortages. Until then, we'll figure it out. It'll be a small shipment, at first, for you to test out the quantities you need, and once you have a ... uhh, benchmark, I'll get you the rest."

"A what?" Sorantius asked, unsure if she used a word he didn't know, or if he misunderstood what she had said, since she had half-mumbled over the word.

"Benchmark," she said, almost distantly. "It means a standard point of reference."

"Ohh. I will let you know as soon as I have the ... benchmark, your Majesty," he said, bowing.

Ramirus exited the planning room, wondering for the hundredth time how exactly the Empress and the Consul's ability to communicate worked. The two had never addressed it to him directly, but he'd figured out a long time ago they had some kind of ability to pass information regardless of distance, since any report he gave her ended up with the Consul.

Right now, with the legions so far away, that ability was probably their greatest weapon, since he could instantly get reports from his sources scattered across Carthaginian territory directly to the armies, faster than maybe even Mercury himself. He'd heard about this telegraph Hortensius and Sorantius were working on, which would apparently be able to provide approximating that same power to the rest of them, but for now, it was just theory. An idea that had yet to be realized.

In one of those moments of coincidence, he almost ran into the chemist, who was being led by a servant to the room he just exited, as he cleared the large door. The man's attention was, as usual, not on the world around him, as he barely acknowledged Ramirus's nod in greeting as they passed. In a way, he envied Sorantius his straightforward work, distant from the web of secrets Ramirus was enmeshed in, although he knew the chemist had his own difficulties he had to deal with that Ramirus could blissfully ignore. So maybe switching places wouldn't be that easy after all.

Making his way across the plaza, Ramirus hurried up the steps to the Imperial Forum where he'd been told Llassar and Cormac were spending the day. Sure enough, the old warrior stood in the back, leaning on a column with his arms crossed as a senator droned on below, in the well of the Forum. Ramirus knew Llassar found politics as tedious as he did, though few would be able to tell from the stoic mask the man always maintained.

Less impassive was young Cormac, who lounged on the steps nearby, not even trying to stifle a yawn. The headstrong prince had regularly made his dislike of the endless legal minutiae known, and almost went out of his way to ensure everyone around him knew how unhappy he was to be here.

Catching Llassar's eye briefly, he jerked his head to the side, indicating his desire to speak privately. Llassar raised a bushy eyebrow but peeled himself from the pillar, following Ramirus to an empty alcove some distance away from Cormac's lounging form.

"I've heard concerning rumors swirling around the barracks and training yards. It seems our young princeling has been making the rounds, subtly inquiring about the troops' thoughts on our current military leadership," Ramirus said, dropping his voice to almost a whisper.

Llassar's expression remained neutral, though Ramirus noted the way his jaw tightened almost imperceptibly.

"Apparently, he's been engaging the men in hypothetical discussions about changes he would make, were he in charge," Ramirus continued. "Specifically questioning the decisions the Consul, Empress, and legates have made."

Llassar said, after a moment's thought, "He's made no secret of how much he chafes at what he sees as a ceremonial posting in the capital while real warriors fight elsewhere. Since that isn't possible, he likes to at least discuss military matters."

"I think it goes beyond that, however. He isn't just talking about the strategies and having hypothetical conversations about them. He's suggesting our military is being poorly led and that men's lives are being wasted, and asking not-so-subtle questions about support for a 'change of leadership.'"

A rare frown appeared on Llassar's face as he said, "If the prince has truly been making such inquiries among the men, it is concerning. Whispers that our leaders are incompetent or might be mismanaging the war effort is not good for these men who are soon to be fighting. This kind of thing can spread through the ranks quickly."

"My thoughts exactly, especially with some of the recent losses in Germania."

"Do you believe Cormac intends treason?" Llassar asked bluntly. "Or is he simply frustrated at his lack of authority and seeking to prove himself through hypothetical boasting?"

"I don't know," Ramirus said, considering his words carefully. "It's possible he's simply venting and doesn't mean to undermine the Empress's authority. I'm just concerned about the effect his words could have, especially if they reach soldiers whose morale is already shaken. They could see him as sympathetic to their hardships, a prince who understands their plight, even if that's not his intent."

"Soldiers gossip worse than fishwives," Llassar grunted in agreement. "They'll embellish a tale to make it more dramatic with each retelling. Before long, Cormac's hypothetical musings could morph into promises to relieve incompetent generals when he takes power."

"Exactly," Ramirus said.

The two men fell silent for a long moment, the distant chatter of the Forum drifting faintly to them.

"So the question becomes, what do we do about it?" Ramirus finally asked. "The last thing we want is to antagonize Cormac needlessly. His father is behind the alliance, but his house is still new and a lot of the nobles, some of whom were very recently in support of the Carthaginians, don't support it. We have to handle this delicately."

Llassar was quiet for a long stretch. Enough that Ramirus wasn't sure he was going to respond. Ramirus had dealt with many reticent men before, but none who could stonewall as well as Llassar. In this instance, he needed the Caledonian's input. Ramirus only had a few men installed in Ulaid and none yet inside the king's inner circle, which gave him a limited view of how they thought or might react. Llassar had both a past history with the Ulaid and Conchobar specifically, and recent dealings with them. Conchobar hadn't picked him to lead his son's education in politics and military matters lightly, which meant he had the king's ear. It also meant Ramirus needed Llassar's ear to deal with this problem and didn't have time for the warrior's normal stoic response.

Finally, though, the Caledonian crossed his arms and said, "If we're going to his father or confronting him directly, we need to be sure that your suspicions are correct, or at least have a foundation in fact. I suggest you discretely task some of your agents to interview the troops, to gauge how far the prince's influence has spread. We need to know if this is idle gossip or something more dangerous taking root."

"I've done some of that already, and so far it's only been a handful of the men he's talked to. We can go back and interview more, and perhaps slip a few men in as new recruits or returning veterans to train them, and see if they can get the prince to address them specifically."

"He's not a fool. He won't talk to anyone he hasn't developed a relationship with during his training, and he's smart enough to smell something if I start pushing him toward newly arrived men. Still, it's worth the attempt. In the meantime, I also suggest you keep a close eye on him. Track his movements, learn his patterns. I know you have men watching him, but you need to know every person he talks to, and perhaps put someone on those men as well. If he's covertly trying to find allies, there will be a web for you to discover."

"That's clever. You sound more like a spy than a warrior."

"Keep your curses to yourself," Llassar said, in a tone that could be taken as either joking or serious.

"Right. Sorry," Ramirus said, looking back toward the main part of the Forum, considering.

The crowds had thinned out some as a new speaker took the rostrum, though Cormac still lounged on the steps and was now chatting with a young man Ramirus recognized as the son of one of the Roman senators.

"Perhaps you should speak with some of the Caledonian troops here in the capital, either in the Praetorian barracks or those training outside the walls," Ramirus suggested, turning back to Llassar. "He's mostly been speaking to Ulaid and Caledonians, I guess seeing them as less likely to have a knee-jerk response supporting the Empress than a Roman would. Since they're new, they'd also be more willing to question decisions and probably assume someone as highly placed as a prince knows something they don't. But use discretion. We don't want word getting back to the prince prematurely."

"Fine," Llassar said, following Ramirus's gaze to Cormac.

When it became clear the Caledonian wasn't going to add anything else, Ramirus said, "I have things to attend to. Send word if you learn anything."

Llassar just nodded, not looking away from his young charge.

Germanica, Belgica, North of the Rhine

The distant rumble of thunder woke Matho from his light slumber. He sat up on the bedroll he'd thrown under an old tree, where he'd laid down for a short nap while scouts went looking for the raiders that had been pestering his column for a week now.

The sound came again, a low boom that rolled across the countryside. Matho's brow furrowed. The sky had been clear when he laid down to rest. Picking himself up, he moved to look over the camp, where most of his soldiers had done the same as he had, knowing enough to get rest when they could, since battle was always just around the corner.

Beyond his temporary camp, all he could see were trees and rolling hills, although he knew a series of rivers lay a half day's ride to the east.

"Rouse the men," he said to one of his aides, who'd made his way over when Matho had gotten up. "Get them formed up."

The officer departed as more booms sounded. As Matho watched, a ripple of movement passed across his army as the resting soldiers readied themselves for combat. Matho listened closely, judging the thunder's direction. A probe, he suspected, but its intent still unclear. After the initial fight just before winter, the Romans had avoided a straight-up fight, choosing instead to pick at his supply lines and harass him rather than attack directly, which suggested their army wasn't as large as the previous commander in this area had reported, before his execution for his failures.

He stood there, on a small rise near the center of their sprawling encampment, looking northeast, as the distant thunder slowed and then fell silent. It wasn't a surprise when, ten minutes later, a group of scouts came riding through the tree line and into the camp.

Matho's commanders gathered around as the scouts rode through the army and up to the command group, where they slowed their horses and dismounted, the lead scout removing his helmet and tucking it under his arm. He was weathered from years in the saddle and had a jagged scar across his left cheek marking him as a veteran.

"Report," Matho said, interrupting the aide who moved to intercept the scout.

"We encountered the Romans, sir. We found their army about six stadia northeast, near the convergence of two streams. They number no more than a thousand by our estimate, although they kept in tight formation and their thunder weapons kept us from getting closer. As soon as they saw us, they began to pull back, through the narrow strip of land between the two smaller streams, toward the Visurgis."

"How many troopers did you lose?"

"Only four. They only used the large tube weapons. None of their soldiers used the thunder weapons they carry, although they held them at the ready, I guess in case we decided to risk a frontal attack. Although most of their weapons missed, one impacted near a group of my riders, which is how we lost the four men. They were busy trying to fire and then roll their weapons back as they retreated, which probably accounts for their poor aim."

150

"They're frightened and outnumbered," Sabnius, one of Matho's commanders said.

"Could it have been a scouting element for a larger force?" another commander asked. "We've seen they prefer to stand behind their defensive works, trying to slow our men down while they use their new weapons. Catching them in the open like that, this could have been a forward unit."

"They don't scout with legionaries, and a thousand is a sizable chunk of their overall force here. Our sources all say they have, at most, twenty thousand men in all of Germania, not counting the barbarians. If they were pulling back to the Visurgis, that is probably where their army is camped, in between it and the two smaller rivers. They've trapped themselves. All we have to do is march in and crush them. They can't run away from us this time."

Matho remained silent, contemplating as he visualized the terrain from the scout's description. A thousand men was far fewer than anticipated. The previous commander had reported the Romans amassing a force of nearly ten thousand before his ... removal.

"What about their barbarian allies?" Matho asked. "Any sign of them?"

"No, general. Only the Romans."

"Because they've abandoned the invaders," a third officer said. "After we showed them that the Romans, even with all of their magical weapons, couldn't stop us from raiding and burning their villages, the tribesmen have abandoned them."

"Exactly," Sabnius said again. "They're weakened and trapped in a valley with rivers on all sides. We should march in now and crush them."

"Did they turn and run, or was it a slow withdrawal?" Matho asked.

"A slow withdrawal. They would pull back, fire once or twice, and then hold until we edged closer, at which point they'd pull back a little further and fire again."

"Because they didn't want to be trapped, but they didn't know if you were scouts or a forward unit, so they couldn't just push out of the valley," Sabnius said. "We should attack now! We outnumber them ten to one. There won't be another chance to destroy them like this."

Around him, most of the commanders nodded as Sabnius spoke, murmuring their agreement. Matho remained silent as his commanders clamored for an immediate attack. He recalled General Tabnit's warning: "Do not underestimate these Romans and their magical weapons." Matho suspected this retreat was too convenient, too enticing. They had used a similar tactic before.

"A bottleneck," Matho mused aloud, interrupting Sabnius's impassioned call for battle. "While it does trap the Romans in a confined area, with little room for retreat, it would trap us as well."

Sabnius scoffed. "With respect, General, they are outnumbered and cowed. We will crush them between our forces like grain between millstones."

Matho shook his head, a grim smile creasing his weathered features. "And they'll funnel us into their weapons' maws, Commander. In tight quarters, our numbers advantage disappears, and we don't know where their barbarian allies are. They've shown us time and again that they know this land well enough that our scouts could walk right past them, and never know it. If we move into the valley between the rivers, I think we'll find the rest of the Roman forces, ready for us to charge headlong into their thunder weapons. When we try to retreat, we'll find all of those Germanics blocking our escape. We'll be the ones caught on an anvil."

Murmurs rose from the other commanders, some in agreement with him, some still thinking they should attack. Matho raised a hand for silence.

"Their withdrawal was slow, sounding almost methodical. Meant to be seen, to entice attack. Why show themselves at all if retreat was their goal?" he said, beginning to pace. "We hit another village two days ago. Why would they wait until now, if they were here in force, to at least make their presence known? Why keep a thousand men just hiding out here, waiting."

"The emperor's decree was clear," Sabnius said, the man barely suppressing a scowl. "We are to pursue and destroy the Romans aggressively. This retreat is surely a sign of their weakness. We cannot ignore his command!"

Matho's expression hardened as he turned to face the impetuous commander, "Mind your tone, Sabnius. I am well aware of the emperor's orders. I also recall the punishments meted out when those orders are not achieved. Look at what happened to General Bomilcar. His entire family was executed after his defeat in Britannia. His wife, his young children, even his elderly parents ... all put to the sword."

The executions, following the loss of Britannia, had gone on for days and had not been limited to the leaders of the defeated army. Punishment went down as far as the families of men who commanded individual units, with wives, children, cousins, and grandparents being put to death for their failure. Matho went on, keeping his gaze fixed on Sabnius.

"So believe me when I say none wish to destroy these Romans more than I. But I have no intention of letting zeal turn to folly. We've seen what comes of generals who become overeager and have their commands destroyed in the process. Entire armies lost, tens of thousands dead. Tell me, will the emperor be understanding if we gain a momentary victory only to be annihilated afterward? Will the shame be wiped away if you can say you obeyed his commands, yet failed utterly?"

Sabnius' face reddened but he held his tongue under Matho's withering stare. Other commanders shuffled uncomfortably, properly cowed.

Matho stepped back, "No. Recklessness and blind obedience help no one. We will press the Romans, harry them, and if the opportunity arises, destroy them. But we will not fall into one of their traps. We hold the advantage in manpower. The longer we force them to hide behind their walls and weapons, the more their barbarian allies will doubt their resolve, and the weaker they will become. No, we will not be baited. Instead, we will spring their trap against them."

Pointing at the three senior commanders, he said, "Have the army pull back and dig into separate camps, each spaced apart by an hour's ride. Sabnius, your men can take the one facing where the two smaller rivers come together, but further west. Ortho, your men will take a position northeast of Sabnius and Edom, position your men to the southeast. This will allow two sections to swing around and hit the flanks and rear of any Romans attacking the third section. Send our mounted forces west with orders to continue burning villages."

If the Romans wanted to battle, they'd have to come to him. If they wanted to continue to wait, they'd have to live with more burned villages and dead allies. Eventually, they would have to give him a stand-up fight or lose all of their support here on the continent. Either way would give Matho the victory he needed.

Chapter 15

North of the Pyrenees, Sixth Fort Construction Site

Velius walked slowly across the muddy ground, surveying the scene before him with a grim expression. Bodies of Carthaginian soldiers were being hauled away by the grave detail teams, stacked in careless heaps before being tossed into mass burial pits. Though they had given far worse than they got, the sight of so many dead still turned his stomach. This was the fourth assault they had beaten back as they constructed the line of protective forts, and Velius was certain it would not be the last.

The men had done well, working tirelessly, building impressive fortifications with stunning speed, even in the face of constant attacks. His pride was tempered somewhat by the sight of the Britannians' own losses, lined up awaiting burial.

The problem weighing on him was the size of his protective force. When the string of forts was completed, they would become the rapid reaction force, moving between strong points to counter Carthaginian incursions. But their numbers were dwindling at an alarming rate. Carthaginian raids and ambushes were taking a toll; even when his men emerged victorious, the situation was unsustainable.

Finished with his rounds, Velius spotted Gordianus, his face smeared with blood and dirt from the recent fight.

"What's the count?" Velius asked, catching up to his second in command.

"Sixty-two dead, this time around, and another two-hundred and twelve wounded, although the majority of them have minor wounds. Most will recover in a few weeks," Gordianus replied.

Velius nodded, thinking. Considering the hundreds of dead on the Carthaginian side, it was a stunning victory, but the Carthaginians could afford such losses, and he could not. They weren't going to survive many more of these victories.

"At this rate, we'll be bled dry long before the Carthaginians run out of men. Our defensive lines are stretched perilously thin and get thinner with each fort, since we have to leave behind a contingent at each one."

Gordianus nodded, "More concerning is how swiftly they're able to mount these raids and ambushes. The last intelligence sent to us from Devnum said that the main part of the Carthaginian forces were still amassing at their port on the Middle Sea. They have to run out of men at some point."

"I've come to the conclusion that the Carthaginians will never run out of men. Send an urgent request to the Empress in Devnum. Tell her we desperately need additional support if we are going to stay in the fight. It doesn't have to be full legions; we'll take whatever men are currently trained and available."

"They could take that to mean a few centuries, which wouldn't be enough to change our distribution of forces," Gordianus pointed out.

"I know, but I don't want them to wait until they have a legion ready to go. That could take months, and we don't have time to wait. I want them to send us whatever they have. As soon as we get them, we can slot them into our existing units. When we have enough, we can then look at breaking them out into their own command. While we're at it, send word to the Consul in Germania. Apprise him of our situation and implore him to detach whatever auxiliary cohorts he can spare to reinforce us."

Velius knew reinforcements would likely take weeks to arrive, if they came at all, but it was his only option. This area was mountainous, not terribly hospitable to human life, and only sparsely populated before the Carthaginians showed up. After a hundred years of their control, it had become almost barren. There had been tribes further north, in Gaul, but that had also been the location of most of the Carthaginian forces on the western end of the continent, which had the effect of either depopulating or completely cowing the populace that remained. He wasn't going to find local allies like the Consul had.

"I don't think we'll have any more luck with the Consul," Gordianus said. "We just received that report that stated his men were spread out, trying to deal with the Carthaginians' new strategy of burning out anyone who supports us. That's a lot of land for them to cover, even with his additional legions."

"I know, but we won't get anything at all if we don't ask. Still, I'm not going to sit back and wait on either of them to save us. Send word back to Port Invictus. I want two of their cohorts sent to join us, which should be enough to keep us going if the reinforcements never come. If we do get reinforcements, they can keep enough of them there to bring their force back up to strength."

"Speak your mind," he said to his second in command, seeing the man's troubled expression.

"Pulling our reserve cohorts from Port Invictus leaves the port dangerously exposed. If the Carthaginians target it while the bulk of our legions are spread thin ..."

He left the implications unsaid. He wasn't wrong, and Velius understood the risk he was taking, but saw no better options before them.

"I know, but we don't have a choice. Once these forts are built and manned, we'll be able to counter the largest Carthaginian forces and have more flexibility. Considering the small number of men we have to carry out our mission, it's the only way I see us accomplishing it. Right now, we're between the Carthaginians at their base and Port Invictus, so we should have some time or at least warning if they head that way. We just have to hold on until our reinforcements arrive."

Gordianus looked unconvinced but did not protest further.

"Let us hope the Empress responds swiftly then," he said quietly, saluting and leaving to carry out his orders.

Velius watched him trudge away. While he didn't disagree with his subordinate, there wasn't much they could do about it. They had a job to do, and they were going to do it, reinforcements or not.

Devnum

The busy streets of Devnum bustled under the midday sun. Vendors called out their wares, travelers hurried to their destinations, and citizens went about their business. Hidden among them, Claudius blended into the crowds, discreetly following the priest Vesnius through the maze of city lanes.

Claudius wore the simple garb of a common laborer, his Praetorian armor traded for rough-spun peasant clothes. With his hood pulled low, he was just another anonymous face passing through the busy thoroughfares. Still, he kept a watchful eye on Vesnius ahead of him, trailing the priest at a careful distance.

It was an unusual assignment, and one Claudius felt was better suited for one of Ramirus's spies instead of himself. Being a blacksmith's apprentice, a Praetorian guardsman, and an optio commanding a small guard, working as part of the city guard, didn't exactly prepare him to follow anyone, let alone do it stealthily. He'd actually made those arguments to Faenius when he'd been given this assignment, since he'd honestly prefer to be with his men, clothed in the garb of the Praetorians. He'd worked hard to get where he was, and he liked the respect his position gave him.

Unfortunately, it seemed good work often resulted in more duty instead of rewards. His commander was impressed that he'd recognized the problem Vesnius had presented in the marketplace and how he'd chosen to handle it, keeping the situation from devolving into a riot. He told Claudius he needed someone with that kind of decision-making skills to handle this assignment.

So here he was, tracking the old priest through the city, trying to keep an eye on him without being seen and, more importantly, without anyone else noticing that he was following the priest. Faenius had told him they thought someone else was inciting the priest, who had always been difficult but never considered an agitator, into giving the inflammatory speeches. They hoped that Claudius or one of the other men tasked to follow the priest might see who that person or persons were.

Ahead, the priest paused, looking around, forcing Claudius to lean into a stall like he was looking at something. Watching the priest out of the side of his eye, Claudius saw him look around once more before turning down a smaller side street. Setting down the small bowl he'd picked up and had been pretending to examine, he ignored the shopkeeper and quickened his steps, determined not to lose sight of the colorful vestments that stood out even in the crowds.

It said a lot about the man's ego that, even trying to be discreet, as his antics a moment ago suggested, he still wore his full symbols of office. It did make him easier to track, for which Claudius was thankful.

Claudius kept his head down as he maneuvered through the alley and back onto a busy street, focused on not losing sight of Vesnius's colorful vestments ahead of him. The priest navigated the crowded lanes with familiar ease, weaving between merchants and shoppers until he turned down another empty side street. Staying back, Claudius glanced around before following.

He slowed his pace as he reached the narrow alley, cautious of being seen. Vesnius had stopped halfway down the shadowed passageway, speaking with a figure in a dark, hooded cloak. Claudius slid into an alcove, near some crates and a stinking pile of garbage, holding his breath as best he could, but unwilling to move since this was as close as he could get to them without being seen, and hoped he'd be able to overhear their conversation.

From his position, tucked in tight against the rotting vegetables and refuse, he could peer through small gaps and catch intermittent sight of the pair. That was how he caught a glimpse of the hooded figure as her hood slipped, revealing the face of Medb, the consort of the Ulaid prince. She'd become a figure of note in Devnum, regularly creating a spectacle when she went out, always dressing flamboyantly with retainers in her wake. To her credit, she'd managed to have more sense than the priest, scaling down her dress for this meeting, matching Claudius's costume as just one of the mob, instead of something memorable like the priest wore.

"... ever wanted to come here. I was forced to by his damned father after they took my people," Medb was saying in a hushed but impassioned tone.

"And yet you are here. Had I known it was you that sent the message, I would have never come," Vesnius said, turning to leave, forcing Claudius to shrink back.

There was a rustling sound, followed by Medb saying, "I don't want to be here anymore than you want me here. All I want is to return my people to Connacht, and leave your land to your people."

Vesnius paused, "But you married the prince, and he certainly holds ambitions for my people."

"Only because I was forced to, but he's young and foolish. He only cares about fighting wars and winning glory. He wants to return home too, but he's afraid of his father. He trusts me though. I have his complete confidence. Enough, that he's told me about his father's plan."

"There's a plan?" Vesnius asked, clearly hooked.

"Yes. One that he and Talogren made shortly after the Ulaid were brought into the Empire. They only joined this alliance because they see it as a way to defeat their greatest rival, one they could have never defeated through arms alone. They now control the Imperial Senate and, until the Empress has offspring, there is a place for them in the line of succession. They know that if they get the throne before that, they will have it and two-thirds of the senate. They will have taken over without a drop of blood being spilled. They can then make rules replacing Rome as the primary power, taking your wealth into their own lands and leaving you destitute and reliant on them. That's been their plan all along."

"I knew it," Vesnius crowed before putting a hand over his mouth, as if he suddenly remembered this was supposed to be a secret meeting. "I cannot allow that to happen. The gods will not allow it."

"I know, and I'm willing to help you stop them," Medb said. "All I ask is that once the true Romans are in control of their own lands and the alliance is shattered, you help me regain my people's independence. I know you have no desire to control Ériu

160

any more than my people have a desire to control Rome. We could be partners, allies."

"We don't need any barbarian as an ally," Vesnius said condescendingly.

"No, probably not, but there is still value in trade, and you would owe us for breaking the alliance," Medb said.

The old priest must be some kind of fool, Claudius thought, to not hear the suppressed rage in Medb's voice at his insult. He clearly didn't, though, based on how he responded.

"Maybe you're right, and we would honor any pledge we made in exchange for your help. The gods would require it."

"I know, that's why I came to you. You honor your gods as we honor ours, and you are as furious over your people's betrayal of your gods as I am furious that Conchobar has made my people betray ours."

"I am just a priest. I do not have armies or the power to overthrow an empire," Vesnius said.

"I know, and I've heard how the last attempt to stop her father from creating this Empire ended. I'm not sure outright insurrection is the way to go. This can't be a few rich men demanding a change; this has to come from the people. It's why I came to you. Who else better to represent the people and to speak to them? You're the only one who can convince the people that they must rise up and demand a change, just as you've been doing. Eventually, the Empress won't have any choice but to listen, if she values her throne. She knows as well as you do what can happen if the mob is unheeded."

Vesnius considered her words before nodding, "That's true, and very wise. What would you need from me?"

"For now, just continue as you've been. Let the people know this Empire isn't right and isn't what the gods want. Let them know that they aren't the only ones being offended by this alliance. Tell them that the Empire is forcing this alliance on other people too, and that we want to leave but aren't being allowed to go. Maybe then they'll understand that it's their leaders who are forcing this to happen and realize where they need to direct their anger. Not at other people of their status, but at the Empress and the senators. The people really making the decisions."

"I can do that."

"Good. If you need anything, I still have resources and I have access to some of the Empire's resources. I'll have my messenger check with you from time to time, and will get you whatever I can."

"Fine. As long as we understand each other and what needs to happen in the end."

"We do, now go. We can't have anyone seeing us together."

With one final nod, Vesnius swept out of the alley, as hastily as he arrived. The queen watched him go, her mask dropping when he was far enough away, revealing her repulsion toward the man. After another breath, the ex-queen pulled her hood low and turned, slinking off in the other direction.

Claudius pressed back into the shadows, waiting until Medb was well out of sight before dashing off in the direction Vesnius had taken. Moving swiftly, he trailed after Vesnius, catching up with him as the priest rejoined the crowds, the man's garish robes making him easily identifiable.

Although he was following the priest, his mind was on the conversation he'd just overheard. It was clear she, or her agents based on their conversation, were the ones pushing the priest on his mission. Vesnius was too naive, apparently, to pick up on how he was being manipulated, but it was fairly obvious to Claudius. The question was, to what end? Did she think he'd somehow put her in control? He couldn't see how an uprising in Rome put her back on her throne. The Ulaid had a solid hold on Ériu, enough so that it was all but impossible she'd get followers to win it back.

Besides, if she was right and she had control of Cormac, then there were more options for her. Including somehow getting herself installed as some sort of consort of an Emperor Cormac. That seemed far-fetched, but who knows what people like that plan. Either way, it was above his pay grade. He just needed to follow Vesnius until he got back to the temple, where he could pass the duty off to one of the other men assigned to trail him. After which, he could return to the Praetorian barracks and inform Faenius about what he'd overheard.

Waldhügel, Germania, North of the Rhine

Ky, Bomilcar, and a small contingent of legionaries, along with Ky's personal guard, rode into the central Istvaeones village, one of the few untouched in the Carthaginian sweep of the region.

The recent rains had turned the ground into mud that sucked at their horses' feet, but the villagers, who were trudging along performing their daily tasks, barely seemed to notice. Other than an odd glance here or there, they didn't even seem to acknowledge the arrival of the outsiders, despite it being an unusual sight.

Ky and Bomilcar dismounted outside the largest hut which bore the banners of the Istvaeones chieftain. Leaving his guards unhappily outside, Ky ducked inside the hut, which was filled with tribesmen, and not all from the Istvaeones. Members of several other allied tribes who made their home in the vicinity of the Rhine, and who'd caught some of the Carthaginian fury, had also made it a point to attend this meeting.

Trasundia, chieftain of the Istvaeones, sat cross-legged at the head of the room on a pile of furs. His braided blonde hair fell to his waist, and he wore a necklace of bear claws that marked his station. His pale eyes narrowed as Ky approached, sizing him up.

"Greetings, Trasundia," Ky said respectfully with a nod. "Thank you for agreeing to meet."

"You should have come sooner. You have much to answer for, Roman," the chieftain said.

Ky didn't bother correcting him. Although Rome had never become the global power that it would have in his timeline, people knew about them and still felt more comfortable using that name instead of the name of their new Empire. It probably didn't help that Ky wore the traditional Roman-style armor, or that the rest of the Britannians, even the Caledonians and Ulaid, did too.

"I wanted to discuss the disposition of your men with you," Ky said, settling on the ground across from Trasundia and the other Germanic chieftains in attendance. "We've begun our offensive that will, hopefully, slow down and stop the attacks on your villages and push the Carthaginians out of Germania altogether, but for that to work, we need your help."

"Slow down," Trasundia scowled, his bushy mustache twitching. "When you showed up, you promised to free us from the death worshipers. That you and your mystic weapons would crush them. Instead, you've sat in your camps, teaching the collaborators to walk in lines while the Carthaginians burned our villages and slaughtered our people."

"Damn you," the Angelli chieftain, who led the tribe that had most adopted Carthaginian dress and culture, said. "We did what we had to to survive. Don't act like your people have done differently. Enough of your men joined their armies and killed in their name. Just because you can't adapt to new ways of war, always throwing your men into slaughter, doesn't make us any less than you."

"I'll show you slaughter," Trasundia said, reaching back for a large sword leaning against a wall of the hut.

This was getting out of hand.

"Stop it," Ky said, his voice cutting through the noise as other men began reaching for their weapons. "This is how you lost to the Carthaginians in the first place. So focused on fighting among yourselves that you didn't fight them. Trasundia's right. We haven't done enough to stop your people from being killed, and we're trying to fix that. When we arrived, we promised we'd help free you. We promised we would stand beside you and fight your battles with you. We did *not* promise that this would be bloodless. Yes, our weapons are powerful, but they do not make us gods. The Carthaginians still greatly outnumber us, and just charging into their armies would weaken us to the point that we couldn't do anything to stop the armies that will follow in this one's wake, even if we are victorious."

Meeting Trasundia's glare directly, he said, "What we can't do is fight this on our own. Their leaders have finally started to show some intelligence and won't follow us onto ground of our choosing. They're willing to take losses no one else would ever consider, which allows them to overcome most of the advantages our technology gives us. For our attack to work, we need to keep them in front of us and on clear ground; otherwise, they'll just wrap around us and crush us. We need your men to help pull them into an area of our choosing. They've only seen you in hit-and-run raids and expect you to run when the odds start going against you. They've already shown they're willing to chase you, especially if they think they can press you against a river or hillside where you can't run."

"So, you want us to be your bait?" Trasundia said.

"Yes," Ky replied. "It's not glorious work, and I know your warriors don't like running, but I'm sure they don't like losing their families even more. If we do this right, we can crush this entire army, which will let my people push south and take the ports that allow them to bring in reinforcements."

"And what about my people?"

"Abandon your villages. Send your people north. The other tribes can take them in for a short time. Once this is over, we will help you rebuild. We will give you supplies and techniques to allow you to make your lands even better. To grow more crops. To build sturdier homes. We aren't your allies just in war, and we will be here with you in peace as well. But for that to happen, we have to win first. Which means you need to get back into the fight, even if it means losing more of your wives and children. It's cruel, I know, but if we lose, they'll all be sacrificed anyway, either directly or by being sent to serve in one of the Carthaginian slave armies."

"It's easy to ask our people to die or surrender their homes for your war," Givellan, the Vandili leader, said.

"It's your war too, unless you want to continue living under their yoke," Bomilcar replied, finally speaking up. "We could have sent all of our forces far to the south, instead of splitting them, but we recognized that we need allies and were under the impression your people were willing to fight to be free. We are sacrificing Britannic lives here, just the same as you, fighting for your lands. I understand having your women and children in harm's way isn't the same thing, but the only way to actually protect them is to win. So I ask you, what would you have us do? Put a contingent in every village along the front? How many men would we have left to take the fight to the Carthaginians after that? Spread out like that, would we have enough men in any one village to fight off a Carthaginian attack? We'd be inviting them to make small meals of us, eating our forces up a little at a time until we had nothing left. Is that what you think we should do?"

None of the tribesmen had anything to say to that, most looking away, not making eye contact. It was one thing to demand someone do something, but these were their people's leaders, and they had to do more than just demand 'something.' They had to make the actual plans and lead their people to execute them, and should have known what they were asking for was impossible, or at least ill-advised.

"I know this is hard," Ky said, taking the lead back. "I know our progress has been slow, but we have made progress. How many of your villages feared a visit from Carthaginian overlords, and now are free to plan for the future? For every village along the front that is in danger, how many are behind us, safe? They are attacking your villages because they know our attacks have weakened them, and they need to stop us. They want us to pull back to protect your people, giving them time to resupply and get reinforcements. This is what we've been waiting for. It's a signal for us to attack. A few victories and the line will be south of the Rhine, and your villages will be safe."

After a beat, the chieftains leaned back, whispering among themselves, arguing. While Ky could hear every word they were saying, he neither wanted them to know that nor felt it was his place to interject. He needed them to join willingly if this alliance was going to work long-term, which meant letting them come to this decision on their own.

Besides, there wasn't an upside to letting them know everything he could do.

Finally, they leaned back, and Trasundia said, "Very well. We will support your strategy for now and go where you tell us to go. But know that our loyalty has limits. We have to answer to our people just as you have to answer to yours, and if our losses grow too large, we won't have enough people left to keep fighting. If you're going to stop them, you need to do it soon."

"I understand. If our attack is successful, we should push them back over the river, and maybe even further, if not scatter this army entirely. There are enough of them that it's unlikely they'd stay scattered for long, but it will give us breathing room. If we keep the pressure up, there won't be time for more attacks against your villages."

Although the conversation went on for another thirty minutes, the decision that mattered had been made. Everything else was logistics and bargaining.

As they left, Bomilcar said, "That could have gone better. They might have agreed, but what they said wasn't just hedging their bets. They gave us one chance to get this right, and if we fail, they will pull their support. For good this time."

"Well then, we'd best not fail. Ready the men. We have a war to fight."

Chapter 16

Outside Factorium

Lucilla sat in the carriage, watching the familiar countryside roll past in a blur of green and gold. She'd taken this trip so many times that she was almost comfortable with the bouncing and jostling, although they were turning for a detour, heading to the new work camp south of the manufacturing city. She was both eager and apprehensive about inspecting the new labor camp.

It was a necessary solution to their critical worker shortage, but the security complexities still troubled her. That was why she'd insisted on seeing the facility for herself, over the objections of her guards.

Glancing across from her, Lucilla studied the stern, chiseled profile of Praetorian Prefect Faenius who, along with Ramirus, was giving her a tour of the facility. The stalwart commander sat rigidly upright, fully armored even for this routine journey. She didn't know the commander well, relying on Ramirus for most internal security matters, as he took care of coordinating most issues with the Praetorian. Apparently, Faenius had something on his mind as well.

As soon as he saw her turn her attention toward him, the commander said, "There's something we must discuss regarding the priest Vesnius."

"What did he do this time?" she asked, annoyed that she was going to have to once again deal with the troublesome priest.

"Last week, my men observed Vesnius meeting secretly with the consort Medb near the market, where they conspired in private in a side alley."

"What do you mean by 'conspired'?"

"My man overheard only part of the conversation, but it was clear she was inciting the priest to continue his attacks on your rule and pushing him to do more. It was evident to my man that she was manipulating him, and Vesnius was buying into it."

"Why am I just now hearing about this?" Lucilla asked.

"My men don't spend much time with imperial guests. I wanted to have my man see Medb when she made one of her trips out of the palace, to confirm that the person he saw was indeed the Ulaid consort. He only confirmed it was her yesterday."

Medb. It made sense. Lucilla knew the former queen harbored ambitions of power, though Cormac seemed oblivious to his wife's true motivations. It also explained Vesnius's xenophobic tirades as of late. The high priest had always been naive, but she hadn't considered he'd be this easily manipulated.

"You're certain that what your man heard was Medb pushing him to preach more dissent?"

"Yes, Your Majesty. Claudius is a good man. Smart and reasonable. I trust his report implicitly. I also believe this matter demands our swiftest action, before their schemes progress further. I can't imagine she's doing this just to cause trouble. She has something specific in mind."

Lucilla looked out the window, contemplating the report. She had hoped to avoid direct confrontation with the irritating priest, but Faenius was right. This secret collusion with the scheming Medb was alarming and could not be ignored. Decisive measures would be needed to suppress the brewing rebellion and maintain stability in the kingdom.

"Very well," she said finally, turning to meet the Praetorian's gaze. "Have your men arrest Vesnius immediately, but do so quietly, away from any crowds. We cannot risk inflaming tensions by making a public spectacle of it."

Faenius inclined his head, "Of course, Your Majesty. My people will be discreet."

"See that they are," Lucilla said. "Make sure he's comfortable, but keep him away from anyone else. He's always been a true believer, and if she's warped his mind, we won't be able to change it back. At least not quickly. We need him off the street and not causing any more trouble until I deal with Queen Medb."

"I understand, Your Majesty," Faenius replied, serious.

Lucilla gave him a nod. He was a good man, and she knew he'd take care of it. Now she just had to figure out what to do about Medb. This situation was rife with political and security risks. Ulaid citizens were still pouring into the capital, and they loved their prince, who in turn loved his wife.

He'd already been causing problems, almost certainly provoked by his wife. Now she was out there provoking the priest and who knew who else. She was definitely working on a plan, and it would result in people getting killed.

No, Lucilla definitely needed to deal with the queen. She just had to figure out how to do it right.

"We're here," Ramirus said, interrupting her thoughts.

Lucilla looked across at Ramirus and out the opposite window, catching her first view of the work camp.

She had to hand it to them, the large fence was impressive. The design was provided by Sophus when the project to build the prison camp started, it was unlike anything she had seen before. Strings of the new steel wire Hortensius was manufacturing were criss-crossed in a pattern making diamond-like shapes stretched between two metal poles, with the pattern then repeating to the next and the next pole, until it formed a see-through wall that encircled the new work factory.

When Sophus had first suggested it, she'd been skeptical. It hadn't seemed that this chain-linked fence, as her disembodied friend had called it, would be strong enough to hold anyone in, but when wrapped tight against the metal posts, which were dug deep into the ground, it appeared to be surprisingly effective. The metal wire was extremely hard and made an effective boundary.

To make it difficult to scale, they had topped the fence with another addition provided by Sophus called barbed wire. This was more of the wire used for the fence, but with regularly spaced sharpened protrusions on it, like the thorns on a rose. It was rolled along the top of the fence in long coils that would both cut into anyone trying to climb over it and cause them to get wrapped up in it, since it wasn't pulled tight, but only looped through the top set of gaps in the chain link. A second fence was then built outside of the first with a several-pace gap in between the two, meaning that anyone scaling it would have to scale one, and then scale another to escape.

That was only the external wall. The camp was also subdivided into sections, with a long prisoner barracks separated in one area, also with fencing around it, and a separate factory area. The entire complex was a maze of metal wire and walkways, with guards spread throughout, both on the ground armed with clubs and in towers, armed with rifles.

Yes, it really was impressive at first glance.

"Welcome, Your Majesty," Ramirus said, coming around the carriage toward the main gate of the compound.

"This is very impressive," she said, echoing her previous thought.

"I agree. The notes the Consul left you on this new fencing material are really what makes this possible," he said, a sly smile on his lips as he continued. "Hortensius was particularly impressed with the new galvanizing procedure. I had to sit through a thirty-minute lecture about all of its benefits and his plans to rework one of his foundries to specialize in galvanizing large amounts of steel."

"He gets enthusiastic," Lucilla, who'd been forced to sit through many of those lectures, said.

"Let me show you the camp," he said, extending his arm toward the open front gate.

It had taken some doing to get her guards to agree to this tour, since there were obvious risks to putting their leader this close to so many prisoners, but she was still concerned about this entire notion of using them as workers and wanted to see what Ramirus had set up first hand. In the end, for them to agree it had required Faenius and a hundred of his men to be present, in addition to her guards and the normal camp guards, as well as having every prisoner locked into their barracks, which was in turn locked behind the wire fence. In spite of all that, her men and Faenius looked nervous as they started the tour.

There was still one unoccupied barracks as Faenius continued to vet those prisoners who volunteered. While it wasn't exactly comfortable, with rows and rows of beds, a small chest at the foot of each, where dozens of men would sleep at a time, it was preferable to the tents and dirt floors they'd used in the camp outside of Devnum. That had started as a temporary solution and they didn't have the cleared land there to build something large like this. One of the reasons the site of Factorium had been selected was the available land not being used for farming that could be used to expand into. It also helped that this was only a small portion of the prisoners they currently held. There were just too many captured Carthaginians to make this kind of thing practical for all of them.

The factory itself was more concerning. Although it was in its own fenced-in area, the building was set up like all of Hortenisus's other factories, except that instead of being devoted to one thing, it was larger with sections to produce each of the products from his other factories. At first, she'd thought they might have some kind of protective walls here, but the more she thought about it, the more it was clear that wasn't possible. So many pipes and metal shafts ran across the building that it just wasn't possible. What that meant, however, was that this would be the largest concentration of men in the complex, and they would be using sharp tools and fire, and they weren't blocked from moving around freely in the building.

The only different feature was a series of catwalks near the ceiling, presumably for armed guards. It was unlikely they'd have enough bullets to kill everyone on the shop floor if everything fell apart. Possibly it was a deterrent, since they could kill some of the prisoners, and no one on the floor would know if they would be one of the unlucky targets.

"I'm worried we may have made a mistake here," she said, turning to the two men with her. "This seems impossibly risky. I can see a dozen tools that could be used as a weapon from right here, and I'm sure there's more I'm not taking into account. Things could get out of hand here faster than the men we'll have guarding them can react."

"I agree, it's a problem," Faenius said, looking from Lucilla to Ramirus. "My Praetorians are spread too thin to properly vet each prisoner volunteer as it is. We're relying on secondhand information from other prisoners and gossip, which is far from ideal. The only troublemakers we've been able to weed out are the ones who've given my men trouble directly or who my men have seen cause problems firsthand. It's unlikely that we've kept all of the real problem cases out."

"Both valid concerns, which is why we've built in all the precautions we have," Ramirus said. "Yes, it's possible that we might get violence or lose control of the prisoners. That's a problem even in the holding camps where these men have all been living since being captured. If anything, we have more control of them here than we do in their current camps. Even if it does get out of control, the building itself is locked down. The prisoners are contained within the double fence. At best, they'd take the building, but we'd be able to take it back."

Lucilla remained unconvinced. The vast space of the factory was filled with heavy machinery, assembly lines, and vats of molten metal. She could see the potential for chaos if a riot broke out among the prisoners working the machinery.

"I'm going to be blunt," Lucilla said. "I think we moved too fast on this plan and may have jeopardized security in our haste to address the urgent labor shortage."

"The realities that drove us to this decision haven't changed. We could shut everything down, but we'd be right back to falling dangerously behind on producing what we need for the war effort," Ramirus said, and then paused a moment before continuing carefully. "Are you ordering me to shut the work camp down?"

Lucilla pressed her lips together. She was stuck. As much as the risks worried her, they didn't really have much of a choice.

"No," she said finally. "But I want you and Faenius to go over all of the security arrangements again. Make absolutely certain we have contingencies in place in case things go badly here."

She turned and surveyed the sprawling factory grounds, her sense of unease not abated. The web of chain-link fencing might seem secure at first glance, but people could do amazing things, especially when they were desperate. The insurrection and the waves of attacks by her brother's loyalists had all but proven that.

In the end, it came down to a balance of risks. They had to win this war, or the Carthaginians would make a prison uprising look mild in comparison to the death and destruction they would unleash. It's why she'd agreed to this in the first place, despite her better judgment.

Seeing this place in person, with its fences and guard towers, and this large open factory floor, she was worried she was being forced into a mistake by her own desperation. But ... they were still desperate. Maybe not in the same way they were when the Carthaginians were right outside their walls, but the stakes were just as high even now.

She could only hope that they'd made the right choice ... and brace for the consequences if they hadn't.

Belgica, Near the Rhine

Ky rode his horse through the dense woods behind the rows of legionaries, their formation broken by a mass of trees. Although this was part of the plan, he was uneasy. This was exactly the type of terrain he'd been trying to avoid fighting in since arriving on the continent. It limited the use of his rifles and made cannons all but useless. Cannonballs would only go a few dozen meters before hitting a tree, deflecting and plowing into the ground, and canister would hit more trees than people. Since they broke up the front shield wall, he'd been forced to leave the artillery in the rear, waiting to be called up. Worse, it also limited the usefulness of his rifles. He still had enough of them to kill many of the enemy, but the trees would also break up the enemies' formation, making them less massed and less vulnerable to volley fire.

All of which meant there was no way to avoid hand-to-hand combat, and in that, numbers mattered. His men were good, but there were just too many of the Carthaginians to hold out against that kind of fighting. Unfortunately, he'd been left with little choice. For two weeks, he'd been dancing with their army, trying to pull them into a fight on open ground. He'd had his local allies picking at their edges, trying to pull them into the fight he wanted, but the enemy had gotten too smart. They knew what a battle against firearms could do on open ground, and they weren't willing to meet him on his terms. Every time he challenged, they pulled back into defensive positions deep in the forest and waited.

With the pressure from the tribes to stop the burning of their villages, Ky couldn't just wait them out. He had to draw them into battle … and he had to win. Which meant taking serious risks to his army.

After their last unfruitful clash, the Carthaginians had pulled back to the spot they currently sat, sending out raiding parties to attack any locals they could get their hands on. He'd kept watch on them using the drone, but could really only see the camps closest to the Rhine, where the tree line thinned out. Beyond that, there were just too many trees to see through the canopy.

The army could feel the tension, marching as quietly as any he'd seen. The joking, talking, and roughhousing that men on the march normally did were gone, replaced by serious soldiers who'd steeled themselves for the coming battle. In fact, the forest as a whole was quiet. The animals that normally lived here had cleared out in the presence of so many men. In spite of the quiet army and absent animals, he couldn't hear much. The Rhine was close enough to hear the water moving, but everything beyond that was silent, like the trees themselves were absorbing the sounds of the two large armies that were about to meet.

Three riders appeared out of the trees, their horses dodging arboreal obstacles, pushing hard. One of the men had a crossbow bolt sticking out of his shoulder, which told Ky all he needed to know. They'd started to see the arcuballista among the enemy over the past few weeks, although that wouldn't help the Carthaginians in this terrain any more than his rifles would help him.

The line parted, allowing the horsemen through. One stopped next to Ky and his command group while the other two headed rearward, presumably to get the wounded man medical attention.

"Report," Ky commanded the trooper.

"They're about half a mille passus behind us. Their scouts must have seen our lines, because they're already in battle formation and marching this way," the soldier said, saluting.

Waving a salute in return, Ky turned to Bomilcar and said, "Send out the word."

Saluting, the general and several of their aides rode back through the forest.

"Make Ready," Ky called to his men, the front line raised their shields while the rows behind them prepared to fire, guns leveled.

Quiet blanketed the area as the legion tensed, poised for contact. Moments later, the ominous tramp of many feet became audible. Carthaginian warriors began to emerge from the trees, marching in dense columns. At first only visible piecemeal through the foliage, soon a solid mass of men stretched across the narrow open space between the tree lines. Clad in a mix of leather and linen, with the occasional bronze armor, their lines bristling with spears and swords, the enemy force radiated menace.

Ky held, waiting. These first moments had to count; they needed the Carthaginians' blood up and their focus forward. The Carthaginians quickened their pace, bellowing war cries meant to terrify, then surged forward in a full charge.

"By the rank, fire!" Ky commanded, his words rippling down the line.

The crack of a thousand rifles roared, sounding as if the world was being snapped in two. And then a thousand more reverberated along the wide front. Again, and again each row fired, smoke covering the woods, making it look as if it were on fire.

Carthaginians fell as if they ran into a brick wall. Hundreds died, and then hundreds more. The Carthaginians were prepared for this, the men pushing the rows ahead of them forward until they became the front row themselves, never stopping, regardless of the losses.

If he had more rifles or more distance, his forces could probably have whittled down the Carthaginians until they ran out of men, but he had neither. For every four bullets that hit a man, one hit a tree, and the ones that missed, instead of hitting a man further back, would bury themselves into wood. That was truer the farther back the bullet had to travel. They were wreaking terrible losses, but there was no way to stop the forward motion of the enemy force.

"Prepare for contact!" Ky bellowed, although mostly to himself, as even his powerful voice couldn't be heard over the noise of the rifle fire.

The Carthaginians slammed into the Roman first rank, pushing the men back as the weight of the bodies smashed into their shields. Men violently stabbed, slashed, and battered at each other amidst the deafening din. Bayoneted rifles stabbed forward and down as the rear ranks continued to hammer out shots, independently now, as chaos reigned.

"On the back step," Ky said to the man next to him.

The legionnaire lifted a small bugle to his lips, one of the minor inventions Ky had introduced, that was significantly easier to wield than the old Roman trumpets. The man blew a series of notes, which was echoed by bugles further down either side of the line. Ky had predicted this outcome and even included it as part of their plan; the men trained tirelessly to learn the precise steps.

As if they were a single organism, the entire formation took one synchronized stride rearward without losing unit cohesion. Carthaginian warriors surged forward to fill the gap, sensing weakness. The rifles fired again, into the front ranks, before the Carthaginians slammed into contact again.

"Again," Ky commanded.

Again, the entire line backed up and the Carthaginians surged forward, fell, and regained contact. As each rank fired, they stepped back in unison, rifles reloaded with practiced efficiency. Then the shields came up, and the macabre dance began again, the enemy surging forward to exploit the gap, only to be scythed down by another deadly volley.

All around Ky were the unmistakable sounds of close-quarters combat. The rhythmic clash of metal on metal, the grunts and cries of effort and pain, the thick, cloying smell of blood and smoke. Men fought desperately, their lives hanging in the balance.

A well-timed shield bash or sword thrust spelling the difference between victory and death.

Despite their losses, the Carthaginians showed no signs of relenting. For every Roman that fell, it seemed twenty enemy warriors remained. They flowed around and past their own dead like a raging river hitting a dam, an inexorable tide seeking to overwhelm the thin Roman lines through sheer force of numbers.

Ky could see the inevitable outcome; his men would be overwhelmed by the sheer mass arrayed against them if something didn't change soon. The plan called for this, for the losses to be taken as his men continued their slow, steady retreat, forcing them to bleed for every inch, their focus completely captured. If their timing was off, the Carthaginians would roll over them, pouring around their sides like so much water.

In fact, it had already started; the first signs that their position was worsening had begun to show. On both flanks, the weight of Carthaginian numbers was beginning to wrap around the ends of the Roman formation. If they managed to get around behind them, his army would be encircled and destroyed piecemeal.

"Pull the flanks in, curve back toward the center," Ky bellowed to one of his nearby officers. "We have to refuse to be flanked, bend but don't break!"

Messengers rode off in either direction to pass on the orders. The legions on the edges angled their formations, trying to present a corner rather than an edge to the enemy tide. Like bending a stiff rod, it threatened to snap their cohesion, but they had no choice. The integrity of the main line had to be preserved.

The ends could only bend for so long, however. They would either break or roll up on the rest of the formation, allowing the Carthaginians to encircle them, giving the enemy the Cannae that every general hoped to achieve.

A horse thudded toward Ky, one of the messengers who'd left with Bomilcar and his detachment.

"Where are they?" Ky demanded. "We're being flanked; we can't hold much longer!"

The messenger saluted. "They are nearly in position, sir. They should arrive momentarily."

Ky ground his teeth in frustration. Momentarily could mean disaster if the line broke before then. He had no choice but to trust his subordinates, but this was the part he hated the most. Flying a fighter, he was just a part of a whole, only having to focus on his own actions. This was something else. Anything that needed to be done, he couldn't rely only on himself. He could only hope the people he picked were as good as he thought they were, and that they'd deliver on their responsibilities.

"Commander, the left flank," Sophus said, its voice icy calm.

Normally, he wouldn't be able to see either end of his own lines through the trees, but he'd taken his drone in below the canopy, zipping through tree branches under Sophus's control. If a soldier looked up, they might see a faint blue light as it sped through the trees a few meters above their heads, swinging from one end of their line to the other to give them a three-hundred and sixty-degree view of the battle.

As Sophus spoke, the drone reversed course and was crossing the right flank, catching a sudden mass of movement. A mass of axe and sword-wielding tribesmen slammed into the Carthaginian flank, doing to them exactly what they had planned to do to the Britannians.

The attack wasn't coordinated, and there wasn't a solid line like the Britannians had, and there might only be a thousand warriors in total, but the ferocity of their attack and the total surprise they had on the Carthaginians made up the difference.

The Carthaginians reeled back, their flanks compressing toward the middle, taking pressure off the Roman flanks and making the Carthaginians an easier target for the Britannian riflemen, whose rate of fire picked up as the legionaries saw the battle joined.

For the moment, the pendulum swung in their favor, but it wouldn't hold for long. Already, the Carthaginians' surprise was fading, replaced by anger as they began to counterattack, pressing out from the compressed center. There weren't enough tribesmen to hold the Carthaginians for long. He didn't need them to hold for long, though.

"Come on. Come on," Ky mumbled to himself.

And then he heard it. A trumpet in the new design, like the ones he'd had signal along his lines, but sounding from in front of him, well on the other side of the Carthaginian lines.

Ky smiled a wolfish grin as the trap was sprung.

Ky watched through the drone's camera as the last pieces of his trap fell into place. Far on the other side of the Carthaginian army, Ursinus' legion appeared through the trees, smashing into the rear of the Carthaginian army. They had made a wide circuit, crossing and recrossing the Rhine behind the enemy's back, while Ky kept the enemy's attention focused on him.

"Send orders to the flanking legions. Support the tribesmen and wrap around the enemy until we meet up with Ursinus's flanks on either side," Ky said to messengers who saluted and rode away to pass the orders.

Pinned between the anvil of Ursinus' advance and the hammer of the Roman flanks, the Carthaginians realized their peril too late. They tried to turn and face the new threat, but the press of their own numbers worked against them. Packed in shoulder to shoulder, unable to maneuver, they made easy targets.

The Romans tightened the noose steadily amidst the screams of the dying. What had been an organized army degenerated into a panicked mob searching vainly for an escape. The trap didn't shut instantly, and there weren't enough tribesmen to stop the Carthaginians from escaping out of the sides entirely. Thousands of Carthaginians ran, throwing down weapons and armor to lighten their loads, presumably ready to run all the way back to the Mediterranean. But that was still only a small part of the army. Many more, hemmed in against their comrades, didn't make it out before the Britannian line extended fully, closing the trap entirely. And then the circle began to contract.

Ky watched impassively as the drone recorded the slaughter. Tens of thousands of Carthaginians died in those blood-soaked woods. The Cannae that the Carthaginians had envisioned had been reversed on them. Ky eventually got the slaughter to stop, with maybe five thousand Carthaginians left alive in the end, a small fraction of the army that had marched north. Most would be marched to the coast and sent back to Britannia, going through the same process as the other prisoners. Some would end up joining the legions, some would work, and some would be true believers and held in a prisoner camp until the end of the war.

Most, however, would never do anything again. Their victory had been costly, Ky had no doubt. When he finally got the count of their losses, there would be more than Ky could afford to lose. But this was the only major Carthaginian army in northern Germania. There would be more. There always were. But this victory would cement the loyalty of the tribes and allow him to begin his march south to take the Carthaginian camp.

Chapter 17

Devnum

Faenius walked purposefully into the temple, past the marble columns, intricate mosaics, and frescoes depicting religious tales, flanked by a squad of his best Praetorians, including the recently promoted centurion, Claudius, whom Faenius had been watching closely, as the man had promise.

The thunder of their synchronized footsteps echoed off the high ceiling as the guards fanned out, establishing control of the vestibule. Two temple guards moved to block their path, leveling spears with shaking hands.

Fixing them with an icy stare, Faenius said, "Stand down. We are here on orders from the Empress herself."

The guards exchanged nervous glances, then reluctantly lowered their weapons and stepped aside. Satisfied, Faenius motioned for his men to continue into the temple's inner sanctum.

At the far end of the hall, beside an enormous statue of Jupiter, Vesnius knelt in prayer. Hearing the Praetorians' approach, the High Priest rose and turned. His eyes widened in shock at the armed men.

"You dare desecrate the sacred temple," he said, his voice tinged with disbelief. "Explain this intrusion at once."

"Lucius Vesnius Sacerdos," Faenius said, stepping forward, his face hard. "You are under arrest for treason and conspiracy against the Empire."

"How dare you. I am the Flamen Dialis! High Priest of Jupiter Optimus! I demand to know the meaning of this!"

"You've used your position to spread sedition and treason against the Empire."

"Lies, all of it. You have no proof," Vesnius scoffed, pointing a long, bony finger at Faenius. "You defile this sacred place with your false accusations."

Faenius stepped closer until they were face to face, eyes boring into the priest, "We are here in the name of the Empress. If you resist, we will drag you out in chains."

Faenius nodded sharply, gesturing for two guards to take hold of Vesnius. They grabbed the priest, gripping his arms tightly when the old man tried to yank his arms free. He dug in his heels, but his sandals only slid uselessly along the smooth marble floor of the temple's inner sanctum.

"Unhand me, you filth!" Vesnius spat as he was hauled through the temple's towering entrance and out into the bright sunlight.

The commotion had not gone unnoticed. A crowd was already gathering, commoners and merchants mingling with robed priests and stunned members of the Senatorial class who stared and murmured amongst themselves.

Faenius emerged behind Vesnius, surveyed the scene, and gestured curtly for his men to proceed. The guards holding Vesnius adjusted their grip and marched onward, dragging the struggling priest down the temple's steps to the street level.

Vesnius craned his neck looking around wildly and yelled, "Is this how the Empress's justice is dispensed? To protect foreigners and barbarians, they haul your priests away in chains?"

The murmurs of the crowd grew louder, undercurrents of anger and confusion rippled through the gathering throng. The priest had led the people of Devnum for decades and had always been a trusted servant of the gods. The people were deeply troubled to see him arrested.

Sensing the crowd's budding resentment, Faenius turned, raising a hand for attention, "This man stands accused of treason by decree of the Empress herself. Return to your homes and businesses."

His tone brooked no argument. Behind him, the Praetorian guards formed a tight cordon, shields at the ready.

Vesnius noted Faenius' caution with a spark of satisfaction, struggling against his captors' grips.

"So this is how Rome's protectors address her free citizens? With arrogance and unjust acts?"

The edges of the crowd pressed in, their angry murmurs growing louder by the second. The Praetorians scanned the mass of people, noting the tell-tale signs of a gathering storm. Fists clenching, shoulders squaring, faces hardening.

Faenius quickened his pace, as the situation began to spiral out of control. The sooner they were free of this mob, the better. But the crowd was already spreading to block the intersections ahead. They'd reached critical mass.

A piece of rotten fruit sailed past Faenius' head, splattering against the wall of a nearby insula making a wet smack. More debris pelted in from all sides - clay pots, stones, sticks - peppering the cohort of Praetorians. Faenius pivoted, looking over the throng. Faces blurred together in a mass of anger and suspicion. He couldn't pinpoint the sources of the projectiles.

"Free Vesnius!" an unseen voice yelled out.

Others echoed the demand and it slowly became a chant, serving to build the people's anger more.

Faenius spotted a red-faced man hefting another stone, arm cocked to throw.

"Disperse at once!" Faenius bellowed, pointing at the man, halting him mid-motion. "Return to your homes before this escalates further!"

His warning went unheeded. More debris sailed toward them. One man surged forward, practically spitting with rage, only to be shoved back by a Praetorian's shield. Cries of indignation erupted from the crowd. They were growing bolder, inching steadily closer, testing the squad's defenses.

Faenius steadied himself. He had hoped to avoid this, but the situation had escalated quickly. It was clear they wouldn't be able to withdraw without using force. The Praetorians were outnumbered.

"Form a cordon!" Faenius bellowed.

Immediately, the soldiers tightened their spacing, linking shields to create an impenetrable barrier, lifting the truncheons they carried in addition to swords, bracing for impact.

"Advance!"

At Faenius's command, they began pushing as one down the street. Truncheons swung ruthlessly, driving back those who resisted. Shouts of pain competed with cries of fury as the Praetorians bulled their way forward. Step by step, they gained ground.

The mob attacked the cordon with renewed zeal, raining down blows and clawing at shields. A hurled stone glanced off a soldier's shoulder armor. He whirled, spotting a wild-eyed youth clutching another rock. Their eyes locked for a split second before the Praetorian's truncheon crunched sickeningly across his jaw. The young man collapsed in a heap.

The crowd was a churning avalanche of bodies, threatening to overwhelm them through sheer numbers. The Praetorians heaved back against the human tide, Roman discipline overcoming the mob's chaotic fury.

The Praetorians continued their relentless push forward as the mob clawed and shoved against them. Faenius spotted gaps beginning to form along the edges of the formation as his men were gradually being separated. He barked an order, and the soldiers pivoted, presenting a new face to push the crowd back and close the gaps. Despite their discipline, the sheer press of bodies made it nearly impossible to maintain cohesion.

It was clear they would not make it to the prison with their prisoner intact if this continued much longer. He had to act decisively before things escalated into wholesale chaos.

"Claudius!" Faenius shouted over the din, the centurion turned his head briefly to show he was listening. "Take three men, get Vesnius out of here. We will cover your withdrawal."

Claudius nodded and began barking orders of his own. He and two other guards grabbed Vesnius and pulled him from the mob's grasp. Faenius could see the stark fear on the priest's face as he was dragged away into a side street. Now they just had to buy enough time for Claudius to get clear.

Faenius used the opportunity to issue new orders, "Form paired columns, we're going to sweep this rabble aside and clear the streets."

The Praetorians reconfigured into two columns bristling with shields and truncheons. On Faenius' command, they lurched into motion, bulling their way through the densely packed mob like a plow tearing through soil.

People cried out in pain and fright as they were battered and thrown aside. The Praetorians were careful to avoid killing blows, focusing on swift, debilitating strikes to clear their path. With the priest and his cries gone, resistance quickly crumbled before the inexorable advance of the paired columns.

Within minutes, the last of the stragglers had been driven into side streets or fled entirely. An eerie quiet fell over the agora. Faenius kept them moving at a quickstep, wanting to put distance between them and the mob, should it regroup.

As soon as he reached the palace, he went toward the dungeon where the priest would be held. Claudius would have been able to move fast, but it was possible that parts of the crowd paralleled him, catching up with him short of the protective ring around the palace.

Thankfully, he spotted Claudius emerging from the dungeon just as he arrived, the centurion hurrying over as soon as he saw his commander.

"The prisoner is secure, sir," Claudius said, saluting.

"Well done, Claudius. Have the men with injuries see the medicos and take an hour's rest. I need to report this mess to the Empress. She'll want to question Vesnius herself about these treasonous allegations."

"Yes, sir," Claudius replied crisply, before marching off.

Faenius watched him leave, thinking forward to his meeting with the Empress. He'd arrested the priest, but not as quietly as she had ordered. There was going to be blowback from this action, to be sure.

Daramouda

While he waited for the rest of his officers to finish filing into the command tent, Tabnit read over the scrolls containing the lists of supplies and logistics for the coming campaign, handed to him by one of his aides. Not for the first time, he wished he had some of the flat sheets the Romans invented that they called paper. He'd gotten his hands on a few sheets taken after one of their few victories, and it hadn't taken long to realize how much easier it was to work with than the rolled scrolls that his people used.

"The final shipments have arrived," Tabnit announced when the last of his officers had finally taken his place for the command council. "We now have enough to fill out Atar's section, which means we're ready to start our end of the campaign."

Murmurs rippled through the tent as the officers exchanged approving glances. After months of waiting, everyone was eager to get started. Small harassing attacks had not given many chances for glory, which is what all of his subordinates would need if they were to get commands of their own.

"I know some of you have also heard we've received the shipment of weapons from the Far East the emperor promised us. While that is true, unfortunately, the weapons will all remain with the main body under my command, as we have a limited amount, and we won't use them until we begin our attack on the Romans in earnest. I want them to be a surprise. That's why none of your people have been allowed to see the shipment. I do not want word of what this weapon is leaking out. This means that I expect all of you to hold your curiosity. Do not go looking to find out what it is, and do not attempt to see it for yourselves. I give you this warning once, and I expect you and your subordinates to heed it. At my request, the emperor has sent some of the Acolytes of

Hexitas, who have been instructed to kill anyone not authorized if they attempt to view the shipment. There will be no warnings or second chances. Is that clear?"

A murmur passed along the group. Of all the tools the emperor had to control his subjects, the Acolytes of Hexitas were by far the most feared. Clad in all black except for the skull masks covering their faces, the Acolytes were fanatical, welcoming death if it came in the service of their god. They saw every death they caused as an offering and were brutal in their devotion.

Tabnit did not enjoy having them around, but he knew he'd only get one real shot to make this new weapon work for him, and he had to make it count. If he could push the Romans off the continent, he could turn the tide of the war and cement his place in the annals of the empire.

"In addition to the new weapons, the emissaries from the Far East have brought us something else. Engineers who will teach our men a way to attack their forts without having our men torn apart by their thunder weapons. I do not want to delay starting our march for training, so each group will select men for a detail that will train every evening when the army stops for the night. During our attack, they will direct our men to build the fortifications that will allow us to get within striking distance of their walls. I expect every one of your men to train hard, to be ready for our attack."

Pausing to make sure the men understood him, he continued, "We will be marching quickly. I received word two days ago that our northern army has maneuvered the Romans into terrain that negates their thunder weapons and they have most likely already begun their attack."

Murmurs rippled through the tent as the men reacted to this news.

"We greatly outnumber their forces there, and without their thunder weapons, we will be able to finally crush their forces in the North. I want to push their southern army back into the sea before word of the loss can reach their islands. We will be marching at dawn, and I want your men ready to march. I will accept no excuses."

"Apologies, General, but what of their string of interconnected forts built along the north side of the mountains?" Nabalsa, one of the section commanders, asked. "Our raiding parties have had limited success against them. They've cleared a large amount of land around them, giving their weapons room to decimate our warriors. When we attempted to put them under siege, we were attacked by the forces from the other forts, pinning us between them. With these new techniques, we should be able to get close enough to capture the forts, as long as we keep sufficient forces to counter their reinforcements. Even with all of that, I don't think we can destroy all of the forts in the timeline you've allotted."

"We aren't attacking the forts," Tabnit said. "We will swing wide around them and then cut in between the last two. Once we cut off their port, they will have difficulty supplying them, and they will wither on the vine, being forced to retreat or starve. We only have to worry about the one closest to the port, since they will be in range to support the port and attack our forces. We will keep part of our army turned to take on any forces they send from the rear, while we destroy the port. Other than that precaution, we will ignore them."

He looked around for any other comments and received none. That was to be expected. Nabalsa was a newer commander and had yet to learn the dangers inherent in offering opinions—opinions that might anger a commander, or someone with the power, enough to retaliate or that might be taken seriously and result in the officer being responsible for a plan that could fail. Silence was the safest strategy for most of the men most of the time.

"Good. Prepare your men for the march. We leave in the morning."

The officers saluted and left, leaving Tabnit with only his aides. The general looked over the map, tracing a line to the sea. This would work. With the new ways of war from the east, he would finally crack the Roman defenses and push them off the continent for good.

Mediterranean, Pillars of Hercules

Admiral Valdar stood at the bow of his flagship, the Britannian ship Bellona, gazing out over the glittering expanse of the Middle Sea. A stiff breeze filled the Bellona's sails, driving the sturdy ship forward at a brisk clip. Around him, Valdar could see the many other vessels of the Britannian fleet sailing in tight formation. After months of preparation, they were finally embarking on their mission against the Carthaginians.

It seemed like a lifetime ago that he'd sailed these gentle waters, back when he was just a merchant, before he linked his future with the Britannians. Now he was back, but trade wasn't the thing he had in mind anymore. He knew the risks they faced were great, venturing into the very heart of enemy waters. His ships might be far superior to anything the Carthaginians could put on the water, which didn't even consider the addition of the cannon he carried, but they had hundreds of ships in these waters. He had twelve.

Still, if they succeeded here, they would block the Carthaginians from shipping in and out of these waters, destroy the bulk of the Carthaginian navy, and force them to march around the world in order to reinforce their armies on the continent. It would turn the tide of the war.

"Enemy ships sighted off the port bow!" the lookout bellowed.

Glancing upward, Valdar saw the Bellona's lookout gesturing wildly from the crow's nest high above the deck. Following the lookout's pointed finger, Valdar spotted a number of tiny dark shapes emerging from a harbor perhaps ten mille passus distant.

Valdar snatched a spyglass from his belt and trained it on the distant vessels. Through the lens, he could make out dozens of Carthaginian galleys sailing out to meet them.

"Signal the fleet," Valdar called to his first officer. "Form in line and prepare for battle!"

Moments later, colored signal flags were soaring up the masts of the Bellona, quickly mirrored by the other ships. The great vessels began shifting into neat rows, their crews rushing about making ready for the imminent confrontation. Cannons were rolled out along the gun decks as marines took up positions with their rifles.

Valdar clasped his hands behind his back, his gaze fixed on the approaching Carthaginian fleet, gauging their speed and formation. They were attempting a double envelopment, trying to get some of their ships close enough to board his and take one of his ships intact. It had been their standard tactic ever since they learned of the existence of the Britannians' cannon. It had worked on some smaller merchant ships, but so far, they hadn't even gotten close to the Britannian warships. It didn't mean they'd stop trying.

"Steady lads," Valdar called out, feeling the pre-battle nerves that always swept through the crew right before a fight. "Remember your training and trust in your shipmates. We'll send these bastards to the bottom!" A ragged cheer went up from the surrounding sailors and marines. Valdar allowed himself a tight smile. The men's morale was high, their courage steeled for the fight ahead.

"Full sail," Valdar ordered. Moving fast would allow him to blow through the Carthaginian formation, giving his ships a chance to rake their ships without giving them a chance to get his boats to grip. The ship surged forward as still more sails were unfurled from the masts above. The rest of the Britannian line matched the Bellona's acceleration perfectly, keeping their line tight.

The two fleets closed on one another with startling speed, faster than Valdar had predicted. He lifted his spyglass again, looking over the enemy ships. It wasn't hard to spot what was out of place. The Carthaginian galleys had new sail plans, clearly modeled after the Britannian designs. While the actual hulls and structures of the Carthaginian vessels remained inferior, the addition of the new style sails allowed them to harness the wind as never before. Though still less maneuverable than the Britannian ships, due to their bulkier builds, the sails were enabling the Carthaginians to close the gap faster.

If they didn't do something, they would intercept his fleet, and his cannon wouldn't have a good angle to damage enough of them to stop their own destruction.

"Adjust formation, prepare to turn!" Valdar ordered. Signal flags soared up masts, and every sailor on the Britannian ships leaped into action. Hands flew across lines, sails were trimmed, and rudders kicked over as the sleek warships heeled into tightly arced turns. Decks tilted at precipitous angles while sailors held on for their lives, expertly navigating the ocean swells.

The Carthaginian ships attempted to turn with them, to avoid the swinging broadside, but their ungainly vessels couldn't copy or counter the maneuver. Had the Britannians been even a few ship-lengths slower, they would have exposed their vulnerable stern and been shredded by Carthaginian rams, brought to grips, and boarded.

The Carthaginians continued to close the distance, the easterly wind helping push their small craft on even as the Britannian ships cut hard southwest into their arc. They were getting too close.

"Hard a-lee," he called out, ordering his ship to cut even harder, turning back into their own line. "Order the ships to break the line. Make easterly and fire as they bear."

The entire line breaking and turning back would, hopefully, allow them to get the distance they needed to keep the Carthaginians from getting a hold on them. His flagship, riding in front, was in the greatest danger, as the rest of his ships were further back and had more time to turn. They wouldn't get the full fleet-wide broadside that he wanted, but it would save them from disaster. Sailing into the wind would allow him to put distance between his ships and the enemy and then they could come at them again, without the surprise of the updates to their ships upsetting his plans.

His ship passed within a hundred paces of each of the closest Carthaginian ships. So close Valdar could see the sailors with his naked eye. Ropes arced out of the closest ships, trying to grapple onto the sides of his ship. Most missed by a wide margin as his ship's sails expanded as they turned with the wind. But not all of the lines missed, those from the closest ship managed to latch on.

"Repel boarders," he called out, pulling his sword and running to the nearest line. Arrows flew past, one embedding itself a hand span away into the forecastle. Accuracy with a bow was nearly impossible on a rolling deck, but enough arrows were being fired to be a danger, and he saw sailors here or there fall, a shaft sticking out from their shoulder or chest.

He hacked at the line, his steel sword cutting through the thick rope after two whacks, sending the men scrambling up it into the ocean. The rifles of his marines fired, picking off archers and sailors on the other ship, as his sailors cut lines and hurled whatever they could at the men trying to climb onboard. It wouldn't matter. As the galley pulled itself closer to his ship, to allow more men to try to board, it put itself exactly where it didn't want to be. Directly in the path of his broadside.

His gun captains didn't wait for the order. Fire and smoke erupted out of the side of his ship, hiding everything from sight. The thunderous sound was deafening, drowning out even the shouts and screams of maimed men.

When the smoke cleared, a scene of devastation followed in its wake. Masts and rigging lay in tattered shambles floating in the waves. The ship that had been trying to gain a hold of his had all but vanished as every cannonball hit it, smashing it to pieces.

More cannon fire echoed, drawing Valdar's attention. Instead of following his orders and all turning to the east, his ships had continued the arc that his fleet had been on before he gave the command, although at a much tighter angle. The sharper curve and the fact that they were further behind put more distance between them and the enemy ships. Valdar's sudden maneuver to avoid being boarded worked in their favor, moving his ship out of the way and giving the rest of the fleet a clear field of fire, which they used to devastating effect, sending the remaining boats chasing the Bellona running for the sandy bottom.

The Britannians had inflicted hellish casualties, but these were just against the front ranks of the Carthaginian fleet. The ships further behind had more time to arrest their onward momentum and turn back towards the Britannian line at an impressive speed, attempting what their comrades had failed to do.

The danger was over, however. The Bellona continued to swing around and rejoin the column, which finished its arc and straightened out as the enemy got within range, allowing for a perfect firing position. He didn't even need to order his men to fire. This was the exact scenario they had drilled endlessly for. The gun captains on each ship watched their batteries and timed their ships' barrage for when it had the best chance to strike. As he watched, more Carthaginian ships disintegrated, ripped apart by salvos of Britannian cannonballs.

Seeing their fleet decimated from what must have seemed like the very edge of success, the remaining Carthaginian captains desperately attempted to disengage and flee the battle. Valdar watched the enemy ships scattering in all directions, torn between wanting to pursue them and holding his position. With the advancements the Carthaginians had made to their sails and rigging, they wouldn't be able to track them down quickly like they had before.

He believed his ships were faster than the enemy's, so he was confident he could still track them down, but they would be able to run farther before his men could catch them. Chasing the fleeing Carthaginians meant destroying more of their navy, but it would also force him to divide his own ships as they spread out in pursuit.

Considering their willingness to lose men and material, that very well could be their plan. Let the Britannians split their fleet and then jump them one at a time, when they had no support from any other ships. Even if it wasn't a trap, the ships were scattering in all directions. It was unlikely that his dispatched ships would chase down more than one or two of the enemy before the others made good on their escape. The risk versus reward just wasn't worth it.

"Signal the fleet to hold position. Let them leave," Valdar commanded.

Valdar watched the enemy ships dwindle into the distance, unable to prevent their escape but satisfied he had made the strategically sound choice. As frustrating as it was to let some of the Carthaginians flee, preserving his fleet took priority. The smoking wrecks and floating debris left behind in the wake of the battle made it clear he had inflicted a decisive defeat on the Carthaginian navy this day.

Watching the enemy ships run, he was still bothered. Though still inferior in design, their new sails and rigging had allowed the enemy galleys to maneuver far better than anticipated. If they got out of the Middle Sea and into Oceanus with these ships, they would be able to run down the Britannians' merchant ships, which would be a disaster. He didn't have the ships to blockade the entrance to the Middle Sea and continue into the sea to hunt down the Carthaginian navy. His orders were clear, but his duty was equally clear.

"Order the fleet to take up positions to blockade the entrance to the sea and stay in range to support each other should the enemy sally again," Valdar said, continuing to stare out toward the sea.

This was a holding action to buy him time to think. He had thought of a solution that would allow him to take up both the tasks at hand, but it would take some planning.

Chapter 18

Gaul, North of the Pyrenees

Velius gazed out the flap of the command tent, watching as the last crimson rays of dusk disappeared below the horizon. Around him, his commanders shuffled into the large tent, still wearing their armor from that day's ride.

"It's been four days since the last Carthaginian patrol was spotted near our forts," he said, facing the men once they were all seated. "Almost a week since the last skirmish or raid on our supply lines."

"You think they're up to something?" Sepurcius, the commander of the legions' artillery, asked.

"I do. They weren't this quiet over the winter, let alone at any other time since we landed on the continent. The question is, what? If they've pulled their forces back, they've done it for a reason. Their probing attacks on the forts haven't worked, and their losses when they tried were heavy, but we know their current commander is a lot smarter than the generals we've faced in the past. He's not going to just keep throwing men into a strategy that isn't working. If he's pulled his men back, then it's because he's decided on a new course of action. But what? Do we even have any idea where the Carthaginian army is at the moment? Or any of their detachment?"

"No," Micon, the commander of the legions' cavalry, said. "We've had patrols ranging pretty far, and we've sent messages up and down the line of forts via the semaphore. We haven't even run into any scouts, let alone their army itself."

"And none of the forts have seen anything?"

"Not since our last message yesterday," Gordianus said. "We have sent another request, but the forts that have responded so far have repeated the same message. No sign of the enemy."

"Fine, I want to send riders to …" he began before a commotion at the entrance to the tent interrupted him, drawing the eyes of all of the commanders.

A messenger was whispering to one of the guards, gesturing energetically towards the legion commanders.

"Let him in," Velius said, waving the guard aside. "What's so important?"

The messenger rushed into the tent, his face flushed.

"Sir. An urgent message from Port Invictus," he said, handing over a piece of paper showing the rapid scrawl of one of the semaphore messengers.

"Damn," Velius said, waving off the messenger. "We've found the Carthaginians. Their army marched out of the hills and has surrounded the port. Based on the message, it sounds like it's the entire army."

He paused, letting the information sink in. The commanders exchanged uneasy glances.

"But how?" Gordianus asked. "We should have seen them."

"Not if they went south of the range and around. Slower going, but our scouts aren't ranging over the mountains. They just had to leave a small harassing force in front of us until their army passed, and then pull that in behind them."

He paused and looked back to the message.

"It gets worse. They've worked out a way to at least partially counter our cannon. Aelius reports that they've dug long trenches to keep their men partially protected from our rifle fire, and they've got some kind of log pile that can absorb or deflect our cannonballs. He reports they're inching their way closer to the walls every day. We have weeks, at best, before they are under the guns and up against the walls."

"We can make it by then," Gordianus said. "We bring the legion down from the north, over the mountain, and hit their forces from behind. Trenches and log piles won't protect them when they're trapped between us and the fort."

Velius grimaced, "They've thought of that too. Aelius reports Carthaginian forces extending far into the mountains, with ambushes prepared to intercept any reinforcements we send. Our only choice is to attack them in force from the rear, but with the numbers they're reporting, it's going to take time to push them back."

"Do you think it's a trap? Maybe they held forces in reserve to hit us from behind?" Gordianus asked.

"Maybe, although the forces close to the mountains suggest it isn't. Still, the last thing we want is our legion getting bottled up between two Carthaginian armies. Worse, we're going to be even more outnumbered than the last time. We've split our forces up among the line of forts, giving us just over one full legion between this force and the two cohorts in Port Invictus itself, while they have an even larger force. You're going to have to move carefully, since you'll also lose any mobility you have."

"Me?" Gordianus asked, surprised.

"Yes. Even if there is just the one army, with their defenses and preparation it's going to take time to squeeze them out, and they'll be pressing into Port Invictus the entire time. I'm going to take one century and go a roundabout route to come into the port by ship, to assist Aelius in the defense. With so few men, I can move more quickly than the full legion. Do not let yourself get pinned down if there is another force out there. Keep scouts out and use the terrain to your advantage. From the mountainside, you should be able to fire down into their trenches, at least the ones closest to the mountains. If our riflemen can't engage the men in the trenches with room to fire, don't take them in too close. If the worst should happen, it's imperative that we keep the legion mobile. Fall back to the forts for protection."

"Even if we scatter them or are able to rake their trenches, we aren't going to be able to cut them off. We don't have enough men to completely surround them with enough strength to hold them in place, even if we were on flat, even terrain. In the mountains like this, it's even worse."

"Don't try to hold them in place. If they pull out of the siege of Port Invictus, retreat and see if you can get them to follow you. If something happens to Port Invictus, your supply lines will have to stretch north to the Consul's forces and the ports he's using. If they are able to use their new tactics to negate Port Invictus's walls and they're successful, you might have to abandon the line of forts altogether. If that's the case, it's best to head north and link your forces up with the northern army."

"If they go against the forts we built here, they won't have the mountains to protect them and we'll be able to attack from all sides. Port Invictus's location makes it easier to besiege than any of those. I don't foresee that happening. I also don't think that just because they get close, they'll be able to scale our walls. Logs might deflect shots at a distance, but point-blank canister will devastate them if they ever come out of their trenches, and it can stay supplied by sea for a long time, so the siege won't starve them out. They might have new techniques, but they've picked the one target a siege can't stop."

"I tend to agree with you," Velius said. "But they've become very clever of late, and it won't help us to start underestimating them. Hope for the best and plan for the worst, as the Consul always says. I want you to keep your men agile and prepared to retreat north should things go to hell. First to the forts, and then to the northern army if need be. Is that clear?"

"Yes, Legate."

"Good. I'll be leaving tonight with one of Viridius's centuries. I expect you to have the men on the march in the morning. And set up a semaphore station on the mountainside when you get in position. It will allow us to communicate across the siege."

"Understood, Legate," Gordianus said again.

"Good. Then get to work. I want you in position in two weeks' time."

Port of Kalb, Southern Tip of Hispania

The waters of the Middle Sea shimmered with reflected midday sunlight, a slight breeze pushing in from the west, but not enough to upset the gentle waves. The perfect day for the residents of the port was marred by the harsh sound of thunder, not from the cloudless sky above, but from the four Britannian ships outside the harbor.

Billowing cannon smoke drifted across the waves as the cannons spoke again, deafening thunder echoing through the harbor as round shot smashed through warehouses and homes along the waterfront. Flames and rubble marked where the ships' rounds had found their marks.

From his vantage point, Valdar could see several Carthaginian ships burning at anchor after being caught helpless at the onset of the attack. Others listed heavily in the water, settling into the muddy harbor bottom with only their masts and rigging still visible above the surface. The docks, once lined with tall ships bound for trade, now stood shattered and abandoned.

Amidst the smoke and wreckage, Valdar saw a cluster of lateen-rigged galleys making a break for the harbor mouth, oars rising and falling swiftly.

"Signal the Seadreki to intercept that squadron attempting to escape!" Valdar called out to his signal officer.

Flags snapped in the wind as coded instructions were relayed to one of the patrolling frigates. Moments later, the Seadreki sheered off her station-keeping patrol and moved to cut across the path of the fleeing Carthaginian ships. As soon as she had closed within range, her sides erupted with cannon fire, splintering oars and punching holes through the thin hulls of the galleys. The ships not sunk outright were soon dead in the water, useless to the defenders.

Valdar allowed himself a grim smile of satisfaction. Though brutal, the attack had been successful so far in bottling up the remainder of the enemy fleet and asserting Britannian dominance over this strategic passage. Kalb was one of the Pillars of Hercules, the narrow gap between Hispania and Africa that connected the

Middle Sea to the open ocean. With his remaining eight ships blockading the narrow gap, it would be nearly impossible for Carthaginian reinforcements to cross from the Atlantic into the inland sea. At least not without braving the gauntlet of Britannian warships blockading the route.

Their blockade of the strait might be a solution to stop the ships that might harass his supply route back home, but it didn't solve his immediate problem. He needed to be able to get his fleet into the Middle Sea and begin clearing it of Carthaginian shipping. That shouldn't have been a problem, with their supply ships rigged with the new sail design, allowing them to outrun and dodge any galley. At least, it wasn't a problem before he'd found out that the Carthaginians had managed to, at least partially, copy the sail plan for their own galleys. Still a little slower, they were fast enough that it was possible he might have his supplies choked off, causing his fleet to become easy prey as their powder and food ran dry.

With only twelve warships, he couldn't leave half his fleet sitting in the strait to protect their shipping and achieve his goal, but a possible solution sat in front of him. A small, fortified port, able to act as a staging point for supplies, with one or two of his ships, could hold the entire strait and limit the number of supply convoys he needed to sail all the way back to Britannia.

It was something he'd considered ever since clearing the Carthaginian fleet from the strait and entering the Middle Sea. His main problem was, he could damage the port, but he couldn't take it with the small number of sailors and marines he had on-board.

Another volley of cannon fire erupted from the Britannian ships, the smoke momentarily obscuring his view. As it cleared, he saw more of the waterfront in flames, wooden buildings shattered by round shot.

"If I had just a few soldiers, maybe a century, I could take and hold it," he said, thinking aloud.

"Admiral," Ingolf, his first mate, said, perplexed.

"What? Oh, I was thinking if I had a handful of soldiers, I could take the port easily. With the terrain as it is, it wouldn't take much to hold it. Some cannons, a century of riflemen, and they'd be able to hold off any land-based attack. A few ships here and we'd have a protected staging point for our supplies and a nearby refuge for the supply ships to run to if the new Carthaginian galleys showed up."

"You want to land and take the port?"

"I'm seriously considering it. We didn't take into account the Carthaginians copying our sail design, and it's going to upset our plans if we don't make an adjustment. Short of leaving half the fleet here, there's no way to keep our supply ships safe while we move deep into Carthaginian waters."

"All of our legions are on the continent, and we needed almost every bit of our merchant shipping just to move them across the channel between Britannia and Gaul. It's going to be hell moving an entire legion down here."

"We don't need an entire legion. The port lacks a garrison, and it was never designed to be fortified. Why would it need to be this close to Africa? Aside from some pirates, who would bother them? With a single century, I could take and hold it. From there, we could fortify it and have a base to take on the rest of the Middle Sea. Send a signal to one of our support ships. I want them to prepare to sail back to Britannia with my request to the Empress directly."

"Is that wise? You know how hard it was to get the supplies we needed, and how short they are on manpower. Do you think she'll listen?"

"We can only hope. Otherwise, we're going to have a very hard time shutting all of their shipping down, and the legions up north are going to have a much bigger fight on their hands."

He watched through the spyglass as his ships fired again. No, this was the right course of action. He was sure of it.

South of Factorium

The line of Carthaginian prisoners shuffled down the dusty road toward Factorium, prodded along by the stern Praetorian guards. Bostar kept his eyes lowered, not wanting to draw any unwanted attention. The chains binding his wrists chafed with each step, a constant reminder of his captivity.

As a junior officer in the Carthaginian army, Bostar had once commanded respect. Now he was just another prisoner of war, stripped of rank and dignity. The past few months had been grueling, marked by back-breaking labor constructing the Britannians' new factories. The Praetorians showed no sympathy, shoving the prisoners to walk faster whenever they slowed. Bostar focused on putting one foot in front of the other, trying to ignore the throbbing in his feet. Bostar yearned to rest his aching muscles, but he knew the day held nothing but more of the same drudgery.

Or, at least that's what the Praetorians had planned for them.

Glancing around, Bostar met the eyes of several of the most trusted of the other men. Men he'd been cultivating before they even heard of the work camps. Men he'd convinced to volunteer for this new work. A subtle nod passed between them. All in preparation for today.

Bostar gave the signal, a subtle lift of his chained hands. At once, two prisoners near the front of the line suddenly lunged at each other, viciously grappling and throwing punches. The Praetorians shouted in alarm, rushing to break up the scuffle. But as they moved in, the brawl was revealed to be a distraction.

With lightning speed, Bostar and a dozen other prisoners produced tools and makeshift shivs hidden in their clothes. After weeks of marching the men back and forth from Factorium, the Praetorians had gotten sloppy and stopped checking them so closely. Not everyone was armed, but enough managed to sneak makeshift weapons out to give them a chance. Before the guards could react, the Carthaginians were upon them in a whirlwind of violence. Bostar slammed his cudgel into the back of the nearest Praetorian's head, dropping the man instantly. Around him, the other Carthaginians set upon the outnumbered guards with brutal efficiency.

Cries of pain and rage split the air as prisoner and guard clashed in a bloody melee. Bostar wrenched a short sword from the grip of a fallen Praetorian and pivoted, ramming it through the chest of another who charged him with a shout. Hot blood sprayed over Bostar's hands as he kicked the dying man free of his blade.

The Praetorians were trained warriors, but so were his men, and the ferocity of the surprise attack had caught them off-balance. They reacted with discipline, attempting to form up and take Bostar and his men as a unit, but they'd been too spread out when the attack was launched. The prisoners enveloped them on all sides; each Roman forced to fight on his own against a dozen prisoners. Bostar glimpsed their centurion bellowing orders, only to take a savage blow to the neck from a prisoner wielding a blacksmith's hammer.

All around, the cries of the wounded and dying competed with the ring of steel and the sickening crunch of cudgels crushing bone. The dirt road ran red with blood as bodies fell. Not all the blood belonged to Romans. Here and there a prisoner was cut down by Praetorian steel, but the Carthaginians pressed their attack relentlessly. This was their chance to taste freedom, and they seized it with a vengeance.

Bostar found himself fighting back to back with Gelu, a broad-shouldered infantryman who had been among the first to embrace his plans. Together they held off a knot of Praetorians trying to consolidate their defense. Bostar parried a thrust from a gladius and slammed the pommel of his acquired sword into his attacker's face, crushing bone and dropping the man.

Beside him, Gelu gave a gurgling cry as a Praetorian ran him through, but Bostar was too hard-pressed to aid his comrade. He could only knock aside a wild sword slash and gut the offending Roman with a quick thrust. Fighting with his wrists chained was difficult, but luckily they were not wearing leg irons like they did in the camp, probably to keep the march from the work camp to Factorium from taking half the day. All around him, the melee seethed, prisoners and Praetorians hacking and stabbing at each other in a vicious close-quarters fight.

Bostar took a glancing blow to his shoulder that numbed his shield arm. Gritting his teeth against the pain, he traded blade-strokes with a burly Praetorian. The Roman was an experienced fighter, but desperation could push a man to extreme feats, and Bostar was very desperate. He smashed his shield into the man's face, then stabbed him in the armpit as he reeled back.

The centurion was still bellowing encouragement to his men, fending off two prisoners with his gladius. But more Carthaginians were surrounding him. Bostar started toward the knot of fighters, determined to cut down the leader.

Suddenly, a galloping horse plowed into the melee from the side. One of the mounted Praetorians, which had been Bostar's greatest worry. The men didn't carry the rifles as they did on the towers at the work camp, probably fearing they might have them taken if something like this occurred. It made the mounted men the most dangerous.

Bostar ducked as the mounted rider's sword sliced through the space where his head had just been. With a roar, he slashed at the animal's legs with his stolen gladius, causing the animal to rear back and dash away from the danger, its instincts overriding its rider's commands.

All around, the roar of battle reached a crescendo. The prisoners fought like cornered beasts, ferocious in their desperation. Despite being chained and lacking armor, they had the advantage of numbers. For each prisoner cut down by a Praetorian's blade, two more seemed to take his place.

Near him, a great bellow split the din. Bostar risked a glance and saw the centurion had broken free of the men surrounding him. Covered in blood, the hulking Roman hacked down two prisoners in quick succession. Those near him fell back before his whirling blade.

With a shout, he rallied a knot of Carthaginians to surge toward the centurion. They met in a clash of shields and blades. Bostar found himself pressed up against the centurion's massive frame, trading furious blows. The Roman's greater size and strength began to tell.

Desperate, Bostar smashed his forehead into the Roman's face. Pain reverberated down his spine as he made contact, but the damage to the Roman was worse. As the man stumbled back, a hand going to his crushed nose, Bostar rammed his gladius home under the centurion's raised arm. With a gurgling cry, the centurion sank to his knees. Bostar wrenched his blade free and turned to find more foes.

More chaos. The rider had gotten control of his mount and charged again, bearing down on Bostar, his sword raised for a killing blow. Bostar flung himself aside, the blade barely missing him. As he rolled back to his feet, readying for another assault, two prisoners managed to reach up and grab the Roman as he rode by, dragging the Praetorian down. Stolen blades stabbed down, ending the man's life as his horse, now free of control and who'd had enough of the noise and smell of blood, galloped into the distance, reins flying behind it.

The few remaining Praetorians were trying to retreat, hampered by prisoners pressing into them. Now was the moment. With a shout, Bostar rallied the remaining prisoners. Sensing victory, they attacked as one. Down to a handful of men, the centurion leading them couldn't hold the assault back any longer. The last Praetorians were battered down in a frenzy of clubbing weapons and stabbing blades.

In moments, it was over. Bostar stood panting amidst the bloody corpses. Of the hundred prisoners who'd begun this desperate gambit, barely fifty remained. But against all odds, they had won their freedom.

The taste of victory, and the respite it offered, would be short-lived. Soon the Romans would realize this work detail was overdue. They would come searching. There were too few of them to make it to one of the ports, overpower the locals, and steal a ship. The Romans would suspect that and send men to the closest ports. Even with a head start, the Romans would be on horseback and would probably beat them to it, since he didn't know exactly where those ports were and the Praetorians would.

No, their only hope was to flee inland. Hide in the hills and forests until the initial Roman search had passed. After that ... survival. Take what they needed, and survive until the war returned to the island. If it didn't, cause enough disruption to hurt the Romans' war effort here, or make for a small fishing village once the search for them slackened. Steal a boat and run for the continent then.

"On me!" Bostar barked, gesturing the for ragged band of survivors to gather.

Amazingly, they still followed his lead even after the bloodletting they had just endured.

"The Romans will be on our trail soon," Bostar said urgently. "Let's make for the southeast hills. We'll find a place to hide, and decide what to do from there. Agreed?"

Heads around him nodded as the men seemed to collectively decide to continue following him.

"Good, let's get moving."

Chapter 19

Port Invictus

Velius stood atop the walls of Port Invictus, surveying the sprawling Carthaginian siege works encircling the city, taking in the trenches and barriers dug by the enemy to protect themselves from the Britannian artillery. Despite this artillery, the Carthaginians had made steady progress toward the city walls. At the rate they were gaining ground, Velius estimated they would be close enough to assault the walls and get clear of his artillery in a few weeks' time.

He squeezed his eyes shut for a moment, pressing against his eyelids, trying to smother the headache that had been gaining on him. A week of hard travel without much sleep, spurred on by the desire to get to his men, was starting to catch up with him.

The cohorts defending Port Invictus were battle-hardened but depleted, slowly being whittled down by the need to man the line of forts and protect supply trains. Even if he'd had a full legion here, he lacked the numbers for a direct sally against the Carthaginians. Gordianus had arrived with his legion in the mountains the evening before, but they might as well have been on the other side of the world, what with the sea of Carthaginians between them.

His only hope was that they could hold out until their massive foe was whittled down to the point they were forced to pull back. Even with their trenches and log barriers, they were losing hundreds of men a day, by Velius's estimate, and that was before

Gordianus got fully engaged. Still, it would be weeks before they finally killed enough to force them to retreat.

At least he still had supplies coming in from the sea, so he didn't have to worry about starving.

As if in answer to his thoughts, in the distance, fire erupted from Gordianus's legion camped on the mountainside. Shells smashed into the Carthaginians, mostly into the ground around the trenches on the mountainside of the Carthaginian positions, as his gunners got their aim, with only a few landing on the trenches themselves. The ones that did hit the trenches destroyed everything mercilessly, throwing bodies and material into the air like dolls.

Unfortunately, the Carthaginians had laid their defenses out well, with the trenches going to the foot of the mountains and stretching a ways back before opening up to a middle position between the two wide sets of trenches. From Gordianus's present position, their artillery could currently only reach part of the Carthaginian forces encircling Port Invictus. They couldn't reach the middle section which was unprotected by trenches and filled with tents and supplies for their soldiers.

When Gordianus pushed forward, he'd be able to rain shells there, destroying the Carthaginians' safe area between the two sets of cannon. Of course, to push forward, Gordianus would have to deal with the Carthaginians already on the mountainside. They were the ones set to perform the ambushes Aelius had mentioned. Through his glass, he could see men moving toward Gordianus, up the mountainside, angling in on where the cannons were firing.

Gordianus was an experienced soldier, though, and had prepared for it. As the Carthaginians scrambled up the mountain, smaller puffs of smoke appeared all across the crest as riflemen, probably the legion's best shots, began picking them off. With impressive rapidity, bodies began to roll back down the slope, like shells dropping from a fishing net as it lifted into the air.

The Carthaginians weren't going to be able to dislodge the seventh legion from their position. Not with cannons and rifles able to fire down the slope. What they could do was slow their progress down the mountainside even more.

It was frustrating.

"Sir, look," one of Aelius's tribunes said, pointing down towards the closest trenches.

Velius looked through his spyglass, following where the tribune was pointing. A group of Carthaginian soldiers rushed forward, pushing large, wheeled catapults toward the walls of the port, but were still inside the trenches. It was unclear if they would be able to launch their payloads from there, but Velius doubted they'd have deployed them if they didn't think it would work.

"Target the catapults!" Velius yelled to his gunnery officers. "Concentrate fire on them!"

The wall cannons roared, belching clouds of grey smoke as they fired. Shells arced through the air and smashed against the Carthaginian barricades. Wood and dirt sprayed into the air where the shells impacted. Several balls found their targets, landing past the barricades and into the trenches themselves. Two of the catapults disappeared in blasts of fire and shrapnel.

But more machines were already being pushed forward, weaving through the trenches to replace the ones that had been destroyed. His cannons were too few to cover the entire encircling siege line and many of the wall positions didn't have a good angle on the newly erected barricades sheltering the catapults.

Whenever he knocked out one position, more machines were brought up to take their place. The Carthaginians were willing to absorb losses to get their catapults in range of the walls. Once there, they could begin bombarding the walls and city in earnest.

The walls could take the pounding, as could the port itself. Whatever they destroyed could be rebuilt. If they rained enough stones, they could create enough casualties to make it impossible to hold the port. Which had to be their plan. Worse, if it was flaming rounds. Most of the gunpowder was in protected stores, but they had to have cartridges with the cannons. A few fabric balls soaked in tar and lit on fire could destroy entire positions, taking whole chunks out of the wall if they hit the gunpowder near a cannon.

And he couldn't just take their ammunition away. Without the cannons' continual fire, the Carthaginians would charge, attempting to take the wall.

"Increase the rate of fire. Destroy those catapults," he ordered.

The order wasn't needed. His men saw them and understood the danger. It was more a sign of his own uneasiness with the situation. It wasn't enough to stop the Carthaginian effort. Several of the catapults had their arms pulled back, ammunition being loaded into their baskets.

"Brace for impact," he ordered. "Have the gunners secure their ammunition as best they can. Possible incendiary rounds."

There wasn't much they could do, but at least they'd be warned.

As he watched, a catapult arm slapped forward, sending its payload sailing through the air. As soon as it cleared the trench, a part of Velius's mind recognized that something was different. It wasn't a large ball of rope soaked in tar, nor was it a stone. It looked like a large clay pot, which was unusual. He'd heard of pots full of oil being thrown, prior to flaming rounds, intended to increase the damage caused. That kind of thing wouldn't damage the walls, and the Carthaginians would know that. Yes, it would increase the chances of gunpowder being set off, but it didn't seem likely the Carthaginians would know that.

He was still trying to process what he was seeing when the unthinkable happened. The container smashed against the wall and exploded, expanding out in a ball of flame. Chunks of masonry blew away from the wall, leaving a gouge in the side of the wall. It took a moment for the sheer shock of what he was seeing to pass and his brain to work again. He was still in disbelief that the Carthaginians could have gotten gunpowder, but it wasn't exactly the same as theirs. If that container had been even half full of Britannian gunpowder, the explosion would have been larger, which meant either the container was practically empty, which was possible but didn't seem likely, or it was weaker than what they used.

Velius didn't understand the substance fully, but he'd had a conversation with Hortensius the previous year when they were developing it, and he remembered the manufacturer talking about testing to find the right ratios to give just enough explosive power. Even weaker though, it was still a huge danger.

Velius's worry was proven correct when two more pots sailed through the air. One exploded prematurely, well away from the walls, suggesting there was some kind of pre-lit fuse on the pots, but the other landed close to one of the cannons. Close enough that the fireball itself, or perhaps some flaming debris, hit the cannon's supply of gunpowder. The explosion showed just how different their gunpowder was from what the Carthaginians were firing.

The explosion shook the ground under Velius's feet halfway across the port and obliterated not only the cannon and its crew, but an entire section of the wall. The cannon tube itself flew high into the air, smashing to the ground outside the walls, as chunks of masonry flew in all directions amidst billowing smoke and dust.

His other cannoneers recognized the danger and intensified their fire against the catapults, but it was a losing battle. He didn't know how much gunpowder they had, but they weren't keeping it all with the catapults. He could see a pair of men running through a trench with one of the containers using his spyglass, along with more catapults being wheeled into position.

With that one shot, the entire chain of logic for his defense was crushed. The gap in the wall from the cannon explosion didn't reach to the ground, but it was large, and it wouldn't take much more pounding to rip a sizable hole in the entire wall or send that section crumbling to the ground, and that was one hit. They wouldn't last until Gordianus pushed into the Carthaginian line. Port Invictus was going to fall.

The only question that remained was how many of his men he was going to lose before it did. Even as his mind raced for solutions, two more rounds impacted, one outside the wall and another just inside the wall, ripping the men it landed among to shreds, the shards of the pot like shrapnel, cutting down men outside the blast down like wheat.

"What the hell was that?" Aelius asked, rushing up from the interior of the port where he'd been directing the men's movement.

Instead of answering the legate's question, Velius said, "Prepare to pull your men back to the docks."

"What?" Aelius asked, a shocked look on his face. "We're giving up the port?"

"Yes. We can't hold it, not if they're throwing explosives. We could keep pounding at their catapults as they bring them up, but they only need one lucky shot for a breach, and they'll storm us. If the wall breaches, there's no way we're going to hold it. We need to save as many of our men as we can. I'm not throwing away the lives of two cohorts for a fort we can't hold."

"I can stay, lead the defense here ..."

Velius cut him off with a sharp wave of his hand, "You will take the bulk of the men and evacuate to the ships in the harbor. I will remain with two centuries of volunteers to ensure your escape."

"But, sir ..." Aelius began to protest.

"That's an order, Legate," Velius said firmly. "Gather the men swiftly and board the ships. We don't have time, so don't bother with supplies, just get as many men onto the water as possible. I will keep the Carthaginians occupied as best I can to make sure you get clear."

Aelius's expression made it clear he didn't agree, but an order was an order. As more explosions boomed outside the walls, he turned and stomped off, bellowing orders to get the men moving.

Waving a messenger over, Velius said, "Send a signal to Gordianus to pull his legion back to the first fort. Have him alert the Consul about the enemy's new weapon and await further instructions from him. If the enemy approaches the fort, abandon it and withdraw to the next in line in a fighting retreat. On open ground and mobile, they won't have a chance to dig trenches, and his cannons can outrange their catapults. He is to conduct a fighting retreat, but he is not to endanger his command until the Consul responds."

The messengers raced off as more clay pots streaked overhead and burst against the walls. The crumbling section of the curtain wall trembled under the impacts. They were clearly focusing their fire on the already damaged section, hoping to create a breach they could exploit. And it was working. Already, the gap was widening.

Velius addressed the men nearby, "I need two hundred volunteers to remain as a rear guard while the rest escape." Only the grimmest determination showed on the faces of the men that stepped forward. They knew the likely outcome yet stood firm.

"Form up on the inner curtain, with the strongest defenses opposite the breached outer wall. Abandon the outer cannons. They will shortly be in enemy hands regardless. I want you to go to the gunpowder magazine and pull all of it out," he said, indicating about a third of the men waiting for orders. "I want it all mounded by the inner wall. Every bit of it. Everyone else, make for the docks. Move."

An explosion thundered deafeningly close, blasting another section of the wall in a hail of stone fragments. Looking over his shoulder, down the sloped ground to the docks, he could see boats already making their way out to sea, towards the caravel and supply ships waiting in the harbor, with more men stacked up on the beach, waiting to join them. With only two cohorts, it wouldn't take long for all of the men to be evacuated.

Another series of explosions rocked the battered fortifications. The deep rumble of falling masonry followed each blast. The air filled with dust and smoke, reducing visibility to a grey haze.

Velius returned his focus to his tiny force manning the secondary wall, trusting Aelius to get the men out. Then, he began to move with the rest of the men to the inner curtain.

With the cannons no longer firing, the Carthaginian firing intensified. Explosion after explosion sent showers of stone raining down as the breaches in the outer fortifications rapidly widened and then finally broke, leaving a wide gap in the outer wall.

The Carthaginians sensed their moment. Through the smoke and dust, Velius could make out a mass of figures spilling out of their trenches like ants from an ant pile. They charged the wall, pouring through the gaps and into the space between the inner and outer walls like water through a crumbling dam. Sharp cries and exultant shouts rose from the enemy as they sensed victory close at hand.

"Prepare for assault!" Velius bellowed, his voice hoarse from breathing the smoke-filled air. The remaining men rushed to take up positions along the wall walk, weapons at the ready. With their men this close in, the catapult firing stopped, not that they'd need it. He didn't have the cannon and the number of men to hold the wall from their scaling attempts.

The first ladder smashed against the wall, the metal latches at the end of it clattering against the battlement to hold it in place. One of Velius's men brought his sword down on the wood connecting the metal hooks, starting to cut it through. Another legionnaire leaned over his rifle, pointing down and firing, hopefully killing a man climbing up. More followed, thudding into the stone facade of the tower at the corner of the wall. Velius watched enemy soldiers start to swarm up the parapets.

The area between the walls was filling with men, thousands of them, with more pressing against the gap in the outer wall, trying to get in. His two hundred men weren't going to hold this for long. Already, bolts from Carthaginian-style arcuballista were sailing over the wall, and Britannians started to fall, increasing the already impossible odds.

A husky Carthaginian warrior hauled himself over the crenellations, pushing past the body of the legionnaire he had just gutted. With a wordless cry of rage, he charged. Velius met the charge, knocking aside the sword swung at him. His shoulder slammed into the larger man's chest, driving him back over the parapet.

It didn't matter. None of them were going to survive this. He was just buying time for Aelius to get the bulk of the forces away and to let the Carthaginian forces build up, pressed hard against the wall. He wanted as many inside the curtain, or just outside of it, as he could get.

Which was exactly what was happening, as men packed in, shoulder to shoulder, attempting to make it up the inner wall at the same time.

"Light it," he yelled to the legionnaire below, standing next to the entire supply of powder left in the port, originally intended for the legions and other forts.

Pallets of filled cannon charges, hundreds of barrels of loose powder, and boxes of pre-packaged rifle rounds by the tens of thousands. A massive supply of gunpowder, all stacked together. And a legionnaire with a lit torch.

The man paused, which was only natural, considering what he'd just been ordered to do. To his credit, the hesitation only lasted a heartbeat. He knew what he was fighting for and what the stakes were. Looking up at Velius, his face scrunched tight, and he threw the torch into an opened barrel of gunpowder.

The world seemed to freeze for a single heartbeat as Velius watched the torch fall. Then the powder ignited in a flash more brilliant than the noonday sun. The eruption expanded outward, enveloping barrels, crates, and men alike in a tidal wave of destruction.

Chapter 20

Devnum

Lucilla sat on her father's throne, her throne now, and tried to radiate calm despite the rage churning inside of her. Everything she'd feared when they'd decided to start the new prisoner work gangs had come to pass, and she needed answers. However, she recalled her father's words that a monarch must be calm and balanced at all times. Revealing her hand too readily, even to allies, only weakened her position.

It had been a hard-learned lesson, controlling her emotions, especially on days like this when she longed to scream. But she understood that emotional outbursts would not garner the results she required.

Faenius marched in first, stern-faced as ever, with his characteristic stiff-backed walk. Beside him was the other man she'd summoned. Ramirus was in every way a contrast to Faenius's military bearing – unassuming, almost looking like someone's grandfather, unless you looked into the man's eyes.

Both men stopped before the throne and bowed with their equally charismatic manners.

"You sent for us, Your Majesty," Faenius said.

"I did. I want you both to explain this failure," Lucilla demanded.

"Your Majesty, this was not a fault of the design of the camp or prison factory, both of which have worked well," Faenius said. "The men escaped from the crew working on the new facilities in Factorium. I said we didn't have enough men to properly vet ..."

She cut him off curtly, "I don't want excuses. I want to know how this happened and how you will rectify it. When we first discussed using prisoners as laborers, you both claimed the camp was as secure as it could be. Now a dozen praetorians lie dead and fifty prisoners roam free."

"Your Majesty," Ramirus began evenly, "I accept full responsibility for the escape. Faenius is right that we didn't have enough resources to check each of the prisoners who volunteered for the detail. We were still checking them, although we also knew these men were all soldiers and this was always a danger. It was a risk, but one I was willing to take. Even with the losses we suffered and the manpower it will take to find these men, I still think it was the only option we had. Several of the factories Hortensius requested are finished and are starting to produce, which wouldn't have been possible without using the prisoners to do the work. Their labor in the prison camp has already started to produce goods, helping relieve some of the strain we've been experiencing."

"What Ramirus says is true. Even with us interviewing everyone, all of these men are prisoners and all are trained soldiers who came here to kill as many of our people as possible. It's always been a danger. That being said, we've made some adjustments to our security procedures to prevent this type of thing from happening again."

"Your assurances of the effectiveness of any security procedures would mean more if you hadn't said the same thing last time," Lucilla said, her wrath on full display.

Faenius looked down, worry creasing his face, but Ramirus seemed unfazed. Lucilla hadn't doubted she wouldn't be able to cow him. He'd known her for her entire life, literally, and he still looked on her as the little girl who rolled her eyes at her brother and learned at her father's knee. At times she found it comfortable, a connection to her father, but other times, such as now, she was annoyed her ire bounced off of him.

"Your Majesty," he said, still calm. "Our assurances were only that we were making the best choices that we could, balancing resources and manpower with the protections we'd need. We fell short, but that was the risk we took. We are readjusting our security procedures, which will cost us more in other places, but it needs to be done. Is it going to be enough? Who knows? I think so, but it could fall short again, and we'll have to pull yet more resources from other critical areas. We're in a war for survival, and this is just the nature of it. Too many critical things that cannot be compromised and not enough resources to keep from compromising them. If you're concerned that we aren't doing enough, we can do more than we have planned, but there will be a cost involved. You could decide to end the entire project, but that too has a cost. It's your decision which we pay for."

Lucilla frowned at him, furious the old man made so much sense. Every time she doubted they were doing enough, that was his argument. There were too many people who needed Praetorians, wire, and all the other security apparatus, not to mention the factories and legions. She wanted to be furious, to blame the escape and deaths on someone, but she knew the dangers and the needs, and made the decision. She was mad at herself, as much as either of them.

"What are these new procedures?"

Faenius gave a side-eye glance at Ramirus and said, "Our biggest vulnerability, as we saw, is when prisoners have to go outside the wire, where we lose the ability to control them as easily. We discussed no longer using the prisoners for outside projects at all, but Ramirus believes this is impractical. We've already received two requests for work on additional projects today, and it is likely that will continue on most days. I am …"

"The main reason we started using prison labor force was for these outside projects," Ramirus said, clearly seeing Faenius hedge. "The work factory inside the wire was a later add-on and not the primary need for them. So yes, unless ordered otherwise, we have little choice but to continue these work details."

"I assume you were going to talk about the new procedures for these work details?" Lucilla asked Faenius, ignoring Ramirus.

"Yes, Your Majesty. Going forward, we will rotate prisoners in smaller groups for any outside labor to prevent mass escapes. We will also be increasing the Praetorians guarding them, with more mounted men. That is going to primarily come out of the units assigned to the city guard, at least until we can recruit more guards. We will also conduct more thorough searches for weapons before we take the men out of the work camp. It will slow down the process of getting them in and out each day, but we found several work tools at the site of the attack, which they must have used to initiate it."

"And what about the men that escaped?"

"Patrols are searching the hills to the southeast, where our trackers have indicated they ran, but the terrain makes them difficult to locate. We suspect they are trying to flee deeper into the wilderness."

"I want every last escaped prisoner recaptured. We cannot allow these men to start causing unrest. Not after we finally quelled the insurgents. Nothing takes precedence over capturing them. Am I clear?"

"Yes, Your Majesty," Faenius said.

"Good, now ..."

Her next words faded as her attention was drawn to a commotion near the entrance to the audience chamber, where one of her guards was speaking in hushed tones to a frantic-looking man she recognized from his many stops at the palace. She'd never spoken to him, but he was a runner and messenger from Devnum's semaphore station and often delivered messages.

"What's that about?" she said loudly, causing her guard to turn.

With a gesture, the guard released the man, who sprinted into the room, skidding to a stop next to Faenius and Ramirus, both of whom were watching him intently.

"Your Majesty!" he said, his voice trembling. "Terrible news from Hispania. Port Invictus has fallen to the Carthaginians and Legate Velius is dead."

He held up a note, showing the scrawled message from the semaphore, which Ramirus took from him and read, his face going pale as he did.

"The message is from Aelius, which he sent with one of the supply ships that had been at the port. Velius arrived to help lead the defense of the port, as he indicated he would in his last message, and Gordianus brought his legion up through the mountains to attack the Carthaginians from the other side. The Carthaginians dug deep trenches in the ground and used lightweight barriers to absorb and deflect cannon fire, to allow their men to get into range. Once they got close enough, they brought up catapults, and began hurling what Aelius believes were pots filled with gunpowder, which exploded, setting off our own gunpowder. The explosion created a breach in the walls around Port Invictus, at which point Velius ordered Aelius to take all but two hundred men and escape to the ships in the harbor. Shortly after, there was a gigantic explosion from the fort, although it's unclear what caused the explosion."

Lucilla felt as if a blow had struck her. She stared blankly at Ramirus, struggling to fully comprehend his words. The loss of Port Invictus and Velius, along with so many of their soldiers, was a devastating blow to their war effort. She also considered Velius a friend, not to the level of Hortensius or Ramirus, but a friend nonetheless, and one whose loss she felt deeply.

"So we don't know if Velius is dead for sure?" Lucilla said, clinging to a small amount of hope.

"If the explosion was as massive as the legate describes, it's unlikely he survived."

"Does he give any indication of what he's doing now? Returning here? Heading north to join the forces there?"

"They intercepted a message from the fort to Gordianus shortly before the explosion, ordering the legion to be pulled back to the line of forts, from which they were to request further instructions from the Consul. The orders reiterated that he is to continue falling back, all the way to the northern army, if need be, to protect the legion until he receives new orders. Aelius indicates his intentions are to sail north with the men rescued from the port and drop them further north in Gaul, where they will march and link up with Gordianus. That is all the message indicates."

"I see," she said quietly, before turning her attention to the messenger. "Thank you for your service."

Seeing he was excused, the man practically ran from the audience chamber, probably thankful he didn't have to get caught up in the aftermath of such bad news. Lucilla hoped that was not what he was thinking. She'd strived to not be one of those leaders who blamed the messenger for the words they carried.

"You can also go. I need some time," she said to her two advisers. "You have your orders. Fix our security issues and find those missing prisoners."

Faenius bowed and departed, but she could see Ramirus wanted to stay. She knew he'd worked out she could communicate with Ky and he was smart enough to know that was exactly what she was intending to do now. This kind of news couldn't wait for a messenger, since it was going to completely upend their entire strategy on the continent. She could appreciate her advisor's desire to be present, but she wanted this moment with Ky, just the two of them. Ky had been friends with Velius as well and would take the news just as hard as she did.

Besides, it wasn't like he could hear what Ky was saying, and even if he suspected she could communicate directly with Ky, she preferred not to confirm it.

"Not now. I will send for you," she said.He gave a nod and departed. Now all she had to do was tell Ky his friend was dead.

Northern Germany

Ky walked out of his tent, numb. The news Lucilla had given him, of the loss of Port Invictus and the death of Velius, had shaken him to the core. While it was a devastating loss to the legions and a military setback, he also mourned the loss of his friend. Velius had been a stalwart companion ever since Ky arrived in Devnum and joined the Roman cause, and he'd shown his immense capacity at every turn. His death was a great loss to the entire empire.

Pausing for a moment outside the tent flaps, Ky closed his eyes and steadied himself with a deep breath. Waving an aide over, he sent for the command staff. There would be time to properly mourn later; for now, action was required.

Within minutes, the legates and their staffs were assembled. All were still in good spirits from their victory over the Carthaginians, crushing the bulk of the forces sent to push them out of Germania. Only Bomilcar seemed to pick up on Ky's mood, sensing something was wrong.

"I have grave news. Port Invictus has fallen. Velius is dead," Ky said.

The words smashed into the men like a wave, their good mood instantly vanishing. Shocked murmurs rippled through the tent.

Ky raised a hand for silence before continuing, "I know this is a shock. Unfortunately, we still have a war to fight and don't have time to mourn the loss of Velius and the men with him. Thankfully, Velius's last act was to ensure our losses weren't crippling. He managed to get the bulk of his forces out, only losing two hundred legionaries while, from the reports, taking a large number of Carthaginians with him. Aelius and the cohorts he had at Port Invictus when it was first put under siege along with the bulk of the Seventh Legion have all fled north to the line of fortifications they've built. The men are going to be demoralized, but they're still in this fight. That's not all. The Carthaginians have also managed to acquire gunpowder. It's not clear if it's the same as the gunpowder that we use, and they aren't using cannons or muskets."

More murmurs spread across the room.

Pointing at the map table showing an overview of Europe, Ky said, "Bomilcar, I want you to head south with Auspex's legion, where you'll meet up with Gordianus and the remnants of the Seventh Legion, and you'll take command. I'm naming you as the legate of the Seventh Legion. Auspex, your legion is to back him up, along with Aelius's legion, or what's not assigned to one of the forts. Protect the forces we have left and counter the Carthaginians in Hispania. With the trenching they did around Port Invictus, they were able to get their catapults into range, even with the cannons, and throw their explosives over the wall. Speed and mobility will be key. Do not allow yourself to be bottled up. Stay out of fortifications and static defenses as much as possible. You have the range on them, which will negate their new tricks. For now, all of your supplies will have to come from here."

"Understood," Bomilcar said.

The aged general didn't need more than that. He understood what needed to be done, and Ky trusted him to take care of it.

"Good. Don't wait for us. Gordianus should be at the first fortification already, and the losses Velius caused will slow the Carthaginians down, but not for long. I want you both in play when they move. Good luck and may the gods watch over you."

Ky turned back to the remaining commanders once Bomilcar and Auspex had departed to carry out their orders.

"The fall of Port Invictus means we cannot afford to remain here any longer. Ursinus, I'm leaving you and your legion here, to coordinate with the local tribes to suppress any remnants of the Carthaginian army. Now that the bulk of their army is shattered, they should not pose a major threat. Your priority is to keep the tribes armed and have them scout the territory, searching for any new Carthaginian incursions, and protect the region from brigands and the like. If the Carthaginians do return, you're to concentrate your forces and deal with them. Make good use of your tools and our allies, *and stay mobile.* If the enemy in Hispania has gunpowder, assume they all do."

Ursinus cleared his throat and asked, "What are your plans, Consul? If I'm staying here with my legions, where are the remaining legions going to be?"

"I'll be taking the two legions south, towards the Carthaginian port on the Mediterranean. It's their main source of supplies and reinforcements at the moment. If we put pressure on it, the Carthaginians will have to respond, which will pull their army between us and Bomilcar."

"I see," Ursinus said.

"Speaking of supplies, you're going to be responsible for maintaining the supply lines to both Bomilcar and my forces. Work with the local tribes, set up supply convoys, and use whatever tools you need to ensure the provisions keep flowing. Can you handle that?"

Ursinus nodded, "Yes, sir, you can count on me."

"Good," Ky said, glancing around at the other officers. "Any other questions?"

The men looked at each other, but no one had anything to add. Their orders were clear and they all knew what was expected of them.

"Very well. Let's get moving then. We've got a lot of work ahead of us, and time is of the essence."

The men began to disperse to carry out their orders, the tent emptying swiftly. He'd hoped to be more methodical about his assault on their port, but they'd forced his hand, and he was going to make sure they paid the price for the death of his friend.

Port Invictus, Hispania

General Tabnit walked carefully through the ruined streets that once made up Port Invictus, his leather boots crunching on broken shards of cement and stone. All around him, teams of laborers and engineers worked to clear debris and salvage what they could from the devastation. The Romans had picked a good location, and this could be a kickoff point when they were ready to re-invade the Roman islands. Although, for the most part, their labor was to keep the men busy while they sat here, day after day, waiting.

It had been nearly three weeks since Tabnit's army had besieged and conquered the fortified port city. Though they had ultimately succeeded in capturing it, the victory had come at a brutal cost. The Romans had fought ferociously to defend Port Invictus, manning the walls with rows of their deadly thunder weapons. He'd countered those with the trenches and barriers described by the Far Eastern engineers, allowing him to get catapults into range and finally pay the bastards back for all the deaths they'd wrought.

What he hadn't expected was the massive eruption, apparently caused when they set off their fire powder, which the Easterners called how yow or something. It was hard to tell with their thick accents and harsh language. The interpreter had translated it as fire medicine and had confirmed that the weapon they gave his people was similar to the material being used by the Romans. Tabnit was fairly certain they recognized the thunder weapons and knew more about them, but they pretended ignorance and misunderstanding every time he asked.

Either way, they must have had either a lot more of the fire powder, or theirs was just significantly more powerful, because while his had torn chunks off their wall, theirs shattered as though Hexitas herself had reached up and smote them. Sections of the wall, that weighed as much as a dozen oxen, flew high into the air before crashing down, as did the body parts and remains of thousands and thousands of his men, who'd poured into the breach his weapons had created. Every man within a hundred paces of the wall had been obliterated. More were killed further out by flying shards of stone and cement or ripped apart by the very air. It had been brutal.

Two of Tabnit's senior commanders, Nabalsa and Hasdrubal, trailed several paces behind him, more focused on him than the devastated port. They exchanged worried glances every time Tabnit stopped, surveyed the scene, and frowned.

"This is taking too long," Tabnit said when he stopped again at the body of a man under a giant piece of stone. "We've been here for weeks while the Romans continue to escape and rally. We have them on the run, but that won't last forever, and we won't get a chance to bottle them up like this again, pushed against the sea and vulnerable. The emperor sent us here to free Hispania and the rest of the continent from the Roman incursion, which we're not doing while sitting in these ruins."

"We lost over ten thousand men, with thousands more injured in the explosion and assault," Nabalsa said, a weary expression on his face. "We're recovering as quickly as we can."

"That's unacceptable," Tabnit said. "Our scouts report that the remnants of the escaped Romans have already landed, north of us near one of the cursed forts. It's likely that the legion that attacked us from the mountains, and then ran when the port erupted, headed in the same direction, to combine their forces. While we've sat here, doing nothing, they've united and reinforced. Who knows if they've gotten more men from the north or from their island? If we're lucky, they'll try to hide in their forts and we'll be able to seal them up again. But not if we stay here, never moving."

"Our men are weary and many are still injured," Hasdrubal said. "We lost most of our supplies when the flaming debris fell across our camp. Perhaps we also need to pull back, regroup, and resupply before …"

Tabnit turned, his fingers tightening on his sword, "No! I'm not going to let these Romans grow stronger while we hide and lick our wounds. I will finish the job I started, the one the emperor commanded me to do. I want you to prepare to mobilize the army at once. Leave a small detachment to defend the port, should the Romans attempt to double back behind us. Everyone else should be ready to march at dawn."

Nabalsa shifted uncertainly, "But commander, what of our many wounded? We cannot simply abandon them …"

"You have your orders," Tabnit cut him off sharply. "The port detachment can tend to the injured, but their commander must understand, his priority is to secure this area, not play nursemaid. The wounded are a secondary concern."

Seeing Nabalsa about to protest further, Tabnit slashed a hand through the air, saying, "Enough! You have your orders. Any man too injured to fight will be left behind. We'll be covering harsh terrain, and I've no intention of slowing our pace for stragglers and invalids. If they cannot keep up, they will be abandoned."

When the two men didn't move immediately, Tabnit added, "Go!"

Both men bowed hesitantly before hurrying off. Once they were gone, Tabnit made his way through the rubble toward the field outside the ruined port where the command tents were set up. He had his own preparations to make before they marched.

Chapter 21

South of Devnum

Claudius led his squad of Praetorians through the dense woods, trudging along the damp trail. Normally, he hated the way the ground turned soggy from the endless early summer rains, but now, it worked to his benefit. The ground had been muddy when the prisoners came through, preserving some signs of their passing, enough so that his trackers could follow.

Still, the forest was not where he wanted to follow them. The towering trees blocked out the sun, leaving them in an eerie, almost twilight. The thick stands of trees took away his greatest combat advantage, the range his men's rifles afforded them. Claudius dropped one hand subconsciously to the hilt of his sword as the shadows grew deeper.

"Swords at the ready," Claudius ordered. "The rifles will be near useless once we're deep in the woods."

The Praetorians slid their rifles onto their backs and pulled their gladius free, the scrape of metal on leather loud in the muffled silence of the forest. They could sense the danger, and the banter that had flowed freely when they'd been in more open environments ended. Their steps grew more cautious, booted feet careful to avoid snapping twigs or rustling leaves. It was impossible for twenty armored men to be silent, but they seemed determined to try. Although Claudius knew it was more from a desire to hear an impending attack than to attempt to sneak in unnoticed.

Up ahead, Claudius spotted faint wheel ruts cutting through the muddy trail. The Carthaginians had hit a farm a half-day's ride to the north and taken supplies and a wagon after slaughtering the family that lived there. The tracks weaved erratically, evidence of inexperienced drivers, dodging trees on the rough cart path.

A snapped branch to his left drew Claudius's attention. He froze, fist raised to halt his men. Silence descended, interrupted only by the occasional bird call. After a tense minute, Claudius waved his squad forward, quickening their pace. The prisoners couldn't have gone far on foot. There'd been indications that some of them had been injured in the fight to escape, which was another reason they'd needed the cart.

They'd gone perhaps another hundred yards when the trail opened into a small clearing. Claudius crouched low, taking cover behind a fallen tree, signaling for his men to do the same. Across the glade stood the stolen wagon, traces dangling loose from the harness. No horses were in sight. Nor were there any signs of the escaped prisoners.

Claudius considered the scene across the glade. Either the prisoners had abandoned the cumbersome wagon and continued on foot, or this was an ambush. He scanned the tree line, searching for any hint of movement or glint of metal among the branches.

His hand signals ordered two men to circle to the right, two more to the left. They were to converge on the wagon, rooting out anyone hiding nearby. The rest of the squad would provide cover. Claudius watched his men melt into the brush, proud of their stealth. Moments later, sharp whistles signaled the all-clear.

Claudius stood, gesturing for the others to follow. They crossed the clearing and examined the wagon. The rough ground had broken one of the axles loose, the wheel sticking out at an awkward angle. It wouldn't move without being fixed and the prisoners wouldn't have wanted to stop long enough to do that. Of course, that also meant that they were carrying the wounded with them, since there weren't any bodies left behind. Supplies were strewn about; the escapees had taken what they could carry before abandoning the wagon. Claudius crouched to examine the ground. The tracks were messy, obscured by kicked-up debris, but clear enough to follow.

Claudius signaled his men forward, plunging deeper into the dim forest. Despite the distraction of the abandoned wagon, Claudius remained focused on the trail. Even with the escapees' speed slowed, they could still be far behind them, since they'd had a significant head start. He quickened their pace as much as the rugged terrain allowed.

The trail narrowed ahead, choked with underbrush. Claudius hesitated, weighing the risk. The limited visibility created a perfect spot for an ambush. The trail ran clearly through it, however, with incredibly thick undergrowth and trees on either side. There was no choice but to follow the trail if they were to recapture the escaped prisoners.

Claudius picked his way forward, flanked by his men. The close quarters forced them into a single file. A sound, something picked up by his unconscious mind, drew Claudius's attention, revealing the ambush seconds before it was sprung.

"Ambush!" he yelled, diving for cover as a barrage of stones and crude spears flew from the concealing underbrush.

The makeshift spears thudded into the mud. Stones bounced off armor and shields. Claudius risked a glance around and saw the forest was suddenly swarming with the escaped prisoners.

"Form up!" he bellowed. "Prepare for close combat."

In trained precision, the Praetorians drew their swords. Claudius kicked out at a charging prisoner as he backed up, causing the man to stumble before Claudius ran him through with his sword. Whipping his blade free, Claudius engaged the next man, continuing to have his men back up slowly in the face of the pressure from the onslaught that attempted to overwhelm them.

The initial assault hadn't been avoided entirely. Four Praetorians lay unmoving, their lives lost in the initial surprise attack. Claudius swore under his breath. They were outnumbered, and at the moment the ground favored their attackers.

More prisoners appeared, crude weapons in hand. Claudius slashed and parried, edging slowly backward through the dense trees.

"Back," he commanded over the sound of clashing steel.

Step by step, the Praetorians closed the gaps in their formation, surrounded on all sides.

One of Claudius's men stabbed a man through the chest, while another swept the legs out from under a prisoner, bringing his sword down in a killing blow. Claudius slashed and parried, edging back down the cart path. They moved as one, swords whirling. A prisoner leaped forward, a makeshift spear aimed at Claudius's chest. Claudius sidestepped, knocking the spear aside as the man stumbled past. His sword flashed, and the prisoner fell without a sound.

Claudius risked a glance around as he parried a sword blow from another prisoner. More than a quarter of his men were down, strewn on the ground alongside Carthaginian bodies. They couldn't defeat the prisoners if they continued to sustain losses at this rate. As three more Praetorians fell, cut down by the mob, he knew that they had to seize the initiative.

"Counterattack!" he bellowed.

At his command, the Praetorians surged forward, several drawing their rifles from their backs, bayonets already locked in place.

Claudius led the advance, his sword streaking out to slash across a prisoner's chest. Blood sprayed as the man fell back with a gurgling cry. Around him, the Praetorians engaged with their blades and stabbing bayonets, driving into the confused mob of prisoners.

Rifles cracked behind Claudius as the Praetorians began firing into the fray. Prisoners screamed and fell, some wounded, others killed instantly by the gunfire. The acrid tang of smoke filled the air.

Pressed by the fierce attack, the prisoners began to fall back. Their crude weapons were unable to stand up to the Praetorians. More prisoners fell until finally, they wavered and then broke, turning to run headlong into the woods.

"Break. Don't let them escape," he called out.

They'd trained for this, a squad breaking off their attack and chasing men attempting to flee. The training had been intended to be used in the pursuit of criminals in crowded city streets, but the application was the same. His men didn't need to discuss what to do, pairing off automatically, so that no man fought alone, and they began the chase.

Claudius pursued his group like a man possessed, slashing a prisoner across the back of the legs to send him sprawling. His squad exploded in all directions, anywhere a prisoner might have attempted to run. Unfired rifles tracked fleeing prisoners between the trees, their gunfire echoing through the forest as they picked off the runners.

In minutes it was over, the forest silent once more but for the moans of the wounded. Bodies littered the leaf-strewn ground, blood seeping into the earth. Wounded men crawled and moaned while others lay still in death.

Claudius quickly assessed the situation. Nearly half his men were injured in some way, and seven were dead, but they'd accomplished their mission. Of the escaped prisoners, only a handful remained alive, trembling on the ground surrounded by watchful Praetorians.

"Secure any prisoners still breathing," he ordered two of his men.

The Praetorians moved swiftly, binding the few surviving prisoners with ropes and hauling them upright. Claudius continued his count as he walked. Twenty-eight, twenty-nine ... when he reached the last body, he came to a total of thirty-six. A significant number of the escaped prisoners had been killed or recaptured, but not all of them.

Claudius turned and surveyed his men. Eleven Praetorians remained of his original twenty, and at least five of those were injured. The escapees had put up a fierce fight, more than he had expected.

"Take four men and go back for the wagon. We'll fix the axle and use it to carry our dead and injured," he ordered a group of uninjured Praetorians.

It angered him that good men had lost their lives to such prisoners. But they had done their duty with honor, and he was satisfied that the threat had been neutralized. Only a handful of prisoners remained on the loose. Faenius would demand they find them, but this was a good start. He saw a few older injuries among the fallen or captured, so most of the prisoners wounded in the initial attack had gone in another direction. Which meant a portion, at least, of those prisoners remaining at large were injured one way or another.

Once back in Devnum, he'd request to take another detachment to root out the last of the survivors. For today, however, his duty was done.

Germania, South of the Rhine

Ky watched his officers dismount from their horses, weary and sore, glad for the hundredth time that his body had been engineered to handle the rigors of a hard day's march without the pains they dealt with. What it didn't help him with was the mud, which caked nearly everyone, from the officers on horseback to the legionaries marching through the mud. The parts of him that weren't covered in mud were soaking wet from the non-stop rain. Worse than how miserable it was making everyone was what it was doing to their timetable. They were covering a fraction of the distance they needed to make every day. If it was just the supplies holding them back, he'd leave them and a detachment behind, and the men could make the march on rations, but it wasn't. The artillery was, if anything, worse off with the long metal tubes and the even heavier caisson full of gunpowder and heavy iron shot digging deep into the thick mud.

"Make sure the men dry off as best they can, and that all of them get a hot meal. We're going to have several more days of this, at the very least, and it could stretch even longer. If we need time to make sure the men aren't pushing themselves too hard, I'll accept it. Do the best you can."

Vibius, the senior of the two legates who'd accompanied him south, saluted and turned his horse toward where the men were camping, down the hill slightly from where the command tents were being set up. Marcus, the other legate, was with the rear cohorts, trying to push the army forward while Vibius pulled it from the front, attempting to get every meter they could each day.

Tents were already being broken out across the open fields they'd marched into, the men well ahead of their officers' orders, wanting nothing more than to get dry. They were the lucky ones. The column was so spread out that the rear units wouldn't make it to the camp until well after midnight.

Thankfully, rank had its privileges, and Ky's command tent had already gone up well before he arrived. Giving a few last orders, he left the rest of the camp setup, which the men knew well by now, to his subordinates, and ducked into his tent, shedding wet and muddy clothes by the front flap, setting them on a small stool for one of his aides to deal with, and donning a robe that had been set out for him. It made him feel a little guilty, being taken care of in such high style while his men were still wallowing in the mud, but he did have things to work on that would take him well into the evening, and this pampering saved him precious time.

He and Sophus had spent most of the last several days debating what their strategy would be once they arrived at the port. The addition of gunpowder on the enemy side had changed their calculus on how to handle the assault, since just charging the walls, even after a barrage from the artillery, would be costly. The artillery would have to stop firing when the men got to the wall, which would give an opening for the Carthaginians to start throwing their gunpowder bombs. They'd come up with a solution, but they needed Lucilla's help to achieve it.

"Can you talk?" Ky said quietly, opening a line to her communicator. His Lictores were used to him talking to himself by now, and the steady rain would drown out his words anyway, so there wasn't a real reason for him to be quiet, but it had become a habit. Lucilla, unlike him, couldn't sub-vocalize and hadn't spent a lifetime with a communicator droning on inside her head, developing the skills to hear it and ignore it at the same time. She still had a tendency to jump at sudden transmissions, which had caused her a few embarrassing moments.

"Yes, I'm here, my love," she said, her voice soft and warm. "You're late."

"We're moving slowly. We tried moving the cannons nearer the front, hoping the ground would be more solid for them, but it just slowed the infantry coming up behind, tearing the ground up just as badly as the infantry tore it up for them. Nothing we seem to do solves the problem, and the ground gets wetter every day."

"How are the men?"

"Tired, but in surprisingly good spirits, considering the conditions. It helps that some of the winter harvests have come in, and we took a lot of the enemy's food stores when we sent their army running. Being well-fed and allowing them a full night's sleep goes a long way. The last thing I want is for them to be exhausted and weakened when we get to the Carthaginian port."

He paused for a moment, slicking back water from his still-damp hair, which had started to drip into his eyes.

"Speaking of the port, there's something we're going to need when we get there that I need your help with."

"Anything I can do, you only have to ask," she said.

"Sophus and I have been discussing how to assault the port walls once we arrive. The reports you sent us from Ramirus suggest they've been preparing for us, with a thick center of packed dirt and logs in between the stone. Who knows how long we'll have to pound the walls with our cannons to get a breakthrough, giving them time to get reinforcements or, worse, time to land another army and march in behind us. Normally, I'd skip that and take the wall, but once our men assault the walls, we'll have to stop firing, and they'll be able to use their catapults to launch their gunpowder pots, which will make our losses very high, even if we take the port."

"And you have a solution," she said, as a statement and not a question.

"Yes, a new cannon design. Sophus will transcribe the specifics for you to take to Hortensius, but it's going to look very different from the cannon we have now. It's a short, stubby barrel mounted at a steep angle, almost like an overturned stovepipe, but very, very short. It should allow us to fire over the walls and onto their catapults, eliminating their gunpowder as a threat during an assault."

"I think I understand ... but can't our cannons already fire over walls? I've seen them fire up and come back down on the test range."

"Standard cannons must fire in a flat, or nearly flat, trajectory. While they can fire in an arc, it's a shallow one, unlikely to clear most defensive walls. In comparison, the mortar's steep angle sends shells far higher, in a plunging arc. They can reach targets behind cover or fortifications," Sophus replied.

"More importantly, when our men reach the base of the walls, our current cannons will have to stop firing to avoid hitting them. The mortars, on the other hand, can continue shooting overhead, with the shells falling on their side of the fortification. Even without the gunpowder, the mortars firing will make it harder for the enemy to attack while our legions are vulnerable scaling the walls."

"I see ... I think," she said hesitantly. "But you're already on the way to the port. Can we even make the mortars, let alone get them to you in time?"

"The production itself shouldn't be difficult. The metallurgy is the same as our current cannon, and we already have the gunpowder. Easier, almost, since it doesn't need to be rifled. It's just a matter of casting shorter, thicker barrels and rigging the mounts. Valdar should be in the Mediterranean by now and hopefully has a clear path around to where we'll be hitting the port. At least I hope so since I want him to blockade the port from the other side. With how slow we're moving, you should be able to get a few tubes to us, which is all we need. The design of the powder charges is even easier, as are the shells. We haven't really started on fuses yet, but we can light a timed fuse, which should be good enough."

"How slow are you going? Will you make it there in time? I thought the whole plan was to threaten their supply lines and force their army back to defend it as your armies converge on the port?"

"Slow. A lot slower, actually. While Sophus thinks the rains are only going to last for another week or so, the scouts have also indicated that, after abandoning Germania entirely, the remnants of the northern Carthaginian army may be to our south. If that's true, I'm going to have to deal with them before I put the port under siege. There are still almost ten thousand of them left, so I can't let them get behind us. How long it takes really depends on how long it takes to find them, but it's going to take some time."

"Well, at least that gives us some more time to produce and ship the mortars to you," she said before pausing a beat. "Actually, now that I think about it, there's something I could use your help with. Hortensius came to see me this morning. He's having an issue with the scaled-down steam engine."

"I was worried that project was going too smoothly. It's the only one I haven't gotten an update on."

"He says his main issue is the piston. Because of the smaller design and lower pressure, the piston arms are lighter. Either because there's less pressure and force on the arm or because the arm is lighter, he's getting a lag between rotations that starts to build waves of vibration, which quickly get out of control until the entire thing starts to shake apart. He's tried increasing the pressure, but that isn't solving the issue."

"*A reciprocating design could address that issue,*" Sophus said. "*Implementing a piston that strokes in both directions would provide more continuous power output. Additionally, there is a regulator that can handle additional system feedback, although I have no records of a regulator being used successfully on a train or other mobile platform. There is a potential for additional failures if a centrifugal governor is used on a non-stable platform.*"

"Let's skip that for now and just incorporate a reciprocating design. If it doesn't solve the problem, we can start experimenting with a regulator, but that will take time and a lot more back-and-forth discussion, so if we can take care of it with the simpler solution, that would be better."

"*Once the mortar and charge instructions are transcribed, I will dictate more detailed technical instructions that can be taken to Hortensius to change the pistons to a reciprocating design.*"

"Good. We've given him a lot of projects to work on, and I'm concerned he's stretching himself too thin," Lucilla said.

"I know. Unfortunately, many of these projects are critical, especially if we can't manage to push the Carthaginians off the continent quickly. Being able to rapidly move supplies and troops across land routes will help us counter their manpower advantage."

"I know. I'll get these to him as soon as I can transcribe them. Be careful out there, will you?"

"I will. I love you," Ky said.

"I love you, too."

Chapter 22

Hispania, North of the Pyrenees

The Carthaginian encampment blanketed the hill's base, tents and men sprawling as far as the eye could see. At the center of this makeshift city sat the abandoned Roman fort, looming overhead the Carthaginians from atop the small rise.

The men cheered him as he rode through the camp, which was still being assembled. Certainly, they were happy to not have the fight everyone had been expecting and seemed to attribute their painless taking of the fort to their general's brilliance. Tabnit was much less pleased. He'd wanted this fight, and finding the fort empty had been more than just a disappointment. It was a sign that his strategy wasn't working as he'd hoped.

Nabalasa and Hasdrubal, his two most senior officers, were both already at the fort's entrance, waiting for him. They picked up on Tabnit's expression where the soldiers had not, turning serious as they saw the expression on his face.

"Did we at least make contact?"

"No, general. They pulled back rapidly as well before our approach, their last men leaving the fort over an hour before any of our men got here."

"Were they running? Throwing supplies behind them to lighten their load?" Tabnit asked, his voice so flat that it had become threatening in its lack of emotion.

"No, your excellency."

"Then how did your men not catch them? An hour? That should not have been enough to stop you."

"The scouts attempted to, but their thunder weapons cut down any who got close enough. My men would have to run for hours to get in contact while they walked. They'd be too exhausted to fight once we did catch up," Hasdrubal said, defensively.

"Then have them run," Tabnit said, his voice hard. "Instead, you set up camp around a useless, empty building. We weren't trying to take their fort, we were trying to kill their soldiers before they could join up with any others. Instead, you let them escape and live to fight another day."

Hasdrubal didn't respond, knowing there was no good way to answer. Tabnit knew his anger was displaced somewhat. He'd seen the Romans' weapons in action. They didn't seem to take the effort that bows or swords did, which meant they were not going to lose effectiveness as they marched, while his men would indeed be too tired to fight well. None of that lessened his anger, however.

"It's worse than that," Nabalasa, whose command had been further behind and therefore not expected to keep the Romans in place. "All of their thunder weapons are gone, even the largest ones that must be very heavy, and all of their fire powder. What supplies were left behind are fairly mundane. None of their more advanced weapons or items are here."

"How?" Hasdrubal pleaded. "How could they have gotten them all out? The Romans use entire teams of horses to move them. You expect me to believe they saw our forces approaching, pulled all of their cannons off the walls, loaded all their fire powder on wagons, and got out while our men were still an hour away from their fort?"

"I'm just reporting what we found to the General," Nabalasa said with a slight smirk.

Tabnit, however, looked thoughtful.

"Unless they started loading everything before we saw them? The first fort we came across, allowing the Romans in this fort to flee. No doubt they gave warning, assuming we'd try to attack the next fort in line, and prepared for the retreat before we marched away from the previous fort. Which means they're already arriving at the next fort and pulling their thunder weapons off the walls, preparing to remove them. At this rate, we will capture and kill no Romans. Capture none of their weapons as required by the emperor. Nothing."

Tabnit looked around the fort again, his annoyance growing. After the victory destroying the Roman port, nothing else had gone their way. The Roman legion behind them had escaped. The Romans at the first fort had escaped. And now these.

"We need to quicken our pace. I want us hitting those forts before any more have a chance to escape. They're hauling weapons, supplies, in addition to moving their men. Get your men moving now, on the double march. We've already tarried too long, but if that fort is empty, don't stop. Continue through it to the next one. You can leave a detachment behind to guard the fort, but I don't want you to slow down."

Nabalasa frowned.

"But, sir, at that rate, we cannot scout ahead of us properly. The Romans could lay a trap or escape to the north, to join their armies there. We could lose them altogether. We'll be blind."

"That's a danger I'm willing to accept. I don't think they'll go north. They'll want to collect all of their garrisons first. Even if I'm wrong and they do turn north, they'll be forced to abandon those garrisons, and we can destroy them, but only if we move fast enough. Even if we don't, they'll at least have to abandon their weapons, which we can collect. Maybe learn the secrets of them. There are so many. But only if we move fast enough."

Waving his hand, as if swatting the suggestion away, Tabnit continued, "I've made my decision. The armies are to move as quickly as possible. Anything that slows them down; supplies, the sick or wounded, anything gets bypassed or left behind to catch up. The next fort is a day and a half's foot march, I want it down in a day. If that fort is empty, I want us at the next one in twenty hours. Do you understand?"

Nabalasa opened his mouth, and Tabnit could see another objection forming. He understood their hesitation. What Tabnit was asking for was nearly impossible, moving this many men that quickly, and there were risks. But he was sure this was the right call. He still had the numbers, but the battle for the port had narrowed that lead, and the Romans still had their weapons. He needed to be aggressive if they were going to keep the Romans from consolidating their forces. The vacant fort before him was proof enough of that.

"That's an order, Commander," he said again, fixing the man's gaze to make sure he understood.

"Yes, sir," Nabalasa said reluctantly, saluting. "We'll see to it at once."

Tabnit watched his commanders hurry off, already barking orders at soldiers to break down camp. Tabnit surveyed the crumbling ramparts one last time. This was it. The last one. There'd be no more retreats. No more empty forts.

He was going to catch the rest of this army, destroy it, and then take care of the one up north. Then he could turn his sights to their pitiful little island.

Devnum

"... are concerning. So far, it's limited to a handful of officers, and the questions have been strongly hedged, without him asking anything too pointed. But she's definitely having an influence on him."

"But is it beyond just him questioning and pushing for more responsibility, into him forwarding whatever her plans are? He's ambitious and egotistical, but I didn't get the impression he was this mercenary. His father made it clear he wanted Cormac to learn how to grow Ulaid as part of the empire, so why would Cormac try to tear it apart? Does Medb have that much influence over him?"

"He's also very naive, and Medb is very smart," Llassar said. "His questions so far have been more about opinions on strategy, asking what they need, building relationships, and similar topics. It suggests she hasn't pushed him to supporting her plans more fully, although I doubt she'd ever tell him what she's actually trying to do."

"Which is what? I get she's trying to destabilize my rule, but to what end? She can't believe she's going to rule the empire in my place?"

"No. If I had to guess, she wants her old throne back and thinks pulling the empire down from the inside will weaken Conchobar, maybe to the point of his kingdom falling apart."

"Cormac would never support that, I don't care how naive he is," Lucilla said.

"Like I said, I doubt she'll ever tell him what she's actually trying to do. She'll use him to wreak havoc until she doesn't need him anymore."

"So we bring him in, explain it."

"He's smitten, and he's young. I've sounded him out a few times, and he won't believe his bride would turn on him or use him. Not without irrefutable proof."

"Putting her in chains would be proof," Lucilla said.

"There's a danger he'll see it as proof of our plotting against him, trying to weaken the Ulaid or something along those lines. For him to be questioning soldiers the way he is, she's got him well under her thumb. Arresting her now might cause him to rebel more openly. Conchobar needs us, but he still doesn't trust us. It's why he sent Cormac here in the first place. If his son comes to him with a story of your trying to weaken the Ulaid's participation in the empire, he's going to believe it, at least without irrefutable evidence, which we don't have yet."

"We've witnessed her pushing Vesnius into rebellious actions," Lucilla said, annoyed. "Shouldn't that be enough?"

"I've talked to the legionnaire Claudius about what he saw after the episode with Medb. It's not as direct as that. She was questioning your rule, but she didn't tell the priest to do any specific action. The priest's prejudices wouldn't allow it, which is why she was more circumstantial, but it makes everything weaker. Cormac will hear what she said, and it won't be enough," he said and then paused, choosing his next words carefully. "You've only been empress for a short while, and the empire is less than a year old. It's still fragile. We're still generations away from people thinking of themselves as Britannians instead of Romans or Caledonians or Ulaid. You still have to be careful."

Lucilla looked out the small window, recently fitted with the new glass being made by one of the smaller factories, letting light into the room. It wasn't perfect. Not like the glass Ky had described. It wasn't fully translucent like the glass her people had been making, but there were still wavy lines in it, causing the light to spread out, almost move on its own. She hesitated because he was right. It was hard to face how easily her father's empire, her empire, could fall apart. That, in spite of everything she and Ky had done, they were still one rabble-rouser away from losing it all.

Sighing, she looked back at the Caledonian and said, "Alright, we proceed carefully until we have enough evidence. I want Cormac under close surveillance, though. Medb can cause trouble, but the Ulaid in the city look up to Cormac as their leader. If he starts taking active measures against us, things can escalate quickly. If it seems like he's going to do something drastic, or if he starts causing active problems, we step in."

"I'll speak to Ramirus and Faenius. Medb's not being as subtle as she thinks she is. We'll find something," he said, standing up, making a soft groan as he did.

"Actually, while you're here, I'd like to hear your opinion on something."

She and Llassar hadn't worked that closely together. At first, Ky had most of the interaction with the Caledonian, and then he'd been in Ériu, emptying it of Carthaginians. Since coming back, nearly all of his time had been spent with Cormac, instructing the young prince. But she was hesitant to reach out to Ky, distracting him in case he was doing something dangerous, and Ky trusted Llassar's opinion, so she would too.

"I'm happy to serve," he said.

For most of her subjects, courtiers, and leadership she normally dealt with, that would have just been the language of etiquette, said without being thought about. For Llassar, it was said almost with a wink, poking at the etiquette everyone else relied on.

"I received a messenger from Admiral Valdar this morning. He's requesting between two to four centuries to capture a port he's blockading. Specifically, a port right on the mouth of the

Middle Sea, separating it from Oceanus, that the Carthaginians were using to control access to it. He's currently blockading it, but he points out that the port will cause issues with any supplies moving in and out of the Middle Sea once he continues further into Carthaginian waters. Controlling it will also allow us to keep them from sending any other ships through the Middle Sea. They still have their ports on the western shores of Africa, but we'll have an easier time controlling those than all of the Middle Sea."

"I assume there's a reason not to send them," Llassar said, but from the way he said it, he probably already guessed what the problem was.

"Yes. We've been sending men as they've come out of training, and we have just over two centuries which had been intended for Port Invictus until it fell. We were waiting to hear from the Consul what his next move was now that the port has fallen, and where the new troops would best be served. I know he sent Bomilcar south with a legion to join with Auspex, and he himself is taking two legions toward the Carthaginian Middle Sea port, which means he'll have need for reinforcements soon. Because we've been sending men as soon as they're trained, it will be a month or two until we have enough for another century to send. All of which is to say, if we send these men to Valdar, the armies on the continent will see no reinforcement for months, and their losses already have them weakened as it is."

"I see," Llassar said, cupping his chin in one hand, stroking his salt and pepper beard. "The Carthaginians are getting reinforcements as well, right? One of our biggest issues has always been the disparity of manpower, and up until now, that gap has been made up by the Consul's technological advancements. With their inclusion of gunpowder, they've closed some of that gap. Unless the Consul has some new weapon he hasn't unveiled that's ready to go, the best option is to take away some of their advantages. Which means cutting their reinforcements. That gives Valdar's fleet the priority, especially when you're only talking about two hundred men. That won't turn the tide for the Consul, but if Valdar can use them to close their ports down, it will."

Lucilla was a little stunned. That was, quite possibly, the most she'd ever heard Llassar say at one time. He was also right.

"You're right," she said, echoing her own thoughts. "Your reasoning is sound. I think I knew that, and I was letting my own personal concerns get in the way. I'll dispatch the soldiers today. I appreciate your counsel."

"I'm happy to serve," he said, giving a slight bow.

Again, she wasn't sure if he was being sarcastic or not, his flat measured tone hard to read.

"Just make sure Cormac or Medb don't give us any surprises."

"I'll take care of it," he said, bowing again.

Now she just had to break the news to Ky.

Carthage

The Emperor sat on his throne, clad in imperial purple and gold, not bothering to hide the annoyance on his face. All day, a stream of officials and ministers had come before him with bad news. Ports blockaded, ships sunk, their trade at a standstill, causing shortages in Carthage for the first time in his reign. Not for him, of course, but the already meager living the average person subsisted on had begun to drop to levels that lowered their productivity. Which meant further shortages. Shortages they could not afford, not in the middle of a war.

"Rise, Tariq, and report," he commanded to the latest arrival.

The governor of Iudæa stood, keeping his gaze lowered respectfully. "Your Majesty, the rebellion in my province has been suppressed, the rebel leaders executed as you commanded. The monotheists have mostly scattered, especially after we burned the last of the temples we allowed them."

"I'm pleased to hear that, but if you've managed to finally perform your duties, then why have you traveled all this way?" the Emperor demanded.

"We are short on soldiers, exalted one," Tariq said nervously. "With so many men requested to reinforce the armies on the continent, there are not enough men to properly garrison the province. We're already seeing resistance from groups in the..."

Imilcar raised a hand, cutting the governor's words off. "Do not think to make your failures my concern. You were charged with governing, Tariq, stamping out all resistance to my rule, and you have sufficient resources to do so. If you cannot perform this task with the forces allotted to you, I shall find a governor who can."

The governor's expression shifted, and for a moment it seemed like he might continue to argue. An unheard-of response that would almost certainly get him executed.

He managed to regain control of himself, at least, and instead said, "It shall be done, Your Majesty."

"See that it is," rumbled the Emperor. "You are dismissed."

Tariq bowed and hurried from the throne room as Imilcar watched, his irritation growing. Another disappointment among many. He was surrounded by incompetence and ineptitude, and it was causing his empire to falter. The next fool that came before him was going to feel his disappointment, that Imilcar was certain of.

The doors opened again, admitting the next petitioner, who gave the Emperor pause. Instead of the nobleman or court official normally admitted, it was a young messenger, really just a boy, walking toward the dais nervously. Imilcar was intrigued by the novelty of it, if nothing else. Messengers were normally stopped by a courtier, who'd take the message and relay it.

The boy approached, eyes downcast, and fell to one knee.

"Rise," Imilcar commanded, sitting forward in his seat.

The boy stood, still not meeting the Emperor's gaze, and said, "I bring a message from General Tabnit in Hispania, Your Majesty."

His voice quaked as he held up a scroll. An attendant moved to take the scroll from the boy, but Imilcar waved him away.

"Tell me what it says," he commanded.

The boy gulped visibly and opened the scroll, breaking the seal. His voice was shaky when he started, "General Tabnit reports a great victory against the Romans in Hispania, Your Majesty. He assaulted the port the Romans built on the coast, where he says the trenches and gunpowder did exactly as the advisors you sent said they would. He was able to breach the walls of the port and kill the defenders with acceptable losses. The port was destroyed by the Romans to prevent the capture of their weapons, but everyone inside was killed. The survivors were forced to retreat north of the mountains, and his army is in pursuit."

The boy lowered his eyes again quickly, feeling the intensity of the Emperor's attention upon him. The way the boy spoke, Imilcar had the impression it wasn't a recitation of the message he'd been sent with.

"You were there with the army, weren't you, boy?" the Emperor asked, leaning further forward.

"Y...Yes, Your Majesty," the boy stammered. "I was assigned to the general as a runner and messenger because I can read."

"And did you see this victory?"

"Yes, Your Majesty."

"Describe it to me."

The boy swallowed again, looking side to side as if he wanted an escape. It was understandable. The entire room was designed to make generals and nobles nervous, aware of their insufficiency. It would undoubtedly be worse for such a young man.

"The catapults... they launched the clay jars, which burst into fire as they hit the wall. One of them hit near the top, near one of the Roman Thunder weapons, and a massive fire erupted, tearing a hole in the wall. The general, he ordered that more catapults target that area. I... I took that message to one of the crews. With every hit, the hole widened until an entire section of the wall collapsed. Our army charged in, and then it was like the world itself shook. A massive eruption of fire went high into the sky. It was so loud, my ears hurt. It was like the underworld cracked open and reached up. I think we lost many men, the ones closest to the walls, but I don't know. I was knocked down by it. When I got up, smoke was rising into the sky, and our men were shouting and cheering."

"Interesting," he said. "Very interesting. You can go. Return to the army with my congratulations to the general."

The boy scrambled backward, clearly relieved that he'd been dismissed. The Emperor put him out of his mind and turned to one of the aides standing silently along the far wall.

"Send ships and a messenger at once to our contact in the East," he barked. "He's to open talks with the Eastern Emperor to obtain more gunpowder and whatever other weapons the Far Eastern Kingdom possesses, along with a request for any additional experts they are willing to send to show us the best way to use these weapons. He's to move quickly, with all haste, and is authorized to make any concession short of giving away provinces."

The aide bowed. "It will be done, Exalted One."

As the aide hurried from the room, Imilcar stroked his beard thoughtfully, the folds of his neck moving with each caress. A victory, at least. With more weapons, he could crush the Romans for good and ensure no one else dares challenge his power again. He needed more. He'd strip the treasury bare if it meant getting the tools they needed.

The Emperor clapped twice, the signal for the next petitioner seeking an audience. The doors swung wide once more, admitting the next person who'd come to beg for some scrap or forgiveness. Imilcar barely heard them. In his head, he was dreaming of their next victory.

Chapter 23

Gaul, North of the Pyrenees

An argument was in full swing as Bomilcar ducked through the entrance to the command tent, which came to an abrupt halt just as the general made his sudden appearance. Aelius, Gordianus, and several of their tribunes were gathered around a rough map of the area and had clearly been in a heated discussion about what to do next. Now, all five men were staring at him, shocked.

It was a testament to how chaotic things must have been along this line that he and a full legion had managed to come in from the north and outpace any warning the legates might have had, telling them reinforcements had arrived.

"Gentlemen," Bomilcar said in his deep baritone.

"General," Aelius said. "Thank the gods you're here. Please tell me the Consul sent you with reinforcements."

"He did," Bomilcar said, coming all the way inside the tent, making room for Auspex to enter. "We brought a legion with us, which should bring us up to more than ten thousand men. Not counting the thousands still stationed in the forts."

"It does. With that, we should be able to finally stop retreating and hold the line against these bastards," Gordianus said. "Before the port fell, Legate Velius ordered us to avoid contact and continue falling back until we received orders from the Consul. I was starting to worry those orders wouldn't arrive before we got pushed back to the last fort in the line."

"Tell me what's been happening. We heard of the loss of Port Invictus, but haven't received much information since then."

"The situation has been dire," Aelius said, looking much older than he really was. "Ever since we lost Port Invictus, it feels like we've just been running with our tails between our legs, trying to stay ahead of them. Even with the losses they sustained at the port, they still have massive numbers over us.

"Worse, we haven't been able to use any of our fortifications. We've had to abandon fort after fort just to avoid being surrounded and wiped out. Seeing what they did to Port Invictus, we dare not let them surround us. We can't escape by sea like we did there, and with their trenches and gunpowder, it would only be a matter of time before they'd destroy us. This is the fifth fort we've pulled back to since the escape from the port, and we'll have to leave by daybreak if we want to avoid them. Recently they increased their pace considerably, giving us barely any time to rest the men."

"Which is why we're going to be changing tactics. We aren't going to hold this line at all. In fact, we're going to be pulling off the line entirely. We'll leave only a single century at this fort and those remaining to the north, taking all of the gunpowder and cannons you've been moving from the previously lost forts with us. There, we will wait for the rest of your men to join us."

"The rest of our men?" Aelius asked, confused. "This is all of the men we have available."

"No, it's not. You also have the men in the forts. You're to send a message along the line ordering them to retain one century at their fort and send the rest to meet us, pulling the bulk of their gunpowder and cannons with them. The men left in the forts will continue doing as you've been doing, pulling back to avoid contact, all the way down the line of forts. That includes the century we're leaving here. Their job is to keep the Carthaginians fixated on these forts by making it look as if we're still all here and retreating. They're to leave behind signs of a retreating larger force and pull large wagons weighted with rocks to simulate the evacuation of the guns. Hopefully, the Carthaginians take the bait and continue chasing them, for a little while longer, giving us time to consolidate."

"What are we doing once we do?" Aelius asked.

"Once the forces from the forts arrive, we're going to swing around and attack the Carthaginian forces left at Port Invictus," he said, pointing at the fallen port on the map.

"Why?" Aelius asked, a little horrified. "Why bother retaking the destroyed port? Even if we do recapture it, it will take time to rebuild and even if we do, the Carthaginians can just destroy it again. They've shown us what they can do when we allow ourselves to be backed into a corner."

"We aren't going to hold the port," Bomilcar clarified. "We're removing any enemy forces behind us and making ourselves a threat to the Carthaginians from the west. Once we defeat the enemy at the port, we'll push east again, hopefully forcing the Carthaginians to turn around and come for us."

Moving his finger from the port up to Germania, Bomilcar added, "The Consul is bringing an army down from the north directly toward the Carthaginian port on the Middle Sea. Either the Carthaginians end up between us, or they retreat to the port and we and the Consul's forces will converge, confining them in their port. If the fleet does its job, we'll have them bottled up, where we can destroy them."

"Either way, mobile or with the Carthaginians trapped, it deprives them of their new tactics and weapons," Bomilcar concluded, looking at the men in the tent. "Does anyone have any other questions?"

Aelius didn't seem convinced, but he didn't ask any more questions, nor did Gordianus or any of the other officers.

"Good, then let's get moving. As you pointed out, we don't have a lot of time until the Carthaginians close on this fort, and we need to be well out of the way before they get here. I want the new orders relayed to the remaining forts immediately with instructions for the bulk of their forces to withdraw and join us at the rendezvous point. Make sure the men remaining behind understand their orders. They must ensure the Carthaginians believe we are still retreating down the line of forts. I do not want the enemy to know we've retreated north until it's too late."

"We'll take care of it, General," Gordianus said, saluting.

"Good. They must understand that they need to keep moving, I don't want any of the men we're leaving behind to try and do anything foolish. No heroic last stands. The Consul will be here soon, and they're to join his army until we can collect them."

Gordianus nodded and left the tent, following the rest of the men. They were good leaders and had shown they were capable, carrying on after the death of their commander. Bomilcar had liked Velius, even though it took time for the legate to warm up to him. He and Aelius didn't know each other well, but they didn't have time to go through the same growing pains he and Velius had gone through.

Time was the one thing he didn't have, not anymore. They'd have to operate as a team, without second-guessing, if they were going to get the Carthaginians to fall into the trap. And they had to do it *now!*

Outside Devnum

Cormac made his way through the Roman legion camp, the sounds of men training all around him. The clash of wooden training swords and the grunts of men learning to kill other men. Cormac ignored them, looking down the row of identical tents, searching for his friend Tullius.

At Medb's urging, Cormac had been making friends with the new legionaries training just outside of town. It had taken some time. Most of the men he'd approached had been standoffish, but others had been receptive, and Tullius had been the most interested. He was also popular with the rest of the men. Cormac reasoned that if he could cultivate Tullius, he could use the soldier to reach out to his comrades.

It hadn't been easy, though. Cormac hadn't grown up needing to be subtle or circumspect. He wasn't a spy or a diplomat. He was a warrior, born to a family of warriors. This was important, though. Medb had convinced him that change was needed. His father had tied their kingdom's future to that of the Empire, and Lucilla and her foreign husband threatened that future.

Spotting Tullius concluding a sparring match, Cormac hailed him cheerfully. The soldier turned, surprise flashing across his sweat-slicked features before it shifted into an odd expression. He glanced around furtively before walking over to join Cormac.

"My Lord," he said with a stiff bow. "I did not expect to see you again so soon."

Cormac raised an eyebrow at the man's demeanor, so unlike their past cordial encounters. Tullius's eyes shifted continuously, and he stood with rigid formality.

"I thought we were friends," Cormac chided lightly. "Why so formal?"

He gave the man what Cormac felt was a disarming smile, but Tullius remained withdrawn. Cormac frowned. Something was very wrong. Before he could inquire, Tullius stepped closer, dropping his voice.

"Forgive me, My Lord, but I ... I don't want to have any more of our conversations."

"What's wrong, Tullius?" Cormac asked, his brow furrowing. "Has something happened?"

The soldier shifted his weight and glanced around again. "I shouldn't be speaking to you."

"Come now, Tullius. There's no harm in two friends talking."

Tullius hesitated, clearly conflicted, before saying at a near whisper, "Please, you must go. There are ... instructions to my cohort. We've been ordered to report on any soldiers who are seen conspiring with you."

"What? Ordered by whom?"

"I don't know. There have been Praetorians talking to all of the legionaries. Asking if we've spoken with you and about the nature of our conversations."

That was a problem. Cormac hadn't said anything against his father or the Empire, but if taken out of context, it could sound insurrectionary. Lucilla was a weak ruler and could take any questioning of her ability or fitness as treason. Aside from that, if Tullius wasn't willing to talk to him anymore, it was going to completely derail his plans.

"You haven't done anything wrong," Cormac said. "Questioning the way the war is being fought isn't treasonous. As a soldier, it's what you should be doing. All you want is for the Empire to thrive, for us to win the war."

"It goes beyond that, Prince, and you know it. We've ... I've said things I shouldn't have. Worse, I think some of my friends have seen us talking. I'm certain they've reported it to the Praetorians, who're going to be looking at me now."

"You don't have anything to worry about. You haven't said anything treasonous or even concerning, but I understand this undue suspicion worries you. We can still be friends though, right? You and I?"

Tullius didn't respond, just shuffling his feet, trying to avoid eye contact.

Cormac sighed. "Can you at least tell me why you're supposed to report any interactions with me? I'm still a noble, and I think I deserve to know if I'm under suspicion."

"I don't know, My Lord. I only know we've been ordered to report any communications with you," he said before raising his voice to a normal speaking volume. "I'm sorry, but my loyalty is to the Empire."

With an abrupt nod, Tullius hurried away, leaving Cormac standing there stunned. Why were the Praetorians monitoring him so closely? That wasn't just routine. If he was a soldier or a politician, sure, but he was the son of a king, heir to one-third of the Empire. They wouldn't just start investigating him unless they thought there was something to find. Yes, he'd been asking questions, expressing doubt about Lucilla and her consort, but that wasn't enough to have men spying on him. Asking questions of anyone who spoke to him.

It had to be Llassar. The old fool had been giving him more lectures of late, 'instructing' him on the right way to do things. He'd wondered why the incessant lectures lately, but this could explain it. The Caledonian had apparently decided he was a traitor and had talked his friend, the Empress, into spying on him.

This was the man his father had entrusted him to. The man he was told to learn from. A snake, who slithered behind his back, poisoning those who might work with him.

He had to be careful. He was in enemy territory, and Llassar had the ear of the Empress and her people. His father was a long way away and had given Llassar some semblance of authority over him. Maybe Medb would have thoughts about this situation. She was clever and could see through to the heart of things.

Or maybe not. She'd pushed him to stand up for himself, and he valued her opinion of him. He didn't want her to start thinking he wasn't capable of handling things himself.

He needed to find out what Llassar was up to and why the old man was watching him.

Outside Factorium

Empress Lucilla stepped out of her carriage, accompanied by her entourage of personal guards and aides that seemed to be growing larger every time she left Devnum. In the distance, Lucilla could see the soaring smokestacks and blocky brick buildings that formed the heart of the Empire's industrial complex.

A sizable crowd had gathered, surrounding the large swath of grassland just outside the city, held back by guards, forming a very wide ring. Excited murmurs rippled through the onlookers, some looking in her direction but others observing the workers swarming across the open center area.

At its heart stood Hortensius and Sorantius, deep in discussion as they fussed over the fantastic contraption laid out on the grass. Mounds of fabric stretched out from what looked like a basket made of reeds or sticks; she wasn't sure which. The balloon's pear-shaped linen envelope had been dyed a vibrant imperial purple, which she hadn't expected. The last time she saw it, it was a dull gray, which she had assumed it would still be.

Hortensius looked up as Lucilla approached, his kindly face crinkling into a broad grin beneath his bushy gray beard.

"Your Majesty, welcome!" he exclaimed. "We are honored by your presence."

Lucilla smiled warmly at her friend.

"The honor is mine, Hortensius," she replied. "Ever since I read about this in Ky's notes, I've been excited to see it in use. I just look forward to the day when I can take a ride up in your device and see the sky as the birds do."

"I understand completely. Of course, we have to make sure it's safe before we send a person up in it. For now, we are putting in stones that should approximate the weight of two grown men."

"Very wise," she said, reaching out to squeeze the older man's calloused hand warmly.

Of course, she didn't think he would allow her to take one of the first voyages, not with something this unknown. She did want to go, however. Ky had told her stories of flying through the clouds and stars. While she could never see the amazing sights he had, she could at least experience some of the thrill with this vehicle.

Hortensius gestured eagerly to the balloon. "As soon as Sorantius is finished with the ballast adjustments, we will be ready for launch. With your permission, of course, Your Majesty."

Lucilla granted it with an approving nod. "Of course. This is your show, old friend. I'm simply a spectator. Don't let me delay you."

"I think that's it," Sorantius called out, beckoning Hortensius over.

With one more glance at Lucilla, the manufacturer hurried to join him. The two men worked swiftly. Sorantius lit the small fire contained in the metal burner affixed below the balloon, while Hortensius untied the ropes securing the large linen envelope to the stakes driven into the grass. As the flames roared to life, heat billowed into the purple-dyed envelope, causing it to fill and expand before their eyes, slowly lifting off the ground as if plucked from the ground by the invisible hands of the gods.

"That's it, nice and steady now," Hortensius said, anticipation in his voice.

Around them, the gathered crowd seemed to hold its collective breath, pressed forward but held back by the wall of guards. Lucilla's excitement matched that of the two men and she desired to join them. Only her regal bearing and knowledge that others were watching kept her in place, her face passive instead of filled with awe.

Slowly, steadily, the balloon rose, lifting skyward as the hot air built up inside it. The ropes drew taut, then lifted off the ground. A cheer went up from the onlookers, applause and excited shouts filled the air. Lucilla beamed, unable to continue hiding the pride and wonder welling up inside her.

The balloon ascended, floating nearly at head height, several dozen hand spans off the ground, still secured to the ground by ropes.

"It works!" Sorantius whooped, throwing his fists in the air triumphantly in the biggest show of emotion she'd ever seen from him.

"Patience," Hortensius cautioned, though he couldn't hide the excitement in his eyes. "We've still got a ways to go before we can call this a success. More tests to run."

Lucilla opened her mouth to congratulate them when a chorus of alarmed shouts rose from the crowd. Her head snapped around just in time to see the wicker basket erupt into flames, fire clawing ravenously up the side.

"No!" Hortensius cried.

Before their horrified eyes, the fire spread with terrifying speed, engulfing the basket and ropes in a matter of seconds. The balloon overhead jerked violently as the basket came apart, no longer able to hold the burner's weight. Gaping holes tore through the fabric, flames shooting through the punctures.

Hortensius and Sorantius shouted, scrambling for buckets of water kept on hand should a fire break out, waving over assistants and even onlookers to help. It was too late. With a groan of rending fabric, the balloon plummeted earthward, trailing smoke and flickering scraps of burning cloth. The envelope hit the ground with a heavy whump, its fire-blackened scraps scattered across the grass.

Lucilla tried to rush forward, only to be stopped by her guards, who grabbed her by the arms, holding her back. She could only stand helplessly and watch as a soot-streaked Hortensius desperately splashed water on the smoldering wreckage. The green field was quickly turning muddy as more and more water was applied, although the fire had been all but quenched at this point.

The danger passed, and she finally managed to free herself and rush over to her friend, who stood helplessly among the wreckage.

"Are you all right?" she asked, putting a hand on his shoulder.

"I don't know," he said, his voice hollow with shock and dismay. "I just don't understand how it could have failed so badly."

She watched as he moved slowly among the charred remains of the balloon, sifting through the debris with an expression of profound sadness. Here and there, he paused, lifting a fragment to examine it more closely before letting it fall from his soot-stained fingers. After several long minutes, he bent down and retrieved a twisted lump of metal and melted wicker; all that remained of the burner and its basket mounting.

"The basket and burner shouldn't have ignited like that," he murmured. "The flames were not even touching them directly ..."

He trailed off, brows furrowing pensively. At last, the old man looked up, his trademark curiosity returning.

"The casing overheated," he said, looking over the thin, twisted metal. "With the gauge, I didn't think it would, I thought that the heat would dissipate before it got that hot. Maybe it was the flume, compressing and directing the heat. The restricted airflow might have allowed it to heat more. I don't know. Either way, clearly the metal was too hot to hold anything flammable, which is a problem."

"Can it be prevented from recurring?" Lucilla asked gently.

Before either Hortensius or Sorantius could answer, Sophus's voice echoed in her ear. Or maybe it was as they answered. It was hard to concentrate on multiple voices and streams of conversation as Sophus spoke, its voice and the words of the people around her overlapping and clashing.

"Empress, I may have a solution," Sophus said calmly, its voice almost causing her to jump. *"Creating a porcelain enamel to coat the steel casing may provide sufficient insulation. The casing would still be dangerously hot, but should no longer ignite the balloon's components."*

Lucilla nodded absently, waiting while Hortensius finished talking about restarting the project.

"What would we need for that?" she said, hoping Sophus picked up that the question was directed more towards it than the inventor.

"The enamel and porcelain require kaolinite and other clays, along with quartz, feldspar, and borax," the AI rattled off, its voice clashing with Hortensius who was answering the same question, although as it related to the burner. *"The materials are abundant and should be available on the islands controlled by the Empire but require processing to produce both porcelain and enamel. I can provide specifications."*

"I believe I have a solution to your problem," she said, cutting Hortensius off mid-sentence.

"Really?" he stopped, his eyes narrowing.

After a moment, he gave a small nod of understanding. He had probably reviewed their conversation and realized that she hadn't been listening to him at all. He'd already made comments that he knew she was getting these plans from Ky in a way he couldn't understand, so this would just be another piece added to that puzzle.

Sorantius, who hadn't seemed to catch on, was more surprised, giving her and then Hortensius a curious glance.

"What did you have in mind, Your Majesty?" Sorantius asked.

"I remember seeing something in Ky's notes called porcelain enamel. I have to double-check, but I believe it can coat the steel casing and prevent it from igniting the balloon's components. It will still get very hot, but it won't be enough to catch the basket or ropes on fire."

"That sounds promising," Hortensius said, overriding Sorantius, who seemed inclined to ask more questions about how she knew about it. "As disheartening as this failure is, I'm always pleased to take the opportunity to learn something new."

Lucilla squeezed his shoulder reassuringly. "I have every faith in both of you. Consider this but a temporary setback on the path to success."

The old inventor patted her hand gratefully before turning to examine the wreckage with renewed interest. Sorantius joined him, and the two were soon muttering theories and making plans.

Chapter 24

Southern Germania

Ky halted his army, scanning the valley below through the drone flying high above the heavily wooded area. Using the naked eye, looking down the slope, the scene was serene and peaceful, with the early morning fog, not yet burned off by the morning sun, still covering the canopy.

The drone's thermal sensors told a different story. Nearly ten thousand men hid beneath those trees, the remnants of the northern Carthaginian army, on the run after their loss on the Rhine. His scouts had been hunting them for weeks. From local villagers and signs left by their passing, they knew the men were in the area, but even this large of a group could disappear into the thick forests of Southern Germania.

The legates had urged him to ignore these men, who were clearly disorganized, and focus on reaching the Middle Sea to snap the trap he and Bomilcar had arranged for the much larger and still very dangerous Carthaginian army that had killed Velius. Ky had overruled them. If it had been a few hundred men, then he would have bypassed them, but this many, even disorganized, could be a danger if allowed to remain at their rear. He didn't want this many soldiers available to reinforce the Carthaginians or, worse, assault him from the rear when they finally did close the trap. Besides, his supply lines to northern Germania were long and vulnerable, and these men were as likely to turn brigand as they were to rejoin the war. Either way, it made them a threat.

The enemy, for their part, seemed completely unaware that just over the western ridge of the valley there were ten thousand Britannian legionaries waiting to charge into their camp. As Ky watched, the Carthaginians began stirring, some preparing morning meals, with the rest just meandering around, all of them more or less rudderless. The way they acted it seemed unlikely any higher-level officers had survived the battle, or at least made it with the men this far. This was more of an armed mob than the remnants of an army.

"The scouts' accounts were accurate. There are about ten thousand of them down there. They have no idea we're here," Ky said to the two legates next to him. "From what I can see, they about match our strength, and the tree cover down there is thick enough to really shorten our range with our rifles, so surprise is the key. Once we get over the ridge, I want mounted units up front. They're to ride through, causing as much havoc as they can, without getting bogged down. They are to disengage and loop around to cover our flanks and be prepared to mop up after us. They should keep the Carthaginians from getting organized until the legionaries can engage. I'll go in with the second legion, hitting them straight on. Vibius, I want you to break the fourth legion in half and swing around, hitting them from the north and south. Bayonets and swords for this, gentlemen. They're already demoralized, and the sudden attack should keep them from massing an organized resistance, but all the same, don't let your men run wild. Hold your lines. Clear?"

"Clear," both legates said.

This was one of the things they'd practiced over the winter, once Ky saw how much thicker the tree cover was during this time as compared to his own. It would be easy for units to become intermixed and lose all unit cohesion, which could turn even something as much in their favor as this situation was against them.

"On my signal, send in your cavalry and follow up with your men at the double step. We've got to get there fast. Let's get it done."

Again, the men saluted as one and headed to their commands to begin handing out orders. Ky wasn't concerned. They might be the two newest legates in the legions, but they were both good men and knew their jobs.

Ky waited while the cavalry and legions moved into position. Although it was impossible to keep this many men silent, the soldiers understood how close the enemy was and did an excellent job keeping the noise to a minimum. Orders were relayed instead of shouted, and the normal joking and conversation that usually happened on the march was gone. They were all focused, mentally preparing for the fight that was about to happen.

Once everyone was ready, he signaled the trumpeter, who blew the charge. The Carthaginians began looking around, first drawn by the sound of the trumpet, but truly alarmed by what sounded like rumbling thunder, even though the sky was cloudless and blue. Men slowly reached for weapons, but without officers to guide them, didn't react beyond that until the Britannian cavalry burst from the tree line, tearing through the Carthaginian camp at full gallop. Although Ky could barely see them through the trees around him, he could hear the screams and shouts echoing up from below as the cavalry slashed its way through the surprised enemy.

Through the drone's camera, Ky watched as the cavalry wreaked havoc on the camp. Men scrambled in every direction, many still half asleep and struggling to grab weapons and armor. Horses bolted in terror; supplies were trampled underfoot as the cavalry careened wildly through the camp.

Before their ride was finished and they looped back to take their places on the flanks, his infantry legions erupted from the tree line as well, smashing into men still trying to grapple with the carnage they were witnessing. The legionaries slammed into the disorganized Carthaginian mob, the clashing swords and the screams of the wounded carrying across the valley. Caught completely off-guard, the Carthaginians had no time to mount any real defense or strategy. It was pure bloody chaos down there.

"Push through them!" Ky shouted, urging his men on. "Do not let them break your lines!"

He wanted to keep the initiative and not allow the Carthaginians any time to get organized. The legionaries pressed the attack relentlessly, herding the panicked enemy like sheep. Bodies began piling up on the valley floor as the Romans slashed and hacked their way through the camp.

They weren't, however, unopposed. Despite the element of surprise, the Carthaginians were beginning to rally themselves, pushing back against the relentless Roman attack. There were simply too many of them for Ky's forces to wipe them out quickly, especially since his men couldn't use rifle and cannon fire in the thick forest. Although the occasional rifle sounded, they were mostly limited to sword and bayonet, which allowed the Carthaginians time to regroup.

The chaos of close-quarter combat in the wooded terrain made communication difficult. He relayed orders, but the men did not always respond as directly as usual, unable to see the message flags or hear the trumpet calls.

Small pockets of resistance were coalescing into larger groups as a man here or there barked orders or cajoled his fellow soldiers, rallying them from the near flight they'd been in. This was what Ky had been concerned about. The terrain slowed them too much, and there were enough of the enemy that it wasn't possible to send the entire force into flight as soon as they made contact. The element of surprise was spent. Now it was a pitched battle. The only thing still going his way was that what once was two relatively equal forces had become weighted heavily in the Britannian favor as hundreds upon hundreds of Carthaginians had died in the first minutes of the attack.

Ky weighed his options, watching intently as the battle lines solidified. The Carthaginians were rallying faster than anticipated, digging in and pushing back despite horrific losses. He needed these men taken off the board, unavailable to the enemy when he assaulted their port, but he couldn't afford to take a large number of casualties. With only two legions, he'd need every man he could get when the final battle came.

"Signal the cavalry to rally on the left flank," Ky said, turning his horse toward that direction.

It took almost ten minutes to get the cavalry in place. Ten minutes of men screaming and dying. He watched through the drone as his men fought and legionaries died, fighting the urge to scream at his mounted troops to move faster. The terrain was hard on the horses, and he knew it would take precious time to get into position. Vibius and Marcus were doing their best, and they were still pushing the Carthaginians back. The outcome of the battle wasn't in doubt; the enemy had lost too many men in that initial confrontation and were already demoralized. The only question that remained was how many men Ky would lose, and he wanted to keep that number as low as possible.

Finally, the cavalry was in position.

"For Britannia," Ky shouted, sword held high, as he spurred his horse forward, leading the rallying cavalry headlong toward the Carthaginian lines.

Trumpets sounded and hooves thundered over the forest floor, kicking up mud and debris as the cavalry built momentum for a decisive strike. Ky and the cavalry plunged through the dense trees, branches whipping against armor and tearing at exposed skin. Still, they pressed on relentlessly through the difficult terrain. Ky leaned forward in his saddle, eyes fixed on the point where the Carthaginian flank lay exposed amidst the chaotic melee.

Breaking through the tree line, the cavalry slammed into the Carthaginian flank with earth-shaking force, ripping through their ranks. Horses trampled men, screams mixing with the thunder of their hooves. Swords flashed in ruthless arcs, cutting down anyone within reach. Men were flung aside by the mass of horse-flesh plowing through their defenses. The Carthaginian lines, already struggling under the pressure from the legionaries and the surprise of the early morning assault, disintegrated under the new threat.

Seeing the charge's success, the Roman infantry howled with bloodlust and surged forward with renewed vigor. Any semblance of Carthaginian resistance evaporated as total panic took over. Surrounded on all sides, men threw down their weapons and turned to run.

The ambush had turned completely in the Romans' favor, devolving into utter carnage and butchery. The Carthaginians were lambs to the slaughter.

"Chase them down," he ordered the mounted men around him. "We're not taking prisoners today."

The men obeyed, turning their horses and riding off to chase down the men fleeing in all directions. He disliked such wholesale butchery, seeing it as a waste of life, especially since many of these men had probably been conscripted into service from other conquered regions and didn't have any more love for the Carthaginians than he had. But with limited time and resources, he had no choice. The remaining Carthaginians had to be eliminated as an effective fighting force, and he couldn't spare the men to escort a large number of prisoners west. War was often savage by necessity.

As the last of the enemy were hunted down and slain, Ky's weary legions began gathering their own wounded and dead. Despite achieving a decisive victory, it had not come without cost.

Ky rode through the carnage, finally finding his two legates as they attempted to regain some sense of order out of the chaos.

"Tend to our wounded and recover our dead," Ky ordered solemnly. "I want the army ready to march by mid-day. We still have a war to win."The men saluted and dispersed to follow his instructions. Ky watched the camp burn, smoke mingling with the cries of dying men. With the enemy force neutralized, it was time to press on. A harder fight still awaited them.

Devnum

Llassar sat at the heavy oak table in his chambers, looking over the latest messages from home. Cormac was down with the legions today, which gave Llassar opportunities to catch up on his other responsibilities. While he had to ride herd on the young man when he was forced to listen to the senate debate this or that topic, or when he was with tutors, Cormac needed no urging when it came to his trips to the legions.

Of course, Llassar's giving the young man free rein to visit the legion training camps gave Cormac the opportunity to start questioning legionaries, asking about their loyalty. It was what it was. Llassar's duty to ensure he didn't cause any problems didn't mean his original task stopped. He couldn't follow the prince everywhere. Eventually, Cormac would have to be able to stand on his own, without Llassar looking over his shoulder. Faenius's men were watching him now, and it was unlikely the prince would get much further with his questioning of the legionaries.

For now, Llassar had to update Talogren on events in the capital. As Cormac was his father's direct voice to the Empire, Llassar was Talogren's. While the chieftain had emissaries and senators here who would report to him, they all had their own agendas. Llassar and Talogren went back a long way, and Talogren trusted him to report on things accurately. Today, it was sharing the news that one of their senators was suspected of accepting payments from a Roman businessman to vote against Caledonia's best interests concerning a section of the border still under dispute. This was a case of pure greed and not the treason that Cormac was flirting with, but it still needed to be dealt with.

As of now, Llassar didn't have proof, but he would soon. The man was a fool, speaking in front of servants as if they had no ears. The man had been smart enough to bring Caledonian servants with him to Devnum, which might protect him from Roman spying, but would not put them out of Llassar's grasp. Especially considering how poorly he treated them. It wouldn't be long before Llassar had the proof he needed, at which point he'd let Talogren deal with the man.

His pen stopped halfway through its progress along the page when his heavy door burst open violently, banging against the stone wall. Although he felt safe here in the palace, his hand flew to the sword lying across the table, years of habit triggering his fight or flight response. He relaxed when he saw it was only Cormac.

The Ulaid prince was worked up, storming into the room, his face flushed and eyes blazing. Cormac slammed his fists down on the table, leaning over Llassar menacingly.

"Explain yourself!" he demanded, so angry that spit flew from his mouth.

Llassar was nearly his exact opposite, remaining so calm an unknowing observer might think he was simple and didn't understand the prince's inquiry.

"Explain what, precisely?" he asked mildly.

Cormac's face turned an even deeper shade of crimson. "Don't play coy with me, Old Man! I know you've had the Praetorians investigating me, telling the legionaries they have to report any conversation I have with them. I am a prince. You have no right."

Llassar regarded Cormac calmly, unfazed by the young prince's outburst.

"You were put in my care by your father, who asked me to watch you and guide your progress. I have every right. I'll admit that I have had concerns due to your interactions with the troops," he said in an even tone.

"So you don't trust me then!" he accused angrily. "You've been having me followed and spied upon like some common criminal!"

"How is your wife?" Llassar asked, again causing Cormac's anger to pause as the conversation turned to the unexpected topic.

"What?"

"Your wife? You two spend a lot of time together. Has she shown interest in your standing? Maybe suggesting the war would be going better if you were in charge?"

"What ... I ... No," Cormac stammered.

"She has, hasn't she? Maybe she's suggested you weren't being treated fairly? Was it her idea that you start talking to the soldiers, building connections, or was that your own idea in response to her pushes?"

"I'm offended by your insinuations. She is my wife, but I am my father's representative, and nothing I've done goes against my duties to my people and the Empire. Everything I've said to the soldiers is to ensure our men are as ready for war as possible."

Llassar answered by changing the subject once again, "Did you know that Medb has been going out on her own to speak with people?"

"What? No ... I'm sure she's just keeping busy. She's very concerned with her duties and tries to stay in touch with the common man."

"By speaking to Vesnius, the Flamen Dialis, who's been going around town preaching about the evil of foreigners in Rome and the foolishness of the Empire? When he talks about foreigners, he's speaking about you and me, by the way."

"Maybe she's trying to change his mind? She only wants peace."

"If she is, she's doing it in a strange way. She's been overheard telling him that his fears of foreign kingdoms trying to destroy Rome by joining the Empire and tearing it down from the inside is exactly what's happening, and what your father specifically is working toward. She's told him that the only reason your kingdom joined the Empire was because they couldn't defeat the Romans directly."

"But ... she's a foreigner too."

"She is, which seems to be proof that she's telling the truth, or at least that's how she's portraying it. According to what we've heard, she portrays herself as a victim, forced to marry you and taken from her home against her will."

"I mean, that's not exactly how it happened. She agreed, and over time ..."

Even as he tried to deny it, Llassar could see doubt creeping into Cormac's eyes. He didn't know what the couple said in private, but some of the things he had mentioned were connecting for Cormac. He was very bright. Naive, but bright. Llassar's hope was that, when this moment came, he'd be able to figure out he was being played.

"I know," Llassar said. "The important question is why is she describing it like that? Think about how she's behaved with you. The questions you've been asking and the things you've been upset about, how many of those are because of what she's said to you? Honestly? I know you want more, to have a bigger part, but you weren't this dissatisfied before."

Cormac looked like he was going to argue again, and then sagged.

"Maybe," he said. "If what you say is true ... it's ... I don't really understand why she'd do that."

"Can't you? She was a queen, and now she's been reduced to your consort. Her people have been subjugated and are now your father's subjects."

"Maybe someone manipulated her, convinced her to turn against me."

"Cormac, you're smarter than that. You've spent time with her. Does she strike you as someone to be controlled? We'd hoped she would accept her place, for the good of her people, and to protect her own life. Maybe we were wrong."

"Exactly. You said yourself you could see why she might be dissatisfied. Couldn't we talk to her? Maybe if I went to her, convinced her she was wrong ..."

"Cormac, she's played you for a fool. I don't say this to belittle you. Do you really think she respects or cares what you think about her? What you might say?"

"Maybe," he said hopefully, but the expression on Llassar's face was enough to tear through that hope. "I know this is naive of me, if she really has been playing me, but I don't want her to die. I care for her, and I think that maybe she could love me one day too, given enough time. This all happened too fast, the temptation too great."

"Do you think she would have schemed back home, that much closer to her people?"

"I don't want her to die," Cormac said, almost desperately.

The realization had hit him hard. He was still fighting it, couching his statements in ifs and maybes, but that was just for his own ego. Having it pointed out to him, illuminating everything that had happened under the light of day, it was enough for him to reevaluate it all and see it for what it was.

"I make no promises, but there's a chance. Soon, word of this will get back to your father, and he'll be much less forgiving. From the beginning, he was not completely sure this plan would work, and this undermines his rule as much as the Empress's. You know your father; do you think he'll listen to your pleas?"

"No," Cormac said, almost sullenly.

"Still, there is a chance. The only person your father will listen to is the Empress herself. She has her own reasons for wanting to be rid of your wife, but I've also found her usually to be very reasonable. We can go to her and plead your case. She, or Ramirus, might have a way to ensure Medb's loyalty, end her scheming, and save her life."

"Yes. Let's go. I'm sure once I explain it's all a misunderstanding ..."

"No," Llassar said, cutting him off. "If you do that, she'll conclude you're smitten beyond reason, and she won't listen to you.

The evidence is damning. We've had people following her for weeks, and she hasn't done this just once. She's been plotting, and we know about it. The preacher she talked to has all but confessed. If you want to save her life, you must do it with open eyes and understand the danger she, and you, are in."

"I'll do anything," Cormac said.

"Fine. I make no promises, but we can talk to the Empress and see what she says."

Chapter 25

Lucilla made her way into the palace from the courtyard, prefer-
ring to take the back way in to avoid the throngs of petitioners and
citizens coming and going on business, official or otherwise.

She couldn't wait until the telegraph was finally installed, after
hearing Ky describe what it would be like, enabling communication with a far-off city in an instant. She spent the last four hours
in a carriage on the bumpy roads, returning yet again from visiting
Factorium to give the latest notes to Hortensius and Sorantius.
It was important, and up to her since she was the only one with
a direct connection to Ky and Sophus, but she didn't enjoy the
bone-rattling trips.

"Empress," Ramirus said, appearing almost out of thin air as she
passed through the side entrance. "Llassar is here, asking to speak
with you. He has the prince with him."

Lucilla frowned. They hadn't taken direct action with either
Medb or Cormac yet, but it was coming soon. Llassar and Cormac
being here meant something had changed, which was rarely a
good thing.

"What's happened?"

"Nothing that I know of. They just showed up a little bit ago,
saying they needed to speak with you. It's impossible to guess with
Llassar, but the boy seems nervous."

"Have them meet me in my office," she said, waving the spymaster off and turning into her quarters.

There wasn't time to wash the dust from the road off, but she
could at least change into a fresh stola. She took her time, basking
in the silence for a moment before diving back into the political
mud. With a sigh, she steeled herself and left the peace of her
quarters.

"Alright, let's deal with this," she said to Chief Protector Modius.

Llassar and the prince were already in her office when they arrived. Cormac was pacing nervously, stopping like a deer caught in the wild when she walked in. Llassar simply looked in her direction, unperturbed as always.

"Empress," he said, not rising as many did when she entered a room.

It didn't bother her. She didn't stand on ceremony, and the Caledonian had proven himself as a supporter of the Empire enough times to skip formalities.

"I wanted to talk to you about my wife," Cormac said, before Lucilla had time to sit down, dropping into a chair across from her desk. "Llassar told me what she's been doing. I ... I'm still having trouble accepting it but, if he's telling the truth ... I don't want her to die. I know she's been talking to people, fomenting unrest, which is treasonous. I know she needs to be stopped, but I beg you, there has to be a way to fix this without sacrificing her."

She looked at him, calculating. The boy squirmed under her gaze. She hadn't expected him to accept what was happening so easily, although she didn't know what had been said between him and the Caledonian, nor had she guessed that he'd be so passionate about Medb's survival. Not that she would let his pleading change what needed to be done.

"It's more serious than you know," she said, gesturing to Ramirus.

"We've been watching her closely," the spymaster said. "And the preacher isn't the only one she's been talking to. She's been all over town since winter ended, talking to anyone who's made public statements criticizing the Empire. We may have cleared out the remaining insurrectionists, but there are still people not pleased with the Empress's rule, how the Empire is run, or the Empire's existence in the first place. She's managed to find a good number of them and has had a lot of conversations with them. We haven't overheard all of what they've said, but in the ones we did hear she said about the same things as she did with Vesnius. She's pushed their prejudices and fears, telling them tales of planned foreign invasions and hatred for Rome by your father. She has gone well beyond fomenting unrest."

"I don't know what she's said to you," Lucilla said. "Although Llassar speaks highly of you, it's clear she's been playing you just as she is everyone else. I don't know her end goal, but she's causing chaos which we cannot allow to continue. Not in the middle of a war."

"I ... I didn't know," Cormac said, almost on the verge of tears. "Please. I know she can be good; she's just having difficulty transitioning from being a monarch in her own right to her position now. But that's not all she is. She can be better, I know it."

"You say that, even knowing she's been manipulating you, convincing you to break your oaths, putting you on the brink of treason?" Lucilla asked, a little surprised he'd keep arguing for her even after accepting the truth of what was happening.

"I'm not a fool, Your Majesty," Cormac said, calming himself and turning serious. "I know she's been using me. With everything I now know about what she's been doing, it's impossible to not see it. But I also know the other moments we've spent together. Moments I've seen the real her come through, and she's worth redeeming. Not simply because of how I feel about her, but because she has a lot to bring to the Empire. She's clever, as clever as anyone in this room. Yes, she has ambition, but if that ambition could be turned in our favor, it would be a huge benefit."

"I'm not sure that's as convincing of an argument as you might want it to be," Lucilla said. "Someone with the combination of intelligence and ambition that you describe isn't someone that can be harnessed. Will she ever stop? It's hard to believe. She'll just keep trying, working to find a way to free herself and get back what she lost."

"I know, but I have to hope she'll come around. I... I've never had a relationship like this before. It's not just ... I love her. Maybe she doesn't feel it and maybe she just managed to convince me of it as part of her plan, but in my heart, I hope she feels it a little too. All I know is, I don't want her to die. Please."

Lucilla regarded him pitifully before glancing at Llassar. The Caledonian met her gaze, face impassive, not giving a hint of what he thought. Ramirus, who could be equally stoic, wasn't hiding his feelings this time. She knew what he would do in her position. She also knew what her duty told her to do. And yet.

"I'll give Medb one chance. If she ceases her treasonous activity and gets in line, I will allow her to live," Lucilla declared. "If she doesn't, there will be *no* second chances. However, I don't want to give her that chance, yet. She has done us a favor, in a way, pulling up the rotten portions of the city and pointing them out to us. Before we give her a chance, I want to first make sure we can scoop up all the people who've joined her in treason."

"Maybe if I talk to her ..." Cormac started to say until Lucilla cut him off.

"I've made my decision. You will say nothing to her, and when she's given her chance, I'll be the one to do it. I want to be clear; your actions were not that different from hers, although you were participating somewhat unwittingly. Your first duty is the one your father sent you to carry out, to ensure your people's role as part of the Empire. *Part of the Empire.* If you cannot keep your responsibilities in mind and your personal feelings under control, I will send you back home with a warning to your father about your unreliable nature. This is your last chance, as well."

Cormac hadn't yet seemed to consider his own culpability for his actions. Maybe it was just the way of princes, unable to see their own faults, but she didn't want him to leave without un- derstanding he was in danger as well. Maybe not of execution, which would cause more problems than it would solve, but if his father heard of his actions and Cormac was returned to him, the repercussions would be severe. And Cormac knew it.

The boy slid back in his chair, crestfallen as the realization hit him. She felt for him, but they didn't have time to coddle him. Now was the time for him to show he could handle his responsibility or decide this wasn't the life for him.

Cormac bowed his head and said, "You're right. If I'm being honest, it's not all Medb's doing. I've been blinded by my own selfishness. Of what I wanted, and not what I was entrusted to do."

He paused for a moment, looking at his hands, before raising his head and looking back at her, meeting her gaze.

"Thank you, for giving me a chance to make it right. Llassar has tried to tell me I was failing, but I guess that I really didn't listen until I almost messed up for good. I can't change what I've done, but I'll try to do better. I'll fix this."

It was a hard lesson for any man to learn, much less one so young. But he wasn't a commoner. He was a prince, with the duties that entailed. He didn't have the luxury of waiting to see if he got away with his mistakes.

"Good. I hope you do."

Port of Kalb, Mouth of the Middle Sea

Admiral Valdar stood on the forecastle of his flagship Bellona, one foot propped on the railing as he surveyed the Carthaginian port of Kalb. The city's crumbling stone walls looked back at him, a sad testimony to what they once had been. They had been strong and proud, holding off pirates and attacks for generations, but they were not made to withstand months of cannon fire. To preserve ammunition, he had kept the bombardment slow but steady, never giving the city a moment's peace.

For several months, the blockading fleet had gripped Kalb tightly, strangling the flow of supplies and reinforcements from the Middle Sea. It was important, but it was tedious, especially as the number of Carthaginian ships that attempted to sally out to meet him or run his blockade slowly dwindled. He was impatient to continue with his mission, but he couldn't until he took this port and secured his supply lines.

"Sail ho!" came the lookout's cry. "Ships approaching from the east!"

Valdar raised his spyglass, smiling as he recognized the lean profiles of Britannian caravels tacking toward him. He knew they were about due to roll off the docks, but he hadn't expected them quite this soon. With these additions, his ship count would be brought up to eighteen, which gave him many more options.

"Signal from the Branwen," the signal officer said, looking through his own spyglass at the flags raising and lowering on board the lead ship sailing toward them. "She bears resupply of food and gunpowder and two hundred legionaries, with the Empress's compliments."

"Excellent," Valdar said, lowering his spyglass. "Signal the fleet. All captains are to repair aboard with due haste for a consultation and preparation."

This is what he'd been waiting for. He was more than ecstatic that the Empress had heard him out and decided to send the legionaries he'd requested. With the port blockaded and the armies to the north too engaged in the land war to respond, the port was weakened, and should be easy pickings for rifle-armed legionaries.

Valdar paced his cabin, waiting for his captains to arrive. After months, this was what he'd been waiting for, and he was impatient to get started. Finally, the last of the captains arrived, taking their places in the now much too cramped cabin.

"Before we get started, I have some bad news from the north," he began. "Port Invictus has fallen and the Legate is dead."

Murmurs rippled through the room as the captains reacted to the news.

Valdar raised a hand for silence. "As bad as that is, everything isn't lost. The Consul is marching south with his legions to assault the main Carthaginian port on the continent."

"What are we going to do about it?" Einar, captain of the Aquila asked. "Shouldn't we support that attack? I understand the value of this port and blocking Carthaginian shipping out of the Middle Sea is crucial, but until we shut down their traffic inside the sea, our armies are vulnerable."

"I agree," Valdar said. "Which is why we're going to do both. I'm sending our five most experienced crews, not counting the Bellona, to blockade their shipping and support the Consul's attack. The Aquila, Tyrfing, Seadreki, Bolvastr, and Europa will be under your overall command, Einar. You're to blockade the port and patrol the nearby coast as best you can, sinking any ship you find inside the Middle Sea. Assume anything floating is Carthaginian. You're also to support the Consul and answer directly to him.

I assume he'll want you to shell the city at some point, so be prepared. You'll have to work with him for supplies, since the coast between here and there will still be open waters and I don't trust any of our supply ships to make it that far. Not until we finish sinking all their ships. Is that good enough?"

"Yes, Admiral," Einar said, sounding both surprised his recommendation was taken so quickly and excited he was getting his first independent command.

"Good. As for the rest of us, we are going to prepare to take the port. I'm not sure what kind of leadership the Empress sent along with the two hundred centurions, but it's likely a fairly low-level commander in charge of them. I want to spend a few days discussing the assault with him and, possibly, take a ship and the legionaries back out to Oceanus to find a bare strip of Hispania to do a few test runs before we take the port for real. Until then, let's keep the city busy. I want to increase bombardment, focusing on the western and eastern portions of the port, leaving the center corridor and the docks themselves for our men to move through. Let's turn the rest of it into rubble. I want them too busy to notice us doing anything else. You'll also be given your responsibilities for the landings that I want you to read over and work with your crews to prepare for. Use the bombardment as an opportunity for target practice, especially you men on the newly arrived ships. When we start our land assault, I don't want cannon balls landing on our troops. If you have questions, hold them until you've gotten your assignments."

All of the captains glanced at each other, no one moving. Only a handful of them had participated in the assault on Insula Manavia, so this was going to be a new experience for most of them. He could feel their excitement and nervousness in the air.

"Get moving. We have a lot to do."

Ruins of Port Invictus, Hispania

The Seventh Legion emerged from the wooded hills overlooking the plain, above the ruins of Port Invictus. Bomilcar watched from the edge of the tree line as the legion flowed steadily past him, observing what was left of Port Invictus. It was odd, seeing it from this position. Although hastily constructed the year before, it had been solidly built. Now, little more than tumbled masonry and charred timber remained, darkened by the fire from either the gunpowder pots the Carthaginians had thrown or the explosion set off by Velius.

More amazing was the landscape itself, marred with the trenches left behind by the siege of the port, breaking up the legionaries' formations. Aelius had described the scene to him, the deep furrows winding their way toward the wall, but that description hadn't prepared him for seeing it in person.

The lessons from a past battle were not, however, what his attention was focused on. His real concern today was the Carthaginians left behind to guard what was left of the wreckage. The Carthaginian general had most likely reasoned that the detachment would be a deterrent against a second attempt to build a port in this location. His scouts had reported the enemy pulling back into the ruins of the fort as they approached. A wise move, since the thousand men left behind would not be enough to stop his legion.

The movement in the ruins wasn't hard to spot, as the Carthaginians panicked, moving into positions within the ruins, using the cover to protect them from the Britannian weapons that they'd learned to fear. He could also see the edges of catapults, well-positioned to be protected by the walls. No doubt they would be loaded with gunpowder pots, the same ones that had led to this port's destruction in the first place.

He turned his attention to his own line, watching as his men threaded their way through the scarred landscape. It was good the enemy wasn't concentrated because his army was badly segmented by the trenches. His line cohesion was very poor. It would be worse when they got to the wall. If they had to assault through the rubble, it would be brutal fighting. While his victory was assured, they could bleed him badly in the assault.

Which is why he had no intention of charging the rubble. Raising his hand he signaled the trumpeter near him, whose instrument called out a series of notes. The army responded instantly, pulling to a halt, the men in even rows, or as even as they could be on the broken ground.

"Now ... we wait," Bomilcar said.

The reaction of the defenders to his legion halting was visible confusion. The enemy soldiers shifted about uncertainly within the ruins, likely trying to decide why the massive force marching towards them had suddenly stopped outside the range of their defenses and what it meant for them. They knew they were outnumbered and certainly doomed, which always seemed to breed an odd anticipation. Men, knowing they were going to die, often wanted to get it over with instead of delaying it.

If they were confused now, they would be truly upset when the rest of Bomilcar's plan unfolded. Right on cue, trumpets sounded from the north. Bomilcar glanced up the coastline to see another legion emerging, the Third Legion under Auspex.

Mostly because of the sandy ground and low water table, the trenches had extended from the east, with only holding forces north and south of the fort, giving Auspex's legion a much easier time holding formation. Instead of taking advantage of this, however, the newly arrived legion stopped at roughly the same distance from the port.

For a time, neither legion did anything except face the defenders. Like the strategy of having a delay before the appearance of the Third Legion, this was a calculated pause. What Bomilcar wanted most was for the Carthaginians to just surrender, saving him the bloodshed that would come from having to dig them out.

In an environment such as the destroyed port, it would be all but impossible to blast them out with cannon, which would ultimately mean having to send men in to clear out the remaining defenders. Bomilcar had neither the men nor the time to waste on such an endeavor.

"That should be enough time," he finally said to Gordianus, sitting on horseback next to him. "Roll out the guns and signal the Third."

Having pulled all of the cannon from Velius's line of forts, the legions under his command were now heavily armed with artillery, and he planned to make the most of it. 'Shock and awe' was how the Consul had once described the effect of massed artillery to him, but until today, he hadn't seen it in full effect. They'd used artillery lightly, in limited engagements, or on the defensive. This was the first time anyone, that Bomilcar was aware of, had massed artillery to hammer a single target.

The signal went up, and the cannons started to fire, maintaining their fastest rate of fire for the first ten minutes before slowing to a more steady but maintainable rate. A gentle breeze off the coast helped keep the entire field from being blanketed in smoke, but even that wasn't enough to make the destroyed port visible as shells slammed into it nearly continuously. A thick gray haze of dirt and concrete dust was more or less constant, occasionally broken by a flash of bright orange fire when a lucky shot hit their catapults or waiting ammunition.

The resulting minimal-sized explosion was a testament to Aelius's report of the much lower quality gunpowder the Carthaginians were using. It was still a mystery how they acquired it, but whatever they'd done, it was clearly not to the same level as that used by the Britannians.

After thirty minutes, the cannons ceased firing, another part of the highly choreographed ballet of destruction Bomilcar had arranged. Who knows what the defenders thought about the pause, although perhaps they hoped the Britannians had run out of ammunition.

At least until they heard more bugle calls, this time from the south. The Ninth Legion emerged from the southern hills, joining them outside the ruined port. They halted just beyond the range of the defenders' catapults, joining the ranks of the Seventh and Third Legions, arrayed to the east and north.

Bomilcar watched as more panic ensued inside the fallen port and felt a tiny amount of pity for those men, who must be terrified knowing the destruction about to befall them. Not so much pity that he was going to spare them their fate, however.

With a signal, the cannons of all three legions opened fire once more, enveloping the shattered remnants of the fort from three directions. Again, plumes of dirt and debris erupted continuously as shell after shell slammed into the rubble.

Bomilcar considered the devastating effectiveness of the barrage, realizing it mirrored the tactics the Carthaginians had used against Velius. But whereas they had required extensive trench works to get within range, his legions could unleash their firepower without such preparations.

Either way, what was clear was that once their enemies obtained cannons and firearms like the Britannians possessed, static fortifications and walled cities would be rendered obsolete. Given enough guns, any defenses could be pounded to dust. The age of fixed bastions was over.

Not that destroying them was simple. Even with the destruction raining down on them, the defenders still had not surrendered. Part of the problem was one that his barrage was actually amplifying. The walls of the port were already all but destroyed, which meant most of his shots were just rearranging rubble piles without really clearing them away. On top of that, they were tearing deep gouges in the earth, making more places for the defenders to cower in.

This part, he'd actually considered beforehand. After twenty more minutes of bombardment, he called another halt, giving the defenders another brief breather before the final stage of his plan.

The final act began as one of the armed sloops came into view. It had been sitting and waiting as its captain, Yrsa, watched the battle proceed through his own spyglass until the three legions were in place and had finished their last bombardment of the port. Which was his signal to move his ship into position outside the port.

As soon as it was stationed, one side facing the ruined port, its cannon fired. Most ended up short, smashing into the water or ruined docks. Bomilcar had been clear in his communications with the captain that he preferred the ship fire short, sending its cannonballs into the sea, rather than overshoot, potentially sending its rounds past the ruins and into his legions.

The second barrage, however, was aimed perfectly, the captain having made adjustments from the first ranging shots to find their target. The sloop's broadside smashed into the enemy, who didn't have the benefit of ruined walls to hide from in that direction.

As soon as the ship began firing, his legions' cannon picked up the call and added to the cavalcade, destruction now raining down on the defenders from every direction. That tipped the scales. The defenders had spent the last several hours under massive bombardment, maybe hoping for an all-out charge where they could take some Britannians with them. This newest attack, however, was just too much for them to bear.

Although he missed it at first, having difficulty seeing the enemy through the haze of dust and destruction, Carthaginians began holding up their shields, a sign that they surrendered.

"Signal cease fire," Bomilcar told the signalman next to him, who saluted and ran off to carry out his orders.

It took almost five minutes to get all the artillery to fall silent. There was almost an echo, or maybe just a ringing in his ears, after the firing finally ceased. It had been louder than anything Bomilcar had ever experienced, which meant it must have been hellish to be on the receiving end of it.

"Send a rider out under a flag of truce. They're to throw down their weapons and march out single file, carrying any wounded. Make it known that if we see any weapons or they attempt treachery, all of their lives will be forfeit."

As the aide rode off to dispatch the messenger, Bomilcar turned his horse towards Gordianus, who was back with the command group waiting for orders.

"We'll leave a century behind from the Seventh to guard the prisoners and accompany them as they are ferried to Britannia and the prison camps. As soon as we've checked to make sure the enemy have all been rounded up, I want the legions ready to march. We have a lot of ground to cover to catch up with their army, and I do not want to wait until they've marched all the way to their port, or they realize we've all but abandoned the entire line of forts. I want the army to move with all speed. Clear?"

"Yes, General," Gordianus said, saluting and riding off to follow his instructions.

Bomilcar let a wry smile escape. He may have been made legate, but so far, everyone still called him General. It had become almost a moniker of sorts, instead of his former rank. Knowing soldiers as he did, he didn't take it as an insult. If anything, the men adopting a nickname for their commander was one of the highest compliments they could give.

Now he just had to prove that their faith in him wasn't misplaced. This fight had been simple and the outcome was never in doubt. The next one would be more difficult and much more deadly.

Chapter 26

Port of Kalb, Mouth of the Middle Sea

Valdar stepped carefully from the boarding plank down into the cutter, moving aft to take his place in the stern seat as the small boat began moving for the shore. Despite months of pounding the fortress from the sea and blockading it from resupply, he knew the coming battle would be anything but easy. This wasn't where he saw himself before throwing his lot in with the Britannians. He was a ship's captain and had no place leading soldiers into combat. Unfortunately, the two centurions commanding his assault force were far too green and inexperienced to properly lead the attack themselves. Valdar may not be a soldier, but he'd been involved in many fights, boarding actions, and even looted a city or two. Besides, this was his plan and his responsibility.

The men rowing the boat pulled hard on the oars as cannonballs soared over their heads, into the city, giving the defenders one last pounding before the men landed. His cutter was the last boat in line, pushing steadily across the harbor's smooth surface toward the mostly untouched docks, left intact for exactly this purpose.

He felt the familiar twist in his gut that always came before a battle, that mingling of excitement and fear, eagerness and worry that somehow had become as much a part of him as his own skin. Ahead of him, nineteen longboats, packed with armed and armored legionaries, slowed as the lead two longboats moved closer toward the docks and the several dozen Carthaginians who'd come down from the walled city to try to repel the invaders.

Unlike the boats filled with legionaries, these two held a third of his marine force. Men who'd trained with the new rifles and were familiar with the constant rising and falling of the ocean. While many of their shots still missed, more struck home than any of the legionaries could have managed. Carthaginians began dropping. Their copies of the arcuballista were worthless at the range the marines were using. The marines were firing at them and were picking them off, one by one.

When the marines' boats reached a couple of hundred paces out from the docks, they stopped, their rowers reversing their stroke to hold their boats in position, letting the legionaries, who had started rowing faster as the marines slowed, sweep past while they continued firing.

Seeing several hundred angry and armored legionaries closing on them, on top of their comrades continuing to fall with impunity as the marines carried on with their gruesome work, was more than enough for the remaining Carthaginians. Almost collectively, they decided they'd had enough, turning tail and running back to the crumbling port city, which had caught fire in several places, the untended fires starting to burn out of control.

Valdar's boat landed at about the same time as the marines' boats, men on the dock helped the new arrivals up and then they all fanned out to join the men already in line. The fleeing defenders had to have spread the word that the Britannians were there, and since there were no defenders sallying out to attack them it meant that they were going to hunker down and defend the broken city, making the Britannians fight house by house.

The canon fire from the ships in the harbor ceased as his ships' captains saw that they were all ashore. From here on out, they were on their own. There wasn't much his ships could do to help them now.

It was an unusual situation for an old sea dog to find himself in.

"Centurion," he called out to the commander closest to him. "They're waiting to bog us down, get us trapped in tight streets. We'll split up our force. Fires are starting to get out of control north and west, so you'll bring your men around and come from the east. We'll march straight in, hopefully rendezvousing at the town center, either crushing them between us or pushing them into the burning streets. You'll get half the medics we pulled off the ships and half the marines to care for any wounded and act as runners as needed."

"Understood. We'll see you there," the centurion said, waving his men to follow him, circling around the city.

Valdar ignored them, turning his attention to the task at hand.

"Lead them on, centurion," Valdar said.

He was in overall command, but he was no legionary. He'd leave the actual combat directives to their unit commanders and focus on keeping his men headed in the right direction, trying not to let them get bogged down. For the first few blocks, the narrow streets were eerily empty, many of the buildings burned and damaged from the naval bombardment.

It didn't stay quiet for long. When they reached the first intersection, the Carthaginians sprung their first trap. A handful of bolts sailed out of a ruined building on their left, killing one legionary and leaving another in the dirt, a bolt sticking out of his knee. A dozen rifles on the left side of the formation turned and fired into the rubble. It was doubtful they killed anyone, considering no one had seen where those bolts came from.

"Contubernium left," the centurion called out, causing ten of the legionaries on the left flank to peel off from the main body, slinging their rifles and pulling their swords.

The rest of the body didn't slow down, which was exactly what they were supposed to do. They weren't going to let anything slow them down. By the time they made it to the next intersection, the Contubernium had returned, their swords stained red. Better still, all of the men were accounted for.

That had just been the Carthaginians' opening move, however. At the next street, the Carthaginians didn't just settle for a few arcuballista bolts. The legionaries had just started to enter the intersection when men swarmed out of the buildings on all sides, completely surrounding them.

"Form Square," the centurion bellowed, causing an instant ripple along their line as the legionaries instantly reacted, the lines splitting and reforming in a square.

Valdar, the marines, and medics rushed to get inside the square. The legionaries ignored their rifles and had their swords at the ready as the Carthaginians slammed into them. The attack was doomed from the beginning, despite the element of surprise, with roughly thirty Carthaginians trying to swarm the ninety-eight remaining legionaries. The Carthaginians gave it their all, however, and clashing metal sounded as the men collided, followed by screams of anguish as the first blades found flesh.

Ringing out over the sounds of battle came the occasional crack of a rifle. The handful of marines, not encumbered with defending themselves from sword and spear, picked targets, helping to whittle down the numbers even faster. Still, the battle wasn't one-sided. The Carthaginians' zealous fury took a toll, as here and there along the square legionaries fell beneath the blades. But for each man lost, five or six Carthaginians paid in kind.

The outcome of the battle was never in doubt. After only a few bloody minutes, the remaining Carthaginians finally broke, fleeing back down the streets.

"Reform lines," the centurion called as the medics pulled the fallen legionaries back.

Valdar and his men continued their push through the ruined streets of the Carthaginian city. More small skirmishes broke out as they went, with defenders emerging from the rubble here or there to ambush them, but the numbers they faced were always incredibly small, usually only a handful of men, who were dispatched quickly.

Valdar knew they outnumbered the defenders, but so far there had been far too few of them, which meant there must be a large number ahead. They were still a few blocks out from what he believed was the center of the town, although a small curve in the street blocked it from view, when they started hearing the sounds of battle. Screams and rifle fire carried over the buildings, loud enough that it was clear where the rest of the Carthaginians were, and where the other century was.

"Double time!" he shouted, not waiting for their commander to give the order.

To their credit, none of them were confused. As soon as the order came, the men recognized the sounds they were hearing and realized their comrades were in trouble.

The legionaries broke into a run, rounding the final corner into a scene of chaos. The Carthaginians had concentrated their defense on the open square and were pressing hard on the second century, which was bottled up in the street, unable to bring the bulk of their men to bear. It was a tactic the Britannians had used many times against the Carthaginians, and one that worked equally well in reverse. Or it would have, had Valdar and his century not appeared.

"Charge," the centurion yelled as soon as they saw the fight.

The command almost wasn't needed. The men were already running full out, and they needed no urging to press the attack. His soldiers slammed into the Carthaginian rear. Caught between two Roman forces, the defenders' cohesion shattered. They attempted to flee but found themselves pinned down and were attacked mercilessly.

What had been a pitched battle moments before turned into a slaughter. The square ran red with blood as the legionaries dispatched the last of the resistance. The port city now lay open to them, the defenses broken.

As the men collected the dead and squads were sent to root out any surviving Carthaginian soldiers, Valdar surveyed the bloody aftermath. They might have taken the port, but it was in very rough shape.

Runners were sent back to the ships, which began landing sailors to help get the fires under control while the legionaries provided security, should any resistance still exist.

Soon, the timid faces of townspeople began peering out from cellars and barricaded homes as they realized the fighting was over. With the battle won, it was time to establish control.

Valdar searched out the senior centurion, the man who'd led the other century, who at some point had made it back to the docks where he was directing the movement of men and supplies.

"You did well, centurion," Valdar said when he found the man.

"Thank you, Admiral, although you were the one who saved us in the city square."

"I only shortened the battle. Your men had things well in hand when we arrived. I've already sent a messenger back to Britannia with news of our victory, in which I commended your fine work to the Empress herself."

"Thank you, sir," the man said, flushing.

He was one of the newly trained and promoted centurions and probably didn't expect his name to be spoken to the Empress directly. Considering he was a Roman, that was quite the achievement.

"Your work isn't done, I'm afraid," Valdar said. "I'm not staying. I need to take the fleet north to support the Consul and his legions as they assault the main Carthaginian port in southern Gaul. That means I have to leave you in command here. I know it's a big responsibility, but I have faith you can handle it. In my message to the Empress, I also requested reinforcements for you, along with a senior officer to take over command of this port, but it will be several weeks at a minimum before you receive any more men."

The centurion almost certainly hadn't expected that news, causing him to blanch slightly at the sudden weight of his new responsibility.

"Don't worry, you can handle this. The port is well protected from assault from the north, and the Carthaginians are otherwise engaged at the moment. Other than remnants of the defenders who made it out before our assault or possible brigands, you shouldn't have much trouble. I'm not leaving you without support. Five of my ships will remain behind to protect the port and blockade the strait to Oceanus, which means the Carthaginians should not be able to do to you what we just did to them. You're expected to keep the peace and begin repairing the port. Keep the civilian populace under martial law until you get reinforcements, although I don't predict you'll get much trouble from them. After months of shelling, I imagine they'll be happy to get some semblance of normality back."

"You can count on me, Admiral," the centurion said, sounding relieved to hear he wasn't going to be left entirely on his own.

"This port is going to be getting a lot of use over the coming year as we turn our attention to Africa, so it's important you keep the docks open and get the city back up and running."

"I won't let you down," he said.

"I know. I won't keep you. Go get to work."

The man saluted, which wasn't strictly necessary, since generally the navy and the legions were not really considered equal, but Valdar returned the salute. The man's world had just been turned upside down, so a little confusion was only natural.

Besides, Valdar had a lot of work of his own to do. There were preparations to be made for his departure, which he wanted to happen soon. He was a week behind the ships he'd sent north already, and he wanted complete control of the entire southern coast of Gaul by the time the Consul got his armies to the coast.

Devnum

Lucilla slid off her horse, enjoying the feeling of the crisp fall air on her skin. She spent so many hours cooped up in offices and audience chambers, or stuck in a carriage, it was a pleasure to be outside for a change. Hortensius had tried to convince her to take a carriage, as more befitted her station, but one of the attacks Medb's proxies had made on her was focused on her "feminine weakness." It was a good opportunity to be out pursuing more rugged activities where people could see her.

Looming in front of her was the object the inventor had brought her to see. A tall wooden pole rising from the earth with a thick black rope strung between its apex and another pole further down the gently sloping meadow. More poles stretched into the distance as far as she could see. She knew the rope was actually copper and steel wiring covered with the newly created rubber, which protected the wire from animals and nature. The long row of poles was quite the engineering marvel, with the glass and metal connections on each pole that the wire ran through, which Ky had said would help maintain the signal strength as it passed over long distances.

Hortensius, less used to riding than she was, caught up, sliding off his horse next to her.

"It's quite the sight," she said, still looking down the row of telegraph poles.

"It is indeed. They are much longer than you might think, sunk deep into the ground and secured with concrete in the ground to help hold them upright. I still imagine we will get downed lines from time to time, but we have run tests on fixing broken wire and replacing fallen or cut poles, and it isn't difficult or very time-consuming. A small team of riders can be dispatched from a telegraph station to repair them quickly. Even if a line does go down, repairs can generally be made faster than sending messengers back and forth."

"Excellent. Truly excellent. Show me the telegraph in operation," she commanded.

"Certainly, Your Majesty," he said with a slight bow of his head.

The small group remounted and made the short trek back to the palace. Along the way, they passed small groups of people who had heard about the new marvel and had walked out to see the strange line of poles. It spoke to how unusual the sight was that they barely paid attention to their Empress riding by as they marveled at the poles and the strange black rope traveling between them.

They arrived back at the palace at the small telegraph office installed next to Lurio's office, outside the palace itself but still on the grounds of the complex. The wires ran from the closest pole down through the roof into the room itself. Inside the room, the wire extended down the wall from the ceiling to a desk that held the telegraph receiver. More wires ran from the receiver down to an enclosed box on the floor, which she knew held the battery that made the entire device function. Although she had a basic idea of how all this worked, since she'd been the one to transcribe its functions for the two inventors, seeing it in person was another matter, although one thing hadn't been in the original plans. Part of her mind had marked it as notable when they'd been out observing the poles, but it was more noticeable once she arrived at the telegraph office itself.

"There were two wires on the poles, one on either side of the arm, yet there is only one here," she asked the inventor.

"Yes. We figured that citizens would want to have access to this technology as much as anyone else, once they learn what it can do. Many families are separated at the moment, with fathers here or in Factorium for work while their loved ones are in villages as far away as Londinium. Once they know they can send messages to them quickly, I believe this will become very popular. Because it can only transmit one message at a time, we decided to run two lines, one for official business and one for citizens, who can pay a small fee to send messages, which will help offset the cost of the installation and upkeep of these stations. Sometimes, like here, the lines will go to different places, although I imagine both will often go to the same building."

"Clever. Very clever. Lurio, in particular, will be pleased to hear you found a way to offset some of the costs, although I think we should be careful not to charge too much. This shouldn't be a luxury only the wealthy can afford to use."

"It was actually Lurio's idea, after he heard about what we were doing. And yes, I had that conversation with him already. I've had the men working in Factorium, who know about the project, ask when they can use it, and while we pay them well, I know many send most of their money home to their families and live on very fixed allowances."

"Good man," she said, patting her friend on the shoulder. "Well, let's see this in action."

"Certainly," he said, giving the operator sitting at the receiving desk a nod.

The man tapped his finger on a small metal arm that extended out of the receiver, which had a roundish part at its end. When he hit it, the plate pressed down into a wooden block which had a similar metal plate fixed to it, wires leading back to the receiver. Each time he tapped it, the machine made a notable "clack" sound.

"First, he sends a short series that tells the operator on the other end that a message is coming through. He waits for a reply that tells him the line is clear and to begin sending. The lines can only carry one signal at a time, so this is to ensure that there isn't cross-traffic."

As they watched, a second part of the receiver, that didn't have a long metal arm but was a short, square set of metal plates, moved on its own, making the same "clack" with each sound.

"Sorantius is waiting at the other receiver, so this first message is just to let them know you're here and ready for the demonstration," Hortensius continued. "Normally, they would take your message, transcribe it into Morse code, send the clear signal, and then type out the message you wanted to send. Any replies would be filed here, and a couple of times a day, a runner would deliver them if the person it was intended for didn't come by to pick them up, or to the palace, for this station. The last message of each transmission has a stop word, to let the other end know the message is complete."

The operator clicked out a series of sounds in long and short clicks, and then waited. She was certain this would take more time in normal use, but this whole display had been orchestrated for her benefit, so each end knew exactly what the other side of the transmission was doing, which meant they didn't need a lot of notification that signals were coming or going.

Suddenly, the receiver started clacking again, with the operator quickly jotting down the dots and dashes as it went. It didn't last long, and it only took a few moments before the operator had the message translated.

Ky had mentioned a version of this that could have the machine itself write out the long or short sounds, so that it didn't rely on the person on the receiving end hearing, or not hearing, a given sound, but they opted to start with the simpler version for now.

The man handed the slip of paper to Hortensius, who held it up and read it, "Long Live the Empress. Sorantius."

Lucilla turned to the operator. "Send a reply praising Sorantius for his success and our gratitude for his hard work."

The operator nodded and began tapping out her message. It was an odd sensation, hearing her words being encoded into a series of metallic clicks.

Turning to Hortensius, she added, "You and Sorantius have accomplished something truly miraculous here. I know this was all Ky's brainchild, but it seemed impossible when he first described it. I can't believe you managed to turn it into a reality. You both deserve immense credit for making it work. This is going to change everything. Not just the war, but our entire Empire. Being able to send messages across the entire country in a moment is revolutionary."

"Everything the Consul has given us has been that way. He's the real miracle."

"Maybe, but it wouldn't have been possible if you hadn't made his ideas into a reality. I always had faith in your abilities, but even I am astonished by what you have achieved here. You should take immense pride in this accomplishment, my friend."

Hortensius smiled warmly at the Empress's praise. "You are too kind, Your Majesty. This is just a first step. We're already working on lines to Londinium and up to Caledonia, and it won't be long before other cities ask for their own lines."

"You plan on using Devnum as a hub, like you did for the semaphore stations?"

"Yes. We're looking to convert the semaphore stations themselves, actually, since the buildings are already built, making it easier to convert. We'll also build some intermediate stations, again using the semaphore stations, to allow some of the smaller towns to have access."

"Good. Very good. I imagine your operators are going to be very busy, soon."

"I have no doubt. Even more so when we finish the second phase of the Consul's plan. We've already begun experimenting with the thicker rubber insulating cover, combining it with a steel casing to protect it from sea life, that we'll use to run lines to Ériu and the Continent. Imagine, instant communication across the ocean. I'm still a little skeptical, but you and the Consul haven't steered me wrong yet, so I'm withholding judgment."

"Trust me, I share your skepticism. Honestly, seeing these plans when I first brought them to you, I seriously doubted this would work like Ky promised. I know you're going to make it so that the entire Empire is united by this miracle. Seriously, you've done a fantastic job."

"Thank you, Your Majesty," he said, a little embarrassed by the praise.

She knew the praise made him uncomfortable, but she meant it. This device was going to change everything.

Chapter 27

Gaul, North of the Pyrenees

"This is unacceptable!" General Tabnit said, slamming his fist against the wooden gate of the empty Roman fort. "How could you let them slip through your hands again?"

"My apologies, sir, the terrain was difficult and ..." Atar, leader of his advance units, started to say, until another shout from his commander cut him off.

"Enough excuses! Time and again your men have arrived to find an empty fort, the Romans escaped, taking their weapons with them. I have told you what would happen if you didn't quicken your pace, and still you defy me. If anything, you're getting slower. What should have taken us a day at the most to assault here from the previous fort has taken us almost three. Meanwhile, the Romans were able to run, dragging their large weapons with them, so far ahead of your men that we've yet to even see one of them."

"The men are tired, General. We have been keeping this pace for weeks, with hardly any rest. And the Romans have been leaving behind traps. We've lost more than a hundred men so far. The men are down to fighting one another to keep from being the first one to enter the empty forts. If we could just ..."

"No," Tabnit bellowed. "Cowardice and weakness is what this is, and I can only assume your men learned that from you. You are demoted in rank and will lead a single phalanx. If we ever manage to engage the enemy again, instead of chasing their footprints, and if you survive and show ability, perhaps you can gain back your rank. Otherwise, the emperor will hear who is to blame for our continued failure. Go. Find your new command and get out of my sight."

At the mention of the emperor, Atar blanched and scurried away. The man knew it was no idle threat. Tabnit had been successful so far, but success only mattered yesterday. The emperor expected, demanded, new victories, and there had been none since destroying the Roman port. The day would come soon when he'd have to answer for his lack of new victories, and he was more than willing to hand Atar over as the cause of their failures.

Still, something had been bothering him with each successive fort. Seeing Nabalsa, who'd been elevated to his second in command after his predecessor died in the eruption of the Roman port, Tabnit waved him over.

"No sign of any of their weapons, or anything left behind that might be useful?" he asked.

He already knew the answer to the question, but it was a placeholder. Something to say while he picked at the thought that had slowly been making its way to the surface of his mind.

"No, General. They were as thorough as ever. As with the other forts, there are clear signs that they dragged their weapons with them, although how they're moving so many this quickly is still a mystery."

"That's the problem," Tabnit said, realization finally setting in. "Does it strike you as odd that these traces we're seeing are the same, fort after fort?"

"I'm not sure what you mean, General."

"I mean, we know that each fort had the large thunder weapons of their own, correct? We saw that when probing them over the summer. And we've seen that at each fort, the Romans have removed their thunder weapons. Weapons large enough to leave deep gouges in the earth where they pulled them. They should be pulling dozens of those weapons by now, maybe hundreds, yet the trail they leave behind is the same every time."

"Perhaps they're pulling them in a row, obscuring the evidence?" Nabalsa offered.

"Perhaps, but … after so many forts, we should have seen some sign. No, this feels wrong. They changed something once we destroyed their port and started taking their forts."

"Maybe they fled north, or a good number of them, anyway. They heard what we did to their other fortifications and realized the futility."

"I don't know. Unless all the forts emptied at once, giving the ground time to clear up the signs of their passing, it seems unlikely we wouldn't see any sign of it."

"We could have missed it. Our scouts are as worn out as the rest of the army. We've already had two accidental skirmishes between our own scouts who confused each other as Roman during night-time reconnaissance."

"Possibly," Tabnit said, still not sounding convinced. "We should ..."

Whatever he was going to suggest to Nabalsa was lost, the words trailing off as a messenger, riding his horse hard, rode up to them, the horse's hooves spraying dirt and gravel over them in his haste.

"What the ..." Nabalsa started to say angrily, before being waved off by Tabnit.

"General, a report from some of the straggling units. Romans sighted to the west."

"They got around us?" Tabnit said, shocked. "How many?"

"The stragglers were very spread out and ran when they saw the Romans. We also don't have any scouts with the rear units, so no reconnaissance was done, but the impression our men had was that it was a goodly number, although less than our numbers. Maybe five to ten thousand, although it could be more."

"Ten thousand? That's not men from the forts. Our reports said there were maybe four thousand men spread across their line of forts. Is it the rest of the men that ran from the battle at their port?"

"There were less than five thousand that fought. We're seeing some signs that hundreds, maybe thousands, of men are still evacuating the line of forts to the east. It doesn't matter. They've finally shown themselves, which is what we've been trying to get them to do for weeks. Turn the army around and form lines for battle."

Nabalsa simply nodded and ran off to get the men ready to attack. Tabnit was pleasantly surprised by how quickly his men moved, in spite of how exhausted they claimed to be. There was nothing as motivating as the enemy on their heels to get his men to finally start moving. Not that he let them know he was satisfied; walking up and down the lines outside the Roman fort, he yelled and cajoled his commanders to move faster, in making their preparations.

His phalanxes began to stretch across the open plain in an odd mixture of spearmen interspersed with men wielding Roman-style arcuballista and catapults. Warfare had changed radically in the last two years, although those changes took longer to get to his people, and they still hadn't worked out a tactical doctrine for this new mix of weapons. Not that it mattered much. Even the borrowed weapons from the Easterners and the Romans' newer design of arcuballista for close-in support weren't a match for the Romans' thunder weapons. The new trenching techniques they used at the port worked to negate that advantage for fortifications, but it wouldn't work in the open field where the enemy could circle around him, at least not without a hundred times more men to allow him to not be flanked. No, their only option was still trying to overwhelm the Roman lines with men, absorbing the losses until they could come to grips with them. Men, however, was something he had and was willing to sacrifice.

It didn't take long for the Romans to make their appearance. Across the rolling plains, their army looked small. Deceptively weak. The original estimate seemed accurate, unless they had other men he couldn't see, giving him roughly five times the advantage in men.

"Signal the advance," Tabnit ordered, initiating a ripple of trumpet calls and yelling as his commanders got the men moving.

His army lurched forward, attempting to get within range of the Romans, who'd halted and spread out to meet his men. All they needed was to get within catapult range to even the odds. The Easterners' fire powder had proven how effective it was in countering the Roman weapons.

Of course, he had to get in catapult range to use it, and the Romans once again showed how effective their weapons were as their lines erupted in a wave of smoke and fire as his men approached, at three times the range of his own weapons. A wave of death swept through his packed ranks, leaving hundreds screaming and dead in a moment. Their larger weapons tearing great swaths through his tightly packed lines.

His men quickened their pace, their formations starting to break apart as they charged, attempting to close the distance and return the pain they were experiencing. Not that they needed the tight-packed formations anymore. The Romans were spread out, no longer using their shields as a tight wall for his men to smash against. Their lines had wide gaps in them for their larger weapons, their legionaries in rows of three or five and maybe a dozen and a half men wide. For a moment, he had hope that his soldiers would do it this time, cross the gap between the armies and come to grips with the Romans.

They endured another round of fire. And then another. Steady like a heartbeat, the Romans' line thundered, belching smoke and fire. A blanket of bodies was left behind his army as it ran forward, the men pushing hard. But it wasn't to be. The momentum started to drain away, the charge disintegrating as his men were transformed into a chaotic mob of terrified men. First a handful, then dozens, then hundreds turned and ran for the rear. It was foolish, as they encountered nearly as much devastation in their retreat as they had in their advance, but a man's bravery only lasts so long in the face of that kind of devastation.

For their part, the Romans didn't move as his men ran away, they only slackened their fire and then finally halted it. Why would they move to engage them? They didn't need to go toe-to-toe with his men to fight, and they had the range now. The field in front of them was covered with bodies, macabre markers of where their fire was most effective.

"Again," Tabnit ordered.

His losses had been heavy, but acceptable. They still greatly outnumbered the Romans, and he'd been smart enough to not send the entire army in one wave, knowing what might happen from previous clashes with the enemy.

Tabnit watched as the second wave of men charged toward the Roman lines. The plains rumbled under thousands of marching feet as the fresh troops advanced, though with a lot less vigor than the first line had shown. Seeing their comrades cut down had been demoralizing, gaps opened up in their ranks as some men hung back or slowed, having to be forced forward by officers placed behind them for exactly that purpose.

As with the first attack, once his men passed some invisible line in the grass, the enemy line billowed smoke once more. More screaming. More death. They didn't even get as close as they had in the first attempt, his men starting to waver after the first volley, some slowing or even stopping as their fear overtook them.

Another series of deafening volleys and his second wave collapsed just like the first. Additional bodies added to the bodies from the first wave, creating a nightmarish vista of carnage.

Tabnit's frustration was growing. He had to get close enough and keep them distracted, so he could roll up his catapults, but none of his attacks managed to hold together long enough to get that far. He'd seen their weapons work in smaller engagements, but never in an open battle like this. He had known victory would have a bloody price, but this butchery was beyond what he'd imagined. Still, he needed to make it work.

"Get the survivors back in line and spread us out. I want to wrap around them on either side. Wrap their flanks. They can't mass fire if we spread out enough," he ordered, sending messengers sprinting off to deliver his message.

It took nearly twenty minutes to reform his lines and get the men moving, stretching his lines. The Romans, damn them, just stood in their formation, watching. Part of him had hoped they'd press the attack against him, moving into range of his catapults, but their commander wasn't a fool. The weapons had surprised them the first time, but now they were ready for them and weren't going to allow him to get into range.

Finally, his army marched forward again.

The Romans hadn't stayed static while his men were redistributed. It wasn't hard to figure out what he was planning, and the Roman commander reacted instantly, shifting the wings of his line, bowing them back in on themselves to counter his wider formation. If this had been traditional armies, Tabnit would have considered that a mistake, since it increased the likelihood that his army would completely envelop the enemy, setting him up to repeat Hannibal's victory at Cannae. Their thunder weapons made that unlikely, and again showed how much they had changed the way war was waged.

His soldiers moved slowly at first, recognizing the danger they were walking into, only picking up speed as their officers cajoled and pushed them, knowing that only momentum could push them through the death they were marching toward. Their walk turned into a trot and then a full-out run as the men picked up speed, regiments jogging forward, spears lowered.

Then his men passed the line, no longer invisible but marked with the bodies of the already fallen men, and the enemy line erupted once more, the deadly fire smashing into his men as if they'd run into an invisible wall. Something suddenly dawned on Tabnit as he watched death rain down on his men. Fewer bodies were falling. Not a lot less, with hundreds dying with every volley, but less. The swaths cut by the larger weapons killed fewer men. The only thing that had changed was that his men were spread out more, to extend their line, causing his army to be less dense than before.

He'd had a conversation with one of the engineers from the Far East, after defeating the Roman port and seeing the potential of their fire powder. It had been awkward, as every conversation with them had been, having to go through multiple interpreters who translated their harsh language into Persian, which was then translated into his own language, but it had been enlightening. The engineer explained to him how the enemy thunder weapons worked, with a metal or stone ball in the long metal tubes, with the fire powder behind it. Because the fire powder could only erupt down the enclosed tube, unable to go anywhere else, the power of it forced the ball out the end, sending it to tear through his men. Although the engineer didn't know specifically, he had guessed their smaller weapons, carried by each of the men, operated using the same principle.

The engineer also indicated that the powder they provided did not have enough power to replicate this, except on very large scales, which meant they couldn't give the Carthaginians the same weapons, even though they understood how the weapons worked. Part of Tabnit thought that was a lie, that they did have the capability to copy the Roman weapons, but he wasn't in a place to force the man to tell the truth. They needed more of the fire powder and none of the emperor's artificers had been able to duplicate it, meaning they were beholden to the Easterners' goodwill. Since it hadn't been immediately helpful to Tabnit's goals, he shelved the information in his mind as something interesting but ultimately unhelpful.

This new revelation, coupled with what he learned from the engineer, however, was useful. If the smaller thunder weapons also pushed out small balls, and that was what was killing his men, then it made sense that if his men weren't as densely packed there was a greater chance some of those projectiles would miss, and even fewer deaths would occur since there weren't men coming behind to be killed in the place of their original target.

This could be a key to countering the Roman weapons. Not one he could use now. His men had trained in the phalanx style, where regimented actions were paramount. A man operating independently could cause the entire formation to fail, which had led to a harsh and inflexible training regimen. It had also helped keep the men, most of whom served out of fear and not out of loyalty, in check. It would take time to change their training, adapt a new strategy that could help them win this fight, much like they'd adapted the trenches, but one that could help turn the tide.

For now, his men still died, their lines starting to waver as they hit the first wave of death.

"Keep going, damn you!" he yelled, not that they could hear him.

They could hear their officers, who pushed the men forward, sometimes at swordpoint. More volleys slammed out, but the formation held this time, absorbing the losses as his troops drew tantalizingly close to the Roman lines. They were in arcuballista range, and a few bolts shot out, killing a Roman here or there. Not enough to change the tide of battle, but seeing their enemy finally die cheered the men, pushing them on.

Then the Romans showed their real surprise. He hadn't noticed it right away, but there were more of their larger thunder weapons here than he ever remembered seeing. Two hundred paces out, his men's charge disintegrated as those weapons finally fired. It wasn't the long, narrow lines of death like they had witnessed before. Instead, it was as if a phantom swept across his line, killing every man in the front of his line, and many of the men in the second. A thousand men died in an instant as those weapons fired at once, the sound deafening, almost as loud as the massive eruption that ultimately destroyed the Roman port.

It was enough to break his men, their line disintegrating as his soldiers turned and fled, all semblance of order lost. The Romans, for their part, held their discipline, the staccato pattern of fire barely breaking even as their enemy fled before them. Of course, that might be because he still had thousands of men held back for another charge. They'd already shown they weren't foolish enough to spread themselves out chasing his running men, throwing away the strength that resulted from their defense.

"Pull the men back and prepare to withdraw," he ordered Nabalsa, who'd returned to his side once this latest attack had launched.

"Retreat? We still greatly outnumber them, My Lord," Nabalsa said, shocked that Tabnit would give the order. "Our frontal attacks failed, but we've seen how effective digging the trenches has been. Couldn't we ..."

"No," Tabnit said, cutting him off. "This army isn't locked behind walls. As soon as we start digging, they can march around us, turning our flank. There's also no point at which we can start the trenches that is outside of their range. As soon as we start digging, they'll move forward, putting their weapons in range of our men, still well outside of the range in which we could respond. Entrenching now, here in the field, would be death. Besides that, did you notice anything about this army? Anything unusual?"

"Unusual?" Nabalsa asked.

Tabnit repressed a sigh. Nabalsa was a good man, determined and intelligent, but he was too much like the majority of their officer corps. Stuck in the old ways of doing things; too used to rolling over the enemy without any finesse, substituting brute force instead. They hadn't learned to read the enemy to determine a way to counter them instead of just all-out attacking.

"I was right. The majority of the Romans didn't retreat from their forts. They rendezvoused with this army and brought all of their large thunder weapons with them. Did you not see what they did with them? With them having that kind of power, we won't last in the field. No, we retreat to Daramouda. Send out riders.

Any remaining forces we have in Hispania or Germania are to fall back to Daramouda as well. That's clearly where the Romans are headed, and we can't afford to lose our supply chain to Carthage. We're going to need every man we can get to defend it."

Nabalsa looked uncertain, "But My Lord, if we retreat behind the walls, the Romans could destroy us once we're trapped there, just like we did to them at the port?"

Tabnit shook his head, "While we've been on campaign, several of the engineers from the east have improved our defenses, thickening the walls with layers of wood and earth in between the stone walls. They tell me they are strong enough to absorb the impact of their weapons. If the Romans want Daramouda, they will have to take our walls, finally bringing them into range of our catapults where we can utilize our fire powder. We can shift the balance of power back in our favor. Now, go. Select a unit to block the Romans so the rest of the army can escape. Use most of the mounted forces, they won't be useful in the defense of Daramouda, but their charges could cause the Romans to hesitate, slowing them long enough for us to get away."

"Yes, My Lord, at once," Nabalsa said, bowing his head before hurrying off to carry out Tabnit's orders.

Chapter 28

Devnum

Lucilla arrived for a second time at the large open field outside of Devnum. Though the early fall morning air held a chill that warned of the upcoming winter, a large crowd had already gathered in anticipation of this day's event, again they were held back by several squads of Praetorians. Hortensius and Sorantius were at the balloon in the center of the field, no doubt making last-minute preparations for their launch.

The first test had proven to be a disaster, with the balloon igniting shortly after lifting off the ground, sending burning fragments raining down as the craft plummeted to earth. Thankfully, no one had been injured, but it had been terrifying. Lucilla suspected that was why today's crowd seemed even larger than before. Nothing brought spectators together more than the possibility of a spectacle, especially a disastrous one.

The Praetorians were already struggling to hold back the encroaching onlookers. The audience was excited and parted as she approached the circle, some reaching out to touch the hem of her stola as she made her way into the center of the test area. Modius and the rest of her guards were anxious since she'd been brutally attacked the previous year by a similar crowd that included insurrectionists, but she wasn't going to let that keep her away from her people.

A cheer went up for her as she made her way across the open field to where the two inventors were working, both of them stopping to see what the commotion was about.

"Empress, wonderful timing! We are nearly ready for the launch. Please, come see the improvements for yourself!" Hortensius said eagerly, gesturing to the strange orb resting in a large wicker basket.

She moved next to the basket, peering inside.

"As you can see, we encased the firepot in the new material you described. It held up very well during our testing, getting hot, but not so hot as to set even a piece of paper put against it on fire. It's excellent at dissipating the heat and should keep the basket from catching fire like the last time."

"Well done. I'm excited to see it in action," she said.

"Then please, stand back," he said to her, before turning his attention back to the attendants surrounding the conveyance. "That should be good. Let's get started."

Lucilla backed up as the men lit the firepot and scrambled away. Like the first time, after a few minutes, the fabric began to swell ever so slowly and expand until it finally lifted off the ground, turning globe-like as it rose above the basket. Again, as it had done the first time, the basket lifted off the ground, the ropes pulling tight as it held several handspans off the ground.

Murmurs rippled through the crowd, probably spectators who were here previously telling their fellows that this was when everything went wrong the last time. She waited almost breathlessly as it floated there, and nothing else happened.

"How will we know that it worked and there won't be a fire this time?" she asked, her impatience finally getting the best of her.

"I think that was long enough," Hortensius replied. "We're well past the point where everything went wrong last time. I think we're safe to assume it worked and move to the next stage of the test."

"Next stage?" she asked as Hortensius began waving for men to grab the dangling ropes and pull the balloon closer to the ground.

As she watched, a man trotted over from where a group of assistants stood, and climbed into the basket.

"Yes, the next stage is to test it with a pilot aboard," Hortensius explained. "Pridan has trained extensively for this flight, including learning Morse code and how to operate a telegraph."

"Why would he need to be trained in Morse code to go up there?" Lucilla asked.

Waving her over, he picked up the thick rope that led from the frame holding the basket to a large winch on the ground and pulled the wound rope apart slightly to reveal a pair of rubber-covered wire inside. Sophus had tried to explain why they needed a pair of wires, but it quickly got past Lucilla's understanding.

"So he can use this. There's a portable telegraph machine, essentially just the transmitter, inside the basket with him. Using it, the pilot can send messages back to the ground, reporting on what he sees through his spyglass. To keep the weight down, and because room inside the basket is limited, we didn't include a receiver, so he can't receive messages, but he's also been trained on the flag messaging system we used on the semaphore. Focusing his glasses down toward where the balloon is anchored, he'll be able to read those messages if need be. There will also normally be a second person in the basket, so one can type out what they see while the other continues to observe from the air. He'll also have flags up there with him, should the telegraph stop working. It will be slower, but we can still get messages that way."

"Clever," she said.

Although they had discussed having a way for the pilot to send messages, she hadn't realized Hortensius had progressed this far with the idea or included the telegraph with the balloon itself. Especially not how he had the telegraph wire protected inside the rope attached to the rising balloon.

"All set," Sorantius, who was over at the balloon checking the equipment, said.

"Excellent," Hortensius said. "Please step away from the rope, Your Majesty."

She stepped back as the men around the basket scattered. The men who'd been holding the ropes on the side of the basket released them, letting it spring up to just about head height. On Hortensius's signal, the operators of the winch began cranking the machine, letting out more and more rope. With each handspan of rope released, the balloon climbed higher into the sky. Above the trees, then above the height of the palace and the Colosseum, and it continued to rise.

The crowd clapped and cheered, enthralled by the spectacle of a man reaching heights usually reserved for birds only. Lucilla shielded her eyes from the sun with one hand as she tracked the balloon's progress, higher and higher, until the basket was nothing more than a tiny speck against the blue sky. The much larger balloon was still clearly visible, but it had gone so high as to seem noticeably smaller, much like seeing a ship far out to sea. She marveled at it. That a man was up there, flying.

Suddenly, the telegraph machine resting on a table nearby sprang to life. Lucilla turned her attention to it as clicks and taps sounded out a message. One of Hortensius' assistants transcribed the incoming transmission, hurriedly writing down the translated letters on a sheet of paper.

Handing it to Hortensius, the inventor looked it over, smiling to himself before turning his attention to Lucilla.

"It's a message from Pridan, Your Majesty. He says all is well. He is amazed by how far he can see."

"Please ask him to describe it to us," she said, wanting to both see what kind of detail the man could see using a spyglass that high in the sky, and wanting to confirm the ability to get messages from the ground to him.

"Send the request, please," Hortensius said to one of his other assistants.

Two of the men went to a set of signal flags, one of them picking the flags up while the other looked up at the balloon through a spyglass. There was some back and forth between them until the second man began to wave the flags in the style she'd seen before on board Valdar's ships. A minute passed, and then two, while nothing happened, before the telegraph receiver began to move again, hammering out a message. Lucilla turned her attention back to the assistant as he transcribed this new, lengthier message.

Again, Hortensius took the message, reading out loud this time, "Majesty, the view from up here is magnificent. I can see clear across Devnum. The water in the aqueduct, running from the reservoir, sparkles like jewels in the sun. The crowds at market around the Colosseum look like small insects from this height. I can see the gardens inside the palace, and the park between the buildings with its shade-providing trees. Beyond the city walls, orchards and farmland stretch as far as the eye can see. There is a ship leaving the harbor, looking much like a toy. What a privilege it is to be granted such a perspective!"

Lucilla smiled as she heard the pilot's enthusiastic account, reminded again of the wonders this new invention could provide. Talking to Ky and Sophus, it was easy to accept these wonders as normal ... commonplace. It took a moment like this to realize the amazement they could bring. She just wished she could join Pridan, sailing high above the city and countryside, seeing it all unfold below. Of course, neither Ky nor her guards would ever allow something like that to happen.

"You've truly outdone yourselves," she said to Hortensius and Sorantius, both of whom grinned at the compliment, as they looked from her back up to their invention flying in the sky.

"Thank you, Your Majesty," the manufacturer said.

Turning her attention to Hortensius, she said, "Make preparations to transport the balloon immediately. I've received word that Valdar has captured the port of Kalb in the mouth of the Middle Sea and is sailing ships up to support Ky's attack on the Carthaginian's main port in Gaul. I want the balloon, all of the telegraph receivers and transmitters we have ready, and as much of the insulated wire as possible shipped to him with the next supply ship."

"Of course, Your Majesty. We'll need to dismantle and pack the balloon for transport, but we'll have it done by the end of the day," he said. "I'll also send the technicians with the most experience operating this and the telegraph. I know the Consul doesn't need assistance from someone like me to work these, but I'm certain it will make his job easier."

"Good. Very good. Then I believe we need to begin expediting the building of the telegraph system. Beyond the legions and a handful of other uses, I don't believe we need to devote a lot of resources to creating a large number of balloons, although I'm certain there's going to be some demand for them once word gets out. I'm all for everyone making money on something like this, that'll be profitable, but let's keep our eye on the prize, as it were.

I have an engagement at the palace, so I'll leave this to you to take care of."

"I understand. I'll take care of this at once," he bowed, hurrying off, already shouting orders at his assistants.Lucilla felt a little pity for the man up in the balloon as the winch began to turn, pulling him back to the ground. If she was up there, it was likely she'd never want to come back down. She allowed herself one final glance at the slowly descending balloon before turning back to her carriage, her face turning serious.

An hour later, and much less jubilant, Lucilla sat underneath an open tent in the palace's side courtyard, hidden from public view. Her expression was stern as she steeled herself for what she must do next.

In the center of the courtyard sat the executioner's block, its solid surface scarred from previous uses, stained with dark streaks by the blood of traitors. It was a ghoulish object. She'd once asked her father why they couldn't just use a new block of wood each time, instead of hauling this horrendous thing out. He'd explained to her that executions weren't for putting men to death. That could be done quietly, without all the spectacle around the event. No, they were for the people watching. A warning or a symbol, depending on who was watching, as to what happened when they crossed the Empire. It was why these types of executions were mostly relegated to treason and other very serious crimes, and not just for thieves and murderers, who were normally dealt with much less publicly.

Today's execution had the same purpose, and hence needed the same props. The only difference with that today's spectacle was meant for an audience of one. They'd chosen this courtyard because of its seclusion, a wall of Praetorians and palace guards keeping everyone else away and blocking the view of what was set to happen today.

As if brought on by Lucilla's thoughts, there was a commotion at the courtyard entrance as Medb was led inside, flanked on either side by stone-faced guards. Her steps faltered briefly as she recognized the chopping block and the large man standing next to it, axe in hand. She handled the shock well, walking with forced dignity toward Lucilla's small tent, never faltering. She didn't try to run or cower. The only indication that she recognized what was about to happen was in her eyes. Lucilla watched the emotions play across them as Medb glanced between Lucilla and the executioner's block. Surprise. Fear. Anger.

The guards halted Medb just inside the tent where Lucilla sat, releasing her arms, but not stepping back.

Lifting her chin defiantly, the queen said, "You'll regret this. Killing me will not stop my people's anger over what you've done."

Lucilla regarded her coolly for a moment, before saying, "I think you overestimate 'your' people's anger regarding your fate. Already, their quality of life has improved under the Empire. There have been no protests for your release. No cries for your return. But I think you are mistaken about what's happening today. This isn't for you."

Lucilla had to suppress a grin of pleasure as Medb's facade broke, relief and surprise washing across her face.

"What? Then who ..."

Her question trailed off as Lucilla gestured to the Praetorians walking into the courtyard. Between them, they hauled a struggling man, his well-styled toga marking him as the Flamen Dialis, less regal than it had once been, stained and torn in many places, his feet leaving marks in the ground as they dragged him into view.

"Unhand me!" he screamed. "You will pay for this sacrilege!"

The Praetorians ignored his outbursts as they pulled him toward his final destination. The preacher's thrashing grew more violent as he recognized the executioner's block, his fate suddenly becoming very real. Then his gaze landed on Lucilla with Medb, flanked by the guards, standing next to her.

"Harlot!" he shrieked. "You are a plague upon Rome, a filthy corruption spreading like rot through the Empire! May Jupiter damn you to Tartarus for your sins!"

Lucilla didn't say anything, simply gestured toward the executioner's block. The preacher's curses turned to wails as he was pushed to his knees, his head pressed down on the wood, where a rope was tightened around his neck, locking him in place, his eyes staring at the basket being placed in front of the block.

Lucilla turned her attention from the preacher back to Medb and said, "I know what you've been doing. Your treasonous conversations with Vesnius, fomenting unrest among my people. We know what you convinced Cormac to do, planting more seeds. We know about the dozen others you've been talking to. I know you're doing this in some vain hope that you can turn the chaos created in my Empire into some ploy to get your throne back. I imagine you already know how unrealistic that is, but you've decided to go down this road anyway."

Medb's eyes widened slightly in surprise, maybe not realizing how much of her plan had been exposed until that moment, but otherwise remaining silent. Lucilla let the unease hang in the air between them, punctuated by the screams of Vesnius, holding Medb's gaze steadily.

Finally, Lucilla said, "Cormac has begged me to spare your life. In spite of knowing you've been playing him for a fool, the boy seems to really love you. I have no idea if you return those feelings or if you see him as only a fool, a tool you can use to further your own power. Honestly, I don't care. Cormac and his father are important members of our Empire, but they're not the only reasons your head isn't on that block today. You're smart. A little too smart, maybe, but it's something we need. If we can put your ambition to work for us, instead of against us, I think you could be a great asset to the Empire."

A flicker of hope spread across Medb's face. Hope, and maybe something else. Arrogance? Ambition?

"There. That's what I'm talking about," Lucilla said, calling out Medb's unspoken thoughts. "That is why most of my advisors have argued against sparing your life. They believe that the Empire would be better served by displeasing your husband, and his family, than letting you live. They think you can't stop yourself. I think you're smart enough to realize how close you've come to losing your life. I'm willing to roll the dice and give you *this one* chance to prove you can be as smart as I hope you are. But I'm only going to do this on *my* terms. You get to choose. You can either fall in line and serve the Empire loyally, or your head will be the next one pressed against the headsman's block."

Medb glanced between Lucilla and the executioner's block before looking at the ground, no longer meeting Lucilla's eyes.

"You leave me little choice," she said.

"No, I leave you with the same choice you've had all along," Lucilla said. "You chose wrong the first time, and you were within a hair's breadth of paying the price for it. I'm giving you a chance to make the choice again. Hopefully, you'll choose better this time."

Medb raised her eyes, looking unsure, a battle between rage and acceptance playing across her face, her usual composure shattered.

"I know what you really want," Lucilla said as Medb fought herself. "You crave power. You want your throne back, your kingdom, your old glory."

Medb's eyes flashed, but she held her tongue.

"You have to accept that it won't happen. You lost that option the moment you sided with the Carthaginians, who would have dismantled your kingdom and had you quietly disposed of once you no longer served their purposes. Even if my Empire falls, there is no way for you reclaim your throne. But that doesn't mean you have to become a pauper. I'm willing to provide you some of the power you crave, within reason, if you're willing to accept who you serve. The Britannian Empire will outlast both of us. You can either have your legacy be part of its foundation or one of the names crushed under our boot. The choice is yours."

Medb stared at the blood-stained wood, the priest still struggling, his execution waiting for the Empress's word, the headsman standing, axe in hand, next to the pathetic man kneeling at his feet.

"Fine," she said, an angry resignation in her voice. "What will you have of me?"

"We'll get to that in time. For now, be good to your husband, whose request to spare you is the main reason you're alive. I would not have taken the time to reconsider my initial impulse to have you gone if it weren't for him. Consider that before you take your anger out in that direction."

"Fine," Medb said again.

Lucilla didn't know if her request would help Cormac's fate with his wife or not, but she'd tried. She'd made it clear, talking to the boy, that he was playing a dangerous game with Medb, but he was smitten. Maybe he'd gain her respect and they'd actually grow to love each other, or maybe she'd kill him in his sleep. Either way, she'd done her best for them.

"Let's be clear. If you step even a toe over the line again, there will be no second chance. You will suffer the same fate as the men you duped," Lucilla said, gesturing toward the weeping Vesnius, pathetic and trembling as he knelt before the headsman's block.

Medb's lips tightened, but she gave a curt nod. Her usual superior aura had evaporated, replaced by a wariness that suggested, just maybe, that this time she'd got the message. To set the point more firmly, Lucilla gave a nod to the executioner. The man hefted his heavy axe, prompting Vesnius to thrash against the restraints, his wailing intensifying as the end neared.

The axe swung in a wide arc, ending in a sickening thud as it impacted against the chipped wood, followed by a softer one as the priest's head rolled into the waiting basket, his body giving one final spasm. Lucilla's stomach turned at the sight, but she didn't look away. If she could order the man's death, she would witness her order carried out.

"Don't forget," she said, not bothering to look at Medb as she stood and marched off the field, leaving the former queen in her wake.

Chapter 29

Daramouda

Ky stood, looking at the high walls of the besieged port and the smoke billowing up from inside its walls. The Carthaginians had picked their ground well, even if they hadn't done it on purpose. Almost no high ground existed, at least not within range of the port, limiting his ability to fire into the city. They'd also improved their walls more than he'd thought they were capable of.

He could see wood and dirt through the cracks and holes left by the continuous fire from his cannon, showing a pretty advanced, for the time, improvement in the walls. It also explained why they were unusually thick, compared to the other walled cities he'd seen.

"This is taking too long," Bomilcar grumbled next to him, lowering his spyglass. "We're going to shoot through all of our gunpowder before we get through this wall, and will have to resort to throwing bullets at them once we do."

Ky nodded in understanding. It seemed unlikely that the Carthaginians would realize one of Britannia's greatest weaknesses. They may have figured out that he didn't have the manpower they did, but he doubted they'd know enough about gunpowder to work out how slow their production was or the limit that placed on his ability to bombard a fortification. They'd simply tried to protect their men from his cannon, and lucked into a strategy that played against his weaknesses.

Already, he'd had to restrain his men's enthusiasm, slowing their rate of fire to once every five minutes, to keep the artillerymen from exhausting the supplies they currently had on hand. Not that it would ultimately matter.

"Patience. Between us and Valdar, they're surrounded. We might be short on gunpowder, but with as many men as they've shoved inside those walls, they've got to be running very short on food. I can't imagine they'll hold out for long. Besides, we'll have some new options soon. I've been informed that the new artillery I ordered from Hortensius, along with some other surprises, are on their way from home, and should be here in a few weeks. Once we have those, we can hopefully speed things up."

What he didn't say was the word from home had been Lucilla over the comm and not a runner, who'd managed to arrive ahead of the supply ships coming their way. Not that either would matter in the long run. In spite of Velius's sacrifices, this would probably not be the last time the armies split up. The balloons would give the men not with him some of the same advantage they had when they were with him, thanks to his drone. For now, though, they were all together, which meant the balloons wouldn't enhance his men's capabilities much.

The howitzers would, since they would allow him to fire over the walls, which would solve his current problem of his cannon not getting the elevation they needed to fire over the walls, but it didn't matter. As he said to Bomilcar, with Valdar shelling from the unwalled seaward side of the port, coupled with a total blockade, they wouldn't last long. It was why trying to take the walls by force was never an option for him. That would have been costly and done little but add a few weeks to the campaign season, which would be generally slowing anyway now that winter was approaching.

"What's really bothering me is that they're up to something over there, but I can't tell what," Ky said.

"You saw this through your bird thing, yes?" Bomilcar asked, still struggling to understand Ky's drone.

That was another thing that would change once they had the balloon. As miraculous as it was, the basics of a balloon were understandable and wouldn't instantly devolve into thoughts of magic the way seeing anti-grav in action did. Bomilcar did well, adapting to it as he had, accepting that Ky could just see through the small disc he'd shown the general, and not questioning it at every turn like some other subordinates had.

"Yes. They've had heavy traffic in and out of it for days, but I can't figure out what they're doing. They've got most of the entrance covered, probably as protection from the heat and sun and not to avoid detection, since I doubt they've realized we can see what they're doing, but the effect of blocking my observation is the same. I do occasionally see barrels, but they seem to both be going in and coming out in equal numbers, making it impossible to guess what they're doing."

"Maybe just a place to feed and rest their men on the walls out of the sun."

"Maybe," Ky said. "But I don't think so. It feels like I'm missing some ..."

"*Commander,*" Sophus's dispassionate voice said, interrupting him.

Its warning was too late, with the words barely said when he felt the earth tremble like an earthquake, the ground shifting underfoot. Part of his brain almost dismissed the thought, since there were no fault lines where they stood, making an earthquake unlikely, except the expression on Bomilcar's face indicated he felt the same thing. Ky's brain was still grasping for an understanding of what happened when the entire world seemed to heave and rip apart.

Ky and Bomilcar were launched into the air as a massive explosion ripped up from the earth. He slammed hard into the ground a dozen meters away from where he had stood, only his advanced reflexes allowing him to roll with the impact, keeping him from being seriously injured. He and Bomilcar had been lucky. They'd been on the edge of where the explosion occurred. The center of his line had been shattered, with the bodies of legionaries lying hundreds of meters from where they'd previously stood. Even sections of the line away from the blast had not gone unscathed. In places, Ky could see men crushed by the heavy steel tubes of cannons that had been launched into the air before falling on them.

The blast hadn't been right on his line. The crater it left marked the center of the explosion several dozen meters ahead of the front of his line. It was large enough that the edge of the crater, over a hundred meters from its center, still extended into his line, completely breaking its center.

It wasn't hard to figure out what happened, or how they'd done it. Clearly, the activity he'd seen had been tunneling. Their commander had taken the lesson Velius had taught them and adapted it, moving their stockpile forward under his own line. Considering how high the groundwater table was here, the tunneling itself was an impressive feat, since water would have been a serious problem. They must have also spent their entire supply of gunpowder, since the blast had been very large. Not as big as the one Velius had set off, based on the reports, but still massive.

A groan nearby broke Ky out of his thoughts. Bomilcar tried to push himself up and then collapsed as his supporting arm gave way.

"Ahh ..." the general groaned, clutching the offending appendage.

"Easy," Ky said, helping the man up.

The man's shoulder bent at an unusual angle, not severe enough to be absolutely broken, but definitely unnatural.

"*It appears to be dislocated,*" Sophus offered, superimposing an anatomical display on top of the general's shoulder, highlighting the affected joint and surrounding musculature. "*It will have to be reset into the socket for his arm to be mobile again. If left untreated, the arm will lose circulation and become lame.*"

"Show me how to fix it," Ky sub-vocalized.

In his time, nanos would swarm the area, putting the affected limb in something like a cushion, releasing micro-targeted numbing agents before slipping everything back into place. It would have been nearly painless and happened almost as soon as the joint went out of its socket. Unfortunately for Bomilcar, he didn't have that advantage.

Sophus overlay the steps Ky needed to take.

"I need to put your shoulder back in place," Ky said, putting his hands on either side of the man's shoulder as Sophus's display showed him what to do.

"The line," Bomilcar said through gritted teeth, trying to push Ky away.

"I know," Ky said, already seeing the gates of the city open through the drone feed, Carthaginian soldiers lining up on the other side of the wall, ready to march through. "I need you mobile and leading the men on the wings."

Moderating his force, to keep from causing more injury, he pushed the joint back into place as Bomilcar screamed as the muscle and sinew stretched, the bone and cartilage scraping as it slotted back where it should be.

"They'll be coming," Bomilcar said, as Ky helped him up, still gritting his teeth through the pain. "Following up on the blast."

A thick haze of dust covered everything, limiting visibility, but Bomilcar's years of experience told him what was happening, even if he couldn't see it.

"I know. They're already coming through the gates. I'll get our center back into place. Our line covers the entire arc around of the city, so they can't flank us. They're going to try and push through the hole in our center. I need you to get to the men on the flanks. We're going to be weak and even pieced back together, the center won't hold for long. Once they're fully committed, I need you to bring the flanks in, wrap around them."

Bomilcar's eyes flicked to the side as he visualized the battlefield, something Ky needed Sophus and his advanced retinal displays to be able to accomplish.

With a nod, he said, "The center has to hold long enough for that."

"I know. I'll take care of it. Go," Ky said, slapping him on his uninjured shoulder before turning his attention to the task in front of him.

As soon as Bomilcar was off, Ky grabbed the nearest soldier he could find.

"Go to the reserves, order their cohorts, all of them, to double time to the center of our line to reinforce and plug the hole," Ky told the bewildered man, still trying to make sense of what was happening.

Being given a specific task seemed to be enough to shake the man out of his fugue, his eyes focusing on Ky as he spoke. The man gave a shake of his head, maybe in an attempt to clear it, before running off toward the rear. At least, Ky hoped he shook off his confusion since he didn't have time to go to the rear and get the reinforcements himself.

"Spread out. Grab anyone you can and get them back in line," he yelled at his lictores.

They seemed torn, unable to decide between staying with their charge or following his orders. Strabo finally settled the indecision, yelling at them to follow orders before cutting to the right, grabbing and shoving stunned legionaries as he went.

Ky didn't pay the men any more attention, his focus was on the line in front of him and the drone as he moved toward the crater. The scene of devastation grew worse as he approached ground zero of the explosion. A massive crater yawned open where solid earth had been just minutes before. Bodies and parts of bodies were strewn around the rim and littered the bottom.

Men staggered around in shock, many with ghastly injuries, bleeding and hobbled. Some crawled on hands and knees, while others just sat staring blankly ahead. The blast had shredded the center of the line. Through the drone, Ky could see the enemy closing on the other side of the crater.

"On your feet! The enemy is on us!" Ky bellowed, trying to get through the daze all of his men seemed to be in. "Back in line, now!"

Slowly, some of the men at least began to come to. Ky's words pierced the veil they were under, the danger of their situation suddenly becoming real.

"Move! Form a line!" Ky continued to yell, grabbing men by their armor, yanking them to their feet and into place.

Then the enemy did something Ky didn't expect. Instead of going around the crater, circling the obstacle to get to the still-shattered men, they flowed down into it. Row upon row of Carthaginian soldiers ran down into the center of the crater, almost funneling into it rather than going around. For the life of him, Ky couldn't imagine what they were thinking, but he wasn't going to let this moment pass him by.

"Open fire," he yelled, slapping several men's rifles into their hands, pointing down into the crater. "Pick up your damn weapons."

The enemy suddenly appearing through the haze, right in front of them, did more to get the stragglers moving than any yelling he did. There were less than a hundred of his own men at the front of the crater, versus the hundreds flowing into the crater itself, but at least they were moving. Raising their weapons or finding dropped weapons, resetting the primer, and aiming.

If the messenger he sent did his job, the reinforcements should be here soon. He just needed to hold out for a few minutes. The Carthaginians seemed to be doing their best to help him, putting themselves in the worst possible position, but he needed his men to shake off their shock and get into action.

The first rifle cracked, and then two more. With the throng of enemy soldiers reaching the center of the crater, there was no chance of missing, the bullets punched down into them, causing ghastly wounds as they killed. More and more rifles began to fire as his men finally got back into the fight.

"That's it," he yelled. "Keep firing. Don't let up."

The men fired and reloaded, their training taking over. It was almost like being on the range again. It was also not having enough of an impact. There were just too many Carthaginians and not enough of his own men firing. Their explosion had done its job, ripping apart his line with such devastation that he couldn't bring enough men to bear in time. Carthaginians fell by the dozens, but more pushed in behind them. Ky had to slow them down, to buy time for his reinforcements to arrive.

Drawing his sidearm, Ky carefully placed two precious rounds into the teeming mass below. He had less than a dozen rounds left, and with these, he was now in the single digits, but there was no choice. Once the enemy started up the sides of the crater, his line, and then the entire army, would fold.

The pellets expanded into burning balls of green flame, rolling through the enemy, melting men, twisting armor and weapons, vaporizing skin and bone. Men on the edges of the blast caught on fire as the super-heated air reacted with the loose tunics and treated hide armor. With the men packed so tightly, the fire started to spread to their neighbors; beards and hair, shirts and bindings went up in flames, the tightly packed mass at the bottom of the crater making perfect conditions for the fire. It was like an inferno in the heart of a wooden city, except these weren't buildings, they were people. Too pressed together to run or put out the flames, they burned. Screams echoed from inside the crater.

Ky didn't wait. They had slowed, but not halted, and now more were running from their smoldering comrades than trying to advance the attack.

"Keep firing!" Ky commanded as he scooped up a rifle and ammo pouch from a nearby body and began adding its fire to the growing cacophony.

Seeing their commander's example, Ky's men fought with renewed fury, pouring relentless fire into the crater. The sound was deafening as hundreds of rounds ripped into the tightly packed Carthaginians. They had no room to maneuver or find cover. It was a slaughter.

Their advance faltered, as men tried to find a place to hide from the onslaught, or were gripped with fear at the sudden appearance of what seemed like the fires of Hades itself, magic that overwhelmed their sense of self-preservation.

Ky noticed that someone on the enemy side had gotten things together. He could see through the drone that they had stopped pouring into the crater, instead doing what they should have done from the beginning, circling the depression and attacking along either side of the crater. Through the drone, Ky could see what looked like a banner standard at the other side of the crater, where the enemy was starting to split to either side. Whoever that officer was, he threatened to get the attack Ky had managed to stall reinvigorated.

"Commander," a tribune said, rushing up to him. "I have the thirtieth, forty-second, and forty-fifth cohorts here."

Relief washed over Ky. He had barely a hundred men holding this side of the crater, and he was about to be hit by thousands of men pouring around either side. They would still be outnumbered with the addition of these thirteen hundred men, but it brought the ratios up enough to at least give his men a chance.

"Give me one century here in the middle to keep firing on the men in the crater, so they don't rally and hit us here. Split the rest between either side and prepare for contact. You take the right side. You should see the enemy streaming out of the dust any moment now. Prepare for hand-to-hand combat."

The tribune's eyes widened, but he didn't hesitate, not even bothering to acknowledge Ky's orders before shouting orders to get his men into position. Which is exactly what he should have done. Ky yelled for the men closest to him to follow him, charging down the left flank, arriving just as the Carthaginian horde emerged from the dust and smoke.

He knew what Lucilla would say if she could see him here, in the front line, flanked by legionaries on either side, as the Carthaginians charged toward them. In this kind of combat, the highest casualties always came from the front lines, especially now that most of his men no longer carried shields, armed only with rifles and gladii.

"Fire!" Ky yelled, and the men with loaded weapons who'd gotten into place in time let loose a volley of fire right into the faces of the charging Carthaginians.

As it always did, the impact had an effect, causing the Carthaginian line to stagger slightly as it was hit the wall of lead. Ky also knew that the effect was limited and would only last a second.

"Charge!" Ky yelled, gladius held up as he led off, ahead of the rest of the men.

They crashed into the Carthaginian line hard. He parried the first spear thrust at his chest, then sliced his gladius across the attacker's throat. Another spear glanced off his armor, knocking him back a step. Ky recovered and stabbed under the enemy's guard, dropping him quickly.

Ky was a blur of motion, no longer holding back to keep from scaring his own people. His sword flashed, over and over, cutting through men and material in a blur, churning through men as a thresher would cut through wheat.

Even so, the enemy tried to kill him. Two spears slashed forward at him, Sophus displaying their projected path of progress. Ky's hand shot out, grabbing the shaft of one of the spears in a vice-like grip while parrying the other with his shield. Shoving the spear in his hand back, he sent the soldier tumbling into the man behind him, crashing hard as Ky's enhanced muscles did what no other human on this planet could do.

He wasn't alone. His men may not have been able to copy his feats of speed and strength, but they fought no less hard, bayonets stabbing forward, rifle butts parrying spears. The rear ranks continued to fire over their heads, scything down the enemy ranks and creating small breaks that helped keep the enemy from completely overwhelming them.

It was also clear they were not going to be able to continue this forever. They needed something to break the tide, and Ky knew what it was.

"Push men," he yelled as he intensified his attack, cutting his way into the Carthaginian line.

Ky was a whirlwind of death, carving a path through the Carthaginian ranks. His men fought bravely behind him as he slashed and stabbed tirelessly, his blade finding enemy flesh again and again.

The Carthaginians threw themselves at him relentlessly. A hulking warrior with an axe rushed him, but Ky sidestepped the blow and relieved the man of his weapon arm in one smooth motion. Another came at his back only to find Ky's sword protruding from his chest a moment later.

Step by step, Ky cut his way further into the massed Carthaginians until there were enemies all around him. They seemed as surprised as his own men were, unsure how to deal with the enemy allowing himself to become separated from his own support as he did. If it had been anyone else, it would never have happened. But Ky wasn't anyone else.

Aside from his enhanced strength and speed, he had Sophus, who'd brought the drone overhead, rapidly updating the battlescape for him, allowing him to see attackers that should have been able to attack from behind without ever being seen. Ky let himself fall into the motion assist, becoming almost one with Sophus and his projections, the movement of his own gladius and the stolen axe never stopping. Blocking and parrying in every direction, stabbing and slashing any man that came within his reach.

The Carthaginians' attack slowed as they pushed away from the creature released in their midst, their animal brains taking over, choosing flight over fight. They still attacked his line, but the men within his reach became less and less as the enemy flowed around him, as if he were a stone in the center of a stream.

Ky didn't care, he was a man possessed, and he had a target in his sights. He continued forward, bodies flying as he cleaved men nearly in two, finally breaking into a more open area near the rear of this mass of Carthaginians, right where the battle standard projected over their heads, rallying their men as his own standard rallied his.

The Carthaginian commander's eyes went wide as Ky exploded through the mass of men surrounding and protecting him, covered in gore from the dozens of men he slaughtered to get there, practically dripping with their life's blood.

The man tried to backpedal, almost instinctually, to escape facing a demon, a thing of nightmares, but he was too slow. Too human. With a guttural cry, Ky lunged forward, sinking his blade deep into the commander's chest. The man let out a choked gurgle, then slid off the blood-slicked blade to the ground.

For a moment, Ky stood alone amidst the Carthaginian inner circle, before he resumed his carnage, slashing the junior commanders, giving them the same fate as their general. And then his men were there, crashing through the breach he'd created, a guttural roar going up from them collectively as they fought hard, driven into a killing frenzy.

The combination of the sight of Ky, his men's frenzied fighting, and the death of their commanders was too much for the shattered Carthaginians, who began to fall back, trying to find safety from certain death.

A full retreat, at least where Ky's men were fighting, was brewing. But there were still other parts of the line that were in danger. The tribune on the right was fighting hard, but his men were being pushed back by a wall of Carthaginians, that side of the Britannian line bowing far inward, moments away from breaking, creating the breach Ky'd been fighting to stop.

Just as Ky turned to fight in that direction, plunging back into the Carthaginian line from the small bubble of quiet he'd created around the fallen commander, a trumpet sounded, piercing through the din of battle. Ky sent the drone higher, trying to get a better view of the battle.

Relief rushed over him. Bomilcar had arrived, the flanks of the Britannian line hitting the Carthaginians from either side. Carthaginians were still marching out of the city, their huge army taking time to pour out of their port refuge for the attack that should have crushed the Britannians once and for all. Now, the line of marching Carthaginians was hit on either side by the attacking Britannians. Their march forward stalled as they fought in both directions, desperately trying to retreat into the city.

Watching this play out from the drone, Ky realized they had a chance to end the entire battle right here. His men were exhausted, the strain of battle starting to sap the strength from them, but they couldn't rest yet. He needed a little more from them first.

"Don't let them escape. The port is open. Follow me!" Ky yelled, raising his weapons and charging forward, leaving it to the men with him to follow his example.

Sophus focused the drone's camera, showing Ky that his men, in spite of their exhaustion, didn't hesitate. They understood completely, that their wounded enemy was trying to escape back behind the walls, and that their commander was going to personally keep that from happening.

They'd kept their faith in him through the brutal fight to keep the battle around the crater from destroying their lines. They were now prepared to follow him into the mouth of the underworld. Ky and his men crashed into the long Carthaginian column, fighting straight into it as Bomilcar pressed on either side.

For a moment, it seemed as if the Carthaginian resistance might stiffen, but the attack from three sides along the five-hundred-meter column was too much. They broke just like the men around the crater had broken. This time, there were Britannians on either side to press in on them as their line collapsed. No one escaped the press of death.

Ky's focus, however, was on the gates. Once enough Carthaginians got out of the way, the enemy would try to close them, put the stopper back in the bottle. He couldn't allow that to happen.

Ky slashed and hacked his way through the enemy soldiers. All around him, the Carthaginian column was disintegrating under the Britannian assault. Men screamed and fell before him, but Ky's eyes remained fixed ahead on the open gates. Ky dodged Carthaginian attacks and his own men who were attacking the enemy from his left and right, navigating over and around obstacles with a single-minded purpose.

He ducked under a wild sword swing, then lunged forward, impaling the attacker. He dodged around two Carthaginians desperately trying to get to the safety of the port, cutting them down from behind as he passed.

Ky was within one hundred meters now. Panic was everywhere.

"Through the gates," Ky screamed at the soldiers around him, some from the reinforcements, some the men following in his wake, scrambling over the quickly growing carpet of bodies.

And then they were at the gates, the Carthaginians who'd been manning the massive wooden doors falling back, the pressure from the enemy and their own retreating comrades too much for them.

Ky and his men surged forward, flooding through the open gates. His men made him proud. Even as mixed up as badly as their divisions were, no one officer knowing where any of their men were, they still worked as a unit. The moment they burst through the gates, Britannians fanned out. Some flowed up the steps to the wall while squads broke off and continued chasing the enemy down the alleys and streets, killing any Carthaginians they came upon.

Ky finally stopped, letting his men carry on with the gruesome work. The city was theirs. The Carthaginian army, while still outnumbering them, even now, had completely fallen apart, each soldier trying to find safety. From the drone, Ky could see hundreds running to the docks, jumping into the ocean, trying to swim their way to safety. Valdar would handle them.

There wouldn't be much in the way of prisoners, not from this battle. His men were blood-crazed, and there was no stopping them. Especially the veterans of the Seventh, who'd been one of the units on the flanks. After seeing their leader killed, their men chased for weeks by the Carthaginians, they wanted vengeance, and it would take an act of God to stop them.

The outcome of the battle had been a lot closer than it should have been. What had been a siege that Ky had been certain he would win had almost turned into a disaster. The tunneling and explosion had been brilliant, and it had almost worked. It was only the Carthaginians' mistake of trying to attack through the crater, instead of around it, that had saved the Britannians, allowing the reinforcements enough time to arrive and plug the hole.

There was a lesson to be learned from this. The enemy might be primitive, without the weapons that he'd gifted the Britannians with, and they might be rigid in how they fought, but they could still be dangerous. He only had to look at Bomilcar to realize how intelligent their leaders could be. As they took the fight to Africa, he'd have to keep that at the forefront of his planning.

For now, though, they'd found victory.

Chapter 30

Port of Kalb

Valdar stepped out of the temporary housing he'd been given when the fleet arrived back at the port a handful of days before, stretching and taking in the crisp salty air. He still thought of the cabin of his ship as his home, since it's where he spent the majority of his time, but even he had to admit it was nice to sleep somewhere a little less cramped.

He was even considering getting something a little more permanent, for when he wasn't aboard ships. The weather here was certainly nicer than Britannia, with its incessant rain and cold winters. The weather was definitely cooling as winter began to set in, but it wasn't the bone-chilling cold they had in Devnum. It was even a possibility now, with the new telegraph wires being strung across the continent, allowing him to communicate quickly with the capital instead of having to be there himself.

He took one last look over the construction happening down by the docks before moving toward the large building in the center of the city. It had previously housed the Carthaginian commander and was soon to be the home of the Britannian naval headquarters here in the Middle Sea. With the quickly growing fleet and even faster-growing merchant shipping activity, logistics was becoming more than he and his captains could handle on their own. While Valdar would miss the more free-wheeling early days of the navy, bureaucracy had made its way into his world, and even he had to bend to its will.

It did, however, give him a more convenient place to hold meetings with his captains. If his cabin was cramped to live in, it was downright suffocating when seventeen other captains and their first mates tried to cram into it to discuss strategy.

Today's meeting was even larger, with ship pursers, the newly arrived garrison commander assigned to the port, and his command staff also in attendance. The last to arrive, as was his prerogative, he was once again taken by the diversity among his captains, as the leadership slowly expanded beyond Romans, a handful of Scandi and Caledonians to bring in Ulaid, and even a few Germanics. With how quickly immigration from the freed tribes across the continent was growing the Empire, it probably wouldn't be long until they saw an even larger variety, including tribesmen from Gaul and Hispania. It certainly was a motley group.

"Well, it looks like we're all here," Valdar said, finding his place at the head of the table. "Good. We have a lot to cover, so let's get started."

Turning his attention first to the newly arrived garrison commander, an Ulaid named Niall, Valdar said, "I know you're just getting your feet under you, but there's a lot of work to be done here. The century I left here did good work repairing the damage caused by our shelling and capture of the city, but there's still a lot that needs repair. In addition, I need you to begin overseeing the construction of additional landward fortifications. I know we've managed to push the bulk of the Carthaginian forces off the continent, but a lot of the soldiers who ran from the battles have turned to banditry to survive, and we need to be prepared if they come this way. The Carthaginians built a port here because of how crucial it is in controlling the Middle Sea, and I would not be surprised if they attempted to retake it. Unless they make some major advances in shipbuilding very quickly, their easiest path to doing so would be to land a force and march south. I want you prepared for that possibility."

"I understand," the commander said in his thick accent.

"On that front, we also need to shore up our harbor defenses. We know the Carthaginians have access to gunpowder, and it's not outside of the realm of possibility that they'll soon figure out they can do more than lob it from catapults, which means the port needs to be able to defend itself from seaborne attacks as well. I want two new forts built at either end of the docks to extend our range of fire. With the new, larger cannons that I understand are under development for fixed positions, we should be able to outrange anything they might send our way. This port is the linchpin of our shipping lanes as we expand into the Middle Sea, and I want a well-protected area for our ships to harbor if need be."

"That will require a lot of material," Niall pointed out.

"I know. You'll get it. The next part of the war is dependent on us getting control of the sea before the legions are deployed to Africa. You'll get what you need."

"Good," he said.

"I've also sent a request to Lucan to have one of his senior builders sent here to help with the expansion of the docks. Besides widening the dock space we already have, we're also going to add in one slip for building ships here. The docks in Devnum need to get supplies delivered from the mainland to provide to us for their completion. Considering we've already been contacted by local tribes, who are interested in setting up some trading relationships now that they're free from Carthaginian control, we'll have more direct, and faster, access to those raw materials here."

"But you don't know if the Empress or Lucan will approve this expansion yet?" Dag, the captain of the Seadreki, said. "Aren't you getting ahead of yourself?"

"Maybe, but I want to get this port up and running fast, and I don't want to wait to build the slip until we get approval and our man gets picked and makes his way down here. We're going to act as if we have approval and, if it doesn't happen, we'll deal with that then."

"It's your head," the captain said.

"Back to the topic of the locals. You've probably already noticed the influx of merchants and I assume that's just the beginning. They're seeing the value of trade with the locals and what the sea lanes will do for us, and they can smell the money. I'm all for it, but we need to be ready for the problems that will come with them. We're going to have a building boom outside of the government-run facilities, and I expect the port to expand, so keep that in mind when building out the walls. We're going to also need to find a place for a factor from the capital to deal with collecting the taxes that will start being generated here."

"Are we planning on expanding our presence beyond the port? Taking over territory in the name of the Empire?" Niall asked.

"No. The Consul and Empress have both been clear that we do not want additional territory beyond controlling the occasional port or fort, to protect our interests. They'd rather make alliances and leave the governing of those places to the locals, rather than overextend the Empire."

"I see," Niall said, not sounding entirely convinced.

"On that topic, I have also sent a request to Britannia for a diplomat to be sent to negotiate more formal relations with the local tribes. Until then, I leave it to you to use your best judgment in dealing with the inevitable disputes that creep up."

"I'll do my best," Niall said.

"Good, 'cause on that front, you'll have to answer to the Empress, and not me. Now, as for the rest of us," Valdar said, turning his attention to his captains; "We have a job to do, which will be easier now that we have someone who can deal with things here at the port. Alfhildr, I'm leaving you to fix our ships, plus your own, and to maintain things here. Your squadron is responsible for securing the entrance to Oceanus and patrolling that side of the coast of both Hispania and North Africa. I want your focus on North Africa. With the pillars closed to them, those will be their only ports into the wider world. I want them shut down completely. Shell any operating ports into oblivion and sink any Carthaginian boat you find, I don't care if it's a galley or a fishing boat. This close to their homeland, we're not going to find a lot of independent villages, so assume anyone you encounter is going to be Phoenician and respond accordingly."

"With pleasure," she said in her deep contralto.

Normally, he wouldn't put her in charge of a squadron. She was a bit too hard-natured and would eventually wear relationships thin, but she had the aggressiveness he needed to ensure they maintained their foothold and shut down the Carthaginians' ports.

"Good. You're getting all five of our newest arrivals, so go easy on them. This will be good experience for them, but I don't want anyone resigning because you drove them too hard."

She looked displeased at being called out, especially publicly, but he needed the new captains to get the subtle warning. He hoped he wouldn't get complaints, but it was best to prepare ahead.

"The rest of us will be sailing into the Middle Sea, with the goal of sinking everything floating. Although all of the charts I have of this area are older, there are several islands that we will eventually have to deal with, and I'm not ruling out putting garrisons on those as well. Especially those closest to Egypt and Persia. Until the Consul secures Italy and Greece, we'll be pretty far from any support, so we'll have to look at setting up additional way stations out there. Beyond that, and supporting the Consul's movements, we'll also be responsible for causing as much damage to Carthage's ports in Africa as we can. There are too many to blockade them all, but if we set enough on fire, we can at least slow down any new ships they might build."

"That's a lot of water for thirteen ships to cover," Járnsveinn said.

"I know, and that's why we'll probably split our fleet into small squadrons, but we can't make that decision until we push further east. Prepare yourselves and remember, while we have the entire Middle Sea to deal with, our goal is to keep a path between here and Carthage open for the invasion. Got it?"

The captains all assented, most of them excited by the opportunities coming their way. The larger the fleet got, the more it would be split into separate commands, and it would be those with the most experience leading smaller squadrons that would be picked to lead them.

"Good. Let's go start causing some havoc then," Valdar said, eliciting cheers and laughter from his captains.

Now was the time they'd all been preparing for, and he knew they were as eager as he was to get started.

Daramouda

The sun had just made its way over the horizon as Ky picked his way through what remained of the port. All around him were scars from the recent siege. Collapsed buildings with walls cracked and blackened by fire, charred skeletons of ships partially submerged in the harbor, and cobblestone streets strewn with rubble and debris. The salty tang of the sea still mingled with the harsh smell of smoke. There was also a tinge of decay, in spite of how quickly his men had worked to remove the bodies of the deceased. It would be months before the port started looking like anything other than a war zone.

And yet, it was still bustling. The first temporary dock was already in place, with ships loading and unloading since it opened for business the day before, the activity continuing all through the night. There were other signs of the city being reconstructed. Although the day had only just begun, already the distant ring of hammers shaping metal could be heard. From where he stood, Ky could see makeshift cranes lifting stone blocks and crews of laborers clearing roads and hauling timber.

A cold wind whipped past him, causing some of those laborers to pull their cloaks tighter, sparking Ky's mind to realize yet another thing he could introduce. Although styles of clothing were varied, with Germanics, Britannians, and even tribesmen from Hispania already starting to mix in the city, their clothing was inefficient compared to what Ky was used to. Or had been used to. There were easier ways to stay warm than cloaks and what were essentially ponchos, especially for laborers.

"Now that Hortensius has the new weaving facilities set up, we should send over designs for more advanced tailoring," Ky subvocalized. "Coats, pants, that kind of thing. Something more efficient than the items people currently wear. It'll start snowing soon."

"I will make a note for the next time you or Lucilla have time to transcribe the instructions, although snow in this region is unlikely for several more months based on recorded historical averages," the AI said, correcting him.

"Fine, but it's still a good idea."

"If you say so, Commander," the AI replied.

Its tone remained emotionless, but Ky could feel the sarcasm in the statement all the same. Sophus's progression hadn't stopped since its transition into sentience, and the AI had recently started to be almost snarky at times. It was strange to get attitude from the machine, although it felt even stranger since the snark was devoid of emotion, almost making it more cutting.

Ky put the thought aside as he pushed open the door to the former Carthaginian barracks, which now served as the legion headquarters. The building was just as bustling as the rest of the city, handling the feeding and organization of nearly twenty thousand legionaries camped around the city. Idle armies, even loyal ones, tended to become rancorous if left to sit for too long, which meant they needed to set up training and tasks to keep them busy, which in turn generated a fair amount of work for their leaders.

Ky escaped the bustle as he made his way to the central chambers, where his legates and their tribunes were gathered, including Ursinus, who had made the ride down accompanied by several of the Germanic chieftains. This even included the chieftains of two local tribes who'd joined them after the Carthaginians were finally defeated. The first, although hopefully not the last, of the southern tribes to sign on to the alliance.

Making his way to the head of the table, Ky cleared his throat, quieting the murmuring in the room as all eyes turned to him.

"Thank you all for gathering here today. You've all done extraordinary work this year and, with the help of our new allies, we've cleared the entire western half of the continent from Hispania to the northern sea of the Carthaginian scourge. Hopefully for good. We've weakened them, taken away a major source of innocent people they can conscript into their armies, and a large portion of the resources they could steal from the land, but they aren't out of this fight yet. Now that winter is nearly upon us, it's time to start planning for the coming year's campaign, to ensure they never return."

A murmur of agreement rippled through the group as Ky turned to Bomilcar.

"General, you and the Seventh Legion will remain in Daramouda. You're to work with our new allies here and, hopefully, reach out to other tribes to continue to expand the alliance. Valdar, or his people, are going to be doing the same from the port to the south, so hopefully, between the two of you, we can build something here the way we did in the north. These people have been under the Carthaginian boot a lot longer, so they're going to need help to recover and find their way back to self-governance. I'm sure that will come with growing pains, so I want you to ensure we maintain order, help with rebuilding efforts, and keep watch for any Carthaginians or their supporters in the area. I'm not sure if the Carthaginians will send any forces up through Greece or Italy to try to reclaim the region, but you should be prepared for that possibility. Keep your scouts out and get what assistance you can from the locals."

At Bomilcar's nod, Ky moved on. Of all his commanders, he trusted the former Carthaginian to make the right decisions and keep the large swath of southern Europe and Iberia under control through the winter.

Turning his attention to Ursinus, Ky said, "Ursinus, you and the Fifth Legion are to hold in Germania. Although I doubt they'll send any significant forces that far north, they still control the land to your east, so be alert. Continue to work with our allies and assist them with any requests they might have, within reason. I know this is their second winter out from under Carthaginian control, but the enemy did a lot of damage in the spring that has seriously affected the harvests. The Empress is already aware of the situation, and Britannia is standing ready to send relief supplies as needed."

"Thank you, Consul," Bernie, the chieftain of the Anarti, the furthest east tribe they'd allied with, said.

337

"It's what allies do," Ky replied. "If we hope to build an alliance across the continent and keep anything like the Carthaginian scourge from happening again, we'll have to work together."

"I assume you're calling out our legions specifically for a reason," Bomilcar said, jumping beyond Ky's announcements.

"Yes. I'm leaving the defense of the continent, at least over the winter, to the two of you. I'm returning to Britannia with the Second, Third, Fourth, and Ninth legions. We'll reinforce both of your forces from their men before we leave, and they'll get the new recruits currently training in Britannia to make up for those losses. We'll spend the winter replenishing our ranks, retraining with the new men, and refitting, in preparation for the spring campaign."

"Do you already know where you plan on attacking in the spring?" Givellan, chieftain of the Vandili, asked.

"Yes. Our first targets will be Italy and Sicilia. By the time we win those fights, Valdar's fleet will hopefully be in control of the bulk of the Middle Sea, allowing us to launch an invasion of Africa itself. We will most likely be taking all of our legions for that campaign, which will leave you to protect your own lands, although we will ensure arms shipments continue to assist with that, in line with the terms of our alliance."

The legates already knew this, or at least suspected that would be their next move, but the allied tribal leaders all seemed pleased at the revelation. While they needed the Britannians, and more importantly the Britannians' weapons, some of them had spent a lifetime living in occupied territory. The last thing they wanted was to exchange one overlord for another, regardless of how friendly that lordship seemed to be.

Turning back to Bomilcar, Ky said, "I will be meeting with Faenius as soon as I return to Britannia. I am giving the Praetorians control of the line of forts built by Velius. They'll be more lightly manned than originally intended, but we can use them to establish secure lines of communication back to Britannia using the new telegraph system. We can then extend that line as our forces move east."

"What about Port Invictus?" Aelius asked. "If my understanding of how these lines work is correct, you'll be turning it north and then across the most shallow part of the water between the continent and Britannia. Port Invictus is in the wrong direction."

"You're right, it is. We're abandoning Port Invictus. It made sense to take it during our initial invasion, but it's redundant now that Valdar's taken control of the port of Kalb. Kalb will serve as our main supply hub for the time being. There is another project I've been pushing that will allow us to rapidly transport supplies over long distances. I'm hopeful we can get it to a functional point before winter ends, which will make whatever port we use closest to Britannia our main crossing point. Working on that project is another reason I am returning to Devnum."

The meeting went on for several more hours, mostly with questions from the chieftains, trying to determine how much support they were going to get moving forward, what was going to be asked of them, and trying to determine how much danger they were in now that they had openly declared for the Britannians. Ky was able to set a lot of their fears at ease, but some of the questions just couldn't be answered. In spite of their technological advantages and the rapidly weakening position of the Carthaginians, a lot was still up in the air. War could be unpredictable, no matter how the battlefield looked, and Ky was unwilling to give assurances about the unknown.

"You've all done tremendous work so far and should be proud of everything you've accomplished," Ky said as the meeting broke up. "I want you to prepare yourselves. The Carthaginians are weakened, but they are not out of this fight yet. There's still a long road ahead of us. Don't let yourselves become too confident now that the momentum is starting to shift in our favor. Let's not allow it to fall apart now. Stay strong."

He paused to look at each of the men, making sure his message was getting through.

"The gods willing, we're about to enter the last phase of this conflict. For Britannia!"

The legates jumped to their feet, fists slamming into the table, echoing, "For Britannia!"

To Be Continued ...

About the author

Travis writes science fiction, fantasy, and thriller novels (and the occasional coming-of-age story), with the hope of transporting and enthralling readers. Publishing novels since 2015, Travis's passion is creating worlds and characters that live and breathe, and experiencing the joy of those stories with his readers.

When not writing, Travis enjoys connecting with readers and other writers, managing the popular Complete Marvel Reading Order website, where he works on his other passion for comics and graphic novels, and spending time with his family.

If you have enjoyed this book, please consider taking a moment to rate or review it wherever you found your copy, as it helps new readers find my works and ensures I can continue writing book into the future.

Find out more at:
amazon.com/TravisStarnes/e/B072YBDC3S/
Or visit
https://tstarnes.com

Signup to get free previews and notifications of upcoming books at
http://tstarnes.com/preview-notification-newsletter/

Also by

John Taylor Stories

Rebirth
False Signs
The Wrong Girl
Burying the Past
Family Ties
Election Day
Danger Close
Extraction
Designated Target
Border Crossed
Desperate Rendition

Country Roads Series

Playing by Ear
Fanfare
Dissonance
Elegy
From the Top
Center Stage

Imperium Series

Shattered Lands Series

False Start Series

The Veilguard Saga

Stand Alone

www.ingramcontent.com/pod-product-compliance
Lightning Source LLC
Chambersburg PA
CBHW070625260626
47161CB00007B/2588